MW01634257

THE
DORIANS

ALSO BY NICK CUTTER

The Troop

The Deep

The Acolyte

Little Heaven

The Breach (audio only)

The Handyman Method (with Andrew F. Sullivan)

The Queen

THE DORIANS

A NOVEL

NICK CUTTER

G

GALLERY BOOKS

NEW YORK　AMSTERDAM/ANTWERP　LONDON
TORONTO　SYDNEY/MELBOURNE　NEW DELHI

Gallery Books
An Imprint of Simon & Schuster, LLC
1230 Avenue of the Americas
New York, NY 10020

For more than 100 years, Simon & Schuster has championed authors and the stories they create. By respecting the copyright of an author's intellectual property, you enable Simon & Schuster and the author to continue publishing exceptional books for years to come. We thank you for supporting the author's copyright by purchasing an authorized edition of this book.

No amount of this book may be reproduced or stored in any format, nor may it be uploaded to any website, database, large language model, or other repository, retrieval, or artificial intelligence system without express permission. All rights reserved. Inquiries may be directed to Simon & Schuster, 1230 Avenue of the Americas, New York, NY 10020 or permissions@simonandschuster.com.

This book is a work of fiction. Any references to historical events, real people, or real places are used fictitiously. Other names, characters, places, and events are products of the author's imagination, and any resemblance to actual events or places or persons, living or dead, is entirely coincidental.

Copyright © 2026 by N.M.D. Precious Cargo Inc.

All rights reserved, including the right to reproduce this book or portions thereof in any form whatsoever. For information, address Gallery Books Subsidiary Rights Department, 1230 Avenue of the Americas, New York, NY 10020.

First Gallery Books hardcover edition May 2026

GALLERY BOOKS and colophon are registered trademarks of Simon & Schuster, LLC

Simon & Schuster strongly believes in freedom of expression and stands against censorship in all its forms. For more information, visit BooksBelong.com.

For information about special discounts for bulk purchases, please contact Simon & Schuster Special Sales at 1-866-506-1949 or business@simonandschuster.com.

The Simon & Schuster Speakers Bureau can bring authors to your live event. For more information or to book an event, contact the Simon & Schuster Speakers Bureau at 1-866-248-3049 or visit our website at www.simonspeakers.com.

Interior design by Erika R. Genova

Manufactured in the United States of America

10 9 8 7 6 5 4 3 2 1

Library of Congress Control Number: 2026935110

ISBN 978-1-6680-7956-0
ISBN 978-1-6680-7958-4 (ebook)

Scan here to get book recommendations, exclusive orders, and more delivered to your inbox.

To Aunt Kathy & Uncle Randy
Gratefully, The Suck

The boundaries which divide Life from Death
are at best shadowy and vague. Who shall
say where the one ends, and where the other begins?
—Edgar Allan Poe

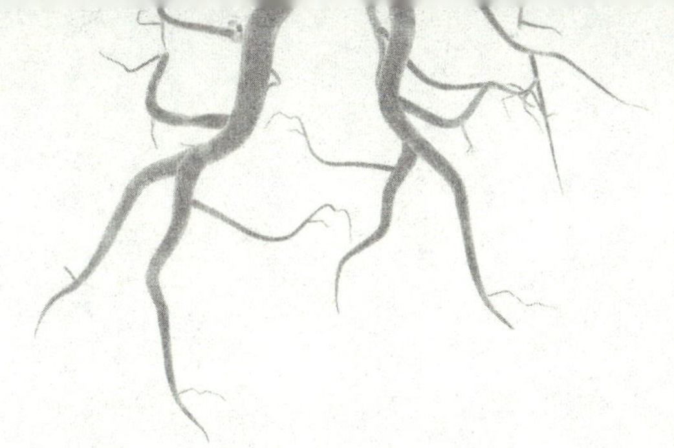

PART 1

BROKE-DOWN MEAT MACHINES

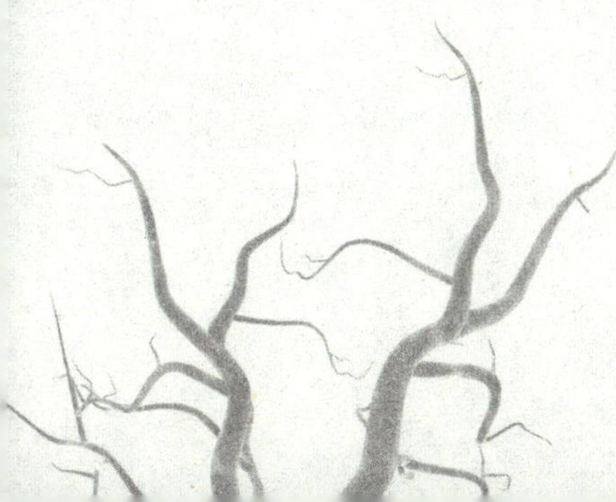

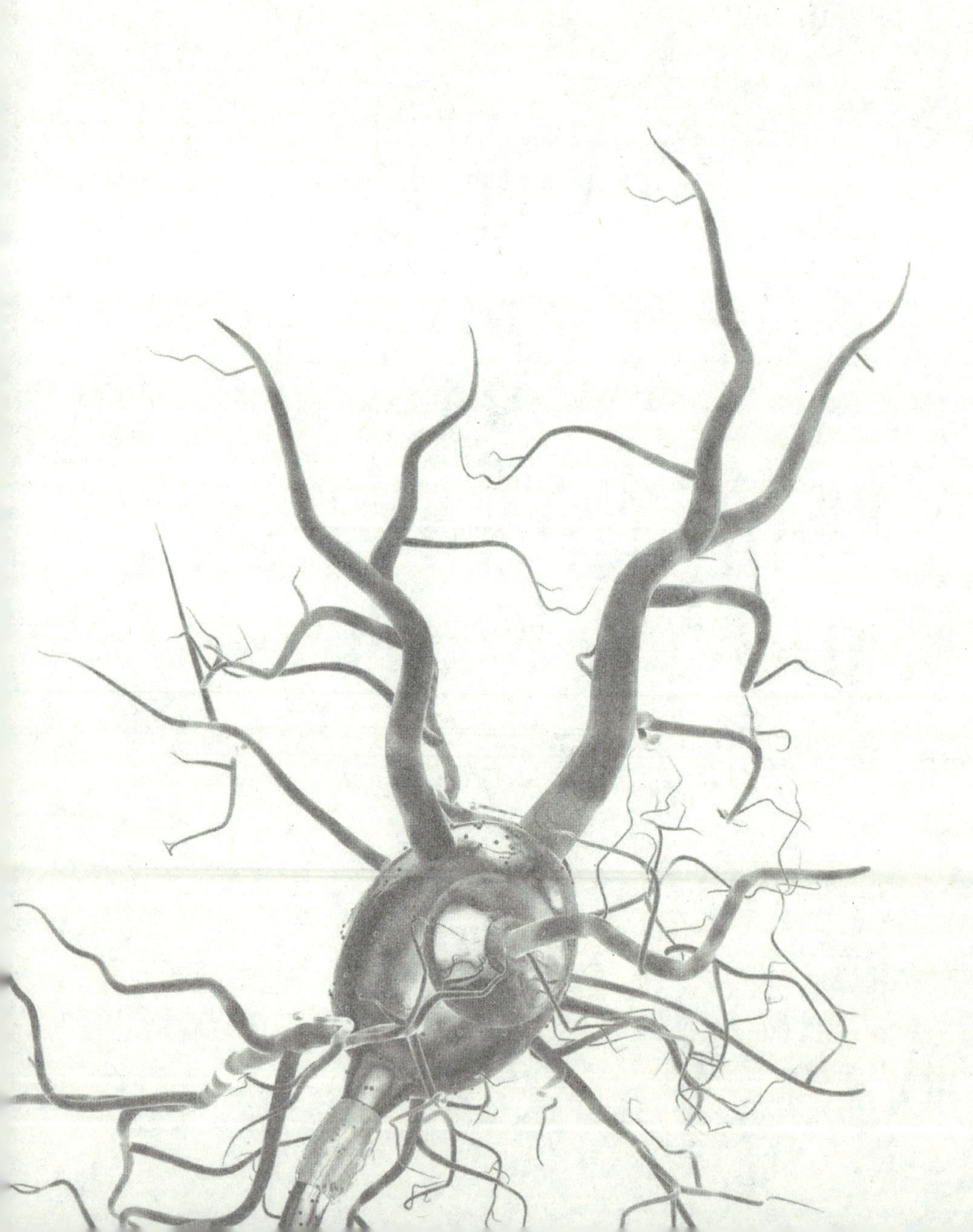

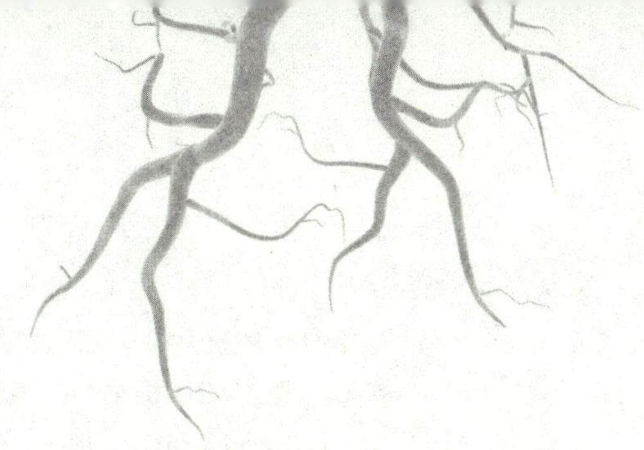

one.

 be joining you?"

The sawbone's name was Parkman, or was it Peterson . . . no, wait, Pierson? Ah hell, who gave a royal rip? There was nothing the matter with Frank's brain, but after nearly seventy-eight years' worth of diligent service, it ought to be forgiven for forgetting a name or two.

"Nope, nobody else coming," Frank told the doctor—*Pastern!* Hell yeah, there it was.

Four people occupied the hospital room with a view of the Gardiner Expressway leading into downtown Toronto. Joining Doc P was a nurse practitioner whose name tag read KELLY and a social worker who'd introduced herself as Pam. That left only him, one Franklin Eugene Doyle, whose remaining minutes could be measured with an egg timer. Nurse Kelly handed Dr. Pastern a folder.

"Everything's in order here," the doctor announced, tapping the folder with one finger. "Mr. Doyle's completed the forms for a medically assisted death. He's gotten assessments from his family doctor and a cardiac intern at St. Joe's."

Frank lay propped up on the bed pillows, wheezing away like a torn accordion. His heart shuddered behind his ribs. Frank had come to picture his heart as a leather wineskin, something Vikings once drank from, all shriveled and cracked.

"Hell of a thing, getting old," he said. "Happily, no longer much of a concern for me."

"Would you like me to go over precisely what's going to happen today, Mr. Doyle?"

"Oh sure thing, why not? And call me Frank, would you?"

"Frank it is," Dr. Pastern went on. "Now shortly, you'll receive four injections. Number one's a sedative, close to Valium. That'll relax you. Next will be an anesthetic that we use in the ORs to put patients out before surgery. That one will lead you into a deep sleep."

Frank was ready to die. Every atom of his being told him so. But Jesus, to watch that lethal fluid slip into his vein and know an everlasting line had been crossed, no take-backsies . . .

"After that, we'll administer a powerful muscle relaxant. Once that has taken effect, we'll inject the final cocktail."

Cocktail. Such a funny euphemism for a substance designed to end one's life. *Ready for your last cocktail, Frank? There's no pineapple slice or tiny paper parasol, I'm afraid. Just a quarter ounce of pure killing juice that'll obliterate your heart, hah-hah—bottoms up!*

"Shortly after that, Frank, you will stop breathing. Then your heart will cease its function and you'll pass on. But you'll only feel yourself going to sleep, if even that."

Amazing how calm Frank felt. Probably not much different from the final stages of hypothermia, when the experts say you freeze to death with a blissful grin on your mug.

Dr. Pastern said, "Any final questions for me?"

"Um . . . shouldn't I be wearing a pair of rubber, y'know . . . ? In case—?"

"Ah. No, no, you won't lose control of your bladder or bowels. That doesn't happen when we use this method."

"Oh. Okay, that's dignified, then."

Dr. Pastern pulled a sheet of paper from the file folder and pinned it to a clipboard. "We need to confirm informed consent."

Frank's vision wobbled; there were two Doc Ps when there ought to be one. Maybe he'd kick the bucket before they could stick the needles in him.

Frank hoped not; he'd had to fill out a lot of friggin' forms to kick the proceedings along to this point.

"This is now me informing you of your rights, Frank," he heard the doctor say. "Our cardiac surgeon has assessed that your natural death due to congestive heart failure is now reasonably foreseeable. But I need to make sure you're aware that there are palliative measures available to ease your way to a different kind of passing, while stressing that *both* options are considered natural."

Frank refocused. That second, phantom Dr. P vanished. "I know about the other options," he replied evenly. "Not interested."

"So, Frank: Do you confirm consent to receive this specific care measure?"

Frank gritted his teeth against another coughing fit. God, his organs were rattling around inside his chest like chicken bones in a tin can.

"My wife, Annie. I mentioned her, didn't I?"

Pam said, "I don't believe so, Mr. Doyle."

"Annie passed eight years ago. Took just about every good part of me with her. Some men, you know, it's really their wives who hold them together. Sometimes I think the weight of keeping me up through my down spells is what weakened her, let the cancer get in."

Frank glugged water from the jug sitting on the overbed table. He hadn't spoken such a long string of words in months.

"Towards the end I begged her: 'Annie, can we put your pain away? You're so damn strong, but this thing is gonna eat until you can't feed it anymore.'" He covered his eyes with one liver-spotted hand. "She was sixty-three pounds when she went." Frank lowered his hand and looked at everyone present, thinking this was a fact that ought to be acknowledged. "And we never had kids on account of my genes—I have a skinny urethra, turns out."

Frank's laugh wasn't much of a laugh at all. More the chuff of a rheumy-eyed old hound who could no longer summon the breath for a solid bark.

"Once Annie was gone, in truth, I began to wait on death. I want to see her again, you know? If there's such a place as heaven, I hope to meet Annie there . . . or gaze up at her from hell, I don't much care anymore."

Frank eased back onto the bed. The pillows were nicer than the regular hospital ones. While Nurse Kelly laid out four hypodermic needles on a rubber-bottomed tray, the social worker stepped forward.

"Would you like to hold hands?"

Warmth pushed through Frank's defeated heart. "Yeah, actually. I'd like that very much. Thank you, uh . . ."

"Pam, like the cooking spray."

"Right, Pam. I won't forget it again, promise."

As Pam grasped his hand, Frank Doyle's life would have soon come to its lonesome end were it not for the man who eased the door open, stepping inside the room with them.

"Sorry for interrupting," the intruder said. "I come with an opportunity for Mr. Doyle."

"This is a private affair," Dr. Pastern told him. "Frank, do you know this man?"

"Never seen him in my life, Doc."

The man didn't budge. He held a phone. Frank could see a face hemmed within its screen. A woman—wait, was that a *girl*?—with wintergreen eyes.

Months later, on the island as things began to go hinky, Frank Doyle would wonder if it was the uncanny green of the young woman's eyes that had overmastered his common sense. Or maybe he'd found the whole thing vaguely hilarious in its absurdity and had thought: *What the hey, let's play out this string.*

What else could it have been? Why, when that unknown man propped the phone on the overbed table so that Frank could stare into those ineffably green eyes . . . why hadn't Frank just gotten on with dying?

"Dr. Pastern, listen," he heard himself say. "Give me a minute here, will you?"

"That's your right, Frank," the doctor said, holding his tongue on whatever he may've been thinking: *Hey, you signed that form, Franky-boy. Are you a man of your word or ain't you?*

Dr. Pastern, Pam like the spray, and the nurse did as Frank asked. The following minutes unfolded as a queer waking dream. The sort of sunlit, wistful daydream an old man might experience at the end of his days. Except it wasn't that, not in any sense. Frank stared at the needles on the tray, the easy death they promised—a painless descent into the everlasting black—then back at the face on the screen.

"Go ahead, then," Frank croaked. "Spit it out."

He listened to what the young lady had to say. No promises were made. No tangible information given. Only an offer, and within it was buried an outrageous hope.

Come to my island, Mr. Doyle. You're still strong enough to make the trip, and we will make every accommodation for your comfort. Or don't. Either way, you'll be making the right choice.

The girl's eyes. The calm ongoing green of them.

I can't guarantee anything other than the following: It doesn't have to end this way.

When she'd finished talking, the strange man offered Frank a courteous nod, picked up the phone, and stepped out. Dr. Pastern and the other two hovered at the threshold, peering in at Frank as they might a species of lizard in a terrarium.

Frank could have called them back in and had them get to work stopping his ticker for good. But instead, he'd leaned back against the pillows, closed his eyes, and thought:

Well, you old bastard . . . why the hell not?

Such are the riddles of the human heart. Yet it was more than that, going deeper than that.

Why me? Why Frank-Nobody-Special-Doyle?

If there was an answer to that question, the universe held it in escrow.

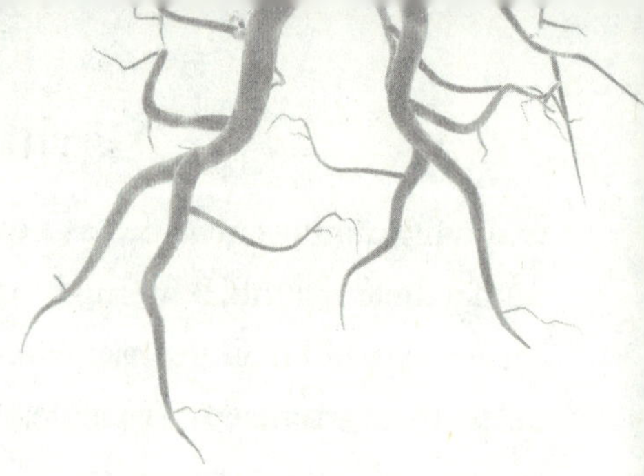

two.

THE ESCALADE motored up the 400, pacing steadily northward. Frank Doyle had never ridden in a vehicle so roomy or that smelled so richly of leather. Could it be *Corinthian*—the king of leathers?

Past the tinted windows, the country rolled out along the highway in tones of green and slate. Here, four hours north of the city, tall pines scaled down the roadside, rising from the cragged rock of the Canadian Shield. The population dwindled, towns becoming hamlets becoming villages, until they were only blink-and-you'll-miss-it townships of a hundred souls or less.

The pines parted to offer a sweeping view of Lake Huron. A shoreline of water-smoothed stones studded with piles of driftwood. Frank's oxygen unit purred beside him, pumping a concentrated mix of medical-grade O_2 into his lungs.

I ought to be dead. It wasn't the first time this thought had come to Frank in the past forty-eight hours. *Cooling on a slab with my lips gray as concrete.*

He'd left St. Joe's hospital two days ago, apologizing (a bit shamefacedly) to Dr. Pastern as he'd risen from the bed, shrugged off his hospital johnny, and tugged his trousers back on. He'd entertained the brief and—to Frank, at least—comical vision of Dr. Pastern chasing him around the ward with a needle, shrieking: "Get your withered old caboose back here, Franky baby! You signed consent! It's time to pay the Reaper!"

Frank had taken a cab back to the Chester Village nursing home, avoiding the eyes of the staff, who'd surely not expected to still see him aboveground. He was mildly surprised they hadn't gone ahead and cleaned his room out and fumigated it of the old-person stink—not that the next guest would've been able to tell the difference, ha.

Frank had taken his luggage out of the closet and packed some belongings. Then he lay in his bed and waited.

The call came early the next day, at the phone kiosk in Chester Village's lobby.

"Still interested, Frank?"

"Am I going to wake up in a bathtub with my kidneys tugged out?"

A gentle chuckle. "You don't have to take us up on this. You're free to refuse."

The young woman's face had come to Frank again. The green of her eyes. The unspoken promise of this island of hers.

"Yeah, I guess I'm intrigued."

"A car will pick you up tomorrow morning."

Presently, Frank asked the Escalade's driver if he knew anything at all about this mysterious business. The driver's name was Gord, and Gord knew jack shit.

"Nobody told me anything other than where to drop you off, sir."

"And where's that, Gord? Satan's hairy asshole?"

A wry laugh. "Well, if not that, then the rough equivalent for city folk. The government dock on the western arm of the French River."

Gord was happy to converse on other subjects: the Blue Jays, the mayoral race, his daughters, Tomasina and Tammy. Frank was pleased for the conversation until his energy began to wane and his eyes slipped shut . . . He bolted up sometime later in a haywired state.

"—*whuh?* Whuzza?"

"Everything's okay, Frank," Gord said soothingly. "You just took a little nap."

I'm not a goddamn toddler, Frank groused to himself. *I'm just old and prone to conking out.*

Frank had been born on a sweltering summer day on July 17, 1945. His mother, dead fifteen years now, delivered him at St. Joe's hospital—the same one he'd visited recently with the intention of dying under its roof. How was that for the circularity of one's mortal coil?

The year Frank was born, a gallon of milk cost twenty cents. A head of lettuce, a dime. William Lyon Mackenzie King was taking a second lap as prime minister. Truman was in the White House and, before Frank turned a month old, they dropped the bomb on Hiroshima.

Frank *was* old, sure. But did that mean he had to be a dusty relic? Christ, Dame Helen Mirren was born the same year he was! And ole Helen could still fill out a bathing suit, too . . . shit, sorry, Annie.

His *hands*. Oh, Frank couldn't stand to look at them anymore. The crepey wrinkles and bulging knuckles and thick yellow fingernails. The hands of an old man with a bum ticker and free-floating snot in his lungs who was reduced to sucking on store-bought oxygen to survive.

Ahh, so it goes. We meat machines, we do slow down. *Entropy* was the word for it; one of Annie's doctors, whom Frank hadn't much cared for, had introduced it to him.

A gradual accumulation of disorder within a biological system was the description that fussy pill peddler had used.

Disorder. Cellular decay. All the tiny subatomic building blocks that were us as humans breaking down and turning against their maker, feral as starved weasels.

Funny how the older you got, the longer the leash you gave to the notion of what *young* meant. As a teenager, Frank used to pass the retirement home on his way to the public pool with his swim trunks rolled up in a beach towel. In the summertime, the old folks would be out in wheelchairs and walkers; some were guided around like bewildered spaniels by the white-overalled orderlies. The sight had filled Frank with pity, and a mild strain of horror. These were *human beings*, same as him, yet they moved slower, their bodies bent, their mouths gummy, the scope of their worlds limited to their retirement villa—or its lawn, if the day was nice.

At his present age, Frank figured anything below sixty qualified as young. Yeah, there came an age (fifty-five, the double nickel, struck him as the year) when your days get shorter, your bodily aches multiply, and it takes longer to haul the trash can to the curb or mow the damn lawn . . . you're not *old*, but you can see the shadow of it. The first time Frank's twentysomething neighbor had come over while Frank was shoving the old Toro Lawn Master around the yard and tapped Frank's shoulder like a baseball coach making a pitching change—*That's it, Ace, time to hit the showers*—well, he'd just about blown his stack. The first time the bubblegum-chawing cashier at the movie theater charged Frank the senior rate without asking—that was another one for the low-light reel. Still, Frank hadn't corrected her . . . and the next time his neighbor volunteered to cut the grass, Frank took him up on it.

The Escalade veered off the one-lane road onto a rutted logging route, the back tires throwing up a rooster tail of dust.

"Whoever hired you better be covering dents and dings," Frank remarked.

"Yeah, no shit." Gord sounded distressed.

The road degraded steadily. Ten miles fled by in the rearview, then twenty, soon thirty. Frank's mind drifted as the SUV's tires burred on the roadside shale, and the odd pine bough whapped its flanks like the rotating brushes at a car wash.

"I was told this dock was accessible," Gord noted grimly. "We're getting pretty tight."

They hit a stretch where the trees had been hacked back into a clear-cut running down either side. They had to be fifty miles off the one-laner by now, and well over a hundred off any major highway. When he checked his cell phone, Frank saw it was down to a single bar of signal, and that one was fluttering weakly.

Nobody knew he was here. There had been nobody for Frank to tell, in truth. Maybe that's why he was chosen for this: Frank was a man untethered, and his disappearance would probably not even be noted. After all, he *was* supposed to be dead. For the first time since the drive started, a note of fear zizzed through his wheezy heart.

The road declined toward the water. The smooth dark expanse of a waterway rolled out to the northwest. No houses or shacks frilled the lakeshore.

There was a dock. That was it. A concrete dock crooked into the bay like a dead gray finger and a pilot boat, silver with brass striping, reflected the late-afternoon sunlight.

Gord maneuvered the SUV in a tight-turning radius until the hood was pointed back up the road. "Finally, we arrive. You need a hand getting out, Frank?"

"I'll manage, thanks."

Gord looked dubious, but only said, "I'll grab your luggage."

Frank got out with his oxygen machine. The monitor read 15 percent full. He'd need to pop a refill in before long or he'd be gasping like a boated fish.

"I'm sorry, I can't tip you," he said when Gord set his bag at his feet. "I never thought to get cash out of the machine."

"I'll cover the tip, Mr. Doyle."

The voice came from the pilot boat. The slant of sun on its windscreen had obscured the fact that a man was perched behind the helm.

It was the same guy who'd barged into Frank's hospital room and altered the trajectory of Frank's life, whatever might be left of it. The guy was dressed differently now: waterproof pants, a simple white tee, and a knife sheathed at his belt. He stepped from the boat, nodding in a friendly manner to Frank. Money changed hands between the man and Gord—a nice fat wad, by the looks of it.

Gord waved goodbye. "Nice meeting you, Frank. You be well, okay?"

"You too." Frank waved back. "And give our mayor a kick in his embezzling ass if you see him."

The rear tires stuttered as Gord worked the SUV away from the dock. Frank turned to face Mister Urban Outfitter.

"Mr. Doyle. Good to see you again," the guy said. "I'm John Salters. I work with Dr. Marsh."

"The woman on the phone? She's a *doctor*? She didn't look old enough to vote."

A man with nothing to live for is capable of anything. Frank couldn't tell you who'd coined that phrase, but it zipped through his head as clean and clear as the wind off the river. Christ, he'd always been a sensible man, hadn't he? To a fault, yeah. Storm windows, pet insurance, paying the dealer premium for TruCoat undercoating on his Volvo (a sensible Swedish sedan), even though Annie said that shit was as useful as a screen door on a submarine.

Stable Frank. Make-No-Waves Frank. So it arrived with a belated thunder-clap just how friggin' *insane* his choice was. The fact that he'd set aside his carefully planned end-of-life agenda . . . God, why? On account of some girl with her cat-green eyes. That snap decision, one that flew in the face of the man Frank had always been, had landed him in the ass crack of nowhere, on the bank of a serpentine river that cut miles through the northern Ontario wilderness, talking to a stranger with a bowie knife lashed to his pants with a rawhide string.

John Salters said, "We're waiting on one more. Once he arrives, we can go."

FRANK USHERED his oxygen machine to the end of the dock. He bent—the knobs of his spine went off like muffled firecrackers—and scooped water into his cupped palm. Before it could drain through his fingers, he impulsively drank a mouthful. The cold hit the back of his throat. It tasted of shaved steel, thrillingly clean. He could drink a gallon of this stuff.

Peering down through the darkening layers of the water, he caught the dart of a small fish, followed by the broader flash of a much bigger fish arrowing from under the dock to strike . . . his machine started beeping. He moved haltingly back to the end of the dock, unzipped his duffel, found a replacement cartridge, and thumbed it into the unit.

By then a second SUV was approaching. A man stepped from it. Frank's age within a year or two. He didn't bear a signature of his illness as Frank did with his machine, but as he moved painstakingly toward the dock, Frank saw the telltale shakes of Parkinson's.

"Mr. Bassiano," Frank heard John Salters say. "Would you like—?"

"I'm fine, damn it," the man replied, molars grinding as a spasm ran up his neck.

While Salters dealt with the driver, Frank ambled over to meet the new arrival.

"My name's Frank."

Stupidly, Frank stuck out his hand.

"I could try, Frank, but my handshake's not what it used to be. It'd only embarrass us both."

"Aw, shit." Frank winced. "Sorry."

"Ah, it's shithead behavior *not* to shake. Teddy Bassiano."

Teddy's voice was unaffected by his condition. The voice of someone used to being heard and obeyed. His eyes fell to Frank's machine. "Heart?"

Frank nodded. "Parkinson's?"

"Bingo. Look at us, the Cowardly Lion and the Flailing Scarecrow." Teddy's smile was warm and genuine. "No offense."

A smile slipped across Frank's face. "None taken. I always rooted for that lion."

"So, what do you figure we've been brought all the way out here for?"

"I was about to ask you the same thing."

Teddy's headshake had the jittery cadence of an impulse sprinkler. "Fuck me for a clue. And believe me when I say"—gnawing his way through another spasm—"I've made inquiries. Whatever's going on out here, the powers that be have the plan locked up tight as a crab's asshole. And that, my phlegmy new friend, is *water*-tight."

"You think it's a scam?" Frank asked. "What am I worth to anyone? You want my triple-mortgaged bungalow on the shit side of the city? Go ahead, take it."

Teddy's shoulders hitched. "I don't think it's a scam, Frank. I wouldn't have dragged my ass to Timbuktu if I didn't believe there was something interesting going on out here."

"Interesting how?"

"Can't say. Wouldn't wish to incriminate myself. But ahh, what can we be worth to this backwoods outfit, anyway? Last I checked, old-fogy meat was selling for only fifty-five cents a pound at all disreputable butcher shops."

Frank felt an immediate kinship with Teddy, which hit home as a warm glow in his belly. When was the last time he'd made a *real* friend? At some point, often by their fifties, but most assuredly by their sixties, most men stop making new friends. They cling to the ones they have, but over time even those get snatched by the vagaries of illness or fate. Frank played cribbage with a few guys at the care home, just passing time while keeping his true self hidden. He hadn't really shown his true self to anyone since Annie passed.

But real friends, it had always struck Frank, were formed out of a spontaneous reaction, two like-minded souls meeting in a big bang: an instantaneous cellular reaction.

Salters now drew near to them, having already stowed their bags in the boat. "Gentlemen, shall we? The island awaits."

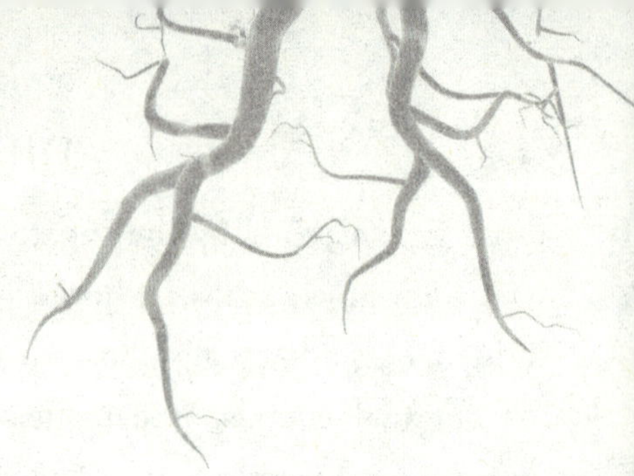

three.

TWO OLD farts and the sea.

The phrase flitted through Teddy Bassiano's mind as Salters untied the pilot boat and got the motor humming.

He sat on a marine-proofed seat next to this Frank fella. Who seemed a good enough guy, if a little dim. The pilot boat moved out into the river system.

Teddy had employed a lot of Franks. His company, MountainCrest Builders, had been putting roofs over the heads of mortgage-approved families since 1977. Teddy was seventy-nine now, but by the time he founded his company at the tender age of thirty-two, he'd been working construction for over a decade.

He'd joined his first crew only a week after graduating high school. Teddy's folks were always one paycheck away from the dust bowl, so no way he was going to college—but Teddy'd have gone crazy around those bell-bottomed beret-wearers, anyway, stuffing daisies down the barrels of hardworking soldiers' rifles.

Instead, Teddy had learned how to mortar a foundation, nail a crossbeam, level a basement pad, run electrical and water—the whole shebang. He loved working outside in the sun, shirtless, stomach taut, arms swollen from countless hammer swings.

But gradually, a superiority crept into him. He *liked* his construction chums all right, yet he couldn't shake the sense he was better than them. The smallness of their existence . . . it bugged him. Their mousy wives and snot-nosed kids, their tract houses with postage-stamp lawns. The way they wolf-whistled at every piece of ass who sashayed past the building site, as if that taxed the limits of their imagination as to how far they could get with a beautiful, sophisticated woman. Teddy figured he'd have those women eventually—them, others just like them, as many as he pleased—and it sickened him that his brothers-in-arms were content to harass them from behind a hurricane fence.

But on the backs of such men were empires built. Teddy was always friendly. Hell, he'd even sneak a cheeky beer on the site with them. Teddy *did* respect these guys. Not their dead-end lives, Christ no, but their pigheaded work ethic and strong backs. Since Teddy was charismatic, and had this spooky ability to peer into the heart of his fellow men and glimpse the outline of their desires—Teddy thought of it as his X-Ray Specs (*Gag Gifts! Fool Your Friends!*)—when he founded his company, he was able to poach several bonded and shop-ticketed guys from his old boss, who was blindsided by his apprentice's betrayal . . . not that Teddy gave a shit. He was a shark swimming up current, eating the dumb little fish as he went.

Teddy shook free of these thoughts as the pilot boat cleared the dead-wake zone. John Salters cycled the motor, and the vessel moved into the heart of the waterway. The river shaded from brown to green, and finally to an impenetrable black that told Teddy solid rock must be running under the hull, not mud mixed with leaf muck.

The hillsides fringing the river were rock, too: wind-scoured and bare in spots, or else overgrown with tenacious lichen. The trees clinging to the highest elevations were starved-looking specimens that reminded Teddy of malnourished Biafrans, the ones Sally Struthers used to shill for on those TV infomercials.

"Smells good up here."

Teddy turned to Frank, who had taken off his oxygen mask to pull in a whistly lungful. Frank was right. The air had a buoyancy . . . it wasn't *heavy*, the way city air was. To breathe this was to inhale something life-affirming, silly as that sounded.

"How far out are we going?" Teddy asked Salters.

"Oh, it's a ways still," Salters replied without facing him.

"The dock back there—that's the nearest landing spot?"

"You got it."

Teddy hadn't spotted any kind of dwelling—not so much as a hunting shack—once the driver of his Escalade had turned onto the logging road. It was at least a forty-five-minute drive from the dock to the main road . . . and the dock was out of sight now, eaten in the boat's wake.

Well, it's not like I'm capable of making it back under my own puff anyway, he thought. *Someone would have to carry me like a backpack full of Mexican jumping beans.*

Teddy's body shook constantly. Full-body tremors he was helpless to fight. Pills were his existence—he carried them in a caddy, a tackle box for his multicolored and hateful life-sustainers. Sometimes he had dreams where he was strapped to a chair and force-fed pills by faceless sadists. The pills started out as small as the buttons on a doll's dress, but got bigger and bigger, until he was swallowing linty horse capsules that got jammed sideways in his throat.

He needed one of those damn things now, but he was liable to spill the whole container as the boat skiffed across the waves; they'd go rolling around the hull like Tic Tacs. So Teddy kept his shaky ass parked and let his memory—now the strongest part of him—spool back in time.

Teddy's fledgling company had nearly gone belly-up in its first year. Months passed when he ate practically nothing but beans on toast. But those early hardships passed, and he made his first million by the age of thirty-five. His second came a year later. By then he'd gotten married, had two boys (whom he loved dearly despite their now-evident uselessness), gotten divorced, married again, had another kid: his daughter, Francesca, smart as a whip.

By 1985, he was a millionaire five times over. Wifey #3 hired Katrina and the Waves to sing at Teddy's fortieth-birthday party. He'd sat there with a party hat strapped under his chin while Katrina Leskanich crooned, "Happy Birthday to *yoooouuu*," and could only think: *So this is my fuckin' life, huh?*

That day, Teddy came face-to-face with the fact that his existence wasn't much different from the men he used to work beside. Yeah, there were more zeros in his bankbook, but the things about those guys' lives he'd found depressing—their passionless marriages and absentee parenting, the ceiling capping their existences . . . in a horrible irony that only proved God must be a moron—*he'd* inherited all that, too.

Jesus Hopalong Christ, *how*? Teddy had played it smart, played it close to the bone, and, okay, played it a little ruthlessly from time to time. And what had it earned him? A life he sort of despised.

Teddy had been young enough to change right there at his fortieth birthday party. He could've put an egg in his shoe and beat it. Sold his company, renounced his fortune, and wandered the earth doing good deeds like the Littlest Hobo. But he felt shackled to his obligations. So he'd stuck with Wifey #3 for thirty-six years, until they both went soft in the gut and Teddy, feeling the Reaper's shroud riffling at his heels, got a quickie divorce and married Wifey #4, Tiffani, thirty years his junior and built like a brick shithouse. The sex was great (God bless those little blue pills, which were the only pills worth a tin shit), until one afternoon Teddy's hands started to shake and he couldn't figure out how to stop them.

Parkinson's worked its grim magic on his nervous system. He visited doctors, got tests, tried wacky new age therapies, necked a mountain of medications. His libido went straight into the piss-tank: even those blue pills and all of Tiffani's cathouse efforts couldn't convince his Jolly Roger to fly. Not that it mattered: he was about as horny as a homo at a Mary Kay party.

Teddy had gone to his first assisted-suicide appointment alone.

Goddamn, he'd wanted to die. That cold, sunless certainty swept over him. He felt age in every part of him. He'd give half his fortune to take a proper shit, the sort he used to drop in Port-o-Lets at worksites without ever taking note of what a grand pleasure it was.

And then, after his final MAID appointment, this Salters guy had shown up. Salters and that apple-cheeked doctor on Salters's cell phone.

And now here Teddy was, in a boat with another terminal man—Teddy could see death crawling all over poor Frank—off to some island in the god-forsaken hinterlands.

The prospect held no fear for him. What was he leaving behind? A pair of middle-aged sons who'd inherit his company and burn it to the studs with their stupidity, but *ah well*, he still loved those dim-witted lunkheads. Francesca, the only thing he'd felt true pride of creation for, but long estranged, sadly. Wifey #3 remarried to a florist and living in Palm Springs. Tiffani would be well compensated for her pains when he kicked the bucket.

All that remained was the open water and an unknown offer this cherubic doctor had hinted at the edges of without ever clarifying.

Salters said: "There it is, hard off stern."

It's the old clapboard church.

This was the sense that reached out to Teddy when he saw the island emerge from a low and circuiting fog that rolled off the water. The feeling reached out from all the way back in his boyhood, when he used to attend church with his mother, who'd been dead thirty years now.

As the mist shredded, Teddy saw a landing dock, a boathouse, and, along the spiny ridgeline, a dark monolith: unforgiving ninety-degree angles from end to end, as flat and imposing as an obelisk rested on its side. It had no comparison to the homes Teddy had built for nearly half a century. There was nothing hospitable in its outline. It looked like a place the sunlight went to die.

So why did it summon the same feel of that clapboard church on the hillside near his childhood home? The memory came of sitting uncomfortably upright in a pew beside his mother as she fanned herself with a vespers leaflet and gloomy Pastor Bailey recited the liturgy—the feeling that God's eye was trained on this church with special intensity . . . except Teddy wasn't welcome in this exalted place, safe under the eye of heaven. Instead, there had been this feeling of being assessed and judged.

Why are you here, sinner? How dare you darken this holy place!

Teddy never felt that sort of appraisal when he was *actively* sinning, which he'd done recklessly all throughout his adulthood. But as a boy in that hillside church, he'd often felt . . .

Unclean.

Him. Theodore Horatio Bassiano.

He felt it again now. *He* was the unclean one, coming to sully the sanctity of this secluded sanctuary. A demon slipping in the back door to defile every saintly thing.

How is that possible, though—I'm a dying old man, Teddy thought. *I'm too tired to defile anything.*

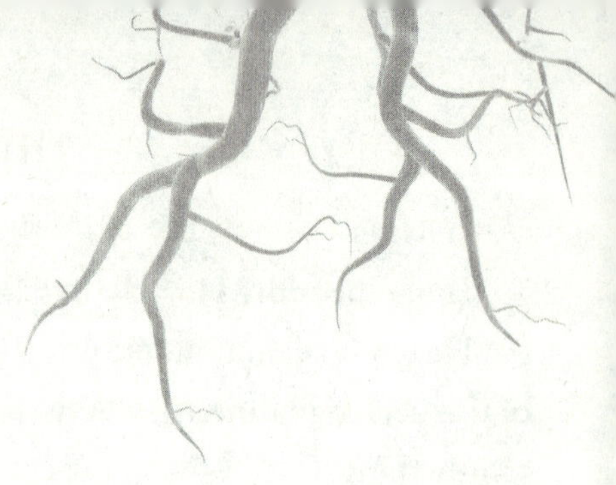

four.

FRANK STEPPED off the boat with his oxygen mask hanging down around his throat; there came a *sssss* as his machine pumped O$_2$ against his Adam's apple.

Did he even need it now? The air out here was crisp and unpolluted, with an alkaline tang that rose off the bedrock of the island. Maybe—

Frank began to cough, which immediately turned into a hacking so wretched that he doubled over, fumbling for his air supply.

Teddy's hand gripped the back of his head, the other his mask, which was placed back over Frank's nose and mouth.

"Thanks," Frank wheezed. "Good looking out."

Teddy seemed unsure. "I got lucky, Franky. Sometimes I can get the shakes under control, but beyond that I'm for-shit, so don't count on me."

Someone was moseying down the dock to greet them. Late forties, trim and weather-beaten in jeans and a coral-green shirt. He had the solitary aspect of a forest ranger who'd spent the last twenty years up in a lookout tower.

"You gentlemen doing all right?"

"Relax—we're not thumb-sucking infants," Teddy told him sharply. "My friend just needed a bit of help with his breathing gear."

The man smiled, unoffended. "Well, okay then. I'm Moses Squires." Extending a hand with squared-off fingers, he shook with Frank and Teddy. "I'll escort you up to the laboratory."

"So that's a lab?" Teddy looked dubious. "Looks more like a five-star penitentiary."

Whatever it was, the building could be reached only by a staircase that ascended from the dock up the ridge of the island. There had to be about a hundred and fifty goddamn steps.

Catching Frank's reluctance, Moses said: "I believe you'll manage. The others made it, and some of them are worse off than you two."

"Thanks for the pep talk there, Moses," Teddy said. "We taking your ark up?"

Moses's smile persisted. "It'll have to be two feet and a heartbeat, Mr. Bassiano."

THE FIRST few stairs were easy enough for Frank. Each was doubly as wide as a standard step, carved into the black rock. But before the quarterway point, Frank's heart was thumping painfully. He felt its sullen weight behind his ribs: an overcooked rump roast swaddled in snot.

The staircase was wide enough for Frank and Teddy to walk side by side. Teddy's face was set in a rictus of agony, hands clenched so tightly that his knuckles were tiny snowcaps. Moses Squires and John Salters followed a respectful distance behind, carting their luggage.

Up and up the two old men toiled. Frank cranked the dial on his machine to full-tilt. Oxygen pumped into his mask faster than he could inhale it; the pure O_2 concentration made him slightly delirious. Teddy's teeth were clenched so tightly that his jawbone was visible; Frank swore he could hear the brittle grind of Teddy's molars.

One foot in front of the other. The sun beat down from a suddenly cloudless sky. Was the staircase elongating? Goddamn thing felt like an escalator running in the wrong direction.

Frank turned and looked behind him, fighting a wave of wooziness . . . Teddy had stopped a few steps back, scrabbling for something in his pocket. Retreating down the stairs, sacrificing some of his precious gains (*Leave him,* yammered a selfish voice in Frank's head. *He's a goner, every man for himself!*), Frank helped Teddy retrieve his pill caddy from his pocket, which Teddy was shaking too badly to grasp.

"Can I help out?" Moses said from behind them.

Teddy could only make an inarticulate note of rage. "*Nyaaah!*" With one trembling finger, Teddy poked Frank in the chest. "*Him.*"

Fishing a pill from the caddy, Frank thumbed it into Teddy's mouth—he had to jerk his thumb back as Teddy's teeth snapped shut.

"Good to go," Teddy said, though his shakes didn't seem to diminish much.

The two of them trudged onward. By the halfway point Frank's heart was shrieking in his chest, a kettle reaching a frothy boil. Either Teddy's meds had taken effect or he was too stubborn to give in to his tremors; whatever the case, he was five steps ahead of Frank by then.

"Don't let the bastards grind you down, Frank!" Teddy called without glancing back.

Only a few days ago, Frank had resigned himself to death. But now—if only to satisfy his curiosity—he needed to reach the doors of the cathedral that loomed tantalizingly above him. There was no goddamn way he could let himself die on the cusp of such a mystery.

Problem was, Frank's exhaustion was making him delusional. How else to explain the fact he'd begun to hear the voice of an old-school Mustache Pete mobster over his shoulder? Frank swore he could smell the pepperoni-stink of the guy's breath on the back of his neck, too.

Nyaah, see, who's dis dirty rat? Let's fit him for a pair of cement overshoes and dump him inna rivah.

That was exactly how Frank's feet felt, too. Two cannonballs dipped in fast-dry cement. His ankles creaked as he lifted one arch-supported shoe, barely sliding the sole over the edge of the next stair before dragging his other shoe up to meet it—

Nyaah, fugget it. Dis old bastid is already dead, he just don't know it yet.

Frank gritted his teeth against that loathsome voice. A hundred and twenty steps . . . a hundred and thirty. Frank's blood slowed to a sludgy crawl; his heartbeat took on the sad mutter of a man screaming inside his own coffin . . . until the staircase met its unexpected end—the summit came so abruptly that Frank swooned, lurching on the balls of his feet as he took the final few steps at a clumsy tilt carrying him up to where Teddy was heaving, his hands on his kneecaps—miraculously, Frank was there.

Frank stood facing a set of double doors. He barely had a chance to give himself a mental pat on the back—*Holy shit, you did it!*—before Moses Squires slid past him, gripped the brass handles on the doors, and pulled them wide.

"Gentlemen, welcome to Spindrift."

FRANK DIDN'T know what he'd expected. But not *this*.

The space they'd stepped into looked no different than a doctor's waiting room. Brown walls and floor, some off-brand art deco chairs, a spider fern in desperate need of watering.

"Flutter flutter, heart be still," Teddy said.

Moses said, "There's more. That I can promise. John will stow your bags for you. We'll join the others, which is when you will all meet Dr. Strauss."

"Wait—I thought the doctor's name was Marsh," Frank said.

"Dr. Strauss works with . . . well, *for* . . . Dr. Marsh. As far as medical oversight goes, it's just the two of them up here."

Off this comment, Moses and John traded a covert glance. Frank couldn't intuit what that glance meant—but it bothered him, just a bit.

"And what do *you* do, Moses?" Teddy asked. "You seem like you ought to be mushing sled dogs through the bush, not working with a couple of Poindexters."

"Once upon a time, I did lead wilderness adventures," Moses told him. "But that's a young man's game."

"Are you Iroquois?" Teddy was eyeing Moses. "I used to work with a couple. Good fellas, kept to themselves."

Moses regarded Teddy with newfound appreciation. "Yeah, that's right. My people are from the Cayuga tribe. As for what I do around here, you could call me a general grunt. Both John and I. If Dr. Marsh or Strauss says jump, we ask how high. Now, if you're ready, please follow along. Everybody's waiting."

Moses led them through a door that opened into a clinical white hallway.

The smell of hot sparks hung in the air. Frank had the sense of unknown industry on the other side of the walls: a leaden bristle, as if a hundred Tesla balls were spitting in that secretive neighboring space. The hallway moved past a series of darkened panes of glass before reaching another nondescript door.

"In here," Moses beckoned.

The room reminded Frank of a portable classroom. Track lights hummed in a popcorn ceiling. No desks, only a few rows of utility chairs. Even a whiteboard.

When he and Teddy shuffled in, all eyes turned.

Eight red-rimmed, rheumy eyes.

It's official, Frank thought with a note of hilarity. *This Dr. Marsh has a type . . .*

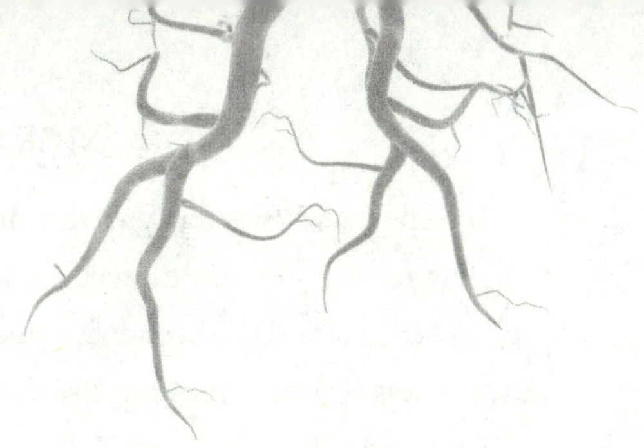

five.

. . . OLD FARTS with one foot in the grave.

The four individuals who sat slumped in the chairs spaced across the room were around Frank's age. Which was to say, old as owl shit.

Frank counted two men and two women. One of the ladies smiled as Frank shuffled to the empty chair beside her. Her teeth were porcelain white; he caught a faint whiff of Poligrip. He could see yards of wrinkled skin draping old bones and could make out the low-profile outline of a bag—colostomy or catheter, Frank couldn't tell—strapped to one guy's leg. A liniment-and-mothball scent permeated the air.

Frank had come out to the wilderness only to wind up back at the care home.

Weird, but some days Frank still felt young. It was an illusion—one look in the mirror would clear that up quick as a lick . . . over the last decade he'd found himself unselfconsciously doing what he considered to be "old person" things. The first time Frank had blown his nose into a Kleenex and stuffed it up the sleeve of his sweater, Lord, he'd nearly shit a brick. But his brain had evidently decreed Kleenexes to be multiuse sometime after he'd turned seventy. He'd noted that cut-glass bowls seemed to magically appear on old ladies' coffee tables, too, filled with pink-and-white chicken-bone candies all stuck together in a sharp ball.

"I feel like I'm back in Sister Fitzgibbons's classroom," Teddy announced. "She's gonna give me the strap when she finds the Bettie Page pinup taped to the inside of my desk."

The man with the bag gave a wan chuckle. Frank could tell the guy used to be bigger—those size fifteen clodhoppers he wore stood testament to that, plus he still carried the broad shoulders—but he was now yellowy and cored-out, those shoulders looking like a wooden coat hanger with a paper ghost fluttering from it.

The door opened. A woman in her mid-thirties stepped in, sliding between Moses and Salters. She took a seat facing the group.

"Hello, everyone. I'm so glad you all made it."

She wore jeans, boots, a cable-knit sweater. Her hair was cut in a no-nonsense bob.

"I'm Dr. Veronica Strauss. I only introduce myself as *Doctor* to separate my role here from that of Moses and John. I'm part of the other side of Spindrift's operation. I'm a bioethicist. Not sure if anyone's familiar with what someone like me does?"

Teddy snapped his fingers. "Damn, why did I let my subscription to *Obscure Jobs Monthly* expire?"

Strauss had an engaging smile. "Very clever, Mr. Bassiano. So, when we're talking bioethics, we're looking at the role of ethics in healthcare. I'm here as a safeguard. When you're driving a car, you want to test the brakes every so often to make sure they're still working. I'm the brakes on this island."

"You're a cop for doctors."

"Yes, Missus Dodds," Strauss answered the frost-haired woman to Frank's left. "That's a great way to put it. I've been onboarded to ensure that research here at Spindrift is done ethically, and that the doctors—or in our case, the single research professional spearheading this project—adhere to upright practices."

Dr. Strauss looked at each of them in turn. "But please understand that my presence should alert you to the fact—before you even exit this room—that the work going on under this roof is groundbreaking, controversial, and yes, it runs the risk of ethical quandary."

"Listen, miss," said the big cadaverous guy. "My last job was at a textile mill. Now I got a pair of busted lungs from inhaling mixed fabric fibers. I don't read the newspaper other than the funny pages, and I dropped out of school after grade nine." He grimaced, breathing so hard he was nearly gasping. "*Quandary? Bioethics?* Just dumb it down, wouldya?"

"I'll try, Mr. Udall," Strauss said. "But some of this stuff *is* complex—I mean, for *me* it's complex, and I've been here nearly nine months. Why don't we introduce ourselves? Just your name, your age, and maybe an interesting fact about you."

Frank found himself slouching deeper in his chair. What was this, first day of class? What next, show-and-tell?

The frost-haired lady went first. "I'm Madeline Dodds. Maddy if you like. I'm eighty-four. Worked in corporate finance. Never married, no kids." Then, as if forced into the confession: "Lyme disease. Tick bite. I went for a walk with my collie years ago, got bit, didn't realize it, missed the treatment window."

The other woman introduced herself next. "Claire Blessings. Seventy-nine. A homemaker. Separated with one child . . . diabetes got its hooks in me. My ex, Joe, said sugar was going to be the death of me. That was just more of his bullshit, because *he* was going to be the death of me. But he went belly-up first."

"Okay! And on *that* cheery note, hey ya! I'm Teddy."

Teddy was in his late seventies, a home builder, divorced a bunch with some kids he didn't see a whole lot of. "And now I'm here with you fine people. I've already met Franky Fast Fingers over there and look forward to hamming it up with the rest of you . . . unless we get dosed on laughing gas and have our organs harvested by the good doctor over here."

Next up was the walking corpse, Hugo Udall. Evidently he was seventy-six, but looked a hundred years old if he was a day.

"Like I say, my lungs're full of fabric junk. I got a lawsuit against my old boss, but my lawyer, this jerk named Johnny Celtina, he's so crooked he has to screw his socks on. Don't hire him, none a you. That bastard is gonna make sure I'm dead before I see one thin dime."

The last man was Davey Jacobs. A big-bellied Christian. Davey had a Bible

("I never leave the house without the Good Book along") conspicuously displayed on his lap. He had some kind of cancer. Bone or blood, Frank wasn't really listening to him.

Frank told everyone his name and age, then clammed up. Just the facts, ma'am. He didn't want to tell the others what he was dying from. Illnesses were all anyone talked about at Frank's care home. Once you get sick, like downward-spiral sick, your whole personhood vanished into your disease. It became your sole notable trait.

Greetings and salutations, I'm Frank Heart Failure. This is my new friend, Teddy Parkinson's. Have you met Maddy Lyme Disease and Hugo Fabric Scraps in His Lungs?

Frank looked straight at Dr. Strauss. "Now, are you going to tell us why we're here?"

"I will, but I can only partially explain. You'll need to meet Dr. Marsh—"

Teddy said, "Yeah, so where is this mysterious Dr. Marsh? She was the one on the phone, wasn't she? Did the rest of you speak to her, too?"

A round of nods met Teddy's question.

"You'll see her after we're done, Mr. Bassiano. And," Strauss stressed, "you can leave at any point. We will have you brought back to the mainland. But if you decide to go forward, we will soon arrive at a point of consequence. Several, in fact, staggered over the next few hours. With those points come decisions, and eventually an ironclad commitment on your end."

"That doesn't sound entirely ethical, Dr. Cop," Maddy remarked. "Sounds like you're trying to force a half dozen elderly and possibly doddery people into something. Or trick them."

"I promise you it's not like that," Strauss said. "But it *is* a delicate navigation. We're on the event horizon out here. You'll soon see that. But I'm telling you that nobody will ever force you to stay."

"I won't agree to anything where I don't know the shape of it," Hugo said. "It'd be like sticking your hand into a box that you don't know what's inside."

"You'll know exactly what you're committing to," Strauss assured him. "Mr. Bassiano, you asked about Dr. Marsh. Does the name *Astrid* Marsh mean anything to any of you?"

Frank had, in fact, googled "Dr. Marsh" on the public computer at the care home. There were over a hundred in Toronto alone. A dozen of them were podiatrists, go figure.

"Dr. Marsh's name is known intimately in specialized circles, spoken of reverently—well, mostly," Strauss went on. "Albert Einstein's IQ was measured in the 160s. Stephen Hawking's as well. The highest recorded IQ is 276, held by a South Korean mathematician."

Strauss paused, her eyes blinking closed for a heartbeat. "Dr. Marsh's is in the range of 290, though more likely the 300s. She's never consented to a full IQ test, but that's the best guess on assessable factors."

"Little Miss Big Brain," Teddy said. "She must be a gas at parties."

"I'd be surprised if she's ever gone to a party. Astrid's barely old enough to drink legally, and I don't believe she's ever had so much as a sip."

A quiver ran through the room. Claire said, "Wait, *how* old is she?"

"Nineteen," Strauss said. "Nineteen years, one hundred and two days old."

"You're saying Doogie Howser runs this place?" said Maddy.

Claire said: "Jesus. My kid is older than her."

"*All* our kids are older than her," said Teddy.

Strauss shut her eyes again. A bone-deep weariness seemed to course through her.

"Astrid had an unremarkable upbringing. Until she was four, there wasn't much to indicate her exceptionality. But by six, she was reading at an adult level. She completed high school in ten weeks, graduating at eight years old. She enrolled at Princeton the same year. Her studies concluded when her professors confessed that she was operating at a higher level of function than they could keep up with or even properly comprehend."

Strauss opened her eyes. "At fourteen, Astrid was granted legal emancipation from her parents. By then she had her own lab, where she was working—largely in solitude, but for a period with another young prodigy— on the process she'll introduce you to shortly."

Strauss twitched her nose, a bunny-like tic. "Astrid Marsh is one of the most remarkable human beings to have ever set foot on this earth. That's my opinion, having spent nearly a year in her company. But she is also the most sheltered and blindered individual—in most ways still a girl—you will ever meet. That's the result of the life she's been pulled into, somewhat against her will. Yet when you are blessed with such gifts . . . the world expects you to use them."

"I think you've described an idiot savant," Teddy said.

"You'll have to make your own judgment. I shouldn't influence you. Not very ethical of me. However, I'd hesitate to use the word 'idiot' and Astrid Marsh in the same sentence."

"Why us, then?" Frank asked. "What's special about us that you dragged us out here with all the cloak-and-dagger?"

Strauss replied, "Mr. Doyle, there was no specific reason it *had* to be any of you. You were all within geographic range and present with maladies common to your cohort. Astrid requested subjects aged seventy-five to eighty-five. She didn't wish this to replicate one of those private rocket flights where only the rich could take part." She paused fractionally before going on. "Plus, you've all elected to receive MAID."

Something passed through the group. A breed of guilt, perhaps, as if a secret had slipped free of their collective heart and gone drifting around the room.

"In fact, it's highly likely that none of you would be alive now, if not for Dr. Marsh's offer." Strauss clapped her hands. "Which I know is still obscure, so without further ado—"

Moses began handing out thick leaflets, one to each of them.

"This is a nondisclosure agreement. If you consent to continue, you'll have to sign it. What lies beyond that door is proprietary intellectual and developmental property."

Hugo snorted in irritation. "Come again?"

"Apologies, Mr. Udall," Strauss said. "In plain English, signing this means you cannot talk to anyone about what you've seen here."

Teddy said: "Can't have us blabbing, huh? Well, these honeyed lips are sealed."

He was already signing. Hugo and Davey and Claire did, too. Frank flipped through the document, which made as much sense to him as the Hong Kong phone book.

"This isn't legal," Madeline said. "You know that, don't you? Who's to say any of us are of sound-enough mind to understand what we're signing?"

"You don't have to sign," Strauss said. "But your tour will end right here in this room should you refuse."

"It's *not* legally binding," Maddy relented, scribbling her name. "Any halfway decent lawyer would use this as toilet paper."

When the NDAs were completed, Moses collected them.

"Let's head off, then," said Strauss. "Dr. Marsh will be waiting for you."

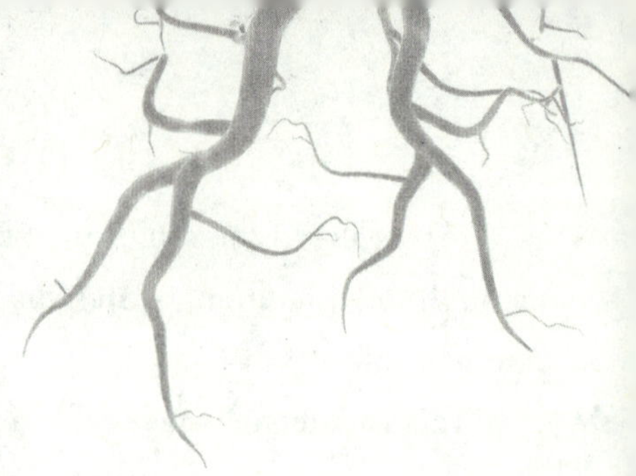

six.

MADELINE DODDS slipped in between Frank and Hugo at the rear of the line. The cocksure one, Teddy, headed the group like an overeager schoolboy. Dr. Strauss was ahead of him. The two Native gentlemen trailed the procession.

As they moved down an antiseptic hallway strung out under humming halogen lights, Maddy found herself deep in thought. She'd always been an analytical type who could—as her underlings once noted—find the angle in a circle. Being the lone woman in the Toronto financial sector during the Gordon Gekko Eighties necessitated that she always be one step ahead. If that earned her the label of a shrew or a ballbuster or even a cunt, well, so what? Money talks, bullshit walks. And Maddy had survived many skirmishes and earned her battle scars while her male competitors fell dead (career-wise, anyway) by the wayside.

Ever since she'd agreed to come to this island, Maddy's ole brain had been cooking; the gears ratcheting, pistons pumping, smoke just about curling out of her ears. It felt good to use her noodle again because for as long as she could recall, Maddy had barely used her brain at all. Chalk that up to the damn Lyme disease.

A tick had gotten trapped in the exposed hem of her panties while she was out walking her collie, Spell, dead three years now. It was a habit she'd stuck to without fail: five days a week, fifty-two weeks a year, through six dogs (Art, Fred, Ginger, Goldie, Wiley, Spell), for her adult life. But it ended when that little parasite supped on her blood without Maddy knowing; within a week she'd felt as if she'd been wrapped head to toe in a lead radiation suit.

By the time she consulted a doctor, the tick's foulness had shot right through her. She'd been seventy-six at the time. No spouse or partner. No children. Few real friends. But there were those millions in the bank. She'd had a six-month intercontinental trip lined up: Australia, China, Singapore, Europe. Maddy embarked on it despite her crippling tiredness, but after a few days found herself weeping on the king-size bed in a Melbourne five-star hotel.

She was so damned sick. So shockingly, frighteningly *old*.

A *tick*. The stupid bad luck of it all! Hadn't she been good, mostly? Shouldn't her resilience in a man's world be rewarded in the form of a long and healthy life?

HAH! laughed the universe. *Instead, the grand prize goes to . . . the tick!*

Maddy had scheduled her first MAID appointment without telling a soul. Truth be told, there were precious few who'd have cared much one way or the other.

Which had led Maddy Dodds here, to whatever *this* was. As far as she could see, a half dozen geezers gift wrapped and delivered to this uncanny island. Dr. Strauss with her NDA. Dr. Marsh, the child genius with her big but enigmatic ideas.

THE PROCESSION arrived at a pair of spotless glass doors, which slid open with an inrush of air. Dr. Strauss stepped into a vast unknown space. The rest shuffled after her.

They stood on a platform overlooking an immense laboratory floor. The facade Maddy had glimpsed from the boat—the black face of Spindrift as seen from the water approaching the island—had given no hint as to its true size. The lab itself was as big as your average Costco . . . larger, perhaps, as much lay shrouded in shadows.

It sprawled out under the cavernous ceiling. Maddy counted at least ten separate work areas, each of them twice the size of a well-funded university lab. Every zone (*pod* was the word her brain settled around) sat in a pool of light cast from high-intensity halogens; corridors of shadow ran in interconnected laneways between each. The interplay of light and darkness gave the lab the gridded appearance of a city block: the pods resembled lit apartment towers with darkened roadways running between them. Her eyes snagged on ill-defined shapes that sat at the fluttering edge of the pods; these could be items or machines of a scientific nature, but as to what *kind* of science, at the service of an as-yet-unstated goal, she had no clue.

Maddy saw a bank of what she figured were supercomputers a short distance from the platform they stood upon. The black, blockish units sat humming in liquid-cooled vaults in the pod beneath her. Another pod hosted an array of clear Lexan cages in which she caught signs of furtive movement. Were those *animals*?

Back in the nineties, Maddy had arranged a hostile takeover of a cosmetics company. Her first order of business was to shut down two animal-testing labs, and she'd taken pains to ensure the animals—those who weren't hopelessly ill or insane—were rehomed in species-appropriate sanctuaries. Whatever was going on here, the use of animals put a bad taste in Maddy's mouth.

The rest of the pods were largely inexplicable to her. *Above your pay grade, darlin'*, as the Bay Street boys used to tell her . . . before Maddy became their boss. A bristling sonic note rose from within Spindrift, a sound composed of many industries, mechanical and organic, that pinged on the sensitive apparatus of Maddy's inner ear.

"That must've set someone back a few bucks," Hugo said.

He was pointing at the cylindrical vessel in the center of the laboratory, stretching from floor to ceiling. A water tank, far bigger than Maddy suspected you'd find in any zoo or aquarium on earth. Within its clear curving glass pulsed what had to be thousands of jellyfish.

Maddy's feelings on jellyfish sat somewhere between awe and *ick*. Of anything on this planet, they seemed most likely to have been left behind by visiting aliens. The formless bells of their bodies and the bloodred beaded stems that trailed from within those bells, the million-skillion tentacles—some of them tipped with poison—hanging limpidly as they drifted in the phantom current inside the massive cylinder . . .

As a girl, Maddy often visited her grandparents' cottage near Shediac Beach in New Brunswick. One morning the tide receded to leave the sand splotched with hundreds of lion's mane jellyfish. Maddy had stepped nimbly between their dinner-plate-size bodies, their tentacles twitching in pools of salt water. She'd poked one with a bit of driftwood. Its rubbery texture reminded her of Jell-O skin.

"Who's footing the bill for this, Dr. Strauss?" Maddy asked.

This wasn't a government- or university-sponsored operation. They wouldn't have the financial means for something of this scale. It would cost hundreds of millions—though most likely capital-B *billions*—to build this, especially in the middle of nowhere. That kind of outlay could only mean corporate interests were at play. Big-money backers, potentially silent ones.

Before Strauss could reply, a voice trailed up from below.

"Did they sign your papers yet?"

At the foot of a staircase leading from the platform to the lab floor, Maddy got her first glimpse of Dr. Astrid Marsh.

DR. STRAUSS had told them Astrid was young, but nothing could've prepared Maddy for the wee elf at the bottom of the stairs. The spray of acne on Astrid's forehead. The fall of lank, colorless hair that flipped out in fey wings above her ears. Her freckled cheeks. The willowy unsexed body. The green of her eyes was as pronounced as it had been on the phone days ago. In place of a lab coat Astrid wore jeans, sneakers, and a *Star Trek* T-shirt.

"Everyone has signed, Dr. Marsh," Strauss confirmed.

Astrid spanked her palms. "Whoa, all right, awesome! I'm so glad you could come. You're looking, uhh . . ." Astrid trailed off, and Maddy guessed it was because she couldn't find anything positive to say about their appearance. ". . . well, hey, this is gonna be a real good time!" She made her way to the base of the stairs. "Come. *Come* down, don't be shy."

Maddy and the others went down to join her. Maddy noticed how Strauss set her fingers on Astrid's shoulder as if to calm her—she also saw Astrid jerk at Strauss's touch, shrugging her fingers off.

"Everyone's excited to hear what you've got to show them." Dr. Strauss adopted the demeanor of a nursery school teacher. "Isn't that right, everybody?"

"Yeah, thrilled to death," Frank croaked.

Astrid missed Frank's lame joke. "Have any of you worked in a laboratory? No? I figured as much. But it's okay! You don't need to know how any of this stuff works. *I do.* Everything would be, like, a complete fucking disaster without me."

Maddy caught Dr. Strauss's pained smile, as if the girl genius was failing a simple social graces test. Spinning on her heel, Astrid strode off into the lab.

"Follow me, gang!" she called without looking back.

They had to hurry to keep up, falling steadily behind until Dr. Strauss called out: "Dr. Marsh, remember that this is a tour, not a race."

Astrid checked up at the perimeter of a lit pod. The one full of cages. Maddy caught the scurry of rodents, which, God help her . . . all creatures great and small, sure, but the order *Rodentia*—rats, especially— stirred an instinctive revulsion in her. Maddy could now see that at least half of the cages contained white lab rats with licorice-whip tails and ruby eyes.

"Do you guys know *why* you're all dying?" Astrid asked abruptly. "I don't mean what *specifically*," she went on, pointing at each of them in turn. "Congestive heart failure—Lyme disease—Parkinson's—chronic diabetes— colorectal cancer—pulmonary edema with associated comorbidities . . . I mean, like, what's going on inside your bodies right now *as* you're dying."

"Young lady," Maddy remarked, "I have to say you lack something in bedside manner."

Astrid's neck flushed at the scolding. "Sorry. I'm . . . always saying weird stuff and making people mad at me."

"An honest mistake," Strauss gently soothed in full nursery school mode. "Missus Dodds doesn't dislike you. Do you, Madeline?"

"I barely know you, Astrid. But I encourage you to please go on and tell us all why we're dying."

"Well, okay then," Astrid said, taking Maddy's directive literally. "You're dying because you've passed a point of cellular senescence. Which is a fancy way of saying that your cells, all the little building blocks of Y-O-U, have turned against you. Nature has decided you've had enough time on earth, and senescence is its way of getting rid of you."

"Mother Nature's way of clearing the decks," said Frank.

"Right!" Astrid clapped her hands. "But not *all* life on earth is subject to senescence. Some animals, like rock bass and tortoises and even seagulls— yeah, they *die*, but they don't *age*. At least, not the way we do. That's a phenomenon called *negligible* senescence."

She spun, orienting herself, and said: "Here's what I mean, right over here."

She led them deeper into the pod, where clear plastic terrariums sat upon metal columns. Maddy's flesh seized in knots as they passed between the rats' enclosures. Past those were some species of golden-contoured lizards, then a pair of tortoises lazing in a pen that appeared too small for them . . .

"Look at these happy fellows in here."

They clustered around a display containing a Habitrail-type system of tubes. At the heart of the arrangement lay four hairless, supremely ugly creatures with yellow buckteeth.

"Naked mole rats," Astrid told them. "Two adults and two juveniles. There's a fifteen-year age gap—and these little guys can live up to thirty years. But guess what? By all key life markers, all four are functionally *the same*. You can hardly tell the difference, right?"

Maddy stared at the fumbling little brutes. They did all look alike.

"Okay, but what does that mean?" Hugo asked.

Astrid said: "If humans aged the same way these mole rats do, we'd look and function like twenty-five-year-olds when we're eighty. These moles' bodies, their whole *system*, have evolved to exist in a perfect stasis. Their brains and hearts and lungs hardly degrade at all, until one fine day, *boom*, they just drop dead."

"Wouldn't be a bad way to go," Teddy mused.

"Yeah, and there isn't the, the . . ." Astrid's gaze tracked over her guests.

". . . the steady decline." She bent, intently observing the mole rats. "So why can't we age that way, too?"

"Because this isn't *Star Trek*," Claire said.

Astrid pirouetted on her heel to face her. "You like *Star Trek*? It's a very good show, isn't it? Have you watched *Picard* yet? You should." She pointed at Claire. "I *demand* you watch it, on penalty of death!" She gripped her thumb on the opposite hand, yanking until the veins bulged on her forearm. "*Hah!* I'm just kidding, miss, um, who are you?"

"Claire."

"Claire, right! Only kidding."

On that, Astrid marched onward. To the group, Strauss said: "It's a big day for her. She's a bit nervous."

"No, I'm *no-oo-ot!*" Astrid shouted back in a ringing singsong.

THE GROUP caught up with Astrid at the base of the cylindrical tank Maddy had seen earlier. It was at least twenty feet wide, ascending fifty feet to the ceiling.

Thousands of vibrantly colored jellyfish wafted in the clear water. The current corkscrewed upward, pulling the jellyfish in a conical trajectory. There were many species of many colors. A few were huge—the main mass of the largest specimen umbrellaed the top of the tank in a diaphanous purple ring; from that ring descended what Maddy had always thought of as a jellyfish's exposed gut sack: this one had both the size and appearance of the human organ system, the naked lungs and liver and intestines, all tinted a violent crimson.

The jellyfishes' tentacles hung down in numberless profusion, each strand curling and licking. The smaller jellyfish—their bodies varied from the size of a manhole cover to that of a teacup saucer—drifted in the shadow of the huge one in the manner of feeder fish sheltering among the roots of a mangrove tree.

The sight was so bizarrely transfixing that it sent a shiver through Maddy's stomach. Somehow, they were worse than the rats.

"Those other animals," Astrid said, "the mole rats, et cetera, they live differently—I'd argue *better*—than we do. But they still die. Every single thing on earth dies eventually, if something doesn't kill it first. All except one."

Astrid directed their attention to a much smaller tank below the huge one. There, visible within the foot-by-foot-wide panes, rested a glowing green fishhook the thickness of a spaghetti strand. Rounded at one end, with a nest of hairline growths sprouting from the other.

As their shadows fell over its tank, the creature tensed in the manner of a muscle contracting: a spasmodic twitch that echoed the crack of a tiny whip.

"What is that?" Maddy asked.

"This is my Hydra," Astrid said reverently. "And it can live forever."

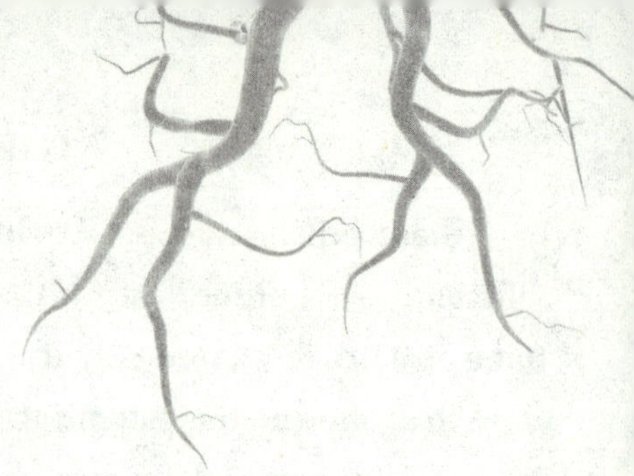

seven.

FRANK DOYLE was standing next to Claire when the doctor spoke those words:

Live forever.

He saw the hairs go quilling up Claire's bare arm.

"Nothing lives forever," Claire said. "Not even universes live forever, do they?"

"You're right," Astrid replied. "But when our universe folds in on itself in a quantum infinity, these magical little guys will be the very last to go."

"How can anything live endlessly?" Frank heard himself ask.

Astrid tapped the Hydra's tank. "This jellyfish is a distant cousin of the ones in the big tank. It isn't usually this big. Typically smaller than a baby's pinkie fingernail clipping, in fact. But I messed around with its DNA coding. Think of this one as a Godzilla Hydra."

Astrid rubbed her head, a seeming tic of hers; Frank was surprised she hadn't rubbed her scalp bare.

"The Hydra is asexual. That's part of its gift. And the Hydra is a regenerator. When injured, it repairs itself."

"Don't humans do that, too?" said Hugo. "When we get cut or break a bone."

"But we don't fix ourselves nearly so well as we get older, do we?"

Astrid pulled a sheet of paper from her pocket, unfolded it, and spread it flat on top of the Hydra's tank. With a pen, she drew a narrow *X*.

"This is a human chromosome. Actually, the chromosome is the top two points of the *X* and the bottom two are the chromatids, and the middle where the two strands meet is called the centromere—do you all follow? I promise there's not going to be a test."

Hugo gave a sigh of bewilderment. Dr. Strauss set a pacifying hand on his forearm.

"Every human has twenty-three pairs of chromosomes," Astrid continued. "Forty-six total. Each protein strand, each chromosome, holds a single molecule of DNA, which is the instruction guide for every cell and function in our body. It's how we get built from the instant our first cell divides in the womb. We're made up of, like, forty trillion cells, okay? It's a lot for our bodies to keep track of. Everyone following along?"

"Just keep going," Hugo said dourly.

"Chromosomes repeat themselves, okay? *Healthy* chromosomes repeat usefully, building new cells. But when a chromosome repeats too many times, its tendency is to misbehave. Its instructions go haywire, and it starts repeating badly and creating sick cells, cancers, and other bad boys . . . which is what getting old *is*, basically. Right, Veronica?"

"I see it more as light switches," Dr. Strauss said. "At a certain time in our life cycles, our bodies begin to shut down. Imagine a school or an office building at the end of the day. You shut off the lights one by one, or by floors, or sometimes all at once."

"They're not *babies*, Veronica." Astrid's neck flushed. "They're in fact the *opposite* of babies. They're *old*, they're sick and dying—you *are* dying, all of you, right where you stand. You don't deny that, do you?" she asked Frank directly.

"Sure, kid, you bet I'm dying," he told her, jaw set. "You got me dead to rights."

"You don't need to be spoon-fed, do you?" Astrid's chin jutted. "Any of you need a widdle baby spoon? You want safe widdle analogies for the hard truths?"

Frank thought: *She's that horrible little goon from* The Twilight Zone.

Anthony Fremont. The boy from that episode of the Rod Serling show:

"It's a Good Life." Frank held a memory of watching it as a kid, cross-legged on the shag carpet in front of his parents' black-and-white Admiral TV with a plate of Lorna Doone cookies on his lap. He recalled the feeling of marrow-deep dread when it was revealed that an isolated rural town sat under the thrall of a mind-reading sociopath: six-year-old Anthony Fremont. A kid who had the power to alter space and time; who could make anything or anyone disappear or else transform them, in Serling's narration, into *a grotesque walking horror*. Little Anthony Fremont turned his auntie into a mute vegetable; he turned a drunk man at a party into a jack-in-the-box. Anthony could banish anyone who displeased him *to the cornfield*. And no matter what atrocity Anthony Fremont committed, everyone in town would give a ghastly grin and say: *It's a real good thing what Anthony did! A real good thing!*

Well, be damned if Frank was going to put up with that same tyranny from this flappy-haired space cadet.

"When I talked that way to my teachers," Frank told Astrid, "they sent me to the office."

Astrid's head cranked over to him. It was not unlike the pivot of a rusty animatronic bear.

"But you see, I'm the *principal*, Frank," she said in a silky tone. "This is *my* school."

"If I gave my ma that kind of lip, she'd have hided me raw," Hugo said, his spine straightening. Hugo looked more puffed up all of a sudden. "Or she'd've called my pops home to whip my ass red on the front lawn—"

"Stem cells," Strauss cut in hastily. "You were saying, Astrid?"

"Oh, right." Astrid blinked. "Thank you, Veronica . . . so stem cells are . . ." She paused, pointing at Hugo. ". . . *you* don't have any stem cells in you anymore. You're way too old. Even *I* don't have many. Our bodies manufacture stem cells early on. When we're young, we're creating them all the time.

"Stems are do-anything cells. Imagine you're building a house, okay? If your building block is a stem cell, it can be a brick or a two-by-four or a nail or a sack of cement. Those are *embryonic* stem cells, but we only create them from our fourth to seventh day as embryos, following fertilization. After that, *poof*, they disappear. Yet those are all we need to build our bodies until our adolescent phase, following puberty. After that, all we have are *adult* stem cells, which are contained in specific areas of our bodies. A marrow stem cell only creates marrow, a kidney stem a kidney. As we get older, even those cells deteriorate. They go senile, start to repeat harmfully, and . . ." Astrid stomped her foot violently. "Blammo!"

"Well, why can't we get some of those into us?" Teddy asked. "Inject stem cells?"

"It won't work," Dr. Strauss told him, "because there's no pathway to deliver them. Our bodies lack the instruction to know what to do with them, sadly."

"But this Hydra knows, okay?" Astrid told them. "It manufactures its own version of embryonic stem cells *endlessly*. It never stops pumping them out, which means it never gets old. And when it gets hurt . . ."

Reaching underneath the tank, Astrid pulled out a platform hidden in a recessed drawer. There were two joysticks wired to a panel.

Astrid settled her fingertips on the joysticks. Frank noted the nasty gleam in her eye.

"Watch this," she said, her tongue piercing her lips as she sank deep in concentration.

A pair of metal armatures rose from the bottom of the Hydra's tank. Robotic arms. At the end of each were pincers resembling needle-nose pliers.

Astrid manipulated the joysticks. The arms darted at the Hydra. The jellyfish evaded the first few strikes, but eventually one of the pincers scissored shut on its body.

"Got ya," Astrid whispered.

Methodically, Astrid pulled the jellyfish apart. Plucked off the tentacles, then clamped the second set of pincers near the first and tore the Hydra right in half.

Done, she pushed the joysticks back out of sight. "Now, watch."

Frank crouched, cotton-mouthed with disgust. Watch *what*? Nothing was happening. The glowing halves of the Hydra drifted weightlessly in the water.

"You killed the poor thing," said Claire.

"No she didn't," Dr. Strauss said in an oddly flat tone.

The larger part of the Hydra began to lengthen, its body filling back in. It was like watching a pea shoot grow in time-lapse. The snipped threads began to push out of it, too, rapidly elongating. The torn-off bits sank to the bottom of the tank, no longer glowing.

An entirely new apparatus formed within the tank. Fresh, from broken parts.

Before too long the jellyfish was alive and whole again.

"The limb regeneration isn't important," Astrid said. "It's just a neat parlor trick. What's key is that the Hydra's injury forced it to marshal its stem cells, and in doing so it both repaired itself physically *aaand*"—pause for emphasis—"made itself *younger*. That's what you just witnessed, okay? A creature, the only one of its kind, that is biologically younger than it was just minutes ago. Its mutilation made it age backwards, against the flow of time."

Astrid winked. "And so I thought: 'Why not us, too?'"

Oaring her arm theatrically, she cried: "Onward, gang!"

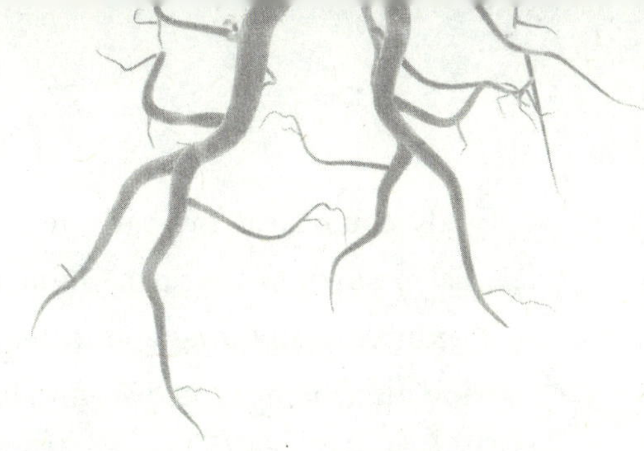

eight.

"HOLD ON! Wait a goddamn minute."

Teddy was dog-tired. He was hungry. He needed to stop moving, stop his thoughts from ping-ponging around his brain.

He fumbled a pill out of his caddy. Teddy hated how he must've looked—an old, pitiable man. Well, fuck 'em if that's what they saw. His brain was as sharp as ever, even if his body shook as bad as a jalopy tooling at sixty klicks down a dirt road.

"This is feeling real Willy Wonka," he said. "You've got this magical candy factory, and boy is it ever nifty. But I'm too old to be led down this primrose path without some more concrete answers, *now*."

His demand earned nods from everyone except the uppity broad, Madeline.

"I get it," Astrid told him. "I'm overexcited, and all this . . . it *is a* lot, isn't it?"

"You ain't kidding," said Frank.

"Should we take a break? Some food?" Astrid called out to Salters and Squires, who'd hung back in the shadows. "Can you whip something up for us, boys?"

Madeline said: "I'm not especially hungry, and I'm not tired, either."

The old biddy stood in the reflection of the tank. The shadow of the biggest goddamn jellyfish Teddy had ever seen drifted over her face, imprinting it with an ugly mottled pattern.

"But I'm willing to stop if Teddy wishes to," Maddy said, looking straight at him.

Teddy could hear the barb nestled in her offer. *If you can't keep up, old feller, feel free to sit this one out.* Ohhh, this was one flinty old bird.

"I didn't say anything about needing a break, did I?" Teddy shot back. "Just don't like being jerked around like a bull with a ring through my nose."

The battle-ax grinned at him. Who let her off the wrinkle ranch? "An intelligent young woman showing you her work makes you feel that way, does it, Theodore?"

The procession got moving again. Teddy shouldered past Hugo, barging to the head of the line. Something within him couldn't help but turn everything into a battle of wills . . . and in Madeline, he sensed an equal. The woman gave off the whiff of Grade-A Bitch.

Squires and Salters showed up with bottles of water and some granola bars. No-name bars, Teddy noted with hilarity. Someone had built a billion-dollar lab and stocked it with food from a soup kitchen. Nevertheless, Teddy wolfed the bar down as the tour came to a set of black-painted double doors. Squires hauled them open. The group stepped into a murky space perfumed with the stink of diesel fuel.

A set of track lights popped on to reveal slab cement walls. A pair of hunter-green Land Rovers tricked out for backcountry driving shone under the lights.

"It's a short drive," Veronica assured them. "Out and back before dark."

SALTERS TOOK the wheel of one Rover; Squires was in the other, pulling a livestock trailer. Madeline, Dr. Marsh, Claire, and Frank got in with Squires. That left Teddy riding with Strauss, Hugo, and Davey Jacobs, clutching that Bible of his for dear life. Teddy was back in his high school cafeteria—except instead of the cool kids, he was stuck at the nose-picker's table.

Salters gassed the Rover onto a path carved through the trees. The sun glossed the island's landscape in a golden-hour light that made the woods look buttery, as if the earth might melt into the water. The path edged out of the trees and meandered along a lonely stretch of the island for a mile or so; the stone that demarcated the island's ridge rose in a black, jagged spine that terminated in a windswept tabletop above the water. It ran much rougher than it had on Teddy's approach in the pilot boat: the surf frothed between half-submerged boulders, and out past the breakwater the water ran dark and depthless.

"Sun sets quickly this time of year," Salters said. "And the cold grips fast."

Teddy was wedged in the back seat with Hugo and Davey, who had Teddy squished up against the door. Davey was sweating, *a lot*, and in the tight quarters Teddy was helpless to get any separation from the big moist doughboy.

"This island extends a long way," Strauss remarked. "I'd say it's what, John, thirty miles from end to end?"

"Yeah, that'd be about right," Salters said. "Nothing much but brush and pine and bog. Then you hit miles of water, then more islands same as this one."

Teddy's arm was slick with Davey-sweat by the time the Rovers swung into a bell-shaped flatland hemmed by pines. A twenty-foot-high chain-link fence ran down the eastern tree line, following a faint bend as it disappeared into the brush.

The group got out of the Rovers and made their way across a stretch of low grass. They huddled together facing the fence. The waxing autumn sunlight guttered between the pines. The air stilled for a span of heartbeats. A waft of breath or something akin to it, strangely sweet, came from the vast woods past the chain-link, and with it, every so often, the cooing of wild grouse. Madeline wrapped her hands around her elbows and shivered.

"My old blood," she said to nobody in particular.

"That so? I feel toasty warm," said Teddy.

Grin and bear it, you mouthy old bag, he thought with grim satisfaction, though Maddy was right: with the sun going down, it was cold as a penguin's dick out here.

Salters popped the trunk of his Rover, hauling out an arm-size object wrapped in black plastic. Meanwhile, Squires unclasped a gunmetal-gray case and removed a rifle.

"If we can get Boots and Diego, great," Astrid told him. "If not, just Boots."

By then, Salters had removed from the plastic a joint of bloody animal meat with the hoof still attached. He slung it over the fence into the enclosure. Meanwhile, Squires slid a feathered dart into the rifle.

All eyes were riveted on the fence. They watched that shank of meat on the furred moss and the wall of trees beyond it. A thin and low-running mist appeared between the trees, burbling across the hummocks . . . within that mist shapes seemed to toss and turn in the manner of overlarge children . . .

When the first one slunk out from under those boughs, it was to Teddy as if he'd crossed the brink into a nightmare.

Teddy wasn't afraid of wolves . . . wait, *was* he? How could he say for sure, seeing as this marked the first time he'd encountered one up close. Before now they'd existed only in fairy tales, where they blew houses down and dressed up as grandmas in order to devour little girls.

This one eased from the woods as living oil, smooth and frictionless despite its size. From Teddy's perspective it seemed a good four feet tall, riding above the ground mist on legs as long and cantilevered as stilts.

"Whoo, that's one big boy," Hugo breathed.

The wolf checked up near the meat. Its coat was black flecked with gray, its ears pointed, its eyes shining goldenly. Its fur rippled in twitchy undulations.

Three more followed. One was nearly the size of the first—Teddy figured it had to be another male. Its pelt was the same bone-white hue as the mist. And two smaller ones, who Teddy assumed must be the female mates. They scissored tightly behind the males in a manner that activated Teddy's primal fight-or-flight drive.

If they decided to attack, he wouldn't make it five feet—it'd be a bloodbath, him and everyone else torn to rags by those beasts. Thank Christ for that fence.

"Canadian timber wolves," Strauss whispered.

"They can't get out," Astrid said. "Believe me, they've tried."

The large male hunched at the meat. Its eyes never left the group of humans. It knew they were there. It must have known well before Teddy and the others had seen it appear, catching their scent on the wind. Its jaws levered open—a cavernous pit studded with teeth—and clamped down on the prize . . .

Squires's dart gun issued a dull *phut*. Passing through the metal links, the dart scored a direct hit. Teddy could see the bright pink feather sticking from the leading wolf's flank.

Skull lowered, the wolf rushed at them. Davey Jacobs let go a girlish shriek as the wolf reached the fence in two heart-stopping leaps. Its fangs slashed at the chain-link as the beast yammered with a note of frustration that Teddy felt as a wire in his blood—if the wolf could get at them, just one chance, it would slaughter them all for the sheer sport of it.

Madeline recoiled, her bony backside colliding with Teddy's hip as the gamy reek of the wolves pushed past the fence. Moses Squires aimed and fired again. This dart hit the second male. It howled and spun, snapping at its flank in an attempt to tug the dart out.

By then the tranquilizer was working on the first male. Its head dipped between its legs as it tottered in a drunken circle, jaws snapping with the *schnick* of hedge shears.

Within thirty seconds both males were unconscious, splayed on the moss. With a mordant howl, the females slunk back into the woods.

Squires and Salters entered the pen through a locked gate a hundred yards away from the viewing party. They whistled and stomped their feet. Teddy figured that was to warn the females off, or make sure the tranquilizers had taken full effect. You couldn't have gotten Teddy to step inside that fence for all the pussy in a Vegas brothel.

The men spread out two tarps. They dragged a wolf onto each.

"You can check them out," Squires offered once he'd hauled the large male back to the Rovers. "They won't bite."

"For now, they won't," Salters added.

Only Claire leaned in for a closer look, but she reared back. "They do have a smell to them," she said.

The men settled the sedated wolves into the livestock trailer and locked the gate.

"You gonna tell us why you're keeping pet wolves?" Frank asked the doctors.

"Other than primates, wolves are the closest match to human DNA," Astrid said. "Eighty-seven percent genetic overlap. Which makes them good subjects."

Teddy said, "Subjects for *what*?"

Astrid only flounced away, coy as a milkmaid, calling over her shoulder: "Get in the Rovers! Back to the lab."

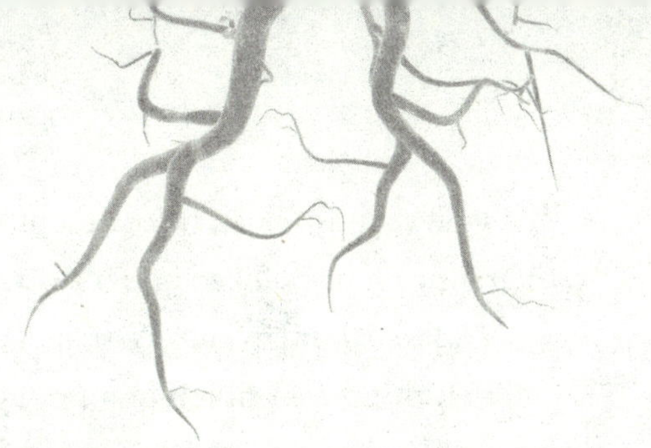

nine.

AIN'T THIS a real ring-a-ding-ding!

The voice and catchphrase belonged to Madeline's dear sainted mother, long gone now. It was her version of *Ooh la la.*

This doc's onto something big, Maddy—a real ding-donger of a ring-a-ding-ding!

Maddy figured her mother was right on that. For that reason, she found herself more energized than she'd been in years. When that wolf rushed the fence, why, Maddy's blood had been set to leap right out of her skin! Strange how the most vibrant colors of life tend to shine brightest when you're cozying up skintight to death.

Beyond the wolves themselves was the question of their utility. Clearly, a Promethean streak was shot through Astrid Marsh's research. The building blocks of flesh and blood, the stuff of life was being snipped and sewn, molded and diversified out here on this island.

The return trip to Spindrift passed in silence. Frank sat to one side of her in the Rover, Claire to the other. Was she trembling, or was it all of them? Maddy was one huge peeled nerve.

ONCE THEY'D parked back in the laboratory's garage, the two hired men—both of whom were eminently capable, but especially the Squires fellow—off-loaded the wolves.

When Maddy saw those same gentlemen next, they were standing beside a glass-topped examination table in one of the laboratory's more distant pods.

The wolves were there, too, laid out side by side on a glass-topped table with their limbs immobilized under restraints.

"Gather round, please," Astrid instructed.

The group assembled in a pool of light beamed down from the vaulted ceiling. The wolves' chests rose and fell as they slumbered. It came to Maddy that they could be dreaming. What were the dreams of such creatures? Wall-to-wall sheep, maybe, or running headlong to bite the moon.

This close, it was clear that one of the wolves was quite old. Its body threadbare, fur thin and hoary. One back leg was kinked, as if it had been broken and healed badly. What were the names Astrid had given them—was it Bruno and Boots? . . . no, *Diego* and Boots. Maddy was pretty sure the older one was Diego. Meaning the younger one must be Boots.

A gray cube the size of a tissue box was connected to a laptop that rested on the edge of the examination table.

"This is an epigenetic clock," said Astrid, touching the box. "It was developed a couple years ago at UCLA. Pretty neat device. By identifying biomarkers, it's effective at pinpointing the biological age of a living specimen." Her gaze traveled over the group. "If you stick around, you'll get very familiar with this clock."

She gave a nod to Squires, who stepped toward the wolves with what resembled an extra-thick Q-tip puff on a wooden stick.

"The epigenetic clock measures methylation in cells," Astrid continued. "Methylation's a chemical process that takes place as a subject ages. Think of it as rust. The more methylation is observable in a cell, the rustier it is, meaning the older that cell must be."

Moses Squires peeled back the lip of the juvenile wolf, Boots. He then ran the Q-tip over its exposed gums.

Squires handed the sample to Dr. Strauss, who swabbed it onto a specimen slide and inserted the slide into the epigenetic clock. The gray cube emitted a soft purr as it worked.

Squires set about Q-tipping Diego, the older wolf. But as he leaned in over its bullet-shaped skull, Diego's lips reflexively skinned back. A growl rippled from its throat.

Squires set the swab down and waited until the wolf's jaws relaxed. He then repeated the procedure, his fingertips less than an inch from Diego's yellowed fangs.

"You got big brass cojones there, pal," Teddy whispered.

Next, the laptop pinged.

A red numeral lit the screen, displaying the age of Boots.

4

"The epigenetic clock can only fix on the nearest year," Astrid told them. "Not months or days . . . not this version of the clock, anyway. But I might remedy that." She shrugged. "Depends if I feel like improving its function."

The specimen slide with Diego's saliva went into the box next. The same faint purr.

Ping.

14

"Wolves can live up to sixteen years in captivity," Astrid said. "So, one of our subjects is the equivalent of a teenager. The other's something like seventy years old in human terms."

Maddy studied the two wolves on the table. Her gaze shifted to Astrid. Something moved through her then—akin to longing, or loss, or desperation.

She's so young, Maddy thought. *How can anyone so inexperienced with life cope with the scope of having so much power?*

"Now here's a tidbit you should find interesting," Astrid said. "These wolves were once the same age. They were whelped in captivity from the same mother, in the same litter. They're brothers, born on the same day just about fourteen years ago."

For a long beat, nobody spoke. What Astrid had said challenged everything they knew about aging and death. Still, there the wolves lay. Boots, the pup. Diego, the weary veteran. One young and healthy, the other old and gray. Yet both were born on the same day, perhaps the same hour, from the same mother, into the same litter.

"Bullshit," Hugo said. "You're lying. I don't know why, but you are."

Not much above a whisper, Davey Jacobs spoke for the first time in forever. "I don't think she's lying."

"It's fair to believe I *am* lying, Hugo," Astrid said. "Honestly, there are days, or at least minutes of each day, when I wish none of this had happened."

"Dr. Marsh," Dr. Strauss said, tight-faced.

Astrid's voice was etched with defeat when she said: "We may as well show them."

Dr. Strauss removed a control from her pocket and pushed a button. The pod's overhead lights dimmed. Next, a flat-screen monitor rose behind the exam table that the wolves lay upon. The dimension of the monitor mirrored the table's polished surface.

Lines of green light crisscrossed the table, spreading under the wolves. A smooth and almost organic-sounding noise kicked up under the table. The thrum of gyroscopes cycling within it, a sound not unlike a heartbeat—there must be a hidden apparatus within the exam bench, which sent its hum up Maddy's legs.

Green grid lines climbed the wolves' bodies, laying faint traceries across their fur; the crisscrossing green lines rectified into a net of squares. The lines crept up and over the animals, from tip of tail to end of nose. The grid lines intersected as the nets grew smaller, the squares of green tightening.

It's some kind of diagnostic tool, Maddy thought. But what it measured, or how, she had no idea.

Soon the wolves' bodies appeared on the flat-screen monitor—only in a defined but hollow outline as yet, two cups waiting to be filled. An X-ray or MRI was the closest equivalent to what Maddy was seeing, but it wasn't quite either of those.

Maddy stared at the wolves' outlines. There was no obvious difference between—

The flat-screen monitor changed. It almost seemed to flex, then pixelate, as new information thundered through its circuitry. Maddy let out a sharp intake of breath.

"That," said Astrid, "is *my* Hydra."

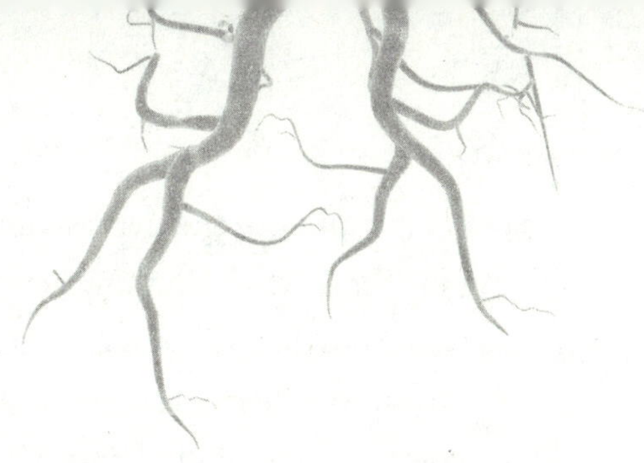

ten.

WHEN FRANK'S eyes settled upon it—they didn't want to, at first; something in the inner mechanics of his eyeballs blotted out the sight . . . when he saw, *really* saw, what was on the monitor, it filled him with dreadful awe. The transfixing awe a pagan may have felt in the days before humanity collected into civilized societies—the darkness of the shoreline, obscene frolics on lonely hillsides, moonlit rites in uninhabited places . . . a shudder passed through him as he stared at what lay inside the younger wolf.

The Hydra. That's what the doctor called it. Same as the jellyfish.

No. She'd said *my* Hydra.

Frank concentrated on the older wolf, if only to have someplace else to put his eyes. The sight of the other one—*Boots*—made his stomach flip over.

Diego's insides were normal. Its bones and organs (which Frank could see clearly on the monitor) seemed typical of its species. The apparatus the wolves lay upon had created a map of their insides; the old wolf's brain and organs were colored in reds or yellows with faint fuzzy outlines—what appeared to be normal blood was moving through Diego's veins. Frank had seen scans like that before. His own medical history was chockablock with X-rays and MRIs and ultrasounds, bones and blood and organs, so this was really no different.

Then his eyes drifted helplessly leftward until he was looking at Boots again. The apparatus peered inside its body with the same intimate detail. Frank could see, at least partially, Boots's organs and bones and venous system, perhaps even the nerves knitted through its musculature . . . but that wasn't all. There was something else inside Boots.

Christ Almighty. What was it *doing* in there?

The thing inside Boots glowed blue, or at least that seemed to be its dominant color—but it shifted through the moodier shades of the spectrum, magenta to violet to emerald green. It had the look of many things one might find in nature, or aspects of those things, but the Hydra didn't *really* appear like anything Frank had seen, or ever wanted to.

The entire length and breadth of the wolf were filled with it. Down each of its legs, inside its chest and reproductive organs, its skull, winnowing up the length of its tail. The wolf *teemed* with it. The sight put Frank in mind of ivy creeping up an endless wall in thick, suffocating threads—or, disturbingly, an infinite plate of spaghetti whose noodles were never at rest, always shifting and expanding, undulating, clenching, invading until they reached but never expanded over the rim of the plate itself, just as the Hydra was barely contained within the wolf's body.

From the outside, Boots looked as a wolf ought to. But inside it was . . .

An obscenity was the ten-dollar word Frank's mind plucked from the ether.

Without being able to say why, Frank felt that what he was glimpsing—as much as the scanner was capable of showing—was but a fraction of the Hydra's whole. The impression came that, at the end of those trillion tapering strands filling the wolf's body in the way of frost spreading across a winter window, there was an endless flowering and diversification that no human eye could chart—something invisible but always at work, the same way an anthill could spread under a house without its owner knowing . . . and in that un-glimpsed subatomic space the Hydra kept flourishing, its alterations and secrets ever more complex as it became smaller and thinner, as microscopic as life could get, delicate enough to slip into DNA helixes at its spinning cores, there to work its unknown magic.

"I can't stand to look at that anymore." Davey Jacobs clapped his hands over his eyes like a kid at a scary movie. "Turn it off."

If anyone heard Davey, nobody granted his wish. Everybody's gaze was riveted on the Hydra, helplessly so, and in their eyes Frank could see reflected his own grisly fascination.

"And you," Madeline said to Astrid, "*created* that? You put that inside this animal?"

Astrid's own eyes were stuck fast to her creation. It seemed to require great effort to pull them away and address Madeline.

"Six months ago, yes," she said. "Back then, Boots here"—gesturing to the younger wolf—"and Diego were the same biological age. Both were nearing death."

"When I arrived at this laboratory, it was as a skeptic," Dr. Strauss said. "I figured the ethical oversight I was hired to offer would be redundant, based on the assumption that the work taking place here was a fool's errand."

"That's me," Astrid said, "a young heart-struck fool."

"As most are at your age," Dr. Strauss said to her. "Foolish and headstrong. But you've managed to create something that has the chance to stand as the greatest healthcare innovation in human history . . . the single greatest human advancement, period."

Frank imagined that old used-car salesman's gambit: jacking a car's wheels up, jamming the transmission into reverse, and pinning a brick to the gas pedal to let the odometer run backward. Had Astrid discovered how to pin a brick to the gas pedal of the human body and forcibly peel the years away—all the damage done, the calcifications and brittleness, the ravages of old age . . . had she discovered a way for humankind to duck the Reaper's scythe? Or was it the same as that salesman's gambit—a pig in a poke?

"I've seen this movie before," Madeline said, vocalizing Frank's concern. "It's the one that starts off hopefully before everything goes to hell in a hand-cart."

"You're right," said Astrid. "The Hydra's been in Boots here for half a year, and as yet, it has worked exactly as predicted."

"Better, in fact," Strauss added.

"But there's no certainty that won't change right this second," Astrid confessed. "It could be happening now, only the damage hasn't manifested yet."

"So then, what the hell *is* that thing?" Hugo asked.

"The engine of the Hydra is too complex to detail," Astrid told him. "But the three building blocks are: one, elements of the jellyfish it takes its name from; two, an aggressive genus of coral called *Lobophyllia*; and finally, a breed of fungal mold known as *Armillaria ostoyae*. It grows underground, but the fruiting spores appear aboveground as mushrooms."

"I hate mushrooms," Teddy said.

"Our particular strain was bio-sourced from the so-called Humongous Fungus, a specimen located in northern Michigan that extends for nearly a hundred miles under the forest floor. It's considered the world's largest living organism." Astrid knit the fingers of her hands together. "Those are its three primary drivers. The jellyfish's component to rejuvenate, the coral's component to colonize, and the fungal component to assist the spread throughout a subject's body."

"So that wolf's got a mushroom-coral-jellyfish inside it?" Claire asked.

"It's much more complicated," Astrid said. "There was a lot of genetic tinkering, chromosomes knocked out and others screwed in." A bright laugh. "The hardest part was creating biological camouflage to trick a subject's body into accepting this foreign entity. In earlier tests the Hydra was either attacked by the subject's white blood cells, killing it in its infancy, or else the subject's body rejected it."

"Same with organ transplants," said Madeline.

"That's right," Astrid said. "The Hydra must enter the very core of its subject, the DNA helix, the code box that directs the assembly of every single cell. Once there, it has to add and subtract to that code, as suits its objective. The Hydra shouldn't *be* there, you see, but your—well, a *subject's*—DNA can't be allowed to know that. So, I had to Trojan horse my Hydra in."

"How did you get it inside that wolf?" Frank asked.

From the pocket of her lab coat, Astrid produced a palm-size disc. She unscrewed the top to display seven silver lozenges. They ringed the circumference of the disc, resembling bullets in a revolver cylinder.

"Take a look," she said, displaying them. "The packets are bio-dissolvable. They degrade shortly after being implanted, releasing the Hydra."

"They're implanted?"

"That's the procedure," Astrid answered Frank. "A small incision at the base of the spinal column. A few stitches to close it up. Powerful local anesthetic, but no need for full sedation."

The disc lay in Astrid's palm. An invitation, a challenge, *something*.

"So . . . you want to put one of those inside us." It was Claire who asked, but she'd only voiced what they all must have been thinking.

Davey Jacobs said: "I've had enough."

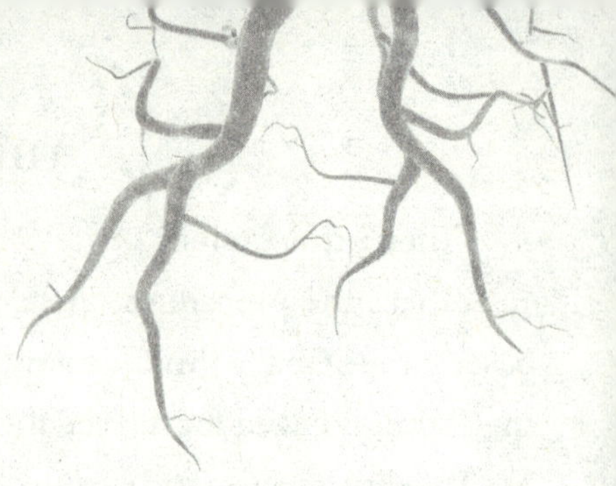

eleven.

TEDDY COULD tell the Bible-thumper had been getting set to cash in his chips.

Honestly, he didn't blame Davey. This whole thing was doing Teddy's head in, and Teddy's bean was screwed on good and tight, fastened right down to the pins.

"I don't want to be here anymore," Davey said. "I'd like to go home."

The two docs didn't seem bothered. They'd probably expected at least one of their charges to pull the chicken cord. And if Teddy was a betting man, he'd've plunked down ole Bessie's last silver dollar that Davey, the human equivalent of a moist towelette, would've been first to have his asshole cave in.

"John will have your belongings put on the boat, Mr. Jacobs," Strauss told him. "We'll have you back on the mainland in a few hours. A car will be waiting at the dock."

John Salters stepped forward, a movement that subtly sectioned Davey Jacobs off from the rest of the group. An excommunication, or so it felt.

"I'm not here to tell anyone how to live," Davey said. "And, uh, I haven't lived the best life. I've sinned. Catted around on my wife. I found God after that, and He forgave me."

Davey stood there pigeon-toed, wringing the Good Book in his hands. "What I've seen here today feels . . . against God. I've come to terms with death. I can face it now without much fear. Just the usual amount. Seems better to me than putting my soul in jeopardy."

"You signed up for a medically assisted death, didn't you?" Claire asked. "Doesn't that count as suicide to your God?"

Davey shrunk. "I spoke to my priest. He said God would understand."

Prodded by Salters, Davey then took a few steps toward the exit . . . but he turned back on the group defiantly, the Bible up above his head—he flapped it at them the way a priest sprinkles holy water at an exorcism.

"*For the wages of sin is death,*" he cried, "*but the gift of God is eternal life in Christ Jesus our Lord!*"

"Oh, get out of here with that, you maroon," Madeline said. "Go soak your head."

Teddy had to laugh. He might just come around on this ball-busting broad.

Davey's shoulders slumped. "I'll pray for you all."

Salters led him out. Within a few heartbeats, Davey's soft shape became one with the gloom. With his departure, Teddy sensed a hardening in the atmosphere. A circle forming into the shape it was always meant to hold.

"Okay, then. Anyone else?" Astrid asked.

When nobody's hand went up, she removed one of the Hydra lozenges from the disc.

Dropping the capsule onto the floor, she ground it under her heel. The sound of the Hydra being crushed—*dying?*—was the fibrous crackle of a dry leaf.

After recapping the disc, Astrid said: "You *can* leave. Any or all of you. Who knows? You could end up envying that guy."

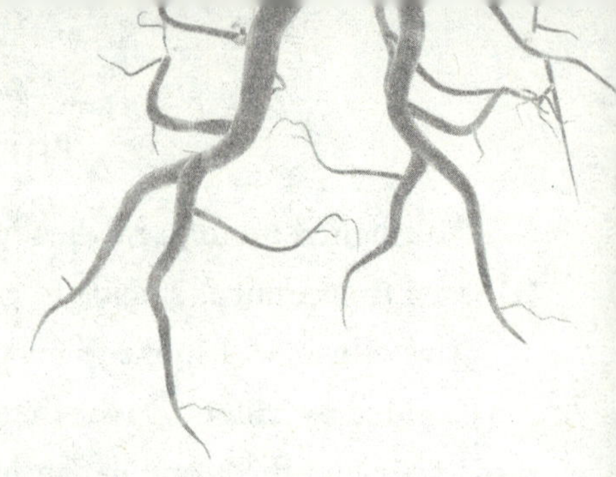

twelve.

THE GROUP fell in lockstep behind the docs as they marched on. To Teddy, this laboratory had the feeling of a maze . . . what did the Greeks call that place where they'd imprisoned the Minotaur? The labyrinth? He'd come to know his way around here eventually, though, even if it meant leaving a trail of breadcrumbs.

The lights brightened as they reached another pod. It housed a ring of vertical tanks: seven glass tubes stood on one end, each appearing capable of holding one human body.

"These are stem Baths," Astrid said. "They're part of the ongoing treatment plan."

The insides of each Bath held brilliant blue liquid. They put Teddy in mind of the Barbicide canisters at his local barbershop, combs and scissors suspended in blue disinfectant.

"The suspension is saturated with stem cells," Astrid told them. "We don't harvest them from infants, I swear! They're bioidenticals—clone cells, but the human system can't tell any difference."

Madeline said: "So we'll be floating in there like dill pickles? If we agree to, I mean?"

Astrid smiled. "Boots and Diego were submersed weekly, but for human subjects it will be a daily treatment."

"Why did you do it to both wolves, if only one has the Hydra in it?"

"That's how science works, Missus Dodds," said Strauss. "All subjects must receive the same stimulus. That's the rigor of it."

"Think of the stem as the fuel the Hydra requires to do its work." Then Astrid corrected herself. "At least, at first the Hydra requires it."

Frank said: "What do you mean, *at first*?"

"I mean that as of two weeks ago, Boots began to produce his *own* viable stem cells. A closed-loop feedback, self-sustaining, meaning the Bath may no longer be required."

"And if Boots continues to create fresh cells," Strauss said, "then it could mean that wolf is the second functionally immortal organism on earth—the Hydra itself being the first."

Astrid curtsied. "Thus ends the tour. Don't forget to tip your guides."

Teddy braced his hands on his hips. "Lemme get this straight. You're saying that if we let you put that thing inside us . . . we can live forever?"

Astrid shook her head. "Oh, no. You could still be killed in every way possible. Shot in the belly, stabbed, burned to a crisp. You *can* die. It is only that, *perhaps*, if it even *works* on humans, it will enkindle what appears to be a reversal in your chronological age."

"Yeah, but to *when*?" Teddy pressed. "We're gonna go back to being babies? I'm not keen on getting Benjamin Buttoned out here in the sticks."

"We were concerned about that, too," Astrid said. "How far back will the Hydra reverse the age clock?" She gestured vaguely toward the wolves in their distant pod. "Boots's age reversed gradually, then quite rapidly—concerningly so—until he reached four, at which point it stabilized. Four seems to be the age the Hydra has settled on for Boots. Perhaps it's the ideal stage of life to maximize all viable life functions. Or it is in lupine years."

"Now see, I don't like that," Hugo spoke up. "You make it sound like that damn thing inside that wolf is doing its thinking for it. Making decisions or whatnot. I don't want anything inside of *me* that's telling me what to do."

"But you have those factors inside of you already, albeit artificially," Strauss told him. "Every pill you take? They all direct or govern you—beneficially, or at least that would be the objective. Anyone who's had a stent or a pacemaker or a beta-blocker. They're all telling your body what to do."

"That's way different and you know it," Frank said. "What Hugo's saying is that *thing* is alive, isn't it? Alive in a way a pill or pacemaker isn't. It's . . ." Teddy watched Frank struggle to find the word. "Y'know, it's—"

"Sentient," Madeline finished for him.

Astrid had meanwhile walked to the nearest Bath. Bubbles scrolled up the inside of the glass, same as in a pint of green St. Paddy's Day beer.

"The Hydra is an organism," she said. "A bioengineered life-form. So yes, it *is* alive, but in the way that yeast or fungi is. Alive, but neither intelligent or agenda-driven. It's a . . . *golem.* In Jewish folklore, you made a golem out of clay. At night, you wrote an order on a piece of parchment and slipped it into the golem's mouth. It would go out and fulfill that wish mindlessly, without thought to morality. The Hydra is my golem. I built it as a health-care tool for the hypothetical betterment of humankind.

"But"—Astrid turned sharply to face them—"I can't promise you the golem will always do what I say, because it may misinterpret what I write on the parchment. I'm human, after all. I can screw up. And you need to understand that."

"Nobody's keeping them here," Dr. Strauss said, her shoulders tightening. "Remember that, please."

"Yes, but they have to know everything."

Claire said: "And what more, pray tell, is there to know?"

"Well," Astrid said, "if you consent to the implementation of the Hydra . . . you'll need to remain on this island for a long time. Years, even decades. You may never leave."

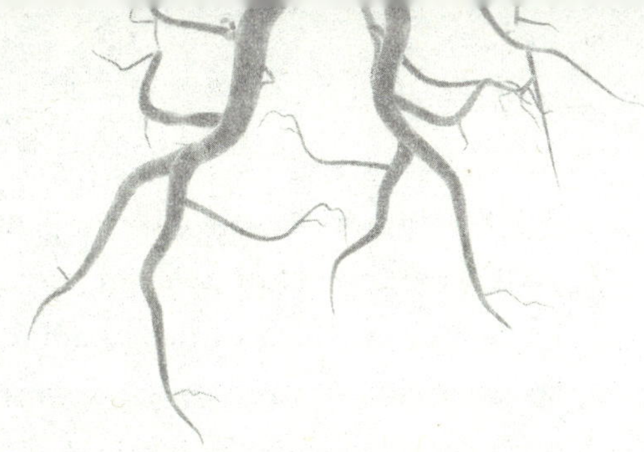

thirteen.

THE SHEATH of Teddy's nutsack sucked tight to his balls. Was this little brainiac bullying her elders, who were old enough to be her grandparents? Threatening them that they could never get off this rock? If so, then as the pervert said to the daredevil as the doughnut went rolling by:

Hey, champ, fuck that.

"I only mean, *if* you consent," Astrid went on. "But it wouldn't be right if we didn't lay out the entire responsibility of it."

"When you say never leave," Hugo said, his walnut-cracking hands flexing at his sides, "just how the hell would you stop us?"

"Take it easy, everyone," Frank said.

Jesus, Frank was the human equivalent of a baby pacifier. The behavior was already grating on Teddy's nerves.

"As Frank says," Claire noted. "No need to get a bug up our asses . . . I mean, not yet."

Hugo mumbled: "I don't like being threatened, is all."

"It's not meant at all as a threat," Astrid said. "But the fact is . . ." And here she looked at them guilelessly. "*If* this works, we have no idea what that might mean for the world at large. If the technology gets into the wrong hands, or goes into widespread use, I can't bear the responsibility of unleashing something for which I simply can't yet estimate the consequences."

What *were* such consequences, anyway? Teddy had considered it based on what he'd just witnessed with Boots. The human population would plummet, he'd bet his last cent on that. Fewer children born, seeing as there would be fewer resources to sustain them—and those fortunate few would get to meet their great-great-great-great-*great*-grandparents. Politically it could be a mess: living under a shit-heel dictator for a decade was bad enough, but if that same fascist could live an eternity, the world would be a living hell. There would be plenty of other variables his tired old brain couldn't cook up at the moment.

"That's what I mean when I say, *if* it works, I'm not sure I can let you leave," Astrid said. "You haven't taken anything yet. But if you decide to, that may be the toll. And not the only toll, because . . . I mean, you could turn out to be a bunch of Algernons."

"I'm not following," Claire said.

"Like in the book *Flowers for Algernon*? The mouse got smart, then dumb again, then it died. And just because it worked on Boots"—Astrid showed them her palms—"well, it's not worth getting into, but you should know there have been *other* wolves, okay?"

"How many other wolves?" Frank asked.

"Are you asking to see?" Astrid said. "I'm happy to show you some security footage—"

"There'll be no need for that," said Dr. Strauss, cutting in.

"Anyway. If it goes badly, we can end it for you," Astrid said.

"You mean take that thing out of us?" Madeline asked.

"I don't think *that* will be possible," Astrid replied. "As to the potential side effects—even if I went through them real fast, like an auctioneer, we could be here a while."

The young doctor impassively observed them. Teddy wondered if this was how the little oddball stared at her lab mice.

"I have no firm idea as to how great a risk you'll be accepting with this treatment. There is no way to estimate that. If there was, I'd have tabulated it. But each of you has consented to MAID, right? And we can administer *that* right here if things go badly—just say the word." Astrid nodded at Dr. Strauss. "She's trained to give the dosage."

Teddy said: "You're saying if we end up on your blooper reel, you'll do us a favor by allowing us to end our lives?"

"I'm just saying"—Astrid seemed honestly perplexed—"if the Hydra's implementation causes you too much pain, or if it starts to feel too unnatural to go on . . . I don't get what the problem is. You've all already decided to die, right?"

"There's dying and then there's *dying*, kiddo," Frank said. "A person's got a right to understand what they're getting into."

"You seem to be missing the ten-thousand-foot view here." This was Madeline, her tone pointed. "If you've accomplished what it seems you have, Astrid, then you've created a piece of medical technology whose worth is impossible to valuate. A piece of tech that, excuse the cliché, will change life on earth as we know it." She spread her arms to the lab and everything in it. "I can't imagine you funded all this with coins scrounged from your piggy bank. Whoever's backing you has absolutely zero interest in keeping that kind of cash cow bundled up here in the asshole of Ontario. So, what power do you *really* have to keep us and your idea tucked away?"

"I'm glad you asked," Astrid said, a flatness overtaking her face. "My one bargaining chip is the fact that nobody else can do what I do. Someone could hijack my files, go over my processes, and try to replicate them . . . but they'd fail. How do I know, you ask? Because they *tried* that already, and failed, *spectacularly*. And now they realize they always *will* fail."

Astrid removed the disc of Hydras from her pocket. "There are six in here. One for each of you, plus one extra. If someone else leaves, I'll destroy another. But even *if* someone laid their hands on a viable Hydra in stasis, they could never duplicate it. The people bankrolling this, *and* Dr. Strauss over there, know that." She eyed Strauss savagely. "*But*, even knowing, they tried to challenge me once before. I guess they thought I was a silly girl and I'd crack all to pieces. Let me show you how I convinced them otherwise."

Strauss whispered: "Please don't, Astrid."

Hooking her fingers under the sleeve of her lab coat, Astrid tugged the fabric up to reveal the naked length of her forearm.

"You have to cut *up* the wrist," she said, "not across. That's the only way they'll know you're serious."

The scar was long and gruesome, carving the inside of Astrid's arm from her wrist nearly to her elbow. She showed them the matching one on her other arm.

"It took some quick doctoring to bring me back. How many pints did they have to transfuse me with, Veronica?" Off Strauss's stony silence: "Pretty sure I was brain-dead for a minute there. And my brain's their moneymaker. But now they know. And I swear to you with all my heart: you'd rather have me in control than *them*."

"What if you succeed the next time?" Claire said. "Where does that leave us?"

"Nothing's certain except death and taxes," Astrid told her. "Didn't someone from your generation coin that phrase? Anyway, I've outlined the offer and been as honest as I can about the risks. If you decide to leave, I can't even say it wouldn't be the smartest choice."

Saying so, Astrid Marsh strode away from the group.

"It's late," Strauss said in the ensuing silence, "and you must be tired. Please follow me."

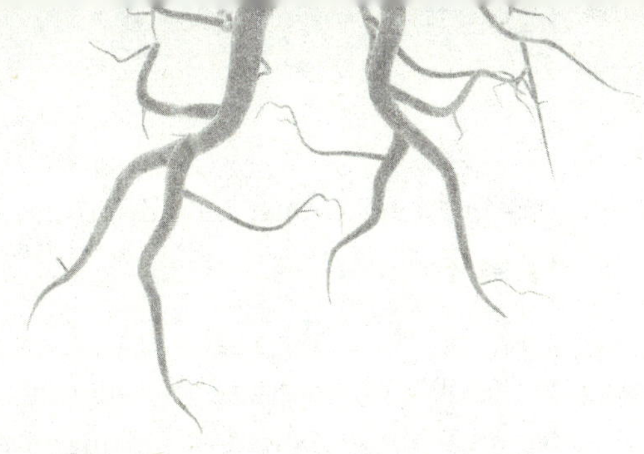

fourteen.

THESE ROOMS, including the one whose bed Maddy presently sat on, had been built under the expectation that she or some other candidate would spend significant time in them.

The rest of our lives, thought Maddy. *As many decades or centuries as that may be. Until this place crumbles to ruins around us.*

The furniture was sturdy, Swedish, redolent of lacquered wood. When she tried the bathroom tap the water ran yellowish, vaguely sulfurish. Maddy had arrived in this room following a brief group meeting in the common room–style room down the hall. These quarters, set off of the main lab, were to be their new home—if they chose to make them so. Claire, Teddy, Frank, and Hugo had sat in the main room with her while Dr. Strauss addressed them.

"I realize this is a lot to take in," Strauss had said. "But Dr. Marsh's work is real and her offer is real . . . and yes, the risks, too, are quite real. There's no rush. You all have private rooms down that hall. Take your time; think about it. As long as you'd like. At such time as you've reached a decision, you can let me know."

On that, Dr. Strauss had taken her leave. Once she'd gone, Teddy was the first to open his big fat yap. "Well, gang, if you want my two cents' worth—"

Which was when Maddy had gotten up and walked away.

Is this real? Maddy asked herself as the latch clicked shut in the room where her name—M. DODDS—was stenciled in black letters on the door.

The whole thing had the feeling of those prank shows that fascinated kids these days. She was waiting for some pimply-faced asshole in a backward baseball cap to bust into the room and bellow: *Surprise, ya dumb old bag, you've been FLORKED!*

Astrid Marsh worried her, too. Those scars running up her forearms. That someone of her demeanor could be in charge of this . . . was Maddy prepared to put what remained of her life in the hands of someone so young and so unnervingly intelligent, who might just be as crazy as a bedbug?

Maddy's luggage sat on the bed. She unzipped her carry-on and began putting her underthings into a drawer . . . that's what they wanted her to do, wasn't it? Unconsciously unpack and make herself at home.

"Calgon, take me away," she murmured.

Opening the closet, she found seven T-shirts and seven sweatshirts hung on the hooks; they were matched by the seven pairs of sweatpants in the dresser drawer. All the same size—women's long—and color: drab olive green. She suspected the other rooms held the same clothes, in the correct sizes for their occupants. In these clothes and in the toiletries in the bathroom lay the impression of a decision that had already been made.

Maddy couldn't say she trusted the bioethicist, either. Dr. Strauss *seemed* sincere, but at whose behest was she here? Assumedly Astrid's, seeing as this island's stakeholders had a vested interest in making sure their pet scientist didn't go slitting her wrists again. But Maddy had been in business long enough to know a few double agents. She'd hired a few herself.

She sat on the bed. Exhaustion lay heavy in every part of her, but her brain was cycling. Of long habit, that brain was trained to make analytic assessments. Profit versus risk. But she'd never faced a ledger like this. And she'd never been forced to put her skin in the game, quite literally.

Maddy spoke to the empty room. "If not me, they'll find someone else."

What *was* the risk? She thought about what other people—her parents and now-deceased friends—had subjected themselves to while chasing the slim hope of survival. Scarring radiation and toxic chemotherapy. Yards of intestine yanked out; a puckered rosebud in their bellies where their partially digested food could empty into a bag. The slow, dignity-stripping slog toward a death that modern medicine could prolong without making anyone that much better.

How many colleagues had she watched die in a narcotic hinterland where they couldn't recognize their own children, reduced to rattling boneyards that tested a mortician's skill to make them look human again for an open-casket viewing?

And for what? Another few months or weeks pushing against an inevitable darkness.

Humans are tough organisms, Maddy thought. *So seldom do we wave the white flag, even when we ought to.*

In that light, even the most profound risk posed by the Hydra seemed one most people in Maddy's situation would accept. As a calculated evaluation of risk versus reward, the reward lay beyond current human comprehension.

Maddy removed her traveling toiletry kit from her luggage. In one of its smallest pockets she found a squeezed-out tube of some magic French wrinkle cream she'd paid a ton of francs for at the Charles de Gaulle duty-free. She'd begun to purchase such serums after turning a certain age—had it been fifty-five, when the crow's-feet had made their inroads at the sides of her eyes?—from shopping center boutiques, never meeting the cashier's gaze. The concoctions boasted *age-defying effects* and *youth-restoring properties*. None of them worked a tinker's damn. The rational part of Maddy realized that time could not be erased and youth couldn't be bottled. So why had she kept buying the shit?

She turned the empty tube over in her fingers. *Could I actually be* young *again?*

There was a fail-safe, too, wasn't there? If the experience became too intense—too *unnatural*, in Astrid's cryptic phraseology—Maddy could inject a syringe of hydromorphone and float away forever.

A knock at the door.

"If that's Teddy, go away."

"It's Claire."

The woman let herself in with the deference of a housemaid. Claire Blessings was short, on the stout side, with candlepin legs. Maddy pictured her as a high school cheerleader. Not the one they tossed into the air; the one who was a stalwart building block at the base of the human pyramid.

"Are you busy?"

"Far from it. Just thinking," Maddy said.

Claire took the chair by the bed and crossed her legs primly. "Can you believe this?"

"It's a trip, I have to say."

"*A trip?*" said Claire. "That barely seems to cover it. Feels like we've fallen down Alice's rabbit hole into Wonderland."

Maddy cocked an eyebrow. "So Astrid Marsh is the Red Queen?"

"More like the Mad Hatter."

"Do you believe her?"

Claire rested her elbows on her knees, balancing her chin in her cupped palms. "Well . . . you think anyone would pay for all this if she couldn't do what she says?"

"Huh. I know venture capitalists who've ponied up billions for far crazier long shots."

Madeline considered Dr. Strauss's comparisons to drugs and pacemakers, all the shit humans stuff into their bodies to prolong their brief lives—yet the Hydra was radically different from those. Unlike a drug, the Hydra was a sentient, perhaps *seeking*, organism. Seeking what, was the question. Perhaps nothing at all. Its constituent parts were subhuman. Coral, mushroom, jellyfish. But those things still had *drives*, didn't they? Every living thing on earth had drives, however basic.

Unlike a pacemaker, the Hydra was programmed to occupy a much larger portion of the human body. It would start as a tiny seedling planted in the base of Maddy's spine, but from there it would flower into every nook and cranny. Maddy would be inviting an unknown guest into the rooming house of her body. She had to trust that guest to leave its dirty galoshes on the mud mat and make the bed after sleeping in it . . . but this guest's job was to spruce the place up. And these repairs were more profound than a new coat of paint or fresh shingles—its function was to gut everything right to the foundation and rebuild it to its former majesty.

Maddy thought: *If we accept this treatment, we'll become hosts.* When you had someone over to your house, that's what you were. The hostess with the mostest. But in the animal kingdom, *host* had a different connotation. Hosts housed parasites. A host was a feeding ground.

"This'll sound silly," Claire said, "but I've been thinking that the part of life we actually live isn't nearly big enough. Like, we only *live* in moments. The rest of existence is just marking time." She smoothed her skirt over her knees. "I made a lot of mistakes in my life."

"Sure. Me too."

Claire looked dubious. "You? Come on . . . I married when I was twenty. *Joe.*" She spat the name out. "The first time he hit me was a month after our honeymoon. I fetched him a bottle of Molson—I'd forgotten to take them in off the back porch and put them in the fridge, so they weren't ice-cold. He backhanded me at the kitchen table."

Her voice became a syrupy mimicry. "*Claire-bear, I had a helluva day. Shouldn't have to come home to a thoughtless bitch handing me a warm beer. I* can still see that flat, questioning look on his face. Like, what was I gonna do about it? Should've taken a knife and stuck it right in his neck. But I thought he loved me. He was just fiery. I'd learn not to disappoint him; it'd be a little blip . . . plus I was already pregnant with my daughter."

Claire was one of those confessional souls who'd tell you their darkest secrets within minutes of meeting you.

"That went on nearly twenty years," Claire said. "Coldcocking, hair-ripping, choking . . . once for not buying the pork butt when it was on sale. Two decades of bad excuses and pancake makeup. My friends, they told me to leave. But I was scared of what Joe would do to me. And to our daughter. Joe promised he'd find us, see. Said he'd chase us all the way to Red China if that's what it took.

"I screwed up the nerve to leave him when my daughter turned nineteen. She'd moved to a new town four provinces away. Still, there was a feeling of Joe dogging me . . . lurking behind the dryers at the laundromat with the fly-swatter handle he used to whip me with, or breathing under the bed of my new apartment. A year ago, an old friend wrote me with the news that the sonofabitch finally up and died. I just cried. Never had I felt such relief."

Claire's eyes found Madeline's. "The worst part? Sometimes I still feel him breathing under my bed. Except Bob's rotting now, his face gassy-purple. He's got worms in his hair."

"I'm glad for you that he's dead," Maddy said.

"Thanks. So am I. Now that he was gone, I was ready to *live*, you know? A late start, but still. Then *I* got sick, which seemed so unfair . . . and now this."

"Right. This."

"If it works, we can go back, can't we?"

"Back home? Seems to depend on factors beyond our control."

Claire shook her head. "No, I mean back in *time*. To the place where we made those bad decisions and make better ones. And not just mark time, y'know? Really *live*, like we should have in the first place." She flapped her hand. "Enough about me. What about you?"

"I think," Maddy replied, "that I spent a great deal of my life focusing on the wrong things."

The admission, which Maddy had never really forced herself to confront, took her off guard. There was something about the energies here on this island she found disarming.

"I was so single-minded that I shut out a lot of experiences. I was— I mean, this was my only real choice as a woman in my line of work—but I was eaten up by things that seemed important at the time. But they weren't, not in the end. My life was lopsided. That work-life balance. I had no balance at all. I regret that. You can't get that time back."

They looked at one another. The bold fact arrowed through the air between them.

Couldn't get that time back . . . until now.

"If I could do it all over again," Claire said, "I damn well wouldn't get married. I'd be like you."

Maddy gave Claire a crooked look. "And how do you think I am?"

"Single, for one. Won't be talked down to." Claire cocked her head. "You don't take shit from anyone, do you?"

"My mother said the first time you let yourself eat shit, you risk developing a taste for it."

"Smart cookie. So, what would *you* do different?"

"Oh, I don't know." Maddy smiled distantly. "I always wanted to have a baby."

She spoke the desire flippantly, but if she had one massive regret in her life, there it was.

"Who knows?" Claire smiled back. "If this Hydra works like the doc says it might, your body'll start producing eggs again."

"Oh Lord."

"Yeah, you said it, sister!"

It wasn't the physical or cosmetic changes, was it? Losing her crow's-feet, regaining the taut muscles that ran down her thighs or the perkiness of her breasts. Those would be nice, sure. But a chance to reexperience her existence in a fundamentally different way, erasing the regrets she had been so sure she'd die holding . . . that was the real carrot on the stick, wasn't it?

"Why us?" Claire asked. "People—like, rich and powerful ones—would give everything they own for this, right? Even if there was a good chance it drove them insane or killed them."

"Dr. Marsh is an odd duck. Maybe it's no more complicated than that? An egalitarian."

"A *what*?"

"She wanted the selection to be arbitrary and fair."

Claire's expression darkened. "Think she'll keep us here forever?"

"If it works and we truly get younger and stronger again, couldn't we just escape?"

"You think she'd just let us?"

"That's the thing about escapes, Claire. Nobody just *lets* you."

"Oh jeezum, could you imagine?" Claire leaned forward in excitement. "Being able to—"

Whereupon she farted. Pinched off, the note of it trembled through the air at a toneless warble. Her eyes widened. "Oh damn," she said.

Maddy burst out laughing.

"Sorry—it's my old plumbing!" Claire cried, joining Maddy in mirth.

"My father," Maddy said, "used to blame them on Columbian barking spiders."

"My dad blamed the dog!" Claire cackled. "You'd think poor Rusty ate nothing but beans, the number of farts my father pinned on him!"

Their laughter subsided. "I really apologize," Claire said earnestly. "You're a classy woman."

Maddy said: "I'll let you in on a secret. I've been known to fart, too."

"Oh yeah? I bet they peel paint. You probably make a point to clear out a room."

"Without a doubt. They absolutely *reek*."

This set the two of them off on another gale.

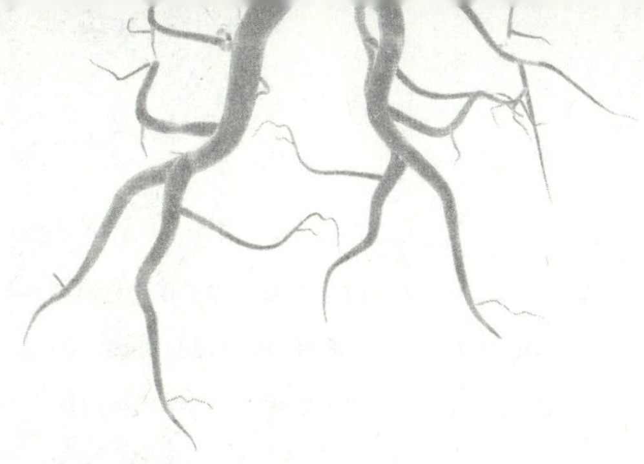

fifteen.

THE SOUND of the women's laughter carried down the hallway. It sounded lovely to Frank.

Teddy said: "Listen to those old hens clucking away." Saying this, he leaned to one side and let off a fruity trumpet blast of a fart. "'Scuse me, I meant to yodel."

They sat in the common room. Teddy seemed elated. His mood mirrored Frank's . . . although there was a flippy-belly feeling, too, a childish sense of eating too much cotton candy and taking too many spins on the Tilt-A-Whirl at the Port Dalhousie fair.

"There was this friend of mine, Dolan," Teddy announced. "He had the most beautiful wife, Elaina. She had a real pair on her, too." Teddy cupped his hands in front of his chest. "I'm talking a neck-and-neck zeppelin race under her no-nonsense cardigan. Understandably, Dolan enjoyed screwing her. And Elaina, she was up for it at all times. Some women have a sex drive that never quits, bless them. The two of them used to go to key parties— remember those? But they never put their keys in the fishbowl. Dolan and Elaina'd just go off and bonk one another."

"I never went to one of those," Hugo said. "Wouldn't've wanted to."

"You weren't missing much. Sometimes you'd roll snake eyes and get matched up with a real Quasimodo. Even on ludes, that's nobody's idea of a good time . . . anyhoo, round about sixty-five, my buddy Dolan stopped being able to get it up. No matter what Elaina did, his faithful soldier hung there between his legs like a wind sock in a dead calm. He went to a plastic surgeon, who convinced him to try a penis pump."

Wincing, Frank said: "I don't really care for where this is going."

Teddy continued as if Frank weren't there at all. "This implant, a little inner tube that runs the length of the shaft. Like one of those inflatable tube men you see at used-car lots. The inflator pump was stashed somewhere in Dolan's ball sack, I believe. Well, be damned if the fuckin' thing didn't explode on him one day."

Reflexively, Frank's hands went to his crotch. Hugo's lips skinned back from his teeth.

"Dolan said the inflator, it kept pumping and pumping until . . . I'm told it sounded like a starter's pistol fired into wet sand. It mangled his dingdong all to hell, but Dolan never said *how* exactly. He never showed me and I would never ask to see, but I imagined it kind of rolled up on itself like one of those birthday party noisemakers."

Teddy shook his head. "Ahh, Dolan's a good sport about it. He can still piss straight, mostly." He settled back into his chair, thoughtful all of a sudden. "It's a goddamn never-ending string of indignities, getting old."

Frank assumed this must have been the point of Teddy's tale.

"A few months ago, I was walking down the street," Hugo told them. "A guy was walking towards me, okay? Young guy, not that big, not any kind of mean look in his eye. But I'm thinking he's gonna *hurt* me, and I won't be able to do anything about it. I didn't know the guy from Adam. Never did nothing to him . . . I can see now that it was his *youth* that scared me. Having all that life packed inside him. I was afraid he'd do something to me and I'd just have to stand there and take it."

Frank sensed this confession was out of character for Hugo, and nodded in understanding. "A lot of days I feel more than just old and used up. More than anything, I feel—it comes over me like a fever, this—being *scared*."

"Yeah, I get it, friend," Teddy told him. "One day you're cock of the walk, next day you're pissing in a bag. Hey, you got a bag hooked up to your back door, too, Hugo?"

"No," Hugo said stiffly.

"Well, *good*. Here's to still dropping the mail the old-fashioned way."

Frank wondered why Teddy had felt the need to ask Hugo that. It seemed pointlessly cruel. That impression was nudged aside by the return of a thought that had plagued Frank the last few weeks. He'd begun to picture his own death. Not a realistic scene, but its edges had recently sharpened.

He was in his childhood bedroom in Timmins. He lay in the cold afternoon light, rain pattering on the windowpane. Lightning forked down from the cobalt-gray sky, so bright it seemed like a crease into heaven. The smell of his mother's cooking wafted under the door. A warm and sure sense he'd be called to dinner soon. He'd sit at the table with his mom and dad and they would talk of small things, his day at school and the upcoming spring market . . .

Except Frank knew he'd die before taking the stairs down to the kitchen. His life would be carried away with one of those lightning strokes that split the sky outside his window, his soul departing with the same polar swiftness—but he felt certain he'd see his parents again in the next flash of light. He'd see his beloved Annie and everyone he'd ever lost and they'd all be shining and happy.

"It's bedtime for this bonzo, fellas," Teddy said with a tendon-cracking yawn. "If you're gonna hoot with the owls at night, it's hard to hunt worms with the robins in the morning. But before I go, let me tell you two things I've learned. The first is that life can take you to the most unexpected places. Even though I don't really know you well yet, I'm glad I'm here with you . . . I think it was foretold to be we five, us and the two ladies."

He looked from Frank to Hugo, then back. "Maybe you won't be here tomorrow when I wake up and go tell Dr. Strauss I'm in . . . but I sure hope you are."

Teddy heaved himself up. The shakes had settled into him again. He began shuffling to his room. Frank said: "Hey, you said there were two things. What's the other?"

"Never play leapfrog with a unicorn," Teddy called back.

After a minute of comfortable silence, Hugo stood up. "An adventure," he said. "What do you think, Frank?"

"I think they come in all shapes and sizes."

"Hm, I like that. 'Night, Frank."

"Sleep tight, don't let the bedbugs bite."

"And if they do, beat 'em with a shoe till they're black and blue."

Alone, Frank beheld the night's canvas through the skylight. Aquamarine and turquoise and gold streaked across the heavens. Aurora borealis. He'd never seen it before. My word, there was so much he'd never seen. Not long ago he'd resigned himself to the fact he never would.

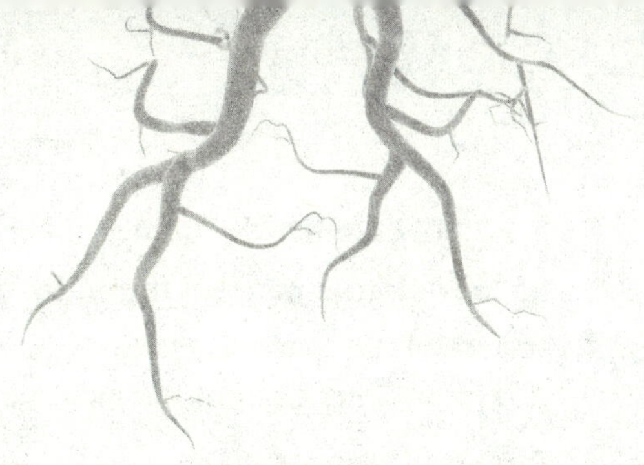

sixteen.

ANNIE DOYLE had died on an unseasonably cool summer day in 2018, in the marital bed she'd shared with Frank for nearly fifty years. He hadn't been with her when she'd breathed her last. He'd been out running errands: the pharmacy, for a refill on Annie's morphine, which she'd hold off on taking until the pain became too immense—especially at night, when Frank swore he could hear her nerve endings screaming beside him in bed.

After her memorial service, Frank returned to the home they'd shared for forty years. Annie was still there in the sugar bowl on the table (she'd bought it from a raw-boned Mennonite woman at the St. Jacobs Farmers' Market); there in the chip on the mantelpiece where she'd struck it with the fireplace poker, a bit tipsy, on some long-ago Christmas Eve. In the ancient home pregnancy kit Frank unearthed at the bottom of her dresser drawer while he was cleaning it out for the Goodwill. An Acu-Test, a brand they probably hadn't made since the eighties, still in its tattered blue box.

A dark ring in the mirror at the base of the Acu-Test indicates you're pregnant, the instructions read. The ring of the test was clear. It always had been clear for Annie and Frank.

Frank put the kit into a cardboard box of keepsakes—a handful of unspent lira from a trip they'd taken to Italy, Annie's university degree, other random detritus of a life shared together—and carried the box downstairs to the basement. He stopped at the kitchen fridge for a can of Diet Pepsi before heading back upstairs . . . halfway down the second-floor hallway he glanced at his hand and instead of the Diet Pepsi, he was holding a can of Tahitian

Treat. The familiar Pepsi logo had been replaced by two palm trees, and as he looked, mesmerized, those tiny palms appeared to sway on the curving surface of the can.

Tahitian Treat. They hadn't made this stuff in years. But it used to be Annie's favorite.

I'm in a dream, Frank thought. *And something just skipped the rails.*

There was no relief in this knowledge. If anything, an edge of onrushing horror.

The bedroom door had drawn closed behind him as he'd stepped out with the cardboard box. That door tended to do so. The hinges were wonky; it always fell almost-but-never-*quite* shut. Now, through that slender gap, Frank could make out noises in the bedroom.

Nobody could be in there. Nobody had been when he'd left it a few minutes ago. Who in God's name *would* be? The house had stood empty save Frank's own shuffling footsteps for going on a week. He was an old man alone in a home that felt two sizes too big.

But something was in there now. What it could be or how it could have gotten in there was knitted to the strain of dream logic that had taken hold. It could have slipped in the back door while Frank was down in the basement—or it could have been *in* the basement, hiding behind the metal bulk of the furnace before zephyring up the wooden steps while Frank's back was turned, up the main staircase, and into the bedroom to wait for him . . . maybe this wasn't even Frank's house anymore. It was an exact duplicate, except little details were tumbling loose—the can of Diet Pepsi turning into Tahitian Treat— exposing the cold fact that this house belonged to something else.

The thing in the bedroom. This was its house, and he'd gotten trapped with it.

Frank didn't want to see whatever was in the bedroom where he once slept with Annie. Yet his feet bore him toward the door. His socks brushed the pile carpeting, the underboards releasing faint squeaks as he set his weight down . . . the door opened of its own accord, as if a little gnarled butler was pulling it from the other side.

Come in, sir, do come in, the unseen gnome lisped. *We've been waiting.*

Annie was lying in bed. She wasn't dead anymore, though Frank clung to the fact that outside of this dream house, she was: in reality, her head was resting on a satin pillow in the dark of her casket. But this Annie lay stark naked on the bedcover, her legs open and her palms on her hips. She was young again. Mid-twenties, the bloom of youth, her skin taut and her hair long and thick where it fanned out across the pillows.

"Annie," Frank said, his voice a croak. "I'm sorry to tell you this, but you're dead."

"Not here I'm not." Her voice was scraping, toneless.

Frank's eyes fled to the window. The rooftops of his neighborhood had been replaced by a scalloped ridge of cliffs and, past those, to water that ran dark and depthless.

We're on the island, Frank realized. *This is the view from Spindrift, isn't it?*

When he looked back at the bed, Annie looked younger still. A teenager now—her age before she and Frank had met. He dropped his eyes from her nakedness; he was an old man and it was lewd to gaze upon anything so young, even the wife he'd recently buried. He could *hear* her getting younger: squealy rubber-bandy notes and a kind of popping snarl like microwaved nickels.

He kept his eyes on the floor at the foot of the bed, where the shadows collected under the box spring . . . something was under there. He couldn't see it (thank Christ), but he heard it knocking around with the sound of dead sticks.

A shape breached the shadows under the bed.

Only a flash before it retreated, but in that flash Frank swore he'd seen the oldest creature to ever exist: its papery scalp worn through in spots, so the bare skullbone shone like the cords on a balding radial tire—its lips nothing but gray worms skinned back from a toothless and inward-caving mouth—its eyes white as sun-bleached seashells, socked into a face that leered out from under the bed at him.

There for an instant, then gone again, but Frank knew (because his dream insisted on this reckoning) what that was under there.

That was Annie #2. The mirror-version of Annie #1. This second Annie was aging in direct contrast to Annie #1 on the bed . . . growing unnaturally old, while the other version grew younger and younger—

"Don't," came the barely intelligible words from under the bed, in a voice of dust and cobwebs and the sour breath of ancient tombs. "My love, don't— don't—*don't*—"

With that, a poisonous undertone leached into that voice, and Frank understood somehow, a knowledge beyond knowing, that whatever was under the bed wasn't *quite* his wife, or anything that had ever been human. He knew he must never speak to it.

"My love," the thing under his bed grated, "don't you want to live forever?"

Frank forced his gaze up to the bed again. Annie was now a child no older than five, her body hairless and her eyes a vibrant blue. She was laughing fit to beat the band, but there was something shrieky to it, the kind of laugh a girl makes when her weird uncle tickles her for too long, that laugh where pleasure and pain bind up into something too terrible to name—which was when Frank started to scream.

He woke in bed. His chest slick with sweat, his legs trembling.

Just after waking with the darkness sucked tight to him, Frank Doyle was terrified he was buried underground in the same coffin as his wife. But when he jerked up and his head didn't bump the wooden lid—when his hands found the sides of his twin mattress—he was able to stop shaking a bit.

Frank swung his legs off the bed and padded into the toilet. His face was pale and constricted in the mirror. Jesus, he hadn't had a dream that bad since he was a boy.

The tremors subsided by the time he crawled back under the covers. But sleep did not come easy.

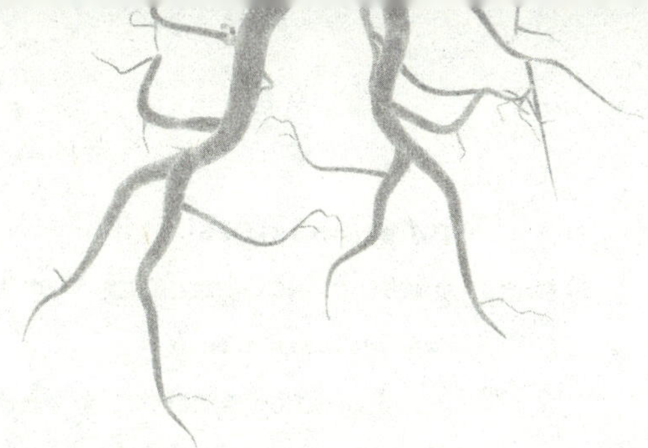

seventeen.

EVENTUALLY, THEY all said yes.

They assessed the risks in their private ways and came to the decision that whatever peril the Hydra posed, it was worth taking. For some of them, it was not much different than their long-ago decision to drink their first beer or smoke that first cigarette. Back then they'd overmastered the shrill warnings of adults: *Those things will turn your lungs black!* and *Do you want your liver to rot to smithereens?* The more a person became used to putting things, especially *dangerous* things, inside themselves, the easier it got. The mental leap dwindled until it was no harder than hopping over a mud puddle.

And if the Hydra posed a risk . . . well, unlike a cancer stick or a snort of cocaine or a six-pack of Miller, it also held the potential to erase the living hell of aging.

THE FIVE subjects came to Dr. Strauss over the next twenty-four hours. Claire first, in the dead of that first night. Teddy and Hugo early the next morning. Then Madeline and, finally, perhaps a little reluctantly, came Frank.

Yes. Yes. Yes. Yes. Frank said, "I guess I do?" like an uncertain groom at the altar.

Afterward, Dr. Strauss found Astrid in the lab and gave her the news.

"It's their choice." Astrid's tone was no different than if she'd said: *It's their funeral.*

"When do you want to do it?"

"As soon as we can have them ready. This is where you come in, isn't it?"

"You asked for me to be here, Astrid. You should do me that fairness."

"Wrong," said Astrid. "I told them to provide someone *like* you, someone to fill your role. Not *specifically* you. I don't care about you."

"Okay. Settle down."

"They should be sedated. Not heavily, but they shouldn't be conscious."

"Why? Before you told them—"

"Why do you need to know? Can't you just do it?"

Strauss held her peace until Astrid spoke again: "I believe the uptake of the Hydra will be . . . um, *smoother*, if they're fully unconscious. With some of the earlier subjects, there was evidence of the Hydra interfacing during initial harmonization. As a result, the subjects' mental processes may have been adversely affected."

"Are . . . are you saying they were driven insane?"

"How should I know whether or not a wolf's gone insane?" Astrid snapped. "Anyway, after that, the subjects have all been sedated. The interface has been seamless."

Strauss's eyes hunted over Astrid's cluttered lab bench, her journals and logs and a stack of library books. At the top of the stack sat a classic. Veronica picked it up.

"A bit of light reading?"

Mary Shelley's *Frankenstein*.

"I reread one passage every day," said Astrid. "The one where Victor Frankenstein brought his Creation to life, but looked away from it in fear. By being a coward, he lost everything."

"What would you have done in his place?"

"When it was born, Victor's monster was weak. He could have murdered it in its cradle. Instead, he ran."

"And kept his monster a secret."

"There are no secrets here," Astrid said. "I've been clear in my intentions."

They beheld one another, two women separated by an ocean of intellect.

"What about the sixth subject?" Strauss asked.

"Don't worry, I'll bring her to you. You and the boys get the others ready for the procedure."

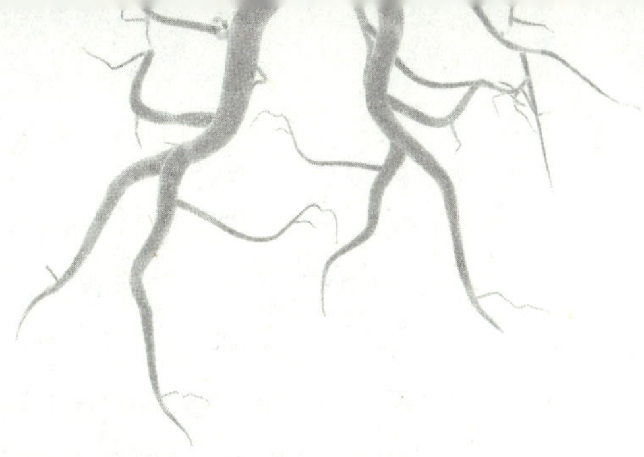

eighteen.

WITHIN THE hour, Claire Blessings, Frank Doyle, Theodore Bassiano, Madeline Dodds, and Hugo Udall were administered a so-called Twilight Anesthesia. The drug cocktail induced a state where they could respond to simple verbal cues but their pain receptors were dampened and, most important, they would be unable to retain any memory of their surgical experience.

One by one, the subjects were wheeled into a sterile room. Mr. Salters and Mr. Squires laid them on an exam table, turned onto their sides with their knees tucked up to their chests. They each looked not unlike a wrinkled fetus in utero.

They were joined by a teenage girl for whom no sedation was deemed necessary. This girl, the sixth and final subject, had been on the island for some time, lying comatose in a private room accessible only to Astrid Marsh. Whenever she wasn't in the lab, Astrid spent her time with the girl. If one listened closely, Astrid could be heard holding animated conversations in that room. Laughing and singing, but only Marsh's voice could be heard.

Six bodies lay on the exam table, naked from the ribs down.

Five old and wizened, one creamy-skinned and youthful.

Dr. Strauss and Astrid stood at the foot of the table. Strauss held one hand out. Astrid set the disc into her palm.

FRANK WAS first. Why Strauss selected him for the initial operation, she couldn't say. Maybe as he'd been the one who'd come to her most reluctantly.

Holding the #10-bladed surgical scalpel in the classic "pencil grip," Strauss positioned the tip over the liver-lesioned flesh covering the basal, or lowest, knob of Frank's spine. The blade opened Frank up in a manner that Strauss found hard to bear—old skin was thinner than young skin, the blood finding less resistance, and a sluggish thread of it tracked from the incision down the cleft of Frank's buttocks.

"Gauze," she told Astrid, pleased to be in charge for once. "Address the blood, will you?"

While Astrid tended to her chore, Strauss removed the first Hydra from the disc. The lozenge felt warm in her latex-gloved fingertips, pulsating like a tumor . . .

Strauss thumbed the lozenge through the lips of the modest incision she'd made. The Hydra's exterior was jacketed in acid-polyglycolic collagen, the same material used in dissolvable sutures. The jacket would degrade over the next several hours, after which the Hydra would "hatch" in the manner of a reptile from a softened egg sac. Knowing this, Strauss expected no visible or even perceived reaction when the Hydra was implanted in its new home—and yet, as soon as the lozenge made contact with Frank's naked tissue, Veronica had the sense of the Hydra locking into place. The sensation of tiny grappling hooks ejecting to anchor the packet inside its host.

Get it out! a voice yammered in Strauss's head. *Before it's too late!*

She dismissed these thoughts. Blood began to flow from Frank's severed capillaries, obscuring the Hydra . . . again there came a sense of it hiding itself, burrowing inside Frank in the manner of a marine worm in the oceanic sand— if she were to try to prize it out, Strauss wondered if she'd be able to locate it.

With a few deft sutures, Strauss finished the operation. No lump under Frank's skin, no evidence other than two strands of surgical catgut that he'd even been cut open.

She repeated the procedure five more times. Each took no more than a few minutes. The subjects' vitals remained stable. Maddy let out a snort near the end of her surgery, shaking her head like a horse with dander up its nose, but the rest of them lay still as corpses.

That changed when Strauss was stitching up the final subject. The girl. Strauss was tying off the remaining suture in the girl's lower back when she woke up.

One moment the girl was inert on the operating table—her posture had been arranged by Moses Squires, who'd undertaken the task of adjusting her limbs with utmost delicacy—and the next, her head cranked on the spindle of her neck and the girl seemed to look directly at Strauss, though her eyes remained shut.

Her eyelids flew wide open. She *was* staring at Strauss, her head cocked at an unnatural angle, her eyes lit with a horror that Strauss had never faced before.

"Astrid," Strauss said in a strangled voice, "this subject was sedated, yes?"

"Of course she w—" Astrid had her back to the surgery, and her voice died when she turned to face the table.

The girl let out a piercing scream. She hadn't moved her muscles in months, so when her arms flared up—her hands hooked into claws that reached for the incision at the base of her spinal cord—they did so with a muffled rubbery squeal as her tendons flexed under her skin.

"Hold her down!" Strauss commanded.

The girl thrashed and shrieked; her hair, thick and luxurious as a bolt of satin cloth, whipped around her head as she flung it back and forth.

"Stop it, Ing!" Astrid cried, gripping her wrists. "It's fine, I'm *helping* you!"

The girl wrenched free of Astrid's grip. Her hands returned to her spine, her untrimmed nails tearing long furrows along her hips.

Moses Squires and John Salters entered the OR. Gently but decisively, Squires eased Astrid out of the way and settled his hands on the girl's shoulders.

"I'll hold her down," he said to Strauss. "You get the dosage lined up."

Strauss bolted to the sedation cart. She'd preloaded several syringes of Twilight Anesthesia as a contingency. Popping the cap off one, she returned to the table.

By then the girl's struggles were slackening. Her screams died out and her mouth relaxed into the same sagging apathy it had priorly held.

"I think she's out again," Strauss said.

"Give her the damn dose anyway," said Squires.

Strauss sank the needle in, depressing the plunger. It was unnecessary. Whatever animus had infested the girl's body, it had now deserted her.

"Let *go* of her," Astrid ordered Squires, who continued to pin the girl down as if under the suspicion she'd spring up again. "Let *her GO!*"

Squires lifted his hands, sticking both palms up in the air. "You're gonna want to check to see she didn't hurt herself."

"If anyone hurt her, it was *you*," Astrid said reproachfully. "If I find out she's broken anything, I swear to God I'll—"

"I saw the whole thing," said John Salters, hovering nearby. "Moses was only doing what he could to help."

Astrid shot both men a glare to melt glass before turning her attention back to the girl.

A follow-up scan would show that the girl's brain wave patterns had returned to the null and void common to those locked in an irretrievable coma. But something *had* woken her, if only briefly. Strauss couldn't say what, but she conceived of a dire note sung down the girl's nerve endings and into the inner recesses of her cortex: *Wake up and save yourself!*

Yet if that was the case (and neither Strauss nor anyone else could make any claim of that), it was to no end. The Hydra was inside of her.

Astrid's disc sat empty on the tray bench beside the operating table. A ring of bare slots, resembling the cylinders of a six-shooter following a gunfight. Each lozenge was now lodged in the spine of the bodies lying in the recovery room.

AFTER THE procedures, Dr. Strauss went outside. The stars shone much brighter above Spindrift than in the city. She lit a cigarette to calm her nerves, but couldn't stop shivering.

"Jesus. What did we just do?" she whispered to herself.

In her mind, she was back in Core Topics for Bioethics, listening to her professor give his thoughts on the human need for death.

THE DORIANS

Few of us want to die. But death provides our lives with structure. As an end point, death gives meaning and significance to time. If time becomes insignificant because our lives are endless, our existence surrenders its value. We become adrift in time.

As a girl growing up in Thunder Bay, a thousand miles north into the snowbelt, Veronica Strauss used to go snowmobiling with her dad. He kept the Iditarod trails, and on weekends they would head out on grooming runs on twin Yamaha Vectors. The Vector would stay zippered to the trail at forty miles an hour, no matter if the snow was pebbled or powder or crack-glazed with ice. On a straightaway, it'd still stick tight at an even fifty. But once you got that sled up to around sixty or so, the front skis started to flirt danger-ously with the ground, and the rear tracks took on a dreamy, glittery lightness where you felt a cold ribbon of air underneath the whole works and realized you'd reached the limit of control. Then all you could do was hope you didn't hit a hairpin turn, because that might end with your brains splashed all over the inside of your helmet. At that speed you could only back off the throttle and pray.

Strauss wished she could do that now. Bring all this back down to a safe speed. But it wasn't her hand on the throttle, was it? She was simply doing her part. What was done was done.

Her professors had never sat at the cusp of an event horizon anything like this. Those old teachers of hers, if they were put in their former student's shoes on this island? They'd be shitting their corduroys.

Stubbing out her cigarette, Strauss went back inside.

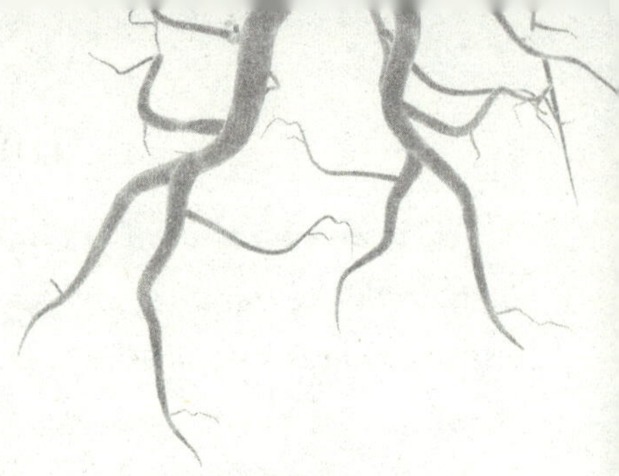

nineteen.

AS VERONICA Strauss gazed at the stars, the subjects slumbered.

Within each of them, the Hydra began to explore.

It was only starting its journey, finding its bearings before forging into the dark promise of those half dozen souls. None of them were able to feel its passage physically or even consciously. The Hydra moved as the slightest breeze through stalks of dry grass, or a shoal of feeder fish in a depthless sea.

Oh, the subjects may catch a spike at the farthest edge of a nerve ending, a phantom sense like a finger plucking a tightened thread, but if they looked for that finger, nothing would be there.

Though the Hydra kept to the deepest channels of their bodies, the subjects were alert to its presence. As with the princess and the pea, the Hydra couldn't hide. But then, why would it bother? It was in them now, and would only hunt deeper. Right to the heart of each of them, in due time.

When their minds finally made their first dim reckoning, it wasn't so bad at all. The intruder—or savior, depending on one's point of view—arrived as a laughing brightness. As sunlight, warm and merry, as nectar and dew and something soft and obliging that awakened a sexual craving they hadn't felt since they were teenagers.

Yet within this brightness lurked an element much darker and harder to grapple with.

For Teddy, it was as cold and lonely as the waking breath after a drug bender.

For Madeline, it came as peals of baritone laughter from behind a board-room door.

Claire experienced it as a vicious and unexpected slap from around a blind corner.

For Hugo, it was something bloated and bulbous that screamed at him in the voice of his dead daughter.

To Frank, a crushing pressure that seized his head in a vise and threatened to rupture his eyeballs in their sockets.

And in the young girl's head? Only calm ongoing blackness, the same as had resided there since that day in September nearly three years ago.

As they slept, the Hydra worked its uncanny magic within them. When they woke—each more refreshed than they could ever remember—it would be to begin the rest of their lives.

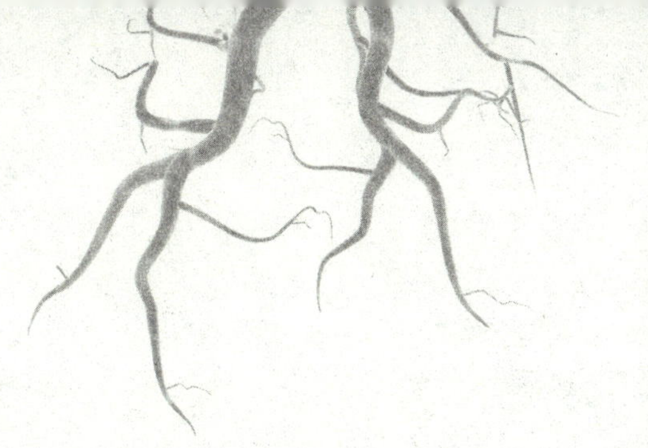

PART 2

DORIAN GRAYS

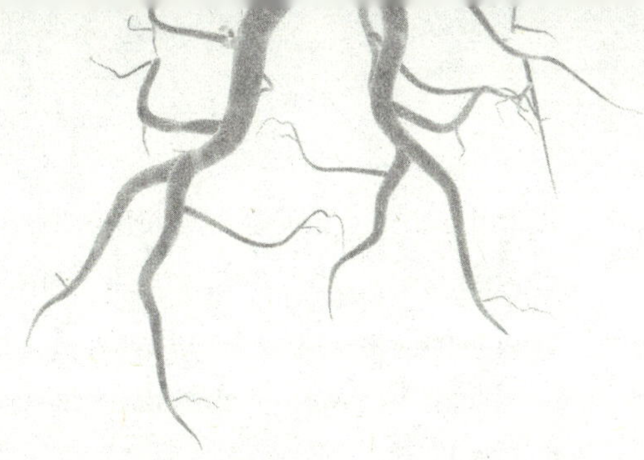

I. *Anno Hydra,* Day 1

FRANK DOYLE woke up in the room with his name on the door. His hands went to his backside, then a few inches northward—the base of his spine. The skin was tender. Sutures bristled at his fingertips.

Dread webbed up from the balls of his feet.

The Hydra. It was inside him.

His first post-op words came out in a dry croak. "You asked for this, Frank."

He swung his legs off the bed. He was too distracted to note then how his kneecaps didn't pop off like little cap pistols, the way they had every morning for the last decade. He stood and paced his spartan bedchamber in the operating gown he'd been wearing when Dr. Strauss had sedated him. He willed his heart to decelerate and his breath to calm.

"Okay," he asked himself. "Tell me, how do you feel?"

How *did* he feel? Any different than before the procedure?

"The same, pretty much."

He wasn't hot or feverish. He flexed his hands. There was no interloper, something to indicate the Hydra had seized one iota of control—not even the slightest hitch between his brain giving the command and his nerves obeying.

"I'm me. Still me."

He stood in front of the mirror, testing that belief. Everything he asked his body to do, it did. Now that the cobwebs had cleared, his brain was clicking along. He felt . . .

"Great." A shaky laugh. "Better than great, actually. *Amazing.*"

He bent at the knees. *Now* his kneecaps went off: *bap-bap.* But once they did, the joints flexed smoothly. Straightening up, he arched his back. It was almost scary. The feeling of a wellspring being uncapped within him to let cool artesian water flood into his veins.

Next, he caught the screams coming from somewhere outside, down the hallway.

FRANK WENT to the door. The screams intensified. Stepping from his chamber, he padded softly down the hall.

Madeline? That was his best guess. High, drilling, somehow insane shrieks.

He arrived at the door with M. DODDS stenciled on the front. It hung open. Frank couldn't help but catch a look inside. Perhaps none of the others had woken yet. Only him . . . and Maddy.

Drs. Marsh and Strauss were in there with her. Astrid must've sensed him at the door, because she flung a glance back at Frank and snapped: "Go away! Back to your room."

But Frank could only stand there stiff as a cigar-store Indian. It was all that blood.

Maddy was huddled in the farthest corner of her room. Dr. Strauss was bent beside her, obscuring most of her body. But Frank couldn't miss the fan of blood on the wall. The air hung thickly with its smell.

"Maddy?" he said haltingly. "What happened?"

When Dr. Strauss turned to him, he could see blood freckling her cheeks. "She'll be fine, I promise," she said. "But you need to give us some space to work, Frank. *Please*, for Madeline, you need to go back to your room."

Frank could hear blood now, too: a silky hiss like compressed air through a pinhole leak.

Astrid stormed over to him, grabbing his wrist in one of her cold hands. "Mr. Doyle, *come* with me." Pulling him roughly along. "I'm not going to tell you again—"

He shook free of her grip. "Maddy?"

Taking another step, Frank caught his first glimpse of Maddy's face over Strauss's shoulder. Her flesh gone white as a corpse's, her eyes big as eggs.

"It moves like us," Maddy said, those eyes rolling in their sockets. "*Exactly* like us. And it eats its young." Her voice rose to a reedy screech. "It *eats its young!*"

Planting both hands in Frank's chest, Astrid Marsh shoved him, *hard*. Frank stuttered back on his heels into the hall. Marsh slammed and locked the door.

IN A daze, Frank wandered down to Teddy's room and found him awake. Teddy was, in fact, standing on his mattress, naked as a jay and grinning like a goon.

"Something interesting is happening," Frank heard Teddy remark. "Oh, yes indeedy."

"Teddy, are you okay?"

Teddy's eyes found Frank in the doorway. They were bright with good cheer. He snapped off a sunny salute.

"Jawohl, mein commandant. I can't say I've ever been better, big fella." He gave Frank a dirty old man's leer. "Fine as cherry wine." He spun a slow circle on the mattress, displaying two pockmarked ass cheeks.

"Maddy . . ." Frank said haltingly. ". . . she's . . . uh, not doing so hot."

"She'll come around." Teddy gripped his penis and got it swinging between his thighs, a fleshy pendulum. "I swear my pecker's grown an inch overnight, Frank-O." He tipped him a stinky wink. "*Width*-wise."

Frank left Teddy, continuing down the hall. Claire's door was shut. He knocked. She didn't open up, but he could hear her warbling a tune off-key in there.

"Claire? Everything okay?"

"We need to be a-*loooone* right now," came her singsong answer.

Hugo's door wasn't open, but when Frank tried the knob, it twisted freely in his grip.

Frank opened the door to find Hugo on the bed, his bulk shoved back against the headboard with his knees tucked to his chest. *He looks like a little boy*, Frank thought with a species of cold fright.

"Hugo, what's the matter?"

The big man was staring at a ceiling corner of the room—his entire focus on that spot.

"She doesn't look the way she used to."

Hugo pointed, his long simian arm extending, the finger at the end of his hand trembling.

"Summer. My little Summer." Hugo's face was as blank as a test pattern. "She's . . ." He sucked in a shuddering breath. ". . . she's all *purple*. Jesus, can't you hear her, Frank?"

Nothing was present in that shadowy corner where the walls met—but for a moment Frank swore he saw something that resembled a huge pot-bellied spider.

"She's just . . . screaming." Hugo pulled his hand back in, wrapping both arms around his bent legs and burying his head between them. "She won't stop *screaming* at me."

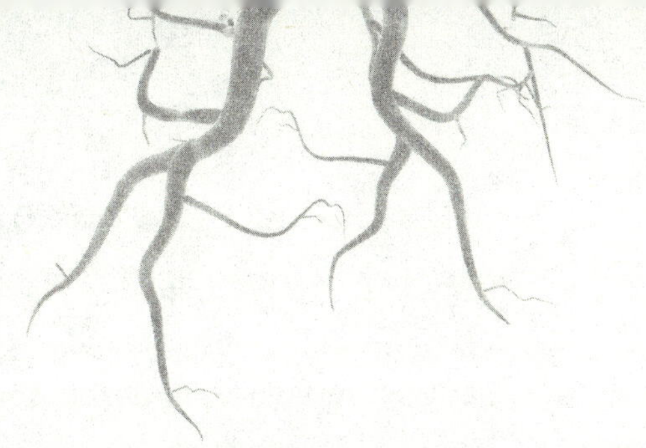

II. *Anno Hydra*, Day 2

<u>**Notes: Uptake and Harmonization**</u>

24 hours since procedure

100% survival rate, no mortalities

Uptake not uniform among participants

Variance observed in initial responses

Individual outcomes TBD

SUBJECT 1: M, 77 (FRANKLIN DOYLE)

Awoke naturally. No adverse effects noted or stated by subject. HBPM, blood oxygen, BP, etc., within safe range of pre-procedure norms.

SUBJECT 2: M, 79 (THEODORE BASSIANO)

Awoke naturally. No adverse effects noted or stated by subject. HBPM, blood oxygen, BP, etc., within safe range of pre-procedure norms.

SUBJECT 3: F, 79 (CLAIRE BLESSINGS)

Awoke naturally. No adverse effects noted or stated by subject. HBPM, blood oxygen, BP, etc., within safe range of pre-procedure norms.

SUBJECT 4: M, 76 (HUGO UDALL)

Awoke naturally. Some psychological/psychic miasma observed during recovery window. HBPM, blood oxygen, BP, etc., within safe range of pre-procedure norms.

SUBJECT 5: F, 84 (MADELINE DODDS)

Awoke naturally. Significant self-harm during recovery window. Subject was sedated and treated. Injuries largely superficial, but psychological underpinning needs to be monitored. HBPM, blood oxygen, BP, etc., within safe range of pre-procedure norms.

SUBJECT 6: F, 19

Did not awaken.

—Dr. A. N. Marsh

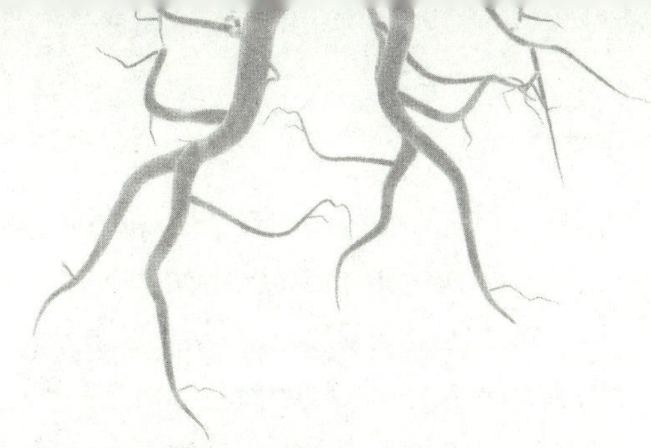

III. *Anno Hydra*, Day 2.5

Dear Cheshire Cat,

I can't say when this will reach you. Snail mail, how quaint. John S. will be dropping it in the mailbox when he next returns to the mainland for supplies.

The procedure was not precisely a success, but you likely measure that differently than I do. At least nobody died, thank God.

For three of them (Franklin Doyle, Claire Blessings, Theodore Bassiano) the implant could be considered a cautious success. Bassiano awoke first, followed shortly by Blessings. I judged both to be in excellent spirits. Euphoric, even. Physically they appeared unchanged, apart from a general flush and elevated heart rate.

Doyle was, to me, wholly unaffected on all measurable levels.

The fourth (Hugo Udall) . . . when I encountered him post-procedure, he was in a state of fright such as I've never seen in a grown man. He was convinced his daughter, Summer, was in the room with him. So far as I could tell, he was seeing her in the corner, high up, as if she might've been floating there.

I now understand that Udall's daughter has been dead for some time. Which was why her being there had him so upset during the post-op recovery window.

I had cause to wonder whether the Hydra had an unexpected and deleterious psychotropic effect on Udall, and if so, whether it would be permanent. But Mr. Udall has since recovered.

The final subject (Madeline Dodds) emerged from sedation in a state of hysterical postoperative horror. Manic, suicidal. So far as I can tell, immediately after waking she grabbed a nail file from her travel bag and set to stabbing herself. Multiple puncture wounds, some quite deep. The file had no sharp edge, but she managed to sink it into her stomach at least six times, some to a depth of over an inch. One strike nearly perforated her small intestine . . . such self-harm is indicative of severe self-hatred, but the subject's psych profile offered no suggestion of that.

My impression at this point? Dodds changed her mind about the thing we'd put inside her and was trying to get it out.

I sedated her and addressed her injuries. When she regained consciousness, she was much calmer. When I asked how she felt, she told me, "Better." We'll have to hope so.

The misgivings I had before coming to this place—ones I made you fully aware of—have only sharpened. Funnily enough, my primary source of calm is Astrid. I have no doubt she will end this project if she gets a hunch it could go sideways. Even if that means burning this place to the ground with her in it . . . there would be nothing you or I or almighty God Himself could do to stop her if she sets her mind to that. There is peace in that knowledge, actually. The belief that someone here (the craziest or the sanest of us, depending on how you look at it) will stop this in the most ruthless of ways, killing the unnaturalness at its root.

The nights are getting longer. I hear strange sounds in the woods. The wolves, maybe?

I tell myself some good can come of this. Some moral grace, even. A way forward for humanity. But that seems so very far away. And the lonely howls of those wolves sound as if they're right outside my door.

—V.S.

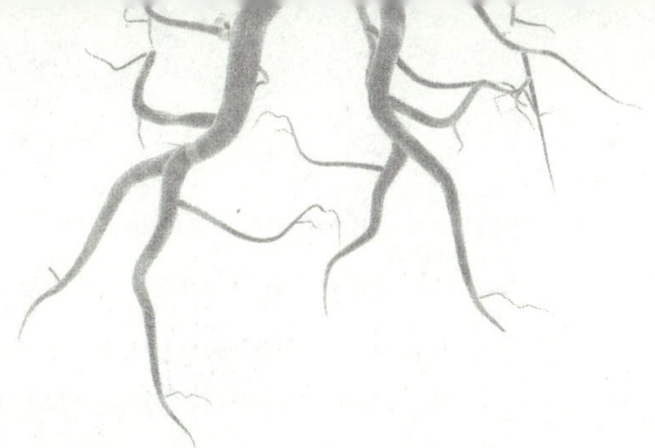

IV. *Anno Hydra,* Day 5

THEY WERE all looking at her, damn them. Their piggish little eyes boring into hers.

They thought she was a freak. A suicidal psycho.

When Maddy was younger, there used to be a term for sloppy drunks. People would say they couldn't handle their liquor.

Well, evidently Madeline Dodds couldn't handle her Hydra.

She faced them now, in a ring of chairs in one of the meeting rooms off the common area. What had Dr. Strauss called these meetings? "Group Encounters." Maddy's bandages rubbed under her overalls. The nail file had been serrated, and she'd acted with desperate intensity. Strauss had done a good job stitching her up, but her stomach still hurt like holy old hell.

"If you don't want to speak, Madeline, there's no requirement."

Maddy smiled sweetly at Strauss, the leader of this mandatory pity party. "What would you like me to say?"

Strauss shared a look with Astrid Marsh, who only shrugged.

"*I* feel just jim-dandy," Teddy bleated, all Mr. Chipper.

Maddy's stomach clenched. Oh, that hateful little man.

"My question is, when can we go outside?" Teddy rocked forward in his chair. "I know, I know, we can't go running off. Believe me, I don't want to! But some fresh air would be nice."

"Not yet," said Astrid. "I'll let you know."

Teddy saluted her. "You're the boss, boss."

Claire spoke up: "I don't know how I feel. I lay in bed most of the day trying to figure out if anything's different." She set two fingers on her neck to check her pulse. "*Shouldn't* I feel something? Isn't anyone else? Is that thing . . ."

Astrid said, "You can call it by its name, Claire."

Claire's jaw crimped. "The Hydra. Is it all through us yet, the way it was in the wolf?"

"It is still integrating," Astrid said. "Investigating and making itself at home."

Frank said: "I don't care for that phrasing."

Astrid's eyebrow quirked. "Care for what?"

"That word, *investigate*."

"I agree with Frank. It makes it sound like the implant inside us is a detective," Maddy said. "It's *deducing*."

"And I like 'making itself at home' even less," Frank went on. "Our bodies aren't anything's home but our own."

"Isn't your body home to your hip replacement?" Astrid asked him. "It's inside of you, isn't it? That's all I meant."

Frank said: "It's not the same at all. People own homes. Homes don't own people."

"I apologize, then. Bad word choice." A tight nod from Astrid. "It's still *harmonizing*. Is that better?"

"I honestly don't know," Frank said. "I appreciate the attempt, at least."

"The epigenetic clock would be the surest marker that anything's changed inside your bodies, or that the Hydra is having any kind of an effect at all," Astrid said. "But I'm holding off on that for the meanwhile."

"Why wait?" asked Teddy.

"Let's allow your bodies and minds to acclimatize," said Dr. Strauss, siding with Astrid.

Maddy caught Frank sneaking a peek at her out of the corner of his eye. The pity in his gaze made her skin crawl. Frank seemed a decent man, but what had *he* done in his life? He had the ways of a factory worker. He'd probably stood on a line for thirty years twisting caps onto tubes of toothpaste. That a man like that would pity her . . . *ohhh*, that was the most galling part of all.

"We'll have these meetings daily," Strauss said. "Along with physical diagnostics and private one-on-twos with both Dr. Marsh and myself. Routine is key. A holistic approach to navigating through the Hydra implant and how it's impacting you."

"I'm hungry," Claire said. "Is that weird? I'm always hungry now, since . . . y'know."

Strauss made a note of that. "Anyone else hungry?"

Maddy was ravenous, in fact. She could eat a horse. But she didn't put her hand up on principle, even when everyone else did.

"Maddy, not you?"

She shook her head. "Not especially. Guess I'm weird."

"Nobody said anyone's weird," Frank said.

Maddy thought: *Oh, just shut your beak, Frank, you play-nice, goody-goody stooge.*

"Anything else?" Astrid said, checking her watch. "This doesn't have to go all day."

Hugo's index finger inched up his chin until it was pointing straight up in the air.

"Question, Hugo?"

"Not a question, but a . . ." The man's eyes pinched in. "Has anyone else seen anything, um, that can't be there?"

Dr. Strauss waited, eyeballing the group. Her gaze lingered a little too long on Maddy.

"Hugo, have *you* seen something?"

"Not since the . . . when I woke up the first time. I, um . . ." He threw his hands up and let them fall to his lap with a soft *flump*. "Frank saw me in my room and so did you, Dr. Strauss. I remember as much, so why are you beating around the bush?"

The muscles cabled down Hugo's arms. Maddy had never really taken notice of just how big the man actually was.

"I imagine Frank wanted to keep your confidence," Strauss told him. "Right, Frank?"

"That's right," Frank said. "It's not my story to tell."

Hugo exhaled. "It's just . . . my daughter, Summer, she was five years old when she, uh, when she . . . died. It happened forty years ago now. She was our only child . . . my wife swore she'd never have another after what happened. I understood. Not sure I could stand the heartache of losing another one, either."

"Why do you think you'd lose a second one, buddy?" Teddy asked.

Hugo gazed at Teddy with such frightening directness that Teddy dropped his eyes.

"Summer, uh, choked to death. On a gumball," Hugo told them. "Y'know, the ones out of those machines in the shopping mall. Put a dime in the slot and give a twist. *I* handed her the dime that killed her. Wasn't paying attention. Your head's always in the clouds at the worst possible moments, isn't it? Gumball must've been in that machine for years. Hard as a rock. My little girl inhaled it by accident. By the time I noticed, she was bent over. I'll never forget the color of scuffed shopping mall tiles, green, *slime green*, and there she was, bent over gagging on them. There was nobody else around—actually, one guy, but when he saw what was going on, the fucker turned and walked away."

Hugo's face went dark. "I still remember that guy's face. He wore a gold earring, right ear. Tell you what, if I'd seen him again . . .

"I didn't know the Heimlich," he went on. "Later, stupidly, I took the course. I was still in that place where if I worked these magical steps, maybe I could fly back through time . . . but when it mattered I didn't know jack shit, so all I could do was pound Summer on the back. Her body rattling as I hit harder and harder, slamming the back of her neck. Someone said later that her spinal column was all crushed up top . . . and as I kept trying, purple strings started crawling across her cheeks and the back of her neck as her air clocked out. By the end, I could have been slapping a big floppy doll."

Claire set a hand on Hugo's shoulder. "I'm so sorry, Hugo."

Hugo drew a shuddering breath. "That's who I saw in my room. Hung in a corner like a cardboard skeleton, dangling there. My daughter. She'd be forty-five today, but she looked like I last saw her, in a yellow pinafore dress her mother bought at Sears, Roebuck. Her face was all black and swollen, her eyes red from the burst blood vessels, and when she opened her mouth to scream at me I saw that robin's-egg-blue gumball way down deep in her throat. How could she scream with that thing jammed in her air pipe?"

Maddy said: "Have you seen her since then?"

"No," Hugo said with relief. "Just that once, right when I woke up." His eyes remained on her. "How about you? See anything when you came to that first time?"

"I didn't," Maddy told him after a pause. "Now whether that's because I've already repressed that memory or because the thing in me doesn't *want* me to remember, well, I'm not the one who'd be in a position to know that."

"The Hydra has no intelligence," Astrid said. "No agenda."

"But it's not in *you*, is it, deary?"

Astrid frowned. "Don't call me that."

Maddy unbuttoned her overalls and parted them to reveal her chest and a segment of her stomach. The rest of them ought to see the bandages. The florets of old blood dotting the gauze.

"I remember the nail file, the . . . sound it made punching into me. But I don't remember *why*. The best I can tell you is it was instinctive, same as a person who wakes up on fire and tries to put themself out." As Maddy re-buttoned her overalls, she said: "I know I must've said some things. Frank— you heard them. Maybe we'll talk about it at some point, but until then I won't know what they were. Could be I'm not cut out for this. What do you all think?"

Teddy said: "I think you're tough as old boot leather, Madeline. You'll bear up."

"Oh, you really are too kind, Teddy." Maddy addressed the doctors. "Since you asked, I'll just go ahead and admit it. I feel absolutely *fantastic*."

Shocking as it was to say, it was the truth. Maddy couldn't recall feeling better since that fateful afternoon when she'd been out for a walk with her dog and that tick had made itself at home in her panties.

"This might be a good point for us to break for lunch," said Dr. Strauss.

"Amen to that," Claire said. "I could eat a pachyderm."

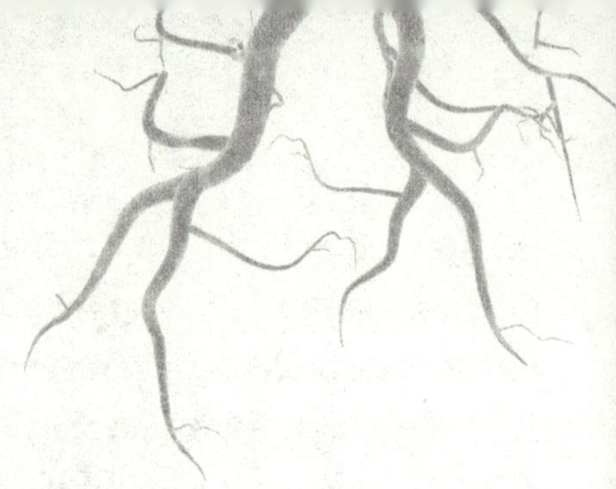

V. Anno Hydra, Day 7

THE GIRL *could hear it screaming somewhere in the endless black.*

It must have caught her scent. Soon it would appear, as it always did: a locomotive of arms and long spindly fingers, but mainly of teeth, and it was those that most terrified her—yellowy teeth, shaved down to points and curved inward like cat's claws.

The teeth of the witch. The one that never stopped hunting her.

And now the witch had found her again.

She began to run. The black stretched out, endless and cleansed of perspective. She prayed for the house to appear, pushing up from the blackness like a weed. Always the same house. She'd walk its hallways with her hands spread against the dark, feeling her way around. Photos hung in frames on the walls. People she may have met at some other place on the continuum—a life (if she'd ever had one) before this.

Unless she'd been born into this hunt? She couldn't remember a time before. The only logical belief was that she'd been born to the darkness, the witch, and that thing's endless pursuit.

And the witch was coming now.

The witch couldn't help but chase her. That seemed true of this place, too: they each had their role, hunter and prey, and all either of them could do was play them.

But if the girl could find the house, the witch wouldn't be able to get her this time.

That was the one rule she'd discovered. If she could get inside the house, she'd be safe for a while. The witch couldn't get in. The witch could only shake and scream and gibber at the threshold, stalking past the windows, her shoulders hunched and predatory, her cloak of thick rags (no, of flesh—the witch was clothed in strips of peeled and cured flesh) rasping against the bricks. The witch could face the girl through the windows and scream in anguish, her nose sharp and her mouth a concave hole like a lamprey's studded with those cat-claw teeth . . . sometimes the girl summoned the willpower to stare back at the witch—even smile at her . . .

. . . but usually, the girl hid under the large bed upstairs, waiting for the thing to go away. She could always tell when the witch had departed because the air became more breathable.

Soon after that, the house itself would disappear. It would emulsify or melt, sinking back into the blackness. And the game would start all over again.

Only once had the witch caught her. At least, the girl thinks so.

All she can remember of that instance is not finding the house. The witch then descended on her. How she'd trembled under that smothering pelt of skins . . . but instead of screaming, the witch had cooed in her ear with a motherly tone.

The girl wondered at the purpose of the endless chase. Was it to kill and eat her, as witches did? Or was it something else?

Whatever the case, the awful thing's closeness terrified the girl. The witch's possessiveness, the way her bony fingers dug into the girl's sides and never let her g—

The house. She'd reached it without knowing. Run right into it, as sometimes happened.

But the witch was there, too, coming fast on her heels—she could smell the choking dust rising from the cloak of stripped skins.

The girl dashed around the side of the house in a frantic search for the door. The witch was there, her ragged fingernails skipping along at her heels. The witch breathing heavily, the snaffle of a sick dog.

The girl's fingertips slipped around the doorframe. She lunged inside and kept running—but the witch didn't scream in frustration, as it always did.

With horror webbing up her legs, the girl turned.

The witch had stepped inside the house.

She had followed the girl all the way in. For the first time ever, the girl got a proper look. The witch wasn't so old, as she'd always thought. Her face was unblemished, but smeared in a rime of oil or soot that made her eyes very wide and white.

"Ingrid," said the witch.

The girl had never heard her own name in this place, but she knew right away that's who she was. Ingrid—her name filling the witch's horrible mouth.

Over her shoulder, the girl felt warmth. Turning, she saw light.

Light, so obscenely bright. A shining coin at the top of the stairs.

Ingrid fled toward it. Behind her, the witch unleashed a shriek.

Faster, step after step. The witch was on her again, so close, trying to stop her, trying to keep her in this place to play the game, the game, forever and ever and ever—

The light swelled. Ingrid's hands stretched out—she could see her fingers for the first time, really see them, her fingernails long and hooked from lack of trimming, too much like the witch's teeth—

The light. Ingrid dove, falling headlong into it—

—LIGHT. OH, too bright, stabbing into her eyes.

Her groan (was *that* her voice?) was the creak of a rusted hinge. Rolling over, something constricted around her body—

arms the witch's arms dragging her back into the blackness

—and she let go a screech, rolling away from those grasping limbs—

"Ingrid . . . ?"

A face haloed in the bright light above her. So familiar. A zag of fear went through her as a pair of arms stretched down for her.

"You're awake. You're actually awake."

Ingrid felt those hands on her shoulder and back, aiding her into a sitting position. Her fear was dimming. There was no witch, was there? It was only the bedsheets. They'd wound themselves around her shoulders, nothing more threatening than that.

"It's me, Ingrid. Astrid. You remember me?"

Astrid . . . the name kindled a timid flame. When had Ingrid known—?

Then, a dam bursting, Ingrid's memories flooded back.

"I'm Ingrid Chevalier." Ingrid's voice was clearer. "You're Astrid Marsh."

Astrid's face lit up. "Uh-huh. That's right!"

It came back so rapidly—a series of flickering shutter flashes—that it was as if the blackness had never been. She was Ingrid Chevalier. And Astrid was . . .

She's my best friend.

Memories slammed into her, shuttling through her brain and slotting into place too fast for Ingrid to keep pace. Amid the blur of scenes and sensations, one word rang like a clarion.

Prodigy.

That's what they were, weren't they? Two child prodigies—but even as her memories rallied, Ingrid understood that she and Astrid were intellects of differing calibers.

I'm smart, aren't I? Like, really smart. This fact entombed itself in Ingrid's brain. *But Astrid is something altogether more, isn't she? She's scary-smart.* This fact registered past dispute, too. *But she's the only person who understands me, and me her. Isn't that right?* This fact was murkier, but it was steamrolled by new thoughts. *We're built to a tolerance nobody else can match. A tolerance that scares a lot of adults.*

Ing and Ast. That's how they'd been known among their older peers, wasn't it? Yes, often sneeringly so. Two peas in a pod. They had shared a room, a laboratory . . .

"Everything." Ingrid's grin widened. "We shared everything, didn't we?"

Astrid's head bobbed. "*Yes!* Oh my God, I can't believe it—I mean, I *can,* of course I can, it's not like I ever had much doubt, but you know, there's always a risk and things can turn out bad, that's just scientific odds, right, but I wasn't worried," she babbled on, "and *hah,* screw you, professors, we did it, didn't we, Ing?"

One of those still-hazy recollections—some key nugget of their shared history—pulsed against Ingrid's forebrain. They'd been working on something together, hadn't they . . . ? Some scientific endeavor everyone else thought was an impossibility. But not Ing and Ast. Their exceptional minds had put the unthinkable within grasp.

"Ing—now that you're back, I can't wait to show you everything."

Ingrid tested her limbs. Her joints felt wonky, packed with dust and grit. Why was she wearing a hospital johnny? Her fingers curved down around her hips—she jerked them away, hissing in pain.

"Why are my legs so skinny?"

"You have bedsores, too," Astrid told her. "I apply ointment every day, but they're tenacious. That doesn't matter now. You'll be up and running in no time flat. Oh—!"

Astrid gripped Ingrid's shoulders, her fingers digging in.

"Don't close your eyes, okay?" Astrid said. "It's imperative that you *stay awake.*"

"I'm not sleepy. I feel like I've slept for a thousand years." It dawned on her. "Ast . . . why do you look so much *older*?"

Astrid plopped herself onto the bed and pulled her heels under her thighs. "Hmm, so how old do I look?"

"Older than I remember."

Astrid's face smoothed out. "Okay, how old do you remember me being?"

Ingrid gave a shaky laugh. "This is silly. You're sixteen. We both are."

"I want you to take a deep breath, okay?"

Ingrid did as Astrid asked. Her chest felt full of Christmas tinsel.

"I'm nineteen, Ing. And so are you. You've been in a coma for three years."

The news didn't come as such a shock to Ingrid. The world simply darkened on the periphery, a pinhole into the blackness she'd been rescued from . . . three years? It felt both longer and shorter than that. An eyeblink and an infinity rolled into one.

"But you're back now, and you're going to stay back—right?"

"I'll try," Ingrid heard herself say.

"*Please*, you can't leave me again."

"How did I end up in a coma?"

Of all the memories that had slammed into her—they were still trickling back, tumbling over one another out of logical sequence—there was nothing about this part.

The door swung open. A woman entered.

"Can't you leave us alone?" Astrid said with a familiar edge to her voice.

"Ingrid?" the woman said in cold astonishment.

"Yes?"

"I'm Veronica Strauss. How are you feeling?"

"I'm sore. Groggy. Kind of like I'm wearing a diving helmet full of cotton batting."

Strauss shared a look with Astrid. "How much has Astrid shared with you about your situation?"

"She says I've been out of commission for three years? In a coma. I'm . . . processing it. My parents . . . ?"

"They're fine and still living in Saskatoon," Strauss said. "They know you're here, although they don't know where *here* is, precisely. Astrid, have you told her—"

"Why do you keep pestering me?" Ingrid could already tell these two didn't get along. But then, Astrid didn't get along with most people. "She just woke up."

"Tell me what?" Ingrid said.

Dr. Strauss cleared her throat. "Your parents, Ingrid. They signed a medical permission form, allowing Astrid, *Dr. Marsh*, to . . ."

Ingrid didn't care for the way the woman's lips were twitching.

"To what?" She turned to Astrid. "What did they let you do to me?"

Cupping her cheeks, Ast gazed directly into her eyes. "The Hydra, Ing. It's what brought you back. Isn't it wonderful?"

As soon as this fact cemented itself—when her fingers dipped back to the base of her spine and felt the freshly sutured incision—Ingrid Chevalier began to scream.

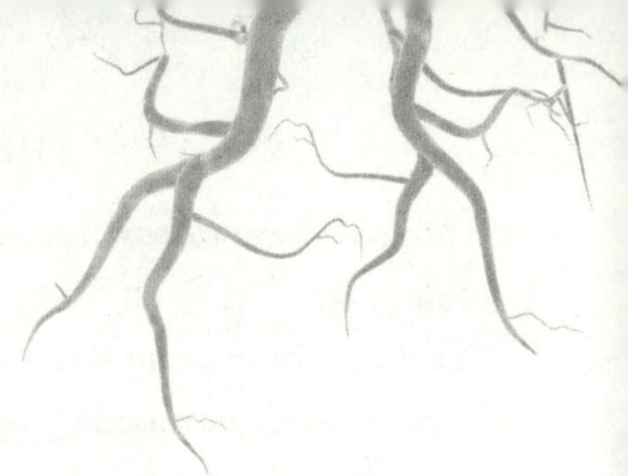

VI. *Anno Hydra*, Day 10

HUGO HUNG suspended in what the docs called "the Bath." This was a daily event. Part of their "Hydra therapy," as Dr. Strauss called it. The subjects needed to nourish the thing inside of them, and this was how.

The Baths were cylindrical glass tanks, rounded off at both ends. Every time he submerged, Hugo felt as if he'd been shrunk down like one of those scientists in *Fantastic Voyage* and stuffed inside a Dristan capsule.

All five of them floated in their liquid Baths, in a ring in one of the maze-like laboratory's many specialized areas. They were naked as the day they were born, which was also mandatory.

Hugo's nostrils were clipped shut with a rubbery clothespin. A breathing hose was stuck in his mouth. He'd never gone scuba diving, and after this Hugo knew he'd never want to. His chest was tight; a million static spiders kept scurrying around inside his lungs.

It helped to focus outside the tank. He wasn't wearing goggles, so he couldn't see far past the glass, whose warp and thickness made it akin to peering out a window smeared with bear grease. The doctors, Marsh and Strauss, were bustling about on the floor of the lab pod, checking the levels on machines that Hugo couldn't make heads or tails of. He kept waiting for them to climb up a stepladder and sprinkle fish flakes on top of his head.

But the stuff drifting around in the Bath wasn't fish flakes, though it looked a bit like that. It was stem cells. They moved around Hugo in soft, lace-edged eddies. Strauss called them *bioidenticals*, which meant they hadn't been snatched from unborn fetuses . . . still, Hugo couldn't push away the god-awful impression that he was floating in a tank full of torn-up little babies.

That would make him the worst kind of vampire, wouldn't it? One that fed exclusively on infants. The Hydra was busily sucking up all these itty-bitty particles through Hugo's pores.

Despite these reservations, Hugo had to confess the Bath made him feel good. On his first dip a few days ago, he'd come out feeling . . . Christ, it was scary just *how* great. His skull had been tingling. There was a warm flow in his bones. He swore he could feel his damn hair growing, fresh strands pushing out of his scalp in the way of grass seedlings.

Hugo couldn't see the ladies from his tank. The men he could, a little. He got a decent gander at Teddy in the next tank over; his wedding tackle bobbed between his legs. Hugo stared down at his own. His ex-wife, Luanne, she'd been a seamstress. She and her sewing gal pals had funny names for fabric colors. Drunk Tank Pink or Goose Shit Green. There was this one color, a lavender gray they all referred to as OMD.

Old Man's Dick, Luanne told him one day. *The color of an old guy's privates.*

And wouldn't you know it? Those gals had been bang on the money. Hugo's crotch was a dead ringer for that OMD shade. Kinda soft and wrinkled, too, like worn-in kid leather.

Hugo didn't feel embarrassed at what he saw, or that Teddy and Frank could see him floating in his tank. It wasn't that he was too old to feel shame at his nakedness. More that since coming to the island, he'd let go of the sense of his body as something vulnerable and fragile and come to see it more as an object frozen momentarily in time.

. . . or moving back through time. That was the hope.

The women floated on the far side of the ring. The positioning must've been on purpose, to keep the sexes from staring at one another's goodies. Hugo wouldn't mind getting a gander at Maddy, or especially at Claire. He liked his women with a little meat on their bones, and Claire sure as heck fit that bill. Hugo considered himself too much of a gentleman to gawk . . . though what to him was a respectful peekaboo might feel like a dirty leer to a woman, especially these days. Honestly, all Hugo wanted was an appreciative eyeful like a swallow of a finely aged wine.

Luanne had left him a long time ago. They'd clung to each other awhile after losing their daughter, Summer, but everything between them had gone to ashes. Hugo hadn't been with a woman since then . . . well, the odd lady of the night. Men had needs, some of them filthy.

Luanne had always blamed Hugo for Summer's dying. Not for the gumball. That part could have happened to Luanne or anybody else. No, Luanne blamed him softly, and for the same reason Hugo blamed himself.

Hugo was a bad man. And bad things happened to bad men. Or to the people they loved.

Hugo hadn't *always* been bad, but those seeds had been sown within him early. By the time he was ten, Hugo was nearly six feet and tipped the scale at a hundred and eighty pounds. Strong, too, with a mean streak a mile wide.

He'd been kicked out of school at fifteen for busting his math teacher in the chops. That same afternoon he wandered down to the local boxing club and started whaling away at a heavy bag. A trainer liked what he saw enough to start working with him.

Despite boxing for nearly a decade, Hugo was never much good at it. His record, six wins and thirty-three losses, said as much. He was a trial horse: decent enough to give up-and-comers a stern test, but never nearly good enough to pose a real threat. Hugo could take a punch and he hit like a cement truck—*when* he landed, which wasn't often.

And back in those sad old, bad old days, Hugo kind of *liked* hurting people. He couldn't explain that desire. Wasn't that he'd had a rough childhood. He didn't go walking around spoiling for a fight, like some people in his neighborhood. It was just every so often he needed to hear someone else's bones go *snap*.

He washed out as a boxer at twenty-eight. Detached retina. By then he and Luanne were a-courting. She was glad to see him leave the ring behind. Hugo wanted to make her happy. He got a job working construction but didn't have his union certificate. He and Luanne could barely make ends meet, and that was before Lu fell pregnant.

As fate would have it—and fate, that tricky bastard, always had it—the local mob had a need for Hugo's services.

The Irish. The Dundas Street boss needed some muscle for his loan-sharking operation, and he knew that Hugo was skilled at hurting people.

Hugo only intimidated the deadbeats at first, but if that didn't work (and as time wore on, even if it *did* work), Hugo hurt them. In ways they'd never recover from, a few times. Left in a wheelchair, pissing in a bag. Brain damage so bad one guy couldn't recognize his own mother.

Hugo told himself he was only doing his job. Except he liked it too much. Luanne, of course, she hated it. But it put money in their pockets, didn't it? She took that, boy howdy.

But when Summer was born, that was it—he stopped working for the Irish. And Hugo suspected a few of those old bog-Catholic micks were happy to see him go, too. Almost as if a greater evil had departed their circle.

So when Summer died choking on that gumball, it slammed into Hugo how circuitous karma was, and how blind its reckoning. His daughter was blameless. She was too young to know evil like her father did, let alone commit it. Didn't matter. The toll had to be paid.

Worse still, because Hugo believed that debt would *never* be paid. Karma had an endless belly. Even if you figured you'd squared the scales (and by Christ, wasn't the death of his little girl enough?), Hugo knew karma, that insane bitch, would never be full. Luanne knew it, too, which was why she'd never consented to carrying another child by him.

Hugo had long ago renounced his violent ways. Got a factory job and began going to the United Church, where he sat in a pew under the stained glass Jesus while the pastor's words droned over him like fat, soothing honeybees. The mindless anger that used to bubble up in him, mangling his thoughts, it went away. But the guilt was like the coffee stains on his teeth; he couldn't scrub it clean. It was there in the carpet fibers in his lungs and in the bad luck to get that shyster Johnny Celtina as a lawyer, who was as helpful as hemorrhoids on a dog's ass.

By the time the doc gave him his terminal diagnosis, Hugo knew he'd die before squaring the scales. But now, as he floated in the Bath on this sleepy island, his thoughts were optimistic.

What if you live to two hundred, Hugo? Or three hundred, or forever?

Would fate continue to harass him over the years? Karma was ageless. But maybe Hugo would be, too, if this pipsqueak doc's therapy really worked.

Hugo hung there in the baby-brine-Bath—

It's not *ripped-up babies*, he told himself. *It's just cells. Little squishy balls of . . . dust.*

—thinking about fate. Thinking more than he'd ever thought before, almost as if the channels of his brain were widening to accept the heavier traffic of these ruminations.

He smiled in the soothing aquamarine. *Ruminations.* A real ten-dollar word, wasn't it? How had it popped into his head? It wasn't a word he'd picked up from the funny pages, that's for damn sure. Beetle Bailey wasn't known to ruminate.

Jeez, he had to piss like a racehorse. Well, could he pee right here in his Bath? Could he get away with it: A kid taking a cheeky piss in a public pool?

Nah, better to hold it. He'd be right back in this thing tomorrow.

His eyes wandered over the Baths until they settled on Teddy. The guy was looking right at him, wasn't he? Eerily, it felt to Hugo that Teddy had read his mind.

You thinking about taking a piss in there, Hugo, you scallywag? Do it, why don't you. Piss or get off the pot, hah-hah.

Come to think of it, Teddy reminded Hugo of a guy he used to chum around with during his loan-sharking days. Pete Gorbel. Pete was a runty guy with a big mouth. He had this way, Pete did, of finding the softest part of you and pinching it. Like this other guy Hugo and Pete used to work with—well, *work* was a flexible phrasing, considering it wasn't like they got a pay stub every two weeks . . . anyway, guy by the name of Logan Hield. Now, Logan had bad teeth. Snaggly and yellow, on account of his folks not bothering with braces when he was a kid. Plus, Logan smoked a pack and a half of Chesterfields a day. They were some ugly choppers, no two ways about it, but why make note of it? Well, Pete Gorbel did. He took to calling Logan "Roman Buttercup": *Roman* on account of Logan's teeth roamin' around in his mouth, and *Buttercup* because of their buttery hue. Wasn't that funny as all hell to Pete? You bet. He'd laugh a blue streak at his own mean-spirited jokes, but if you got on him for it, Pete got all sore.

Aw, stop being so sensitive. I'm just funnin' around! He was always funnin' around and skylarking and having a rib, was Mr. Pete Gorbel.

Well, one sunny afternoon Pete's corpse was found in a roadside ditch near a nonunionized construction site. His skull was stove right in, one of his eyes popped out of its socket. It was never discovered who'd done that, but it sure as shootin' wasn't no accident—unless Pete had the bad luck of catching the business end of a Louisville Slugger ten or twelve times. Nobody was ever convicted for it (fact is, Pete's death was never even reported to the cops), but Hugo always figured someone'd had enough of Pete's funnin' around.

That's who Teddy reminded Hugo of: ole Pete Gorbel with his sneaky ability to find your soft spot and give it a tug . . . yeah, well, maybe someone would shut Teddy's funny old mouth for him one day, too.

AFTER THE session, Hugo stepped out of the tank—a ladder was lowered inside for him—and put on a terrycloth robe. Dr. Marsh didn't want them to shower, even though the residue of the Bath felt like soap scum. She said the stem cells would keep leaking into them, and the way Hugo felt, who was he to argue?

"Today we're going to try the epigenetic clock," she announced.

They padded along behind Dr. Marsh in an obedient procession—Hugo thought they must've resembled ancient schoolchildren being led across the playground. Their bare feet slapped on the floor as they moved through a shadowy corridor between the laboratory pods, past apparatuses whose function Hugo couldn't figure. There arose a prolonged snoring cry from someplace to the right. The acoustics in Spindrift were strange; noises got caught up in the high vaulted ceiling, bouncing around in the girders. It was disorienting.

"That's the male tortoise," Astrid said. "It's a mating call. But we don't have any females here, poor guy."

The snore quit out by the time they reached the pod. It was the same one they'd stood in the first day, after the hired men had tranquilized the wolves. There was the glass table the wolves had been examined on. A shudder raced through Hugo at the memory of the one wolf, Boots . . . the interior of its body revealed on the display, the infinite threads of the Hydra twisting in and through it.

The clock was there, too. *Epigenetic*, Dr. Marsh had called it. Hugo remembered that, too, which was odd, as his memory was generally for shit. The clock, which Marsh had used to measure the wolves' age—the one many years younger than the other, despite the fact they were littermates—was hooked up to the same laptop Marsh had used that day.

"Who'd like to go first?" Marsh asked.

"What if we don't want to?" said Maddy.

"Why would you *not* want to?" Dr. Strauss asked.

"I'm not saying whether I do or don't," said Madeline. "I'm speaking for the group."

Hugo understood Maddy's hesitation. What if they got hooked up to that clock and their age hadn't budged? After getting the Hydra stuffed into them, after floating like dill pickles in the Bath . . . to wind up the same age would be a heartbreaking failure.

"I'm afraid it's not an elective, Madeline," Marsh said. "I'm *telling* you."

"I'll go first, Doc," Teddy said. No surprise there. Teddy, the arse-kissing keener.

Hugo and the others watched Dr. Strauss prepare a specimen slide for the clock. She ran a Q-tip over Teddy's gums and smeared the residue on the glass plate.

"Go on," said Teddy, his voice a little hoarse. "Let's get this show on the road."

Dr. Strauss inserted the slide into the clock. The gray machine whirred. After a breathless span, Teddy's age spat out on the laptop screen.

79

"That's the age on my goddamn birth certificate." Teddy was pissed. But Hugo sensed he was scared, too. "You sure this clock's working right?"

"It's calibrated properly," Marsh told him.

"I'll go next," said Hugo.

Strauss repeated the procedure on him. Hugo's heart thumped away like a tom-tom drum as she covered his spit with a thin glass square, smooshed it over the slide, and inserted it into the clock. The machine made its soft purr.

76

That was Hugo's actual chronological age. Same as Teddy, he had the birth certificate to prove it. The two red numerals disappointed him, but Hugo tried not to let it show.

"No change for Mr. Udall," Marsh commented dryly. He kind of wanted to smack her smart mouth for the tone . . . well, Bad Hugo did.

Frank came back at 77. Claire at 79. The same ages as when they'd arrived on the island.

They were *all* the same according to that stupid clock. Still a pack of withered old turds.

Maddy was last. Disenchantment hung heavy over their heads—even the doctors seemed infected with it—as the clock purred . . . but then it *whirred* at a slightly different treble.

Two numbers brightened the laptop screen.

83

Marsh and Strauss shared a glance. A flush of success, or perhaps pure relief.

"When did you turn eighty-four?" Marsh asked.

"The ninth of August," Maddy replied quietly, transfixed by that number on the laptop.

"Subject Five, Madeline Dodds," Marsh recorded. "Initial recording indicates one year's reduction of bodily age."

Shock. Giddy, almost paralyzing shock. Hugo felt it as a numbness at the ends of his fingers. The whole group was held in that state for a moment, even the doctors. Simply hearing Marsh utter those words . . .

"Holy shit," said Frank. "Maddy, you're a year younger."

She looked at him dazedly. "I don't feel any different." But something on her face said: *Maddy, are you sure about that?* "I'm still old as the hills . . ."

Claire laughed, a sprightly soda-pop hoot. The laughter zinged from her to Frank to Hugo to Teddy, and soon they were all howling, the doctors included. It wasn't that anything was all that funny. The sound was improbable, somehow hysterical, rising to the high dark ceiling.

"Okay, look—we'll have to check again," Marsh said once the mirth died down. "The clock's not perfect, so—"

"Oh, come on," said Teddy. "You just finished saying it was finely calibrated."

"We'll see" was Marsh's terse reply.

Teddy hooked a thumb at Maddy. "So why's it working for her and not the rest of us?"

"Who's saying it's working?" Marsh replied. "It could be a misread. Or it could be that Maddy's the oldest subject. Or something related to her specific body chemistry, or the fact she's a woman, or she's left-handed, or who knows what? It's early. I have no answers for you at this present time."

But the simple, inescapable fact sat before them. That thrilling number.

83

A whole year gone. Erased, scrubbed away, kicked into the gutter. Eighty-*fireballing*-three.

Frank leaned close to Maddy. "Yeah, but do you *feel* any younger?" he prodded.

"Oh, how could I tell?" she replied. "It's like shaving an inch off a giant redwood—can you really see it's gotten any shorter?"

But boy oh boy, was Maddy ever grinning.

"I want to see it," Claire said, nodding at the X-ray board. "How it looks inside me. Same as you did with that wolf. I want to see it right now. That's only fair, isn't it?"

Another look between Marsh and Strauss. Before they could come to a decision, Claire Blessings made it for them.

The robe slipped down Claire's shoulders—such strong, solid shoulders—to puddle on the floor. There was nothing self-conscious in the gesture. Her breasts were large for her frame and gravity had been punishing them for three-quarters of a century, but the fact she didn't seem to care about that, or the shock of gray pubic hair in the cleft between her legs . . . the display activated something primal in Hugo—a shocking jolt from an urge-center that had been so long dormant he'd considered it dead.

Claire climbed onto the board and lay down with her arms and legs starfished out.

"Turn it on," she ordered.

Her demand quilled the short hairs at the back of Hugo's neck. It was that feeling you get at a young age, the first time one of your fellow students disobeys the teacher. A threat to the natural order of things, but that whiff of chaos was as thrilling as it was scary. A voltage zipping around the classroom, little spokes of heat lightning so powerful that the kids swore there must be balls of electricity popping off their fingertips.

And if the teacher didn't rein it in right away by punishing the smart-ass, well, their authority began to crumble. Before long the inmates were running the asylum.

"I'm not sure we ought to quite yet," said Marsh.

"It wasn't on the docket," Strauss added.

Claire didn't budge. Her nakedness was some kind of wager, not much different than a player shoving all of her poker chips into the middle of the table.

Wordlessly, Marsh eased to one side of the table. Her head was cocked at an angle that seemed more birdlike than human. A kind of cold avidity. *She wants to see as badly as Claire,* Hugo realized. *All she needed was a little push.*

With the press of a button, Dr. Marsh activated the diagnostic mechanism within the table. The display screen rose vertically from its berth. It was the same process as had been done with the wolf, except now it was a human body. Spiderwebs of static pulsed across the table's surface while the device warmed up.

The group crowded closer, as if Claire were some rare delicacy laid out on a banquet table. Hugo had the oddest compulsion to run his fingers down the inside of Claire's thigh like a meat inspector on the floor of a slaughterhouse . . . he wondered if Claire might even lick her lips if he took that vulgar liberty.

Go ahead, Hugo, but remember this. Looking's free, but touching'll cost you.

The table emitted a faint glow beneath Claire, more intense at the places (her elbows and heels, the back of her skull, her butt) where her skin made contact with the glass. Greenish strands climbed her torso and spread across her limbs.

Claire squirmed. "It tickles."

Strauss said: "Please stay still."

"Should she be awake?" Hugo asked. "That wolf was conked out."

"It doesn't matter," Marsh said, looking more a child than ever before. "The scan works the same either way."

"But what if it scares her?" Hugo said, meaning Claire. "Y'know, seeing it?"

"Speak for yourself, big fella," Claire answered.

The outline of Claire's body appeared as a cutout on the display screen above the table. A hollow blackness in the exact shape of her body; it reminded Hugo of a chalk outline at a crime scene. Marsh manipulated the control panel. At once, the cutout was full of red threads.

"This is your circulatory system," she said. "Heart, major arteries, veins, and capillaries."

The routes of Claire's blood were more complex than any road map. It amazed Hugo, the machinery of the human body.

A *click* as Marsh twisted a knob.

"This is your nervous system."

An even more elaborate arrangement of green threads was superimposed on top of the red ones. Claire's nerves, their stems and endings, stretching through her.

Another *click*. Claire's body map went black again. Just that hollow cutout of her shape on the screen.

"And this is your Hydra."

Click.

Hugo took a step back as if he'd been buffeted by a strong headwind.

Good Christ. That's what's inside us all.

A billion spiders working tirelessly for a billion years couldn't have spun a web to rival the one inside Claire. If her circulatory system was complex and her nervous system doubly so, the Hydra was a maze without entry or exit—its bluely-glowing architecture was alien, a bit like those endless staircase drawings that made Hugo's head hurt . . . except this was an infinity of staircases hammered together, upside down and front to back.

It was shot all through Claire, from the ends of her toes to the tips of her fingers, fanning in an even denser arrangement across the top of her scalp, barely contained, it seemed, by the bone of her skull . . . the memory of those jellyfish arose, the ones floating in the tank in the center of Spindrift—that's what it looked like, especially up in Claire's head: the thickened bell of the Hydra fanning across the inner dome of her skull, sunk into her brain box, while its unguessable tentacles stretched down to fill the rest of her body.

It grew so fast. So goddamn fucking fast.

Hugo's gorge rose. His revulsion was a symptom of something much more enigmatic that was now transpiring at the deepest levels of his psyche. He wanted to run—to tear his hair out at the roots—to sink his teeth into Frank's neck and rip out a bloody divot.

"Oh my gosh. Isn't it beautiful?" Claire trailed her fingers over her belly with a faint smile, watching the Hydra helix its endless coils inside of her. "I think I'm in love."

Marsh shut the table off. "That's enough for one day."

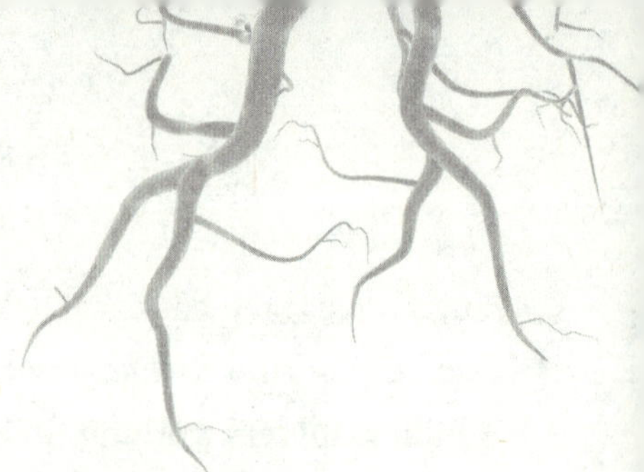

VII. *Anno Hydra,* Day 12

FRANK AWOKE to a knock at his door at the ass crack of dawn.

"Little Frank, little Frank, let me in."

Teddy's voice. Frank slid out of bed and padded to the door.

"Teddy, crissakes, what time is it?"

"Early-bird special." Teddy winked. "Come on, get your puckered old ass out of bed."

Once dressed, Frank trailed Teddy out the main lab doors. The air was still dark, birds wittering in the treetops. Cool, the tracery of woodsmoke from someplace.

Teddy nodded to the hateful steps. "You up for it?"

"Up for what?"

"I talked to Strauss. She said we could take a boat out for a toot around."

"At this hour?"

"Well, yeah, before they start their daily poking and prodding."

Frank glanced over the precipice of that endless staircase. "Can *you* make it down?"

Teddy shrugged. "Took my pill this morning, so I'm damn well gonna give it a go."

They set off. There was no railing on the staircase. The roots of the spindly pines that clung to the upslope knobbed over the stairs here and there. Frank had to constantly check his momentum; once or twice he pitched forward, but at least he didn't go ass over teakettle. Halfway down he was huffing. The mucus packed around his congested heart had it thudding away like a rusted engine—but was it actually so bad? Frank was short of breath, sure, but not gasping. His legs carried him down each step, his pace picking up ever so slightly.

Teddy looked a lot better, too. Not full-on shaking, more the shiver of a fall leaf in a gentle breeze. Frank was having a hard time keeping up with him.

"Slow down," he called out.

"Why? It's not a race, is it?"

"Everything is"—*now* Frank was starting to wheeze—"a race . . . with you."

Reaching the bottom came as a pleasant shock. Frank peered back up their winding route. God, he'd have to climb that again just to crawl back into bed. But as he looked up at Spindrift, the climb didn't feel nearly so daunting as it had been that first day.

JOHN SALTERS was in the boathouse, eating his breakfast by the light of a Coleman lantern. He greeted them with a nod and a genuine smile.

"Did Dr. Strauss clear this with you?" Teddy asked him.

"Yup, sure. Said you could take out the cedar strip for an hour."

Salters pointed toward the dock, to a twelve-foot boat with a fifteen-horsepower motor. Salters had rigged up a pair of fishing rods for them.

"The pike bite can be pretty lively in the morning," Salters said. "Just pull the spoons behind you in the boat."

"Will do. Thanks, John," said Frank.

"Sure. But I wouldn't wander too far. Lots of doglegs and cricks around, easy to get lost. The river bottom's all rocks, too. They like to tear propellers off."

"Frank's an excellent boater," Teddy lied.

A few minutes later, they were puttering away from the dock into the rising sun. "I've driven a boat maybe once in my life," Frank told Teddy.

"Ah, how hard can it be?" He leaned back in his seat. "What did John call this boat?"

"A cedar strip."

"*My cedar strip,*" Teddy sang like an old doo-wopper. "*Ain't she a pip, life's a trip, don't be a drip, let 'er rip—catch a ride with me baby on my nifty cedar strip.*"

A quarter mile across the water with the boathouse still in sight—and Salters at the end of the dock, the faint dot of his lantern—Teddy let the fishing lines out. Frank prayed a fish didn't bite. He would hardly know what to do.

"I feel better," Teddy said after some time. "I thought it was wishful thinking, but it's hung around."

"Me too," Frank confessed. "But I wonder . . . who knows whether we all got the real thing, right? For a trial to be scientifically accurate, doesn't it need a placebo?"

"Yep, and I hate to be the bearer of bad news, but you got it. That's the real reason I brought you out here this morning. The group figured I could let you down the easiest. Sorry about your luck, Frank-O."

"Oh, shut up, would you?"

Teddy slapped his knee. "Long time ago, I went to this dingy clinic and got testosterone supplements. The doc who prescribed it looked like he ought to be selling time-shares on Florida swampland. The stuff's supposed to put the pep back in your step and the lead in your pencil. It wasn't injections; I got this tube of cream to rub on my nipples."

"Your *nipples*?"

"Well, you could rub it anywhere you like. But it didn't do shit-all, Frank! Just made me sweat and, weirdly, fart a whole lot. Real underwear-shredders. Plus, wicked insomnia. So you know what I did when I couldn't sleep? I thought about boobs."

Now it was Frank's turn to laugh. "Whose?"

"Now, here's the thing," Teddy said. "They were anonymous boobs. Big, soft, round, bulbous—"

"Wait, *bulbous*?"

"Don't be a prude!"

"It's not prudish," Frank explained. "I object to you mangling the English language."

"Anyway, yeah, I imagined disembodied boobs. Not my wife's—not any of my exes'—or any boobs I could recall seeing or squeezing."

"And that helped?"

"Kind of, sure," Teddy said dreamily. "Nuzzling them. Drifting off to sleep between them." He snapped out of it. "Who the hell knows? I think it was that damn cream that put me in the frame of mind . . . but like I said, it didn't work at all. All the stuff I've tried since turning sixty—diets, pills, serums, any old shit I could grasp at—nothing's worked."

They motored along with this odd new admission between them. Finally, Frank said: "I woke with an erection yesterday. First time in forever."

Teddy perked up at this news. "Morning wood, huh? An honest-to-God sun-up boner. How was it?"

"What do you mean? You asking for measurements?"

"No, you idiot. What were you dreaming about?"

Frank wanted to tell Teddy he couldn't remember. Most people didn't remember dreams, that was just the fact of it. But maybe it was the crisp air and the tightened lines—it just seemed like a real man-to-man moment— whatever the case, Frank opened his stupid mouth and spoke.

"I dreamed I was really little, like teeny-tiny, and a woman was washing me in the sink."

Teddy's mouth fell open. "Wait just a damn minute. *Beep, beep, beep.* Back the bus up."

"Yeah, so I . . ." Frank's face was heating up. "I was little, but not a baby. Just shrunk down to the size of a Ken doll. This enormous woman was giving me a bath in the kitchen sink."

Teddy whistled. "Holy mommy issues, Batman."

"She wasn't my mother, okay?" Frank said. "Just a big, gentle, I don't know, Valkyrie or someone."

"In full battle regalia?" A beat. "I bet Maddy's got a suit of armor in her closet."

"What's that supposed to mean?"

"Nothing," Teddy said innocently.

"Whatever. Don't you dare use it against me."

"Never!" Teddy seemed genuinely offended. "You've got my unidentified-flying-boobs confession in your hip pocket."

Working the tiller, Frank swung them around in a gentle half-moon. They hadn't gotten so much as a nibble.

"I'll tell you something else," said Teddy. "I like our daily stem Baths. I mean, *a lot.*"

Frank found himself nodding. Yeah, he felt the exact same way.

"Actually, Frank, I *crave* them. The last time, I started to shake before I'd even taken my clothes off. Wasn't the Parkinson's, either. It was anticipation. Did you shake, too?"

Frank pondered this. "No. No shakes."

Teddy kept his peace for a span. "I'm gonna tell you something, seeing as we're being honest Injun here. Thirty years ago, I got myself into cocaine. I lost my second wife to coke." He lip-farted. "I'd never say this to her face, but that was no great loss. But my business suffered, as it would when the boss is a coked-up asshole."

"I never tried that stuff," said Frank.

"It's a real gas right up until the moment it ain't. When your doctor's telling you your septum's eaten through and your nose is on the verge of caving in, leaving a crater between your eyes and mouth. How's that for a wake-up call? So, I quit the stuff."

"What, just like that?"

Teddy fished a pill out of his caddy. His hands trembled, but not nearly as badly as they had that first day. He stared at the pill pinched in his fingers . . . and he flicked it overboard.

"Yeah, just like that," he said, watching it sink. "Cold turkey. No AA, no working the steps. I made the clearheaded choice to say: *Enough of that.* I'd fallen down the well . . . but when I hit bottom, I had two options. Either bounce up, or die. So I knuckled down, dug my fingers in, and just . . . yeah, quit. You believe me?"

"I do."

Teddy leaned forward. The air between them crackled in the new daylight.

"So lemme tell you—I *know* addiction. I know the feel of those claws hooked under your skin. Thirty years back, I had the gumption to stop. But right now? I'm scared—and this may be the only fear left in my soul—that if the nutty little bitch running this show kills off our Baths . . . Christ, I don't know what I'd do."

"Why would Astrid do that?"

"You may've noticed that our dear Astrid is a mite unpredictable? Not to mention that I've gone through plenty of dealers in my time. And that's what they do. Dealers hook you, pal. Give you a taste and then jack up the price."

"She's as invested in this as anyone—*more* invested. Come on, you're talking silly. She wouldn't dare—"

Frank stopped. Teddy was looking at him funny. *You're hooked through the nose same as me, my friend,* that look said. *You're just an optimist, while I'm a pessimist.* Maybe that's all Teddy had wanted to do in the first place. Get a reading on Frank's state of addiction.

"That's not what worries me, Teddy."

"Well, what is it, then?"

"Do you think that . . . maybe this thing inside us, whatever it's doing . . . I mean, these are *our* bodies, but it's inside us now. So, what agency does it have? What have we given it?"

"Agency? It's a *thing*. Brainless. Harum-scarum, hugger-mugger. There's no agency."

"Yeah, I'm sure that's so. Still, it has an end goal, same as that pill you swallow and the canned oxygen I breathe. But it's more powerful. I can feel that, Teddy, just having it in me. The question I keep asking is . . . what if it won't let us die, even if we want to?"

Frank had been thinking a lot about this over the past day or so, ever since seeing Claire's body map on-screen. Less of a conscious thought than something that chased itself through the unlit chambers of his lizard brain.

"I don't want to die," Teddy said. "Do you, Frank?"

"I dunno," he said. "Not now, but . . . forget it. It's stupid."

"Frank. Hey, look at me."

Frank lifted his eyes to meet Teddy's.

"I like these people," Teddy said. "Really, I do. The other, uh, *subjects*. But I've been thinking that it might come down to you and me at some point. I thought maybe Maddy, too, but not so much after the whole trying-to-snuff-herself thing."

"What the hell are you talking about?"

"This thing inside of us—out of everyone alive on earth, only us five have been gifted this opportunity." Teddy rolled his eyes skyward, content to merely paint the edges of his thinking. "Maybe the Hydra has to be *wrangled*, know what I mean? You've got to bust it like a wild mustang or, or *commune* with it, or I don't know—"

"Feed it?"

"No, no . . . I mean, *yes*. That's what the Baths are for, right? And in that case, it's more that we're feeding these achy old bones of ours. We're not feeding *it*, not really—"

One of the fishing rods began to whang madly against the gunwale.

Teddy said: "What in God's name is that?"

"That's a fish!"

Teddy stood up, swaying perilously. He grabbed the rod as its tip danced over the water.

"Get it, Teddy! Reel, *reel*! Reel it in!"

Teddy balanced on the dangerously rocking boat and cranked the reel. Line sizzling, the rod bucked in his hands.

"Be careful, Teddy, or you'll snap the line!"

"Don't you tell me what to do!" Teddy cackled. "I'm the Fisher King!"

The fish appeared as a streak of greenish silver in the tea-stained water, the spiny coxcomb of its fin slitting the surface.

"Yank it up, Teddy, get it in here!"

Teddy hauled it out of the water. They stared at it flopping in the bottom of the boat.

"What is it?" Frank said.

"A fish! A fish!"

"No, you goof, what *kind*?"

"Who am I, the fish whisperer?"

Frank was able to tug the hook from its mouth. As he hefted it in both hands, the smooth and elastic voltage of its body thrummed in his wrists.

"We don't want to keep it, right?"

"I hate fish," Teddy said. "Can't stand the taste."

Frank managed to hold it over the boat's edge without pitching overboard. The fish squirmed out of his fingers, a quicksilver flash returning to the water.

"Jeez, my heart's hammering to beat the band," he said.

"Harder than it has in years, I bet, and you're still kicking." Teddy put one hand over his heart. "So I said to my wife with a wooden leg, *Peg, how's life?* She said: *Oh well, can't kick.*"

Frank grinned. "I'll have you know that I was engaged to a woman with a wooden leg. But we got in a fight and I broke it off. She was stumped."

Teddy's own grin was even wider. "Holy shit, aren't we a couple of losers."

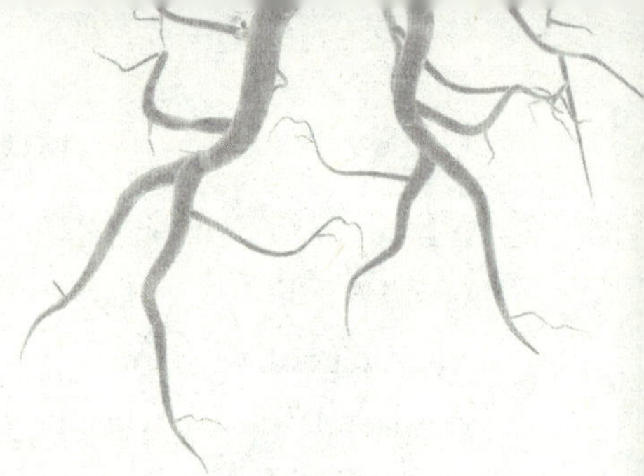

VIII. *Anno Hydra*, Day 14

MOSES SQUIRES had a bad feeling about the wolves.

As a boy, he'd learned all he could about timber wolves. They were animals he felt a great kinship with. By now, he knew their habits as well as any human can truly perceive the ways of wild things. He recognized their markings and tracks and, yes, their spirits. Moses believed all creatures had those, spirits, but not the way city folks fantasized. The Stoic Indian and the Great Spirit. For Moses it was much plainer: a point of connection between all living things, no more mystical than beads on a chain.

Humans were part of that chain, too. But at their worst—and Moses could no longer say what was happening on this island *wasn't* the worst, or close enough to it for horseshoes and hand grenades—humans were the rot in the chain that made everything fall to pieces.

"I've had my eye on the males, Diego and Boots," Moses presently told the doctors. "Neither of them has moved in nearly a day now."

Moses found Drs. Strauss and Marsh in a lab pod in Spindrift's eastern quadrant. They were with the other young woman. Moses hadn't spoken with her yet, but he knew her name. Ingrid. She sat in a wheelchair a discreet distance off, her legs covered in a blanket like a teenage Sir Winston Churchill. Since rousing her from her coma, Marsh had kept Ingrid hidden away, recuperating in private. Her progress on that front was, in Moses's opinion, a lot quicker than might have occurred in a more natural state of affairs. He had no experience with coma recoveries, but in the few glimpses he'd had of Ingrid since she'd awakened, the girl looked almost nothing like the shrunken effigy she'd been before surgery.

Ingrid appeared hale. Her limbs were fleshing out rapidly; it wouldn't be long before she cast off that wheelchair. That was the Hydra's doing, far as Moses could tell . . . as was the moody blue cast that shaded the whites of the girl's eyes.

Dr. Strauss said: "The fact the wolves haven't moved—you see that as a concern, Mr. Squires?"

"I wouldn't bother mentioning it otherwise."

Moses had a soft spot for Strauss. She saw things the clearest out of this bunch. Marsh he cared for considerably less, but Moses did admire her for not giving a damn what he or anyone else thought, so it partially evened out.

"A concern *how*?" Marsh asked him.

"Wolves are territorial," Moses explained. "They mark that territory constantly. And the cold isn't far off. This is the time when they ought to be hunting. Fattening themselves for winter."

"Meaning what?"

"Meaning a wolf who hasn't moved in twenty-four hours is probably a dead wolf."

All four of the captive wolves on the island had surgically implanted tracking units. Dora, Boots, Swiper, and Diego. Dr. Marsh had named them after a child's cartoon show. For someone so smart, she was often a bit silly.

"What wolves are you talking about, Mr. Squires?" the girl, Ingrid, called over from afar. "Ast, what does he mean?"

"In a minute, Ing," Astrid said. "They can't be dead, Moses. Boots *especially* can't be dead."

Moses opened the laptop he'd brought with him. He booted up the tracking program that monitored the wolves' movements. The screen filled with a topographical map of the island. Moses zoomed in on four glowing dots. Numbers Three and Four, the females Dora and Swiper, were currently moving; their dots blipped along a ridgeline on the eastern edge of the wolf enclosure. One and Two, the males, had their dots overlapping each other some distance away from the females.

"That's Boots and Diego." He put his finger on the screen. "Not moving. I've been checking regularly over the last eighteen hours."

"Shit," Marsh said under her breath. "It doesn't make any sense. The Hydra can't be . . ."

Turning on her heel, she walked to one of the pod's lab benches. "Come over here."

Moses tagged behind Marsh. Strauss retrieved Ingrid, guiding her wheelchair over to the bench. Marsh opened her own laptop and toggled onto the program she'd come looking for.

"This is the Hydra inside Boots," she said. "It's still operational. It's *alive.* So by that logic, the wolf ought to be, too."

Marsh's laptop screen displayed the Hydra inside Boots. Its unaccountable essence pulsating and vibrating.

"Am I invisible?" Ingrid said. "Don't I have a right to know what's happening?"

"You do, you do," Marsh said, hunched down over her screen. "But hang on—I don't want to overburden you, okay? You've got to get your strength back."

"It's in *me,* too. You put it there, Ast."

"Please, Ing, not now."

Voices tended to carry here in Spindrift. That's one fact Moses had discovered. There were many darkened spaces within the laboratory where a person could linger, unseen, and listen. Moses wasn't a snoop by nature, but increasingly an air of secrecy pervaded operations on the island—though from the start, much of this project was on a need-to-know basis, and Moses simply hadn't needed or truly *wanted* to know. Yet now it seemed his not-knowing might pose a risk to his life, and John's, too . . . so he had taken to walking softly on the lab floor, and yes, listening. Over the past few days, he'd had occasion to hear the two girls (and that's what they still were, despite their vast intelligence) talking to one another.

Ingrid had questions, as well a girl who'd been unconscious for three years might. How had she gotten here? Why had Astrid put that thing inside her without asking her permission? And—this Ingrid had asked more than once—what was the nature of the incident that left her in a coma?

Astrid had answered these questions truthfully, as far as Moses could overhear. Ingrid had been brought to the island via a medical transport (true: Moses had overseen the manifest himself). Her parents had been made aware, but for now no contact was permitted with the outside world. Finally, as there had been no way to ask Ingrid whether or not she consented to the Hydra implant, her parents' consent had to suffice.

However, Dr. Marsh's answers about the incident rang hollow to Moses's ears. There had been an accident in the private lab they'd shared at the institute. A tank housing jellyfish had burst. Ingrid had been stung. It had happened late one night. Nobody was around. Ingrid's body was discovered, still wet, on the floor of the lab. Marsh's retelling didn't strike Moses as untruthful. Half-told, maybe, but not exactly a lie.

Presently, Dr. Marsh said: "Moses, if you think something's the matter, then go check on the wolves. Take John with you. Bring them back here. We'll run a full diagnostic."

"Even if they're dead, you want them back?"

"At least one of them *isn't* dead. But in whatever state, yes, back here."

MOSES FOUND John in the boathouse. He was at his desk, writing by lantern light.

Every day, John wrote a letter to his wife and daughter. Neither of the hired men was permitted to contact anyone off the island, a constraint they'd both agreed to in taking this job. It paid very well, enough to abide the loneliness. But letters were permitted. John Salters's were long and likely quite searching—Moses found him to be a man of layers. He'd often include small items he'd found in the woods: an arrowhead or owl feather, a vibrantly colored pebble. He mailed them in bunches, twenty letters or more, whenever he returned to the mainland.

Moses and John were not allowed to speak of the work being done here in any personal correspondence, even in vaguest terms. Which was for the best, really, as that kind of news would surely cause undue worry to their wives.

"It's the wolves," Moses said. "The males."

It took a minute to explain. John listened, then nodded to his rifle, where it rested by his cot. "Think we'll need it?" he asked.

"I don't imagine so. But bring it along anyway."

They walked to the garage through the main building, passing down the hallway where the subjects' rooms lay. Moses could hear faint music behind Subject Five's door.

They're not numbers, he reprimanded himself. *They're* people.

He'd only started to think of them that way following their implants. The habit was hard to root out, but he was trying . . . Madeline, then, not Five. She was listening to classic rock.

Hugo (*not* Subject Four) sat alone in the common area. His flat-hanging and somehow primeval face turned to Moses and John as they approached.

"We under attack?" he said with a nod to John's gun.

"Nah," Moses said casually. "Just moving some stuff around."

It disturbed Moses, the quality of Hugo's skin. The man's face looked waxy as a dummy at Madame Tussauds . . . but undoubtedly younger, too. It was collagen. The subjects were producing it again, as heavily as they had as teens. Moses had overheard a conversation to this effect between the docs as they'd huddled over some recent results.

Moses and John moved through Spindrift's darkened corridors, between the lit pods. As they passed within range of the saltwater tank—it was the most direct route, otherwise Moses would have avoided it—the shadow of that massive jellyfish fell across his face. Moses fought the urge to flinch. All living creatures had spirits, and *yet . . .*

When those things die, it'll be no different than a disgusting little light going dead.

They loaded up one of the Rovers and drove outside, down the path leading to the wolf enclosure. The night was still and cool, the stars remote in a cloudless sky. A good night for tracking, not that Moses expected that tonight. The two dots marking Boots and Diego weren't going anywhere, were they?

He'd been a wilderness guide since the age of thirteen. Both his father and mother had done the work, too. There were dozens of lodges up in these parts. Most were frequented by whites from the city, but Moses rarely had trouble with such folks. Those who hired him respected his abilities without question. The shade of his skin and the necklace of bear teeth he wore (fake ones, and purely for show) were enough to convince them he knew what he was doing. He could've walked them off a cliff, and they'd fall to their deaths believing he'd found them a secret Indian shortcut.

Thankfully, Moses *did* know what he was doing. Everything about these islands and the game and fish that inhabited them . . . but wolves, ahh, they were forever unknowable.

Men didn't hunt wolves. Everything else up here, men could and did. Fifteen-hundred-pound bull moose, ornery brown bears—nothing was off the table. Nothing except wolves.

And every so often, they might decide to hunt you.

MOSES PULLED up to the enclosure, he and John exiting the vehicle. The sky was hemmed by the mingled jack pines and elms, whose canopy spread like smooth oil against the horizon; above them, scattered night clouds were pushed across the heavens by a wind Moses couldn't trace down there at ground level—those clouds massed from the east, blotting out the stars that freckled the sky for a heartbeat or two before passing by.

Electricity crackled off the fence, a voltage Moses could feel through the lead plugs in his molars. Opening the trunk, he shouldered a tranquilizer rifle, a backpack with night vision goggles, a fetch pole, and bear spray. John had his .30-30.

John said: "Should I cut the juice to the fence?"

Moses nodded. John's tribal affiliation was farther north, Ojibwe; Moses's people were Iroquois. Their people had been enemies at one point, but none of that bad blood had much mattered for two hundred years now. John was damn good at his job and cool under stress. Moses trusted him down the line.

Opening the power box, John dropped the lever. The grid went dead in a bluish flicker. The sounds of night filled in to replace the hum of electricity.

Moses checked his phone screen. "They're five hundred yards in."

"What about the females?"

"Roaming normally. I'll give you the word if they're closing in. Let's stick tight."

Opening the gate, they entered the wolves' enclosure. After taking a few steps past the fence, Moses heard the gate fall shut behind them, the hasp catching with a dull *clink*.

They crossed a flat expanse of moon-washed rock, slipping under the trees. It was colder under the forest's canopy, darker too, but Moses expected that. What he couldn't account for was the unfamiliar worry. Five icy fingers steepling at the back of his neck. Why? He'd been in woods ten thousand times. Night or day, he could navigate them confidently. He had John, a trusted man, and they were well armed. Most of all, they were smarter than whatever they faced.

Except that thing was out here, too. Not the wolves, who represented a measurable but grippable threat. These wolves—*any* wolves—were at least wise enough to know Moses and John were far from easy meat.

Yet the Hydra made a home inside one of them—put there by the hand of man . . . *that* sat outside natural forms and rhythms. To Moses, all that was unnatural, *uncanny*, ought to be a source of worry. Even for an even-minded man such as he, most especially in the dead of night—

A howl pierced the trees. It rose to a moody, exalted pitch before receding to an echo that shivered the pine cones overhead.

Moses consulted his phone screen again. The wolves were emblematized as four glowing dots. Two were moving along the water's edge now, across the rocky spine of scree that descended to the crashing surf.

"That was one of the females," he whispered. "They're a thousand yards off west."

Moses was about to put the phone away, but something made him watch a bit longer. The females were working their way off the water now, around the perimeter of the enclosure . . . if they continued on that course, they'd scissor in behind Moses and John. Right between the men and the gate.

Were they trying to box them in?

Moses couldn't believe they'd try. Yet as with anyone familiar with these remote territories, he'd heard stories.

It was highly uncommon for wolves to hunt human beings. Bears, sure—a mama bear would attack anything standing between her and her cubs. Moose were known to trample hikers and hunters every year; they often turned back after the initial charge to finish the job, too. But the only time Moses had heard of wolves hunting humans was from an old fur trapper. This man had made his living off the bush, a hermit who was as wild as the country he roamed. He'd gotten snowed in past the picket line. The flurries persisted for a week straight, and when he finally dug out of his hutch, every tree under five feet tall was buried deep. Not long after, the wolves appeared.

A pack of six, by that hermit's count. Winter timber wolves with fur white as hoarfrost. He could hear them outside his hutch in the witching hours— the dark of a forest night was a kind of blindness; human eyes never adjusted to that blackness—snaffling at the chinks in the log walls. The trapper couldn't understand why. Even at their most desperate, wolves didn't eat human flesh. Too stringy, not enough fat. They'd rather eat moose nuggets.

I'd say they wanted to kill me for sport, the trapper had told Moses. *They were bored, or wanted to tell their buddies they'd ripped one of them two-leggers apart.*

The man survived until the melt and made his way to the nearest trading post. The wolves hadn't pursued him—lost interest, probably—but at the time, the hermit was sure they were on his ass like every hound of hell.

They weren't right, those wolves.

The ones Moses was dealing with weren't right, either. At least one of them. It had been *made* wrong, no fault of its own. But now he and John had to grapple with that wrongness.

On his phone, Moses noted that the females had checked up eight hundred yards from the gate. Lying in wait, resting, or something else?

"The other two are up this rise," he told John. "Two hundred yards."

They crept carefully. Dry pine needles crunched under their boots, as loud as pistol shots in Moses's ears. All four wolves knew the men were in the enclosure. They would have caught their scent as soon as they got out of the Rover. There was nothing in their pen these wolves weren't aware of.

"They moving yet?" John whispered.

"Nothing. Dead calm."

He and John topped the rise. The moonlight fell in thin rails between the trees, almost like how water hangs slack between the waves. An uncomfortable feeling went through Moses, something moonlike itself, lonely and lunar, the sense of being a lifetime away from anything he could draw warmth from . . . the awful taste of radiator dust on his tongue.

He found his hand reaching for John's like a lost boy—catching himself, he reeled it back in. *Don't get squirrelly now. Keep your dick dry.*

He held up one hand. John checked up on his gesture. Moses confirmed the load on his tranquilizer gun. Unzipping his pack, he reached for the night specs and pulled them over his eyes.

The specs snapped on with a cool buzz at his ears. The terrain resolved into a grid etched and shaded in greens. He didn't much like the night vision goggles; they cut off his peripheral vision, made it feel like he was wearing a Ski-Doo helmet. But if the wolves were hiding out in a den, they'd be impossible to spot without the specs.

"Get your rifle handy," he said. "No use us getting ripped to shreds by two sick wolves."

"Right." John caught the quaver in his partner's voice. "Safety off."

They advanced on the depression in the earth where the wolves' tracking signal was blipping from. A huge pine had torn halfway out of the stony island soil, lying against its neighbors like the mast of a sunken ship.

"They're under that," Moses said. "The hole left by that ripped-up tree."

Moses adjusted a knob near his left eye. The greens intensified, so bright he squinted before the coloration corrected. He could make out the tangled roots of the tree, dry and twisted into hardened ropes—*like jellyfish tentacles,* but he pushed that jarring similarity aside.

He came forward with his shoulder angled defensively toward the hole; his heart was jabbering in his chest, a painful sensation that made his toes numb. Was he on the verge of heart failure? No, he was barely forty and his family had good hearts, good strong hea—

Something was in the hole. The specs made it clear.

"Get that rifle ready," he whispered. "I can see at least two of them in there."

"Copy that."

Raising his own rifle, Moses took quick aim and fired. He saw the dart through the specs, an arrowing flash of green like a tracer bullet. It sunk into the wolf's hide.

The wolf didn't move. No reaction, no anguished howl.

Moses tensed, waiting for the other male to come rocketing out of the den . . . when it didn't, his brow wrinkled. *What the hell?*

"That one must be dead," Moses said. "Let's give it a minute."

He checked the phone. The females were in the same spot—or had they sidled a bit closer to the exit gate? Could be. Maybe just enough to intercept them as they hauled the males back.

The two in the den weren't moving. Were they *both* dead? Or was the other one dug deeper down the hole, tucked out of sight? That wasn't wolf behavior, that was mole behavior.

But it wasn't a regular wolf, that one. Hadn't been since Dr. Marsh got at it.

Did one of them eat *the other?*

Cannibalism among wolves was unheard-of. They'd rather starve to death. If Boots *had* eaten its pack mate, or Boots and the females had dined on Diego together—even a few timid chunks—it would indicate a madness beyond rabies or distemper, an act against the innate nature of their species.

They've been touched by the Wiijigo.

For the first time in his adult life, the wires of Moses Squires's brain crimped. The bend was subtle, but enough to pull his thoughts over some unreal meniscus curve, warping logic and making childhood nightmares reality, if only for a few heartbeats.

A legend as old as his people. One that many tribes shared—old lineages who'd taken root in wild, dark places in a time before the dominion of Man. A creature roamed the forest primeval in that time before time, altering anything that felt its cold touch.

It was cursed to life forever. And in that glut of time, it became unimaginably cruel.

Moses saw *that* inside the wolves. The Wiijigo . . . ageless, deathless, spreading insanity and unclean hunger throughout its host.

Reaching into his pack, Moses retrieved the fetch pole. He pulled it out in sections—it was telescopic—locking in place a ten-foot length with a noose at the end.

He edged up on the tree. The goggles identified the wolf Dr. Marsh had named Diego. With the fetch pole extended at the end of one arm, Moses looped the noose around the wolf's neck. Cinching it tight, he pulled it from the den.

Nothing else is in here, he realized. *Just this one.*

He dragged the wolf back to John's position. Checked the phone.

"Watch our flank," he said.

The females had gotten closer. Skulking so slowly as to almost be untraceable, but they were on the move.

Kneeling, Moses checked on Diego. Dead as dead can be. Cold, its legs stiff with rigor mortis. Probably a day or more.

The dots on the phone screen . . . the males—they had *both* moved, hadn't they? Yes, when Moses hauled this one out of the den. The other male, Boots, wasn't nearby, but according to the tracking program, he *was.*

"What the hell's going on?"

It twigged. Moses ran his hands over the coarse threads of the dead wolf's pelt . . .

There. Stuck to one of the hind legs above the dewclaw. A tacky little square.

Moses picked it free. The tracker chip. The one belonging to Boots.

John said: "The wolf must've chewed it out or something . . ."

Moses said: "Or else the Hydra *forced* it out."

Moses pictured the Hydra nesting inside Boots. He saw it wrapping its threads around the tracking implant and excising it from Boots's tissue not unlike a rotten tooth, spitting it out of its host's hide . . . no, that couldn't be. Both Marsh and Strauss said the Hydra had no brain, no . . . what was their word? *Agency*. It couldn't think or reason or form a cogent plan.

Didn't the chip in Moses's palm dispute that, though?

A howl bristled over the treetops. This one was lower than the first, a powerful baritone like the rev of a rusty chainsaw. It felt dangerously close to their position.

Boots. He was out there somewhere. And they couldn't track him.

"We go," Moses told John. "*Now.*"

Dragging Diego, they moved down the slope in the direction of the Rover. The trees crowded in, their boughs whapping Moses's shoulders. He tried to breathe steadily—and was failing at that simple task, his nerves gone jangly. He checked the phone. The dot representing Diego moved as they lugged his body behind them. The dots representing the females had split apart, tracking down each side of their present position.

Scissoring tactic, as suspected. Old as the hunt.

"They're on us," he told John. "I can't believe it—they're *hunting* us."

"I believe it," said John. Moses could smell it in the air under the pines, sharp as rubbing alcohol. Their own chemicals—the adrenal scent pushed from the pores of a man in fear of his life—and the gamy, cloying reek of the creatures fixed on ending them.

Hauling Diego one-handed, Moses unsnapped the holster of his Glock pistol. He'd never pulled it on a job, only at the firing range. He knew how to use it just fine, perforating targets center of mass seven out of nine shots . . . but he'd never seen the need for it until now.

"Closing in left," he said tightly. "Right side's holding back, must be waiting."

The trees pushed in, suffocatingly close. Moses couldn't see much past them, even with the night vision goggles; the dark was too choking, the bushes thick and tangled . . . he debated dropping the dead wolf. Maybe that's what this was about. The wolves didn't care for them taking their pack mate, dead as he might be . . . but this was his job, and more than that, Moses could only hope that by bringing Diego back to Dr. Marsh, she might find something that troubled her. Something that would force her to reconsider the entire project. Perhaps she'd have no choice but to shutter Spindrift and abandon it, leaving it to rot into the earth—

Moses retightened his grip on the fetch pole and pulled for all he was worth . . .

. . . he waited for the dead wolf to suddenly gather its feet and spring at him—dead, but somehow *not* dead, animated by the unclean touch of the *Wiijigo* . . .

The fence. He could see it now, the links glowing in a greenish diamond pattern through the night-vision specs.

To his left, John fired. The report snapped between the pine trunks, deafeningly loud. Moses had a brief view of bark blowing off the side of a tree thirty yards off.

"You see one?"

"Might've." John's voice was barely audible. "Just a warning."

Moses's mouth was dry as birch dust. Fifty yards. The gate in sight. Almost there.

"Take the lead and get to the gate," he ordered John. "You're clear if you go now."

Obediently, John flanked ahead. Moses watched him approach the fence, his body a hollow green outline against those diamond links—he waited for something to pounce . . .

John unlocked the gate and swung it wide. He turned back to Moses—

"No, go!" cried Moses. "Keep going! Hit the power box! I'm coming!"

John made a dash for the box. It was on the other side of the Rover, maybe fifty feet from John's present location. Moses took one last glance at his phone—those dots were so close, so fucking close, but not springing—

—were they waiting, and for *what*?

Moses wouldn't remember dragging the wolf over those final fifty yards. Half a football field, yet it felt endless. The corpse burred over the stony ground, bumping along as Moses scanned the high brush, the night flowers shining like coins in a wishing well as the air whistled between his teeth—

Moses froze. His muscles and limbs, the blood gone syrupy in his veins. Unreality washed over him, this feeling that his whole life until that moment had been dreamy camouflage laid over something so much crazier and impossible to reason with—

That wasn't a wolf.

Whatever that was lurking stealthily behind those flowering blooms wasn't analogous to anything in nature . . . except it was, wasn't it?

Moses's fear lay most strongly there. How a thing could be both a *yes* and a *no*, an *is* and an *isn't* . . .

It hunched in the first cut of woods, its wholeness obscured purposefully or even coyly, the tease of a burlesque dancer behind a silk curtain. Moses could see—oh, it *wanted* him to see, of that he was certain—that it was the other male, Boots.

Or had once been.

When a summer salmon leaps upstream, the briefest flash of its fin and silver tanning is enough to know it by. A wolf, the same. That feral beauty, even at a glance. But now it came with a sense of being watched right back by an intelligence not wholly animal or human.

Moses felt abandoned under the eye of the Almighty. Both the Christian God and the pantheon his people honored. Nothing watched over him now.

"Moses, get *out* of there!"

With a final heave, he dragged himself and the dead wolf past the gate. It swung shut behind him. Power flooded the links with a blue sparking as John hit the lever.

Inside the enclosure, the females slunk from cover. John joined Moses at the fence. The four of them stared at one another, two humans and two lupines. The fence between them felt thinner now, though, no better than cheesecloth.

No sign of Boots. But Moses could sense the rogue male someplace near, watching him.

After a considerable pause, the females loped off into the trees. A howl kicked up, bass-y and somehow chuckling.

"You saw him? Boots?"

Moses swallowed. "I saw something. Sure as hell I did."

"You okay?"

He tried to swallow again. Only a dry click in his throat. "I don't think this fence is near high enough."

After loading Diego's body into the Rover and with a few backward glances toward the fence, they headed off in the direction of the lab.

WHEN THE men returned, Ingrid Chevalier knew right away that something bad must have happened out there. The two of them were good at disguising it, mostly. But Ingrid could see—frankly, a blind man could have seen—the shock that still hounded their eyes.

"Your subject is on the loose," Moses announced.

Ingrid knew the men's names. Moses Squires and John Salters. But that was about all she knew about them as of this minute.

Technically speaking, she'd been awake for a week. But she'd barely been conscious for a lot of that time. She'd tried to stay up, but nothing could stop her eyelids from growing heavy. Her sleep was deep and dreamless. Fine, so long as the witch didn't show up. Her appetite came back with a vengeance. She was eating six, seven times a day.

The thing inside her. It *needed* her to eat. Ingrid knew enough about it to realize that.

She knew a whole lot about the Hydra (as Ast had called it, and to the inventor went naming rights), seeing as the project was as much Ingrid's brainchild as Astrid's.

It may have been *solely* Ingrid's idea at one bygone point. Had she come up with it on her own—had Astrid only piggybacked? Astrid was not an idea person. She was better at taking one that already existed and improving it . . . or was that being unfair? Ingrid couldn't remember. Not confidently, anyway. Maybe those memories would sharpen over time.

The fact was that their invention—which had been more of a mad concept when Ingrid had last been conscious—was inside Ingrid now. In a few short days it had rewired the neuronic pathways of her brain as if that were child's play, cleared the blockage that had vexed the half dozen neurologists who'd evidently tried and failed to rouse her from her comatose state, and brought Ingrid screaming back to consciousness . . . at least that was how Astrid's version of the story went. Seeing as there was nobody around to confirm the finer details (Dr. Strauss was obviously frightened by Astrid's volatility, and John and Moses appeared to have been brought on at a much later stage in the project), and since Ingrid was still too reliant on Astrid to ask the harder questions that had started to circle in her mind, she'd decided to accept her friend's side of the story.

And Ingrid *had* come back screaming, hadn't she? Once she understood what Astrid had done to her—made her body into a petri dish, perhaps even a plaything of the life-form she now shared it with . . . well, wouldn't anyone react that way?

Once the men had returned from the wolf enclosure with their eyes hooded in secrecy, the more capable of the two (no shade on John Salters, but Ingrid could see this Moses guy was in his own class) tossed a bloodied tab onto the operating table.

"That's Boots's tracking chip," Moses said.

"So," Strauss said, "you're saying there's no way to know where Boots is now?"

"There's a little more to it than that, which we'll get to shortly. Bottom line: we'd need to trap that wolf and put a new one in," Moses told her. "But since he's figured out how to get his chip out—and isn't worried about mutilating himself to do so—it seems like wasted effort."

Ingrid said: "He's just running around on the island?"

Moses cocked his head at her, then extended his hand. "I ought to have done this a lot earlier. My apologies. My name's Moses Squires, Missus Chevalier. This is my partner, John Salters. Pleasure to officially make your acquaintance."

She felt a blush creeping up her neck at his directness. He was *old*, like forty, but handsome in his grizzled fashion. He shook her hand gently, as if cradling a hummingbird. She did the same with John Salters.

This was her first time meeting either man formally. Astrid had kept her sequestered in the room next to her own until cabin fever forced Ingrid to ask—beg, more like—her friend to let her explore. For the past few days, Astrid had wheeled Ingrid around Spindrift in the chair. She'd caught sight of Moses and John, spoken briefly to Dr. Strauss, and heard voices within the laboratory she suspected must belong to the other subjects . . . but Astrid had not wanted to share Ingrid with anyone. Now, well, she had no choice.

"To answer your question, Ingrid, yes, Boots is untrackable," Moses confirmed. "He's in the pen at the moment, but I'm not sure he'll stay there if he doesn't want to."

"That enclosure was built to contain wild mature wolves," said Astrid.

"It *was*," Moses answered her. "But I got a look at Boots. Just me, as John was otherwise occupied. That wasn't like any wolf I ever saw."

Astrid crossed her arms. "Mr. Squires, have you been drinking?"

"A little," he told her in that same even tone. "A few beers round dinnertime. If you think that's got me seeing pixies, well, go on thinking so if you like, little lady."

Astrid went tense but said nothing. Strauss said: "What about the other three?"

"Diego's dead," John said. "We hauled him out, if you want to take a look."

"Yes, I'd say that's kind of important," said Astrid.

FIVE MINUTES later, the hired men had lugged the wolf inside and laid it on the exam table. Stretched out with its legs hardened by rigor mortis, its paws hanging off the edges of the table.

"It doesn't look as if he's been harmed, though, does it?" Strauss said. "Nothing's been picking at the body."

"Diego must've died of natural causes," said Astrid. "We can get another male and put it in the enclosure."

"You could, but wolves are clannish," said John. "The other three are likely to shun any newcomer."

Astrid stuffed her hands into her pockets, shoulders rounding the way they did when she'd sunk into a mood. "Who says we even *need* another."

Moses put his hands on the wolf, inspecting it in the gentle way an obstetrician might do with an expectant mother. "Can we look inside it with this machine of yours?"

"Why?" asked Astrid.

"It feels light," he said, brow beetling. "Light *inside*."

"Do it, Astrid," Ingrid requested. To Moses: "What do you mean, light?"

"Like there's not enough of the stuff inside of it there ought to be."

"Could it be bugs?" Strauss wondered. "You know, maggots?"

"Could very well be bugs, yeah," Moses said. "But I don't know—I don't feel anything squirming. Also, I don't think enough time's passed for the creepy-crawlies to move in." The crease in his brow deepened. "Like I said, there just ain't enough *there*. Can't say it any clearer, because it doesn't make a whole lot of sense."

"Oh, well then, I guess we'd better hop to it." Astrid's tone dripped mockery.

When Astrid made no move to meet Moses's request, Ingrid wheeled herself over to the exam table. Her joints ground in her sockets like old machinery as she got the chair rolling.

"How do you switch this thing on?" she asked Astrid. "Hey—come on, you gonna make me figure it out? I will, it'll just take a bit longer."

Astrid relented. "*Fine.*"

She toggled through the settings and pressed a few buttons on the table's interface. The board illuminated under the wolf.

"What do you need?" she asked Moses. "Blood or nerve or what?"

"Start with the simple anatomy. Organs, bones, that stuff."

Within moments, the insides of the wolf were up on the vertical screen, each bone shining whitely and its organs outlined in fuzzy greens.

"Lungs, kidney," Moses itemized, pointing to each, "liver, pancreas, gonads, guts, wait . . . is it me, John, or is it missing its heart?"

John's eyes tracked, the color draining from his cheeks. "Shit. I do think you're right."

Ingrid had a passing enough understanding of anatomy to make the same deduction. The biggest muscle in the wolf's body. It was gone. Diego's entire heart had vanished.

"Hold on—how is that possible? Has it been cut open and pulled out?" Strauss asked. "I've heard killer whales eat shark livers—*just* the livers, right?"

"Nah. There's no opening," Moses said. "No cut or wound where it could've been pulled through. No blood, even. This animal is whole and intact."

"Its bones, too," John said, squinting. "Jeez, some of them look skinny as toothpicks."

The wolf's rib bones, and the one running down its left hind leg. They did look thinner, like lollipops that had been half sucked and then abandoned. Ingrid was swarmed by the stupid, insupportable sense that Diego had been . . . harvested.

Gripping the wolf's muzzle, Moses pulled the top and bottom halves of its mouth—its jaw prized open with the shriek of hardened tendon.

The poor creature had no teeth. Every single one was gone—only little stubbed holes in its gums where they used to sit. When Moses let go, its jaw sagged cartoonishly, like a sock after someone had yanked their foot out of it.

Moses's left hand crept up to Diego's eyes. H rolled one eyelid down with his thumb.

Astrid reared back, a muffled squeak escaping her.

"Could parasites have done that?" said John in a strangled voice. "After the host dies, they do go for the soft parts. The stuff that's easiest to digest, the most, most . . ." He trailed off, losing faith in his argument.

"That isn't parasites," Moses said in a dead tone. "Wish it was."

The wolf's eyes . . . the worst part was that they weren't *all* gone. It was like looking into a container of half-eaten vanilla pudding. To Ingrid, it would have been better if the whole eyeball had been plucked out and the socket picked clean.

The impression came again. That something had deliberately sorted through this animal, sampling the tastiest morsels, a plump boy who'd eaten a full meal but was peckish still, peckish and picking away . . .

"Cataracts."

Everyone looked to Moses.

"That other male," he said. "This one's brother. Boots. When he came here, he had cataracts."

"I'd have to double-check," said Strauss, "but I think you're right."

"You can if you'd like. But I'm right."

Moses's logic was so simple that a child could follow along. Boots had stolen his brother Diego's eyes. Somehow, the wolf with the Hydra in it had . . . what? *Fixed* itself using the other one? Something a bit like a mechanic salvaging parts from an old beater to fix a custom roadster.

But animals didn't—*couldn't*—do that. No creature under the sun had that ability.

Except vampires, Ingrid thought with a shudder.

Then again, that wasn't exactly how vampires did their nasty business. But they did drink the blood of their victims to stay eternally young, didn't they?

The Hydra wasn't a vampire. Ingrid knew enough about its genetic background to say so. It had been built out of simple organisms representing the lowest levels of life on planet Earth. It had none of the standard vampiric traits she knew from books or movies. It wasn't cunning or charming or evil.

But it did have an indomitable will to survive. Thrive. Spread. Its base elements—jellyfish, coral, fungi—were highly adaptable and possessed an astonishing capability to endure through unimaginable strain.

A quote from the physicist Richard Feynman—a man who helped J. Robert Oppenheimer build the Gadget—popped into Ingrid's head.

Science describes Nature as absurd from the point of view of common sense. And it fully agrees with the experiment. So, I hope we can accept Nature as She is: absurd.

"You said you saw Boots," Ingrid said to Moses. "Did you get a good look at him?"

"A flash of him through the night vision goggles, yeah."

"You said it wasn't like any wolf you ever saw. So how did he look to you?"

Moses's eyes seemed to dim back into his head, as if they were trying to find a way to unsee whatever they'd taken in.

"Boots had a lot of teeth" was all he said.

"And? That's your typical wolf," Astrid replied. "Grandma, what big teeth you have."

"Not this one here," Strauss reminded everyone. "Not anymore."

"Is that all with Boots? Just teeth?" Ingrid pressed.

"Way more than it ought to have," Moses told her. "Hard to say, just being a passing glimpse . . . what I saw was *mostly* teeth, all crowded into its mouth and pushing its jaw apart."

"You're sure?"

He shook his head. "Nah, not sure. Like I said, a glimpse. We were fixed on getting out of that pen because the two females . . . I had a feeling they were onto us."

"What do you mean, onto you?" said Astrid.

"Hunting us." Moses looked right at her, unembarrassed. "Pinching in from either side as we dragged their pack mate out."

"That's ridiculous."

"I'm not claiming it's not. Just what I saw, little lady."

Astrid pointed at him. "Moses—*that'll* be the last time you call me that if you want to keep your job."

"So how about *you* treat us with just a touch more respect, Dr. Marsh?" said John, stepping up behind Moses.

"Oh, did I hurt your feelings?" Astrid sneered. "Aren't you grown men?"

"Why don't we look at the situation that stands before us," John said to her. "You've got a wolf, currently MIA, with a bit of experimental technology in it. Unpatented and unlicensed technology, to boot. Am I right so far?"

Astrid just stared at him, arms rigid at her sides.

"That fence is twenty feet tall, electrified, running right around the pen. *Should* work to contain wolves. Y'know," John said archly, "your garden-variety ones. So until Moses and I can track the rogue, trap it, and put it in a cage, you'd better alert everyone on this island."

"We have to tell our financial backers—" Strauss started.

"*No!*" Astrid's hands balled into fists. "We're not telling anyone *anything*. The fence is fine, it'll hold." She blew her breath out in a rush. "We can tell the subjects, okay? If the idea worries them, well sorry, that's life. But nobody else." Pointedly, to Strauss: "*Not one soul.*"

Ingrid said: "Can wolves swim?"

Astrid's eyes darted in her direction. "Ing, could you just *not* right now?"

Her best friend looked like a girl right then. Which is what they both were, truly. Two teenage girls, one of whom was in charge of the greatest experiment since Oppenheimer met Feynman in the desert of Los Alamos.

"Yeah, they can swim up to eight miles at a time," Moses told Ingrid, but really all of them. "They got webs between their paws, makes them real good swimmers."

"The mainland's over twenty miles away," Astrid noted.

"Yeah, but plenty of island chains to the south." Moses shrugged. "Some closer than eight miles."

"Could you wrap Diego up and put it in the walk-in fridge?" Strauss asked the men. "We may need to do more tests. A full autopsy."

WITH THE tense discussion done, Moses and John lifted the wolf off the table and moved out of the laboratory pod. The blueprint of Diego's innards and that emptiness where his heart used to be lingered on the screen before fading.

Once they were gone, Astrid said: "Couple of bed-wetting babies, spooked at nothing."

Strauss made a face, but Astrid didn't see it. For Ingrid, this was the Astrid she'd always known. Her skyscraping intellect had made her arrogant even at thirteen, given to bouts of hysteria and unbridled rage. Ingrid had been the yin to Astrid's yang. Their minders at the Institute—older scientists in their late twenties, thirties, forties—had been thankful for Ingrid, the only one who could keep Astrid in line . . . most times, anyway.

The Paperclip Maximizer.

This came to Ingrid the way the vampires had: out of the blue, nastily, and with teeth.

A thought experiment Ingrid had come across by a tech philosopher named Nick Bostrom. It was about machine ethics. The scenario hypothesized that an AI-operated machine could be programmed to achieve goals that seem helpful and harmless, except when subjected to a machine's reasoning. So, take a machine programmed to make paperclips. What if this machine wasn't programmed to value life—human, animal, or otherwise—the environment, or anything *but* making paperclips? If that machine was powered by a sophisticated but unreasoning AI, its goal might be to turn *all matter* on earth, in fact the whole universe, either into paperclips or devices that make paperclips. In this experiment, humans became disposable; when we realized what was happening, we'd try to turn that machine off. But in that case, the AI would rather we were dead. Our bodies also contain elements useful in the making of paperclips, so the AI might see our value solely in terms of how many paperclips *we* could be turned into.

The thought experiment ended in a vision Ingrid found far more horrifying than any movie monster. Our whole world covered in paperclips. Drifts of them rising eight or ten feet deep. The oceans choked and the deserts carpeted. Factories dotting the horizon whose only goal was to make paperclips, more and more paperclips . . . while rockets launched into the stratosphere bearing machine cargo, seeking distant worlds to harvest the resources to make paperclips, endlessly.

The mindless appetite of such a hypothetical machine had always frightened Ingrid. A machine that had no inkling of logic or beauty, that had been programmed to see all matter, living or dead, through the lens of a single blindered objective.

Making paperclips for this hypothetical AI.

... *or* in the case of the Hydra, its sole objective was to reverse the age and prolong the life of the organism it had been placed inside.

What would the Hydra now inside of *her* do in order to make sure Ingrid kept breathing? What or *who* would it harvest to meet its needs?

Could she stop it?

Given the passage of sufficient time, would she even want to?

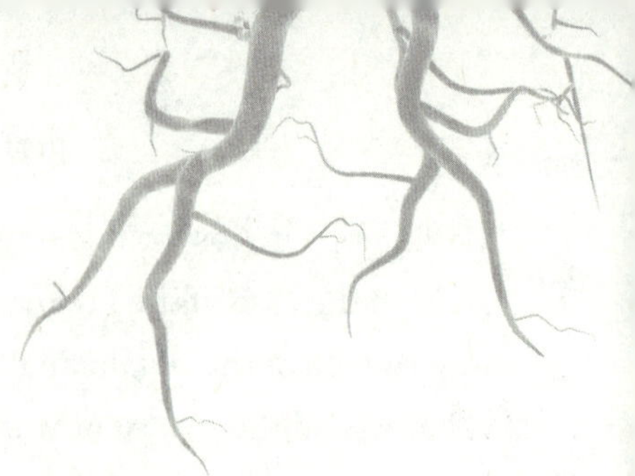

IX. *Anno Hydra*, Day 17

MADDY'S EYES were bluer now.

With age, human eyes lost their luster so gradually that their owner might miss it. Maddy's blue had faded from the piercing hue of her thirties and forties. Her eyeballs had become a pair of Christmas tree ornaments collecting dust in her sockets.

But now they shone as from years before. A penetrating, chilly blue she'd used as a secret boardroom weapon: part strong-arm tactic, part seduction.

Presently, she was lounging with the other subjects after their daily Bath. The residue of her immersion dried under her robe, tacky under her breasts and the cleft between her legs. She wasn't sure why the Bath activated her in the way it did. Why the experience always turned her on, quite frankly. It must have something to do with the new life flooding into her, lighting her up like a pinball machine.

Maddy wasn't the only one to react that way. She'd seen (it was pretty hard to avoid the sight, not that she'd tried) that the men all sported unself-conscious erections while suspended in their Bath units. Teddy's curved upward like a flesh-toned banana; Hugo's was a thick and almost square-looking plug; Frank's forthright endowment struck Maddy as a baby bear's bowl of porridge . . . *just right.*

These notions were an amusement to her. Maddy hadn't thought about sex—at least in an eager and participatory way—in donkey's years. *What's the point anymore?* she'd thought at some time in her mid-seventies, and that thought had never been uprooted.

But now? Things were on the upswing, *ahem,* in that area.

AFTER THEIR Baths, the next step was for all subjects to take turns getting swabbed. Madeline's heart began to thump in anticipation as Dr. Strauss placed a dab of her saliva on a slide and inserted it into the epigenetic clock.

One by one, their genetic ages flashed on the laptop screen.

```
Teddy: 77, down from 79.
Claire: 77, down from 79.
Hugo: 75, down from 76.
Madeline: 79, down from 84.
```

As the results appeared, each of them reacted differently. For Teddy, a fist pump and a whispered "*Yes.*" Claire let out a yelp, hands fisted over her lips. Hugo took it stoically while a disappointed flush reddened his neck. Maddy tried not to show much emotion at all—a maxim from her hedge fund days: *Never let them see you smile and never let them see you sweat.*

Frank came last.

His age appeared on the screen. 77, same as his birth age.

Teddy slung his arm around Frank's shoulders. "Sorry, buddy. It'll come."

Frank seemed to take the news well. "I do feel better."

Supportively, Strauss said: "It may be that your clock is at five minutes to the hour, Frank. The hands are ready to move backwards at any minute."

"Or the treatment doesn't work for every subject," said Astrid, standing off to one side. "No promises. That was never the deal."

"I've said it before," Maddy remarked, "but your bedside manner is for shit, Astrid."

The girl genius peered at Maddy with hooded eyes. "I'm not that kind of doctor, am I?"

Frank shrugged fatalistically. "If it happens, it happens."

But Maddy could see—it was as plain as the nose on his personable face—that Frank couldn't possibly mean that. He was like the child who'd been left behind a grade, putting on a good face for the students moving on with their cohort.

ONCE SHE returned to her room, Maddy slipped out of her robe into something cooler. Her self-inflicted wounds were healing; the largest punctures, the ones above her hip bones, were covered by small square bandages. Underneath them, her skin itched furiously as it knit together.

She was five years younger according to that clock. She'd dropped a half decade in . . . how long had they been here? A few weeks, though she was no longer sure. Time felt nonessential, which was odd to say for someone who'd been a slave to the ticking hands of the clock for much of her life. But she couldn't remember the last time she'd looked at her watch, let alone a calendar.

When she exited her room, she found the others in the common area. Someone had put on the kettle for tea, the air faintly scented with Earl Grey. Welcome to the geriatric Breakfast Club.

The days held a lazy pace on the island. There was no tour guide waving a triangular red flag, no activities coordinator summoning them to bingo or canasta, no nurses coming around with pills in Dixie cups. They could do as they liked, so long as they stayed put. They read a lot of books. Frank was partial to Stephen King; Teddy to Crichton and Cussler; Claire, surprisingly, was a big Leon Uris fan.

When they gathered as a group, they tended to chat about things in a general way. There was one unstated rule: no talk about life after the island. There were two reasons for this: one, everyone knew it would piss Astrid off (and who could say if she wasn't eavesdropping on them; Teddy had once tendered the idea that their rooms could be bugged), and two—and in this, Maddy could speak only for herself—they didn't yet hold a picture of themselves as they might exist *after* the island. They were like developing Polaroid photos; it was impossible to say how they'd turn out quite yet.

Almost against her will, Maddy found herself getting close to the other four subjects. Even Teddy, the scoundrel, who she had to admit was a hoot. It reminded her of the summer camp she'd gone to as a girl. Picturesque Camp Cadicasu, in the foothills of the Rockies. At camp, your cabin was your crew.

The camp enforced this through group activities and objectives. All for one and one for all. It was a bit like that on the island, seventy-odd years later. A bunker mentality. You formed a bond based on a shared experience, even with the people she didn't care for that much.

Susie Flemming, Maddy thought, the memory jumping out at her. *I caught her eating a kneecap scab behind the boathouse like it was a cornflake.*

In her final dream before coming to the island, Maddy had lain inside her own coffin.

It was the same one she'd chosen for herself in real life, selecting it from the models in the showroom of the Bluebird Funeral Home on Coffee Street. The Canadian Eternal, with nonoxidizing brass fittings. She'd already made all the arrangements, not wanting to inflict the chore on anyone . . . though in truth, who else *would* have undertaken that task? Her children would've been the likely candidates, but she had none. No husband, either. Maybe someone at her old firm would've resignedly stepped up to the plate, but—as in every other aspect of her life—Maddy figured she might as well do it herself.

She'd paid for the casket and a funeral plan. A gathering in Foyer B, finger food, coffee, tea, soft drinks. A plot under the elms at Mount Pleasant. Nobody would be put out in the slightest when Maddy tottered off her mortal coil. To the contrary, people would remark: *Madeline took care of every detail, right down to the rubber undergarments. Good ole i-dotting, t-crossing Maddy Dodds.*

There she lay, in this dream of hers. Inside her Canadian Eternal, its innards lined with plumped-up satin. Dead as a doornail, but alert in a way that resisted sane understanding. Her eyes itched. It was the wadding, she realized. The cotton pads the mortician had thumbed over her eyes before drawing her eyelids closed. Her eyes had sunk into her skull, as eyeballs did once a person died; maddeningly, she could feel them pooling at the bottom of her sockets like cracked eggs.

As she lay there, unable to move, she could hear noise above her.

A shovel? The scratch of fingernails? Something, anyway. It was digging its way down. And Maddy didn't want it to find her. In this particular dream, she dreaded it. Whatever was coming, it terrified her. Even dead with her eyes puddled inside her head, Maddy understood this thing could hurt her in ways she couldn't quite imagine. She'd been hiding from it under six feet of gray caliche and green grass, but it had found her now. Its nails scraping at the lid of her casket, hunting for the latch—

DRESSED IN her overalls, Maddy found Frank sitting by the bay window overlooking the woods on the lee side of the island.

"Want to go for a walk, you old layabout?"

He gazed from the pleasing vista to her. "Promise to go slow so I can keep up?"

"Oh, you'll manage. And don't even think about bringing your walking partner with you." She meant his oxygen machine. "Meet me at the entrance doors, and bring a towel."

"Why?"

"You ask too many questions."

The morning was warming. The alkaline smell of the water curtained the island, sending a tingle up Maddy's sinuses. She made her way to a little-used staircase that circumnavigated the southern end of Spindrift; the synovial fluid (the stuff between her balky old joints, the term introduced to her by Strauss) was flowing nicely today, because her knees didn't go off like little Black Cat firecrackers when she took the first step. For the last decade she'd been plagued with arthritis in her hips and knees—even when she over-mastered the damn tick's effects and hauled herself out of bed, her joints would scream bloody blue murder when she planted her feet on the bedroom floor. But now there was barely a whisper of that pain, which was not only tolerable but somehow wistful as her many ailments were forced to loosen their grip on her.

Frank met her with a towel wrapped round his shoulders. He shivered. "My thin blood isn't made for early-morning rambles."

"Oh, quit your bellyaching. Keep it up and someone'll haul you off to the glue factory."

My thin blood. Frank's words. Thing was, Maddy's blood didn't feel thin anymore. It felt *thick*, wonderfully heavy in her veins. The platelets plump, the white blood cells racing around like tiny hard-hatted workmen fixing her cell walls, her brain synapses, the long white rails of her bones.

They walked down a path leading around Spindrift, in the opposite direction of the dock. Before today, she'd taken the same walk with Claire a few times. After covering the small range of topics they held in common—the weather; how strange that their lives should be in the thrall of someone like Astrid Marsh; the unidentified girl in the wheelchair they'd seen in passing once or twice now in the laboratory—their walks became largely silent. It wasn't uncomfortable, but it did express the fact that two people could have an affinity for one another without having much of a real connection.

Frank, though . . . yes, Maddy had to admit she liked Frank.

Funnily, she wasn't quite sure *why*. It wasn't wild lust or obsession; she'd felt those things earlier in life and hoped to again—but Frank didn't conjure lust in her . . . if anyone, Maddy had to admit that leathery rascal, Teddy Bassiano, kindled a touch of heat in her. But she wouldn't let herself go down *that* road.

So what was it about Frank? Maybe it was that she'd met—or refused to put herself in the company of—too few genuinely kind souls in her life. Goodness was a hindrance in her line of work; people sporting such traits were targeted and torn to pieces. But from what she could tell, Frank had gone his whole life retaining an innate kindness, and that was appealing to her.

And the idea that this treatment might not work for Frank—that he'd be stuck here getting older while the rest of them got increasingly younger—made Maddy ineffably sad.

But maybe she could help. Maddy had been paying attention. It was one of her own traits: seeing what others missed, which to her lay in plain sight.

To Maddy, one fact was dead certain: *her* Hydra was working.

It wasn't just the renewed elasticity of her skin or that she could now walk several miles without tiring. She could *feel* the Hydra in her, strangling all evidence of the goddamn tick. The tiny fix-it men in her body were vacuuming up every shred of Lyme with relentless little Hoover Suck-o-Matics, leaving her bloodstream pristine.

. . . and sure, *okay*, there were the nightmares. But they were just the cost of doing business, weren't they?

What about the nail file? came the insidious whisper—muffled, as if it were trapped in a locked box inside Maddy's brain. *What about the twenty-odd puncture wounds from when you did a bit of DIY aerating? What about that, Maddy Dodds?*

Compartmentalization. One couldn't overestimate the value of that skill. Beyond the odd night terror, Maddy slept like a baby. She chalked the nightmares up to the Hydra's influence on her brain waves as it worked its deep magic. A small price to pay for the service it rendered.

So there was that, and the fact she wasn't on top of her emotions anymore. For someone who'd made a living by keeping those in check, it was strange for Maddy to find herself on the verge of tears, or whipped into a rage, or touching herself while thinking of erect cocks floating in a greenish suspension . . . well, there was a reason for *that*.

Another side effect. But surely every therapy had those.

SHE AND Frank passed a patch of earth where the grass rose thigh-high to the west. The breeze fanned the dew-wet tips of that grass, creating an optical trick that turned the plain into a lake, the grass appearing as water, wavelets washing up on a rocky beachhead. Past that illusory lake was the curve of the road they'd taken the very first evening in the Rovers. The one that led to the wolves' enclosure.

"I wonder what that wolf died of," Frank said. Maddy followed the train of his thought: the road, the enclosure, the wolves, and the news—delivered the other day by Moses Squires, surely with Astrid's approval—that one of the wolves, Diego, had passed away.

"Well, it wasn't the one with the Hydra in it," Maddy reasoned. "Diego was the other one. It probably died for the reason all old things do. Age."

"Probably." Frank seemed unconvinced.

Don't be a party pooper, Frank. Don't make me regret inviting you along.

"I ran into Moses and John yesterday," she said. "They were packing up the Rover with motion-sensor cameras. They were on their way to the enclosure with them." She gave Frank a playful punch on the shoulder. "Cheer up, Gloomy Gus. It was an old wolf. The other one's fine. I bet it's *better* than fine, in fact."

She and Frank walked a downslope side by side. He was laboring now, sweating buckets, a real hooker in church—good God, had she just used a Teddy-ism? That man was a bad influence. She could tell Frank was trying hard not to show how much he was struggling.

"This way," she said, beckoning him into the trees. "There's a path, but it's faint."

He followed her into the shadowy dampness. She'd found this path quite by accident

—was anything that happened on this island truly accidental?—

and she hadn't showed it to anyone. Maddy had used it the last five days on her own, but now she figured it was selfish to keep it all to herself.

"Not much farther. A hundred yards."

"What sort of . . ." Frank rasped, his breath gone raggedy, "boondoggle are you . . . dragging me . . . into?"

"It's for your own good, you baby."

The path led onto a sandy wash. A crescent moon of shoreline rung by the rocks. The water sparkled off the crests of the stiff, lapping waves fifty yards off the beachfront.

"Hey, this is nice," Frank said. "Your little"—huff, puff—"secret?"

Maddy heeled off her sneakers and socks. Padding down to the waterline, she dipped her toes into the water. "It's cold as a witch's tit. But that's the point. That's why we're getting in."

"Say again?"

"Go on, strip. You can leave your skivvies on if it makes you sensitive, but it's not like we haven't all seen one another's bits and pieces in the Baths."

Maddy unbuttoned her overalls. Unhooked her bra and pinched her shoulders in to let the straps fall to her elbows. Frank dropped his head.

"C'mon, Maddy . . ."

"Ohhh, come on yourself. Not anything you haven't seen before. Or am I your first?"

Here was another way this all reminded her of summer camp. The illicit stares at bodies glistening in the lake, and those lingering looks *across* the lake to the boys' camp. How you might let the strap of your bathing suit drop accidentally-on-purpose, or let the suction of the lake's surface pull your bottoms down an inch or two . . . the bold, somehow dizzying freedom of discovering your own body and the bodies of others for the first time.

And Maddy liked being looked at. *Admired.* She wanted Frank to *want* to look, too.

She slung her overalls down her hips. Her panties came next; no use getting them wet, was there? The evidence of her self-inflicted wounds was boldly displayed: the haphazard ladder of punctures (healing, she still marveled, with supernatural swiftness under the thick, crusty scabs of a healthy immune system) up her left side; the daisy chain of matching scabs running up under her armpit and down her right arm. They no longer embarrassed her, no more than a cast would: they were simply evidence of something broken that was now fixed.

Nor did her naked body provoke a hint of shame. It never *had*, really. But now, under Frank's gaze (and she suspected he was looking), she knew that the sag of her buttocks or the nets of wrinkles girding her hips were fleeting— her skin was regaining its elasticity, and by next week or the week after, Maddy figured that those wrinkles and liver spots and cherry angiomas would vanish one by one as the Hydra swept them off her skin like a wet rag to a coffee spill . . . the fact that she believed this with the ironclad surety of a cult initiate probably should have worried her, but it didn't.

Turning to the water, she began to wade in. The chill hit her like a sledgehammer, a near-paralyzing coldness that shot right up to her teeth.

"Oh *Jesus*, that is icy."

Frank stood rooted on the shore as she forced herself deeper into the surf. The bottom was sandy, studded with toe-stub pebbles. The water enveloped Maddy to her hips; the cold crawled past her ribs. Pushing off the bottom, she dove. The iciness was so stunning that her brain fritzed out for a moment.

She surfaced and straightened, fully immersed with her toes twiddling the bottom.

"Listen, Fuh-Frank," she said, teeth chattering. "The Huh-Hydra, right? The juh-juh-jellyfuh-fish." She bore down, willing herself not to shiver. "Remember Astrid ripping it to pieces? How it had the ability to r-r-ruh-remake itself? But it had to suh-suh-suh—"

"Suffer," Frank said.

Her smile was a chilled rictus. "*Right*. It had to rebuild it-it-itself out of its puh-pain. So I asked myself, wuh-why is *my* Hydra working so good for muh-me?"

She waded closer to shore, her shoulders and breasts clearing the surface. She felt young in spirit, if not yet in form—seventeen again, her breasts a source of great interest to the boys in her neighborhood, the teeth in her mouth real and not dentures cemented in with Poligrip, her heart under her school uniform a spirited little pony motor chugging away. She took another step, her chest pebbling with gooseflesh until the water stood at her hips.

"It's wuh-wuh-working for me, Frank," she said, "because I huh-hurt myself."

She touched her scabs, pebbled as pig iron. Frank was looking at her boldly now. Was the little hamster wheel in his head turning? Was he figuring out the trigger, the same way she had?

"What I d-d-did . . . when I stabbed myself . . . it *activated* the Huh-Hydra. That's why I'm ahead of eh-eh-everyone else. Not because I'm the huh-*huh*-oldest. Because I'm the most duh-*damaged*, Frank. I kick-stuh-stuh-started it. Gave it something big to duh-do."

She had his full attention now. It wasn't her nakedness, though she suspected—a bit vainly—that was at least part of it. Without speaking, he began to take his shoes off.

"Thattaboy, Fuh-Frank. Get in here. Suffering is guh-good for the suh-soul."

He stripped right down to his underwear before stopping. *Come on, Frank,* she thought archly, a bit inanely. *In for a penny, in for a pecker.* Standing on the shore with his legs crossed, Frank watched her with an intensity she found erotic. But then, so much felt erotic in this eerie place. This sheltered beach, the sand between her toes, the cold invading her chest . . . the shorebirds creasing the sky to the east, the lonely red strobing of that lighthouse marking the way back to the mainland. But most of all, the man there on the beach, gazing hungrily at her. A look that said he might just devour her if he got a chance, bones and all.

Frank tugged his underpants off, stuffed them into a shoe. His body was rail-thin, tendons twisting like gnarled roots up his thighs and chest. He stepped into the water to his ankles.

"Ohhhh, Maddy. It's cold as balls."

Balls, Maddy thought, glancing at Frank's. *They look so silly, don't they, for all the harm they cause? What would it be like to cart those around between your legs all day?*

A cold lake wasn't as effective as what she'd done to herself with the nail file, but if she and Frank did this every day, Maddy was convinced it would help. Under the numbness colonizing the top layers of her skin, she could swear the Hydra was revving even faster, into the red zone. She *wanted* it in the red. Max that damn thing out and feel its furious engine filling her from toe tips to the ends of her hair.

She dove again, forcing herself underwater. When she surfaced, the cold was a living thing in her. "Fuh-fuh-*rank*. Nuh-nothing in life c-c-cuh-comes without stuh-stuh-struggle."

After the briefest hesitation, Frank dove after her. He disappeared under the water—for a heartbeat she thought he'd sink like a sad pale stone—and came up in front of her, eyes wide and hair plastered in wet strings to his scalp.

"My heart, Muh-Maddy," he rasped. "Oh, my uh-uh-old heart."

Toeing herself forward over the sand, her hands reached out to cup Frank's crotch.

Bold move, Maddy, she thought. *You've gone and snatched his soul.*

Bold and weird, too, in that it wasn't something pre-island Maddy would ever consider doing. But she accepted this new behavior because she *had* changed.

"You thuh-think that's helping my huh-h-heart any?"

"I duh-d-don't know, is it?" A vampish grin. "I can buh-buh-barely feel my fingers, and th-th-thuh-they say the h-h-human body collects heat buh-b-between the legs."

"Suh-so you're a huh-heat thief, huh? If I duh-die, m-m-make shuh-sure I don't fuh-*fff*-float away."

"At least you'll duh-d-d-die happy."

I'm cradling a seventy-seven-year-old dick. The cold must be screwing with her brain waves. *Like a hairless baby robin fallen from its nest. Poor Frank'll follow me around like a lost puppy dog for the rest of his days now.*

She floated closer, until her nipples (hard as two bullets) were brushing Frank's chest.

"Yuh-you cuh-can stuh-steal suh-some heat from muh-me, if you wuh-w-want."

Frank's hands may have feathered the spot between her legs, but Maddy couldn't be sure. She was so cold that everything below her hips crackled with dull static. It came to her that she wished she'd done something like this when she'd had the chance—and hell, those chances had been there in her twenties, thirties, forties, and well into her fifties. To meet someone in a palace of mirrors, where everything was possible, it all depended on the refraction of the light.

Maddy brushed past Frank and kicked hard for shore. Frank let out a cry of despair as she vanished under the water.

When she drew herself dripping from the surf, Frank was still floating out there. His face was gray as a gravestone, but he hadn't followed her out.

"Stay as long as you can b-b-bear," she said. "It's good for you."

He lasted nearly five minutes. Longer than she would've bet. When he lugged his bones back to the shore and waded out, she wrapped his towel around his shoulders. She wished she'd brought matches to make a fire, but then one of the others might have seen the smoke and found their secret place. She couldn't have that. This was just for her . . . and Frank now, too.

Eventually they quit shivering and got dressed. They kept their eyes to themselves. The spell that had taken hold in the water not quite so powerful now.

They both then sat on the sand, Maddy's gaze tracking to the horizon. That red light cycled on the southern fringe of the island. A way home, but home was the furthest thing from Maddy's mind right now. *This* was home.

"You know, your eyes have gotten bluer," Frank said.

"Well . . . I tend to intimidate people."

"You don't say."

She gave his knee a slap. "I *had* to intimidate people for a great deal of my life. But the drawback is that I tend to intimidate *everyone*, even people I'd rather not."

She stared directly at him. "I don't intimidate you, do I?"

Frank thought about this. "I think you're very intelligent, and you've lived at an . . . an atmosphere that I can't fully understand. And you're beautiful," he said without preamble or embarrassment, "so yeah, you're a bit intimidating. So what?"

Something warm pushed through her as she broke eye contact with him. "Frank—and I say this with all the kindness in me, whatever iota that may be—you really are a bit of a nerd."

"Am I?" He chuckled. "You're not the first to say so. Ah, so be it."

They sat in silence. The feeling came back to her skin. Little waves lapped the beach.

"Maddy . . . why did you do that to yourself?"

Frank had the good grace to ask this with his eyes averted. There were a few ways she could answer. The deepest truth was, she didn't *know* why she'd tried to stab herself to death. It was almost as though she'd come out of sedation with that nail file in her hands, in medias res, already doing that terribleness to herself. And if there had been some primordial wolves running in the deeper layer of her subconscious, their howls had dimmed by the time she was aware enough to have registered them.

That was one truth. That she simply couldn't remember why.

But another truth (and such things could be multiple, despite what juries were told) was that if Maddy *had* been trying to kill herself . . . it wasn't the first time.

She'd tried once before, when she was seventeen. Over the years, that December afternoon had taken on a smeary, not-quite-real aspect—as happens when a human mind pushes something down deep, to that place where it loses the certainty that it had taken place at all. She couldn't pinpoint a reason for it anymore. Some silly disappointment, the cruelty of a *boy*? Or had an overwhelming blackness welled up inside of her, choking her until ending her life was the only reasonable response?

She'd taken her mother's sedatives while her folks were off at the Playhouse's rendition of *A Christmas Carol*. Snowflakes had battered the bathroom window as she'd taken whatever was in the bottle, maybe half the full prescription. She then ran a bath and knelt on the tiles with her head nodding over the rising steam so that when unconsciousness gripped her, her skull would slip under the water. It all must have felt elegant and clean in her teenage mind. Her parents would find her, and what a holiday mystery she'd make. She'd written no note because even then she was unsure what was gripping her—if anything, a sense that she was not right for the world, or it for her.

At the last moment a survival instinct took over and she'd slung herself off the edge of the tub. With darkness crowding in, she'd jammed her fingers down her throat and thrown up before passing out. She woke later, rising feebly, the partially digested pills lying in a watery puddle on the tiles. She took a shower. Then cleaned up. She was at the kitchen table eating unbuttered toast by the time her parents got home. She never told them. Her mother never asked what happened to her pills.

Over the ensuing decades, as Maddy built her bulletproof reputation, that critical event sat there. Sluglike, tagged to the base of her brain stem. An oddity she couldn't account for: the act of a completely different person, a stranger who'd sunk inside her skin on that December afternoon as a soft snow fell.

Never had she felt the urge to do anything like that again. But that *one time*, she had. That day, Maddy tried to kill herself.

"As I said in our group encounter session," she told Frank, "I can't put my finger on a *why*. Maybe it was my body rebelling at what was inside it— a foreign invader." Maddy shook her head. "But I don't feel that way about it now. Do you?"

"No, I don't think so. It's foreign, but like . . . a helpful foreigner."

"This thing, it's changing our lives. Hopefully it'll change the world. I'm so thankful to be part of it."

"I'm glad it's working for you."

"Oh, it'll work for you, just wait and see." She gripped his wrist. "Frank, listen. When you saw me just now in the water . . . think about unwrapping a present, okay? But each time you do, what's inside gets nicer and, and *fresher*, and younger. Isn't that a good thought?"

"It's a thought," he said, unsure.

"We can come here every day. But . . . let's keep it our secret, okay? You can come on your own, too, whenever you'd like, just—"

"I'd rather come with you."

She let out a trembling breath. "We're silly, aren't we? Two silly people."

They sat side by side, listening to the hush of the offshore waves.

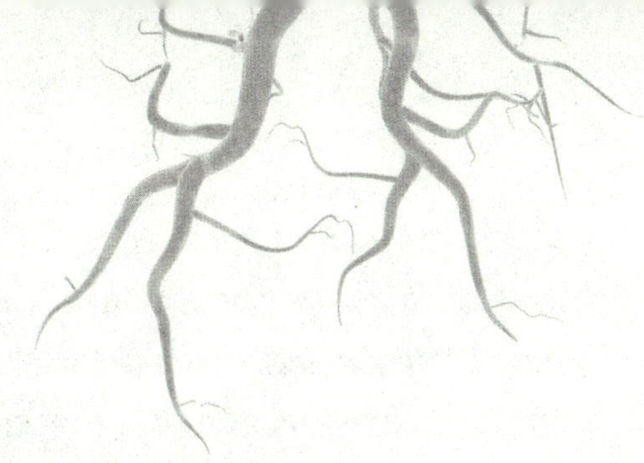

X. Anno Hydra, Day 22

Cheshire Cat:

This is the most astonishing news to pass on. The damn thing <u>works</u>.

Even Astrid is dumbstruck, though she'd never admit it. As headstrong and self-assured as she is, to be the creator of a technology that flies in the face of God? Even for her, that's a lot to take in.

Of course, she's gloating. About how everybody said she'd never do it, all those whispers that she was as crazy as a dog in a cat factory (yes, that's one of her own phrasings), the little princess with fancies of life everlasting . . . as if she didn't have an entire laboratory dedicated to her project, five trusting souls who've willingly put their lives in her hands (plus one who didn't), and an increasingly anxiety-ridden bioethicist at her beck and call.

Does that worry you? The mental state I'm in? Nothing to be done for it now, is there? I can't be replaced unless you've got a cloning machine. Who am I to say you don't? If so, send in the Veronica clone! I'll happily leave this place.

Actually, no. As vexing as all this may be—amazing how an experiment can be more so as a success than as a failure—it's also exhilarating. The air in the lab practically pops and sizzles with the frisson of achievement these days.

I must confess, though, we've had an incident with one of the wolves. I include a detailed report in this envelope, but . . . I'm no veterinarian. I don't DO autopsies. But it was clear when I opened that wolf up that something unaccountable had happened. Its heart was nothing but a stump. No bigger than a pushpin and jarringly smooth, as if it had been sucked down like a hard toffee. The wolf's skin was unbroken, meaning its heart couldn't have been excised from its body. In any case, Moses and John have beefed up security to the wolf enclosure.

On to happier news! They're all getting younger. Every single one of our subjects. The raw data is under Astrid's lock and key, but trust me. Each subject, One through Five, has exhibited a successful reversion of their aging trajectory. The Hydra is working.

The last subject to turn the corner was Frank Doyle, the second youngest after Hugo Udall. Today the epigenetic clock gave his age at 75, meaning he's aged down two years. Finally, may I add, as we were getting a little concerned about what it could mean if the Hydra was having no effect on him.

The others' results are well beyond his pace. It's unclear yet whether their underlying health conditions, Theodore's Parkinson's, Madeline's Lyme, Frank's pulmonary issues, etc., etc., are being addressed by the Hydra. But anecdotally, our microphones pick up a lot less consumptive coughing from the subjects' rooms during the night.

The one unassailable fact is that they're getting younger, and—though returns are still in their infancy—possibly at an accelerating rate. We may need to slow the decline down. If that even proves possible.

Also, it is of note that Ingrid Chevalier is now conscious. This is of interest primarily as it stands as evidence that the Hydra seems capable of addressing a host of human health conditions. While the background of Chevalier's coma was not made transparent to me (do YOU know? If so, why keep it from me?), I do know she'd been sunk in it for three years. The Hydra loosened the Gordian knot in her brain. Her memory seems intact, albeit with same key gaps. She's even walking. Shaky as a newborn foal at present, but still, it must stand as record time to get oneself upright after spending 1,000-plus days in bed. This is the Hydra's doing. It has powers beyond what I could have expected.

I'd like to know more about Ms. Chevalier, up to and including the accident that rendered her comatose. What I do know is, she and Astrid were the best of friends. It's clear that friendship remains strong, if complex. I've been told they met in a cloistered and highly competitive situation at the Institute for Human Advancement, which from what I can tell is an intellectual hostel of sorts. A think tank for ultra-brains. Most of the researchers these girls (as they were then, and remain now) dealt with at the Institute were much older, and male. Ingrid and Astrid would've been well over ten years younger than their closest contemporaries. So, they clung to each other. That much is obvious; they call each other Ing and Ast and speak sometimes in a lingo they've made up, a code just for one another. They spend every moment together. Ingrid is curious about the work Astrid undertook while she was comatose. Although I haven't asked, I suspect she's amazed at how far her friend has brought their research . . . for good and for ill.

Thank you for sending Ingrid's file via John Salters. I see that her IQ is below Astrid's. A top-tier genius, but in their interactions there's evidence of that shortcoming. Astrid makes connections—she's capable of genuine and startling creative originality—while Ingrid appears to have the more meager facility to understand what her friend has done once it's been laid out, and to forecast the implications. Ingrid can see big-picture issues, the view further downstream, better than Astrid. She can see where the stream forks. I'm not sure Astrid likes that. Certainly, she's less willing to look at that fork and contemplate the dangers lurking there.

And then there's Ingrid's "accident," as it's been referred to. The one that left her in a coma. I have questions. You must indulge my curiosity.

But the Hydra <u>works</u>. Know that. And because of that, we must tread carefully.

I will write with more as our situation develops.

—V.S.

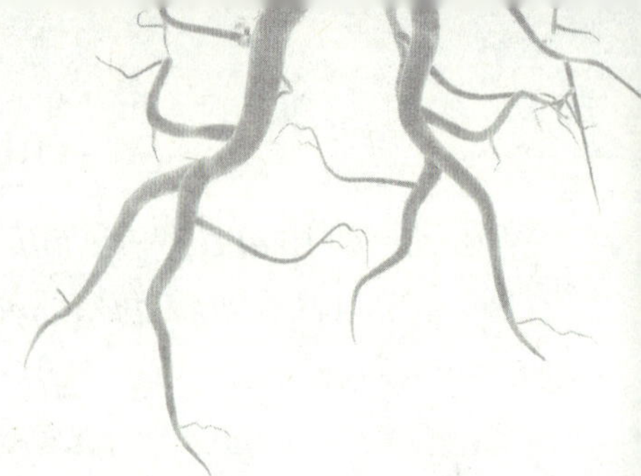

XI. Anno Hydra, Day 23

TEDDY LEANED over the breakfast nook and nudged Frank-O's elbow.

"Congrats, hoss. You're getting with the program."

The big event happened yesterday, after their Baths. *Getting their clocking,* as Teddy called it. Everyone held their collective breath as Frank's spit got graded in the epigenetic clock . . . the laptop whirred and flashed two red-hot numerals.

75

The group raised a *whoop*—a real hoot and a holler. Only Astrid held back, observing them as she might bugs under a turned-over log. Teddy slung an arm around Frank's shoulders.

"You're doing it, y'old bastard!" Another hoot. "Well, not quite so old now!"

Frank, that poor sap, only had eyes for Maddy, who'd gripped his head and planted a kiss on his forehead like she was his great-aunt Murgatroyd.

Okay, that's a bit queer, Teddy had thought as a tingle fled up the back of his neck.

Anytime Teddy got that nagging itch, he took it as the universe trying to tell him something. So he'd decided to do a bit of old-fashioned gumshoeing.

"What's your secret, Frank?" he asked his pal there in the nook.

Frank squinted at his soggy Muffets. He still ate like an old biddy. *Get with the plan, Frank,* Teddy thought sourly. *Steak and eggs, put some iron in that limp rod of yours.*

"No secret, Teddy. The thing's just working now, same as it's been for you."

And hoo boy, had it ever been working for Teddy. He was down to 71 on the clock, and feeling more like an ass-kicking 65. He'd have to beg off the Canada Pension Plan before long!

"That so?" Teddy said breezily. "Man, I thought you'd found a loophole or something."

"No loophole. Just started to kick in."

"Huh, if you say so. I know there's no secrets between us fellas."

Frank didn't reply. The lying ole pussy hound!

Yesterday afternoon, Teddy had put a tail on ole Frank-O. He caught sight of him and Maddy walking a path round the lee side of Spindrift. Trailing them at a discreet distance, Teddy had followed them to a beach edging the water. He then spied on them swimming in the nude together, a couple of wrinkly wood nymphs.

That itch at the back of his neck, right? It never led Teddy astray.

Attaboy, Frank-O, Teddy had thought. *Get yourself a taste of that hair pie. Just watch out for the barbed wire down there.*

Frank's secrecy didn't bother Teddy. The man was entitled to get himself a slice of ass. But not to tell his buddy Teddy *why* he was out in that freezing-cold surf, the wink-wink secret Maddy had let him in on . . . well, *that* wasn't very brotherly.

And damn if Teddy was going to lose any ground to those two stinkers. Life was a game—and Teddy intended to win this round, and every one to follow.

AFTER BREAKFAST, after Soggy-Muffets-Frank and the others had fucked off to their rooms, Teddy moseyed off to find Hugo. He discovered him in the common room, his galumphing body spread out on the couch with his feet over the edge, nose buried in a Mickey Spillane paperback.

"Hugo, my fine fellow, you up for a stroll?"

Hugo dog-eared his page. "Sure, why not?"

They walked outside, stepping onto the same path Teddy had trailed

Maddy and Frank down yesterday afternoon. Now, Teddy wasn't about to suggest he and Hugo go for a watery romp in the buff. He wasn't down for *that* kind of party. But that's not to say Teddy didn't have a plan.

"Hugo, you're looking good. Sitting taller in the saddle, I'd say."

Truly, the guy looked even bigger than he had a week ago. Hugo the homunculus.

"Thanks, Teddy. Spine's feeling a lot better."

"How 'bout those bellows in your chest? Still feeling the fiber fluffs in there?"

"Oh yeah, still there. I coughed up some gunk yesterday, all fuzzy 'n' stuff. Almost as if the thing in me gathered it up and swept it out the door of my mouth, kinda like a maid or something pushing all the dirt 'n' shit out the front door, if you can believe it."

"A maid, hah! I can believe it, you bet."

"You're not shaking so bad, Teddy. Just a little wobble that I can see."

"Yeah, down to ten pills a day. Less than half of what I used to pop."

"Did Dr. Strauss tell you to cut back?"

"We know our own bodies, don't we, Hugo?"

"... if you say so."

Teddy wasn't sure how he felt about this man. Hugo was no dummy, but for damn sure Mensa wasn't battering his door down. Teddy doubted Hugo knew what Mensa was.

Plus he was about as talkative as a stump. If they *were* to chat, Teddy was sure Hugo'd want to kibitz about textiles or tractors or Lord knows what . . . but the itch at his neck told Teddy that Hugo had a dangerous air about him. Not a guy you wanted to piss off.

"This way." Teddy guided them off the path. Off Hugo's look, he said: "I'm not planning any funny business, champ. We'll keep our dicks in our pants, promise."

"Didn't figure you for the type."

Truly, Teddy wasn't angry with Frank-O. Frank was probably scared Maddy would turn off the poontang if he squawked. Some men were happiest with their dick lopped off and tucked securely into a woman's handbag. What-ever the case, it altered the playing field, didn't it? Teddy couldn't trust Frank. Frank was a sap who'd walk a mile for a vertical smile . . . and Teddy had to admit Maddy was looking a lot better. Before long, she'd be a genuine piece of tail again.

"Claire's looking fine, isn't she?" Teddy said breezily. "We've all got a ways to go, but you can see the outline. She's got a great caboose packed on the back of her."

Hugo chuckled. "You could say that."

"Y'know, I heard some young punk referring to a woman's shapely derri-ere as her *turd cutter*. Kids these days. Where's the respect?"

Another chuckle from Hugo, this one ending in a wheeze.

"I'm a tit man myself but I can recognize a quality ass, and Claire's got one."

"Yes," Hugo said robotically. "I agree."

Teddy smirked. *I am Hugo-bot 2000 and I concur that woman's buttocks are very fii-ine.*

"And Maddy's got nice pipestems, doesn't she? Those getaway sticks go all the way up without stopping to take a break. Just gams, gams, gams, and then *wham!* You're looking at her chin . . . I guess that breed of construction-site talk isn't kosher these days." Teddy held a branch so it wouldn't whip back and smack Hugo in the face. "But do you want to know *whyyy* I persist in my ribald ways, Hugo my good chum? I'm what you'd call a toxic male."

"Not sure you want to go around broadcasting that."

"Who's going to tattle on me, the chipmunks? Besides, what everyone's calling *toxic* nowadays was just how it was when I was a kid, and things seemed pretty swell—better than nowadays, I can tell you that! My mom *liked* being in the kitchen. It gave her great joy."

"You sure about that?"

"What do you mean, am I sure? She was my mom!"

Hugo shrugged those big shoulders of his. "Right, just . . . did you ever ask her?"

Goddamn, was Hugo ever a killjoy. To lighten the mood, Teddy broke into song.

> *Do your balls hang low;*
> *Do they dangle to and fro;*
> *Can you tie them in a knot—can you tie them in a bow;*
> *Can you heave 'em over your shoulder like a regimental soldier;*
> *Do your balls—hang—LOW, badda-da-bum-ta-tum!*

Harsh truth was, Teddy's balls *did* hang low. As he'd rounded that hard curve from his late fifties into his sixties, his ole beanbag had developed an unwelcome elasticity. He'd be walking along and be damned if his fellas didn't fall to the bottom of his jockey shorts, brushing softly at his inner thighs. Then one time he sat on a wooden chair, felt an internal crunch followed by a bright flare of gut pain, and realized: *Jesus Christ, I just sat on my nuts!* He'd wondered how long before the damn things were bouncing between his legs like a pair of paddleballs . . . but his boys hadn't been pulling their usual jailbreak from his jockies lately: they sat tighter to his crotch, right about where they belonged. When he took a leak, his piss rang off the porcelain with greater gusto, too.

But it's only the start, Teddy thought. *I need more, and faster.*

TEDDY SHOULDERED through a tangle of brush into a clearing he'd scoped out yesterday. The sun fell in lazy runners through the elm and willow trees that shielded the glade, the air holding a chlorophyll tang in the still morning light. The kind of spot you'd bring a lady for a roll in the hay alfresco and wind up picking timothy grass out of the crack of your ass for a week.

Teddy sauntered over to the tree nearest to him. He snapped off a nice three-foot switch. *This ought to make the grade,* he thought.

"This'll sound weird," he told Hugo, flexing the length of branch in his hands like an oversized conductor's wand, "but I suggest that you and I spend the next half hour or so whipping the holy old dickens out of each other."

Hugo chuffed. "*What?*"

He was too old by the time they became popular, but Teddy always figured he would've been the champ on one of those television survival games. It wasn't about being the biggest or strongest, was it? No, it was about being the cleverest and making the biggest and strongest competitors work for you. Forming alliances, hiding your true face, being willing to drop your best friend like a hot potato the moment it profited you. Such behavior was firmly in Teddy Bassiano's wheelhouse. Some people were born with a knife stuck in their backs. Others were born holding that knife. Teddy definitely viewed himself as the latter.

You see everyone as disposable. Wifey #3 once accused Teddy of this. Not true! Well, not *entirely* true. Now did Teddy see people as *filling roles*—the way Wifey #5 would soon be doing once he got off this island? Sure! But disposable? No, because that would mean Teddy didn't really need them at all.

Interchangeable. That's the word Wifey #3 really ought to have used.

"Hugo," he said, "this thing inside us—it's *working*. You can feel it, same as I can."

"Sure, yeah. Feels great."

"But—and this is a *big* but—we're still old and riddled with disease. We need to ramp this little guy inside us up, make it work harder. It's shagging ass as far as I can tell. The bastard needs to get its butt in gear."

Hugo planted his hands on his hips. "What the hell are you talking about?"

"I've been watching and I've been listening. The thing responds to stress, okay? Stress and injury." He brandished the woody whip. "So we've got to injure ourselves to activate it even more and accelerate its intended outcome."

Finally, it dawned on the big lug. "That doesn't sound like a great idea, Teddy."

"What are you talking about? It's the very best of ideas. Listen, do you always take the exact dosage you're given by the doctor? Come on, be honest."

Hugo dropped his eyes. The big dope. "Yeah . . . I mean, mostly I do."

"So when those lungs of yours are giving you merry old hell, you don't take an extra pill to stop them screaming inside your chest? You're goddamn right that *I* do."

Hugo was looking at the switch now. Good, very good. Follow the bouncing ball, you big goof.

"Doctors purposefully under-prescribe, Hugo. You don't know that? It's an ass-covering move. Doctors deal in half-lives and dosage limits—the drug companies hate it and fight it, fairly in my opinion, but no doc wants to be caught with his pants down if one of their patients goes belly-up. That's what Strauss and Marsh are doing, too. That's not fair to us. It's fucking up our progress."

Teddy tested the switch, bowing it between his hands. "But we can medicate ourselves, my overly cautious friend."

"How? Hurt ourselves?"

Teddy nodded. "Nothing more to it than that. We gotta do some damage and goose the thing inside us up. It'll not only fix what we've done; it'll go into hyperdrive." He gave his leg a rap with the switch; it made a leathery *thwap*. "So come on—you and me, Hugo. Blow for blow, tit for tat. I whip you, you whip me." He tapped his toe with the switch. "I can't summon enough gusto to give myself a good whapparoo."

"I don't know. What they're doing to us is already working."

Teddy tamped down his frustration. Did he want to leave the island? No—at least not anytime soon. But this *had* become a competition. It wasn't simply that Teddy wanted to win—and in this case that meant getting the youngest the quickest . . . it was that he had the feeling that he might *need* to.

"We're at the mercy of a mercurial teenager, Hugo," he reasoned. "Who knows if she might change her mind if one of us blows our nose in the wrong direction? She might even slit her bloody wrists. *Again*, I hasten to add."

Teddy waited for his velvet-tongued logic to sink in. As it turned out, Hugo didn't need much extra urging.

"Huh . . . you make a good point." Hugo cracked his knuckles. "How do you want to do this?"

"Holy smokes—now we're cooking with gas!"

Teddy unbuttoned his overalls, peeled them down to his hips. The cool morning air pebbled his skin. Hugo doffed his own overalls halfway, knotting the sleeves around his waist. Teddy was shocked at the man's solid mass. Jee-zum crow. Hugo the Huge.

"You're beefy in all the right ways, aren't you, pal?"

"Who goes first?" Hugo said leadenly, not caring for Teddy's compliment.

Looking at Hugo's thick chest and walnut-cracking hands, Teddy said: "I'll give you the first whack, sound fair?"

Hugo nodded humbly and presented his back. Teddy pushed his breath out in a series of bull-like snorts to amp himself up. Adrenaline flooded through him—damn, felt a little like doing a thick poodle leg of cocaine, didn't it?

Rushing across the glade, Teddy unleashed a strangled battle cry. "*Yeeeargh!*"

The switch laced Hugo with a flat and viperish spank. Hugo's arms went up and he let out a hiss, sinking down onto one knee. He cranked his head back to stare at Teddy with cold fury in his eyes.

"Hey," said Teddy, backing off, "you told me not to go easy."

Hugo pushed his words through gritted teeth: "I . . . didn't . . . say that."

"Didn't you? I could swear you did."

A fiery red line carved across Hugo's back. He staggered up, reaching behind him to see if Teddy had broken the skin.

"Am I bleeding?"

"Not at all!" Teddy did his best to sound aggrieved, as if his day job was whipping people and he had his technique down pat.

Hugo held his hand out. "My turn."

Reluctantly, Teddy handed the switch over. He was starting to regret this idea a little.

Hugo said: "Where do you want it?"

"Uh, my back, same as you. But before we—"

"Turn around."

Teddy did as he was told. His eyes rolled up to the clouds chasing them-selves across a postcard-pretty sky. His breath whistled between his teeth while his heart crashed behind his ribs.

"Don't flinch," Hugo said, "or I'll have to do it again."

The blow came as did a storm: first the pressure of the clouds splitting, then a raw fork of lightning lashing Teddy's skin, followed by the spank of thunder.

Oh DEAR GOD!

He went down in a breathless crumple. A line of pain sizzled across his back; it felt like he'd been sliced open and some asshole had pushed wasps into the wound. He rolled around on the grass. Hugo stood above him with a nasty smile.

"*Oooooh you,*" Teddy gasped, "*. . . zzzzhhhhiiiiishshsss . . .*" He made a helpless sound like a bike tire emptying out its air.

Cool grass, oh, cool grass . . . and past the pain, down in his deepest centers, Teddy swore he could feel the Hydra clench and expand.

By the time Teddy dragged himself up, warm waves were spreading down his legs and spine, radiating from the lash mark. He felt drugged. The warmth of a narcotic bath.

Hugo had a dopey grin on his face, too. "Not so bad, is it?"

Teddy waggled a finger at Hugo. "You hit me pretty dang hard, you knuckle-beak."

"Hee-hee," went Hugo, and handed Teddy the switch. "My turn again."

Teddy was shaking. It wasn't the Parkinson's; it was the pain burning off, and Jesus, there was a lot to burn. He gripped the switch in dreamy fingers. His brain was firing sluggishly as something tried to break through the fog.

"Wait . . . we should do it on our feet."

Hugo's grin went crooked. "*Feet?*"

"Those snoopy doctors are bound to notice our backs carved open like cold roast beef. Y'know," he said with a giggle, "especially the moody one. Little Ms. Marshmallow."

"Miss Sourpuss," Hugo said.

"Mmmmm-*hmm*. During the Vietnam War, the Cong used to whip POWs' feet with electrical cables. Called the technique a . . . a . . ." Teddy tapped his chin. "*Bastinado.*"

"Okay, so we bastinado each other?"

Teddy tittered. His head was singing, his thoughts pleasantly muddled like in the cartoons, when a character takes a punch and little chickadees go flittering around his head.

"Yeah, that's the ticket. I'm gonna bastinado you real good, you big ole bastard."

"Then I'll bastardly bastinado *you.*"

"Take your fucking shoes off," Teddy growled.

Hugo sat cross-legged on the grass, fumbling with his laces. His thick fingers had gone dumb; they didn't work right anymore. Teddy understood. He felt all numby-happy, too. Not glass-chewy and fight-y, the way he used to get when he snorted the Bolivian marching powder. The Hydra was a real mellow trip, *maaaaaan.*

"We're brothers," he told Hugo, licking his lips uncontrollably. "Whippin' brothers . . . brothers of the lash."

"The Bastinado Boys," Hugo said, rocking back on his ass and sticking his bare feet in the air, presenting them to Teddy.

Teddy danced away, flicking the switch like a fencer's épée. "*We are having a swinging time, my friend!*" He wriggled his hips theatrically. "*We are two wild and cuh-raaaazy guys!*"

He ran up on Hugo, who was giggling like a schoolgirl.

"Quit fidgeting," Teddy hissed. "I'm gonna whip the living shit out of you."

The switch came down on Hugo's arches dead-solid perfect. The *thwack* carried up to the treetops and cracked out over the glade. Hugo's eyes went all buggy, bulging from his sockets. He let out a trouser-shredding fart as he kept on laughing like a donkey.

"Speak to me, oh toothless one!" Teddy brayed, collapsing onto the grass beside Hugo. His skull was on fire. Liquid magma burst behind his eyes. His brain was gonna go jetting out his ears. But fuck him if this wasn't the best time he'd had in ages.

Hugo rolled over. Teddy stared into his eyes.

Chains of cold blue skated across Hugo's eyeballs. Teddy recoiled instinctively.

"What is it, Teddy-weddy?"

". . . nothing." By then, the blue had retreated. "Hey, do you see anything in my eyes?"

"Nothing. Why, is something in mine?"

". . . uh, no."

"Take your goddamn shoes off then."

FIFTEEN MINUTES later, having beaten the daylights out of each other, the two limped out of the clearing. The euphoria had burned off; it was a bit like the sour, maudlin feeling of coming off a three-day drug bender, stepping from some seedy flesh pit on Bloor Street and squinting into the harsh light of day.

Hugo's eyes weren't bulging anymore. They had retreated deep inside his sockets, his eyeballs peeking out like two animals inside a cave. Once he returned to his room, Teddy's good vibes went away as the pain reseated itself. Damn Hugo's eyes. That big ox. All brute force, no finesse.

He wrapped his feet in wet towels. He'd have to wear flip-flops for a while. But he'd whipped Hugo's tootsies to smithereens, so even steven. Good times!

With the pain still singing along his nerve endings, the urge came to do it all over again.

Hey, Hugo, get your big ass up. Out to the woods. Time for another round. Brothers of the lash.

It was always more fun to get high with a buddy. Teddy knew this well. Even if the guy was just a drug buddy, a good-time Charlie . . . or a good-time Hugo.

Teddy lay in bed. His back and feet throbbed. But he didn't feel quite so old anymore. His body thrummed like an overtuned guitar string, but damn if it couldn't hold a note.

"Youth is wasted on the young," he whispered before drifting into sleep.

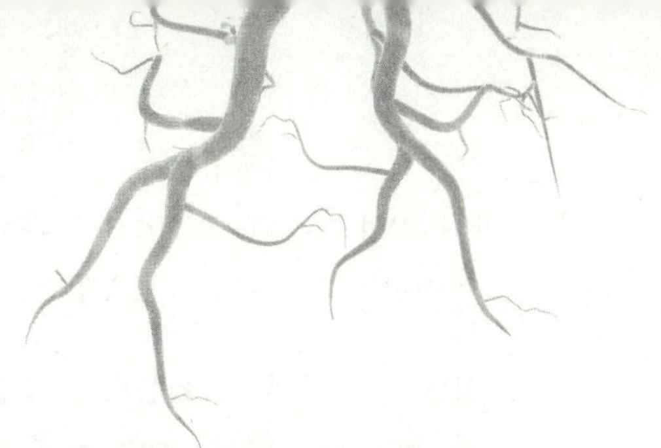

XII. *Anno Hydra*, Day 32

<u>**Notes: Subject Developments**</u>

1 month since procedure

100% survival rate

Uptake harmonized across all subjects within normal range of expectation

Individual outcomes TBD

SUBJECT 1 // FRANKLIN DOYLE, M, 77 — CURRENT GENETIC AGE: 63

Slowest initial uptake. Currently on gradual path of reverse aging. Some facial acne present.

SUBJECT 2 // THEODORE BASSIANO, M, 79 — CGA: 62

Gradual uptake / rapid acceleration. Hydra may be interfering with subject's balance and/or mobility: has become clumsy, especially with regard to tripping/stepping on objects during daily constitutionals, incurring injuries to his feet.

SUBJECT 3 // CLAIRE BLESSINGS, F, 79 — CGA: 60

Gradual uptake followed by rapid acceleration, especially in the last week (declination of eight years, i.e., over a year per day in this period). Some erratic behavior observed. Mood swings, without violent intent. Requires close monitoring by bioethicist Strauss.

SUBJECT 4 // HUGO UDALL, M, 76 — CGA: 64

Acceptable uptake with graduated path similar to S1. Is evidently experiencing the same issues re: balance as S3. Frequently observed limping during past week.

SUBJECT 5 // MADELINE DODDS, F, 84 — CGA: 66

Rapid uptake / rapid acceleration. Has reacted most strongly to treatment, to the point that deceleration via days off from stem Bath may be implemented. Acne present, as in S1 (and other subjects, to lesser degree). Strauss has observed some degree of emotional instability during private sessions. Openly weeping, confusion, etc.

SUBJECT 6 // INGRID CHEVALIER, F, 19 — CGA: 19, UNCHANGED

Still has viable stem cells and overall bodily health, rendering the Hydra's abilities unnecessary to that end. Subject walking again. Happy to be awake. Happy to have her friend back. Relieved to have been rescued. **Grateful to her best friend.**

GLOBAL NOTES

ATP bioluminescent signal detection indicates all subjects are synchronizing available bioidentical embryonic stem delivered to their systems via Bath procedure. Telomeres lengthening, chromosomal decay arrested. Aging process now clearly running in reverse, as observable in age-related biomarkers.

Mood among subjects is light, according to Strauss and my own impression. Lingering signs of emotional distress from the procedure or implant are minimal. Evidence of so-called cabin fever observed, isolation sickness, but subjects understand their position and the logic behind their sequestration on the island.

Subjects' illnesses (Parkinson's, Lyme, congestive heart failure, diabetes, pulmonary edema) and resultant comorbidities on a path of declination in keeping with reduction in genetic age.

Subjects 1–5 have been monitored via halter monitor and wearable brain scan device (SedLine/oximetry).

Heart strength and blood flow improved across subject demographic.

Brain activity shows severe and inappropriate-to-age spikes in dopamine release, as well as significant activity in amygdala area of their temporal lobe. The Hydra is especially active in this area. This is of note as the amygdala is rarely active from age 25 onward, when neural activity becomes concentrated in the prefrontal cortex.

Of note (not concerning at present, but need to monitor), the amygdala is aligned with emotionality, heightened sexual response, impulsivity, aggression, and instinctive behavior.

All subjects are having vivid dreams. Each has independently related this to Strauss.

Nightmares, to be more definitive. A daily occurrence, in most cases. The worst they have experienced since childhood.

—Dr. A. N. Marsh

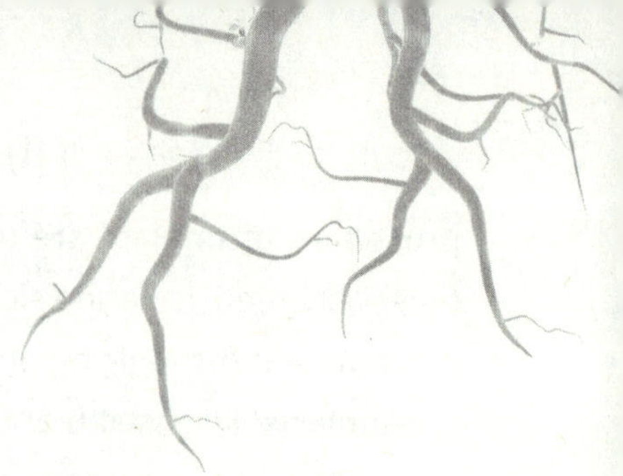

XIII. *Anno Hydra*, Day 36

INGRID ENJOYED walking through Spindrift in her bare feet. The darkness between the illuminated pod stations—she could melt into them, quiet as a church mouse. She relished the direct contact with the floor, the pads of her feet whispering across the tiles.

Still, Ast never failed to hear her.

The pods were mainly dark at this hour, the sun having set. The day's work was done. The Baths completed, the subjects' diagnostics recorded and logged. Dr. Strauss was gone. What did she do in her off-hours? For all Ingrid knew, she dug a hole and buried herself until morning. Only Astrid was left to haunt Spindrift at odd hours, as usual.

Ingrid found her standing in the columnar shadow of the tank. *That* tank. The one Ingrid had hated on sight.

Times were, Ingrid loved jellyfish. The lazy lift and fall of their bodies; the way they seemed to be made of a million small, shifting, intricate parts. Most people loathed them. Same as wasps at a picnic, jellies at the beach were the ultimate mood-wrecker. Nobody wanted to be out in the surf and have one of them—or hundreds, as they tended to travel—brush their chest like a disc of toughened Jell-O.

And, of course, they stung.

Yet jellyfish were among the most miraculous creatures on earth. Ingrid had seen the power in them initially, well before Astrid. Still, she'd never be able to see as deeply as her best friend, or nearly as far. Even if Ingrid lived to be a thousand, Astrid would always be smarter.

"It's okay if you want to stand back there," Ast said. "I get it."

"They unnerve me," Ingrid said to her. "I don't know why."

"They didn't used to."

"Well, that was before."

"Like I said, Ing, I get it."

The implied challenge set Ingrid's jaw. She forced herself toward the tank. When the outline of the huge lion's mane jellyfish drifted across her feet, she tensed. Its shadow sent a hum along her skin . . . but it couldn't hurt her. It was trapped behind glass.

So were the other ones.

Her recollection of those moments—her last conscious ones before the endless dark and the witch—was hazy. Wait, that wasn't quite right: those memories were *compressed.* In her mind's eye, they lay under a huge, disembodied thumb that pressed down on them with relentless pressure, warping their perspective.

They'll rally back eventually, Veronica Strauss assured her. *Most memories do. But the brain is an unknowable organ, and it breaks—and heals—in unknowable ways.*

Buried at the heart of those lost memories—the only clear and present detail—were the jellyfish. The sense memory of them in their large saltwater tank in the laboratory she and Ast shared at the Institute . . . the dozy, thick, somehow *droning* mass of jellyfish on her skin after the tank housing them had burst.

Why, when her mind traveled these dead-end paths, did it settle on the smallest but most deadly of all jellyfish? The Irukandji. Five millimeters long, milky-skinned, with poison a hundred times more potent than a cobra bite. The sting of the Irukandji results in vomiting, muscle cramps, a burning sensation over the face, and, most horrifyingly, a feeling of impending doom. Why could Ingrid feel the feathery kiss of that nearly invisible jellyfish, nothing more than the brush of a spider's gossamer against her skin . . . ?

Her newfound terror of these creatures was why she'd screamed at the discovery of what Astrid had done to her: the Hydra's unnatural design was now twisting through her *own* body.

But she's your best friend. Ast did it as an act of love . . . right?

Love. Control. There were times when Ingrid thought Ast got those things mixed up.

Astrid was occupied now. Her fingers toggled the controls that worked the robotic arms in the modified Hydra's mini-tank, below the much larger one. Ingrid approached her friend just as Astrid took hold of the Hydra. With the pincer arm, she ripped the jellyfish to pieces—slowly, deliberately, a girl tearing up a paper doll. The Hydra seemed to willingly submit to its ruin, steering its body into the grip of those pincers.

"This organism here," Ast said, "has evolved almost since the beginning of time to perform its little trick."

Manipulating the controls, Ast tore another limb off the Hydra.

"Mother Nature allowed it to evolve its talent because it's perfectly harmless, *natural*, when restricted to its phylum. But we've taken it out of nature's hands, haven't we?"

"*We?* I couldn't have done any of this."

"So, this is all on me?"

Ingrid let that one pass. "Why do you keep ripping the poor thing apart?"

"I think it likes it. I give it a chance to show off."

"Should we head out for a walk?" Ingrid asked. "It's a nice night."

Astrid swiveled from the control panel. In the shifting light of the tank, her features were shrunken and somehow goblin-like.

"A walk? Like Oppenheimer and Einstein around the pond?"

"Sure. But which one of us is Albert and which is Robert?"

"You can be whoever you want. I'm neither."

THEY DONNED jackets against the evening's chill and walked around the hub of the laboratory. The path took them past the common room's bay window. Light spilled from the wide pane, which looked in on the subjects. They rung the main table, engaged in a spirited conversation.

Ingrid could identify all five of them, despite not having officially met them yet. Still, she felt a kinship with them, and a peculiar protectiveness: they were her elders, but the Hydra was at least partially her brainchild, and she hoped it wouldn't . . . do anything to them. This worry was mostly form-less, while nonetheless sharp.

Frank and Teddy threw their heads back, roaring with laughter as Madeline pantomimed, her hands fluttering around her face. There was something bright and sunlit to the scene, a sense of an interaction wholly natural and right.

"Look at them," Astrid said. "They're just a bunch of dumb little kids, aren't they?"

"Don't be mean, Ast."

"I'm not." She sounded motherly. "This second chance at life they're get-ting, how happy it makes them . . . honestly, I'm jealous. And I'm glad that, in my way, I provided it for them."

Ingrid watched Claire perform a gliding soft-shoe around Hugo's chair; he shied his eyes at her, his neck shading pink. Ast was right: there was that feeling of children at play . . . or teenagers discovering themselves for the first time. This was an observation in advance of Ingrid's tender years, and yet she felt the truth of it.

"Do you think they know how valuable they are?" Astrid wondered. "That's the annual GDP of every first-world country clowning around in there."

"It's bigger than that, Ast, and you know it," Ingrid said. "You've changed the world. It'll never be the same once this gets out."

Astrid *had* changed the world, hadn't she? She'd used Ingrid's idea to do so . . . hijacked the project while Ingrid lay comatose. Did the betrayal sting? Was Ingrid a bad friend if it did?

"*If* it gets out," Astrid said. "But I suspect you're right. They're priceless, but eventually they'll demand to leave. Everyone does that to me. Even best friends decide to leave."

"That's not fair. It wasn't like that."

How suddenly the old earth could be turned over, exposing the bones of the past. Even for those as young as them, there were bones: moldering, malformed, and perhaps with some life left in them still.

It had been their only real argument, but hadn't it been oh so bitter? Ingrid wanted to leave the Institute. She and Astrid had been sequestered for months, working on their project. The environment under the Institute's roof—the infighting among the ghouls in lab coats; the pipe-busting pressure of Astrid's work ethic—had become claustrophobic to Ingrid.

Just a month away, she'd promised. *Two at most.* Then she'd come back. She and Ast could continue their work together.

But Astrid hadn't believed her intentions . . . and she'd reacted badly.

You'll find new friends and never come back!

Astrid had screamed the accusation in Ingrid's face one of those final nights in their lab, flecking Ingrid's cheeks with spittle. All that hostility and loneliness and fear radiating from her best friend. But that hadn't stopped Ingrid. *Scared* her, yes, but by then she was determined to get the hell out. She had her bags packed, a plane ticket home booked by her folks. And then . . .

. . . and now, with the Hydra safe and sound within Ingrid, Astrid had gotten her wish. Where could Ingrid go now? *Friends forever.* She could still hear Astrid crooning those words, syrupy-sweet, in the dark of the dorm room they shared at the Institute.

Ast and Ing, friends forever and forever friends.

"This would have been so much easier to bear if you'd been with me all along," Ast said.

"What choice did I have? I was comatose."

"I wanted to share my success with you."

"I'm proud of you. You know that. Some people spend their entire lives holding out for a success that never comes."

"Yes, but those are regular people, aren't they? It's different with us."

"I want to meet them," Ingrid said. "The other subjects. Why can't I talk to them?"

Up till now, this had been forbidden. Ingrid was permitted to consort with Dr. Strauss, John, and Moses. But any personal interaction with the subjects had so far been out of the question.

"Why? They're old. They're boring as dirt."

"But they're having so much fun."

Mercurially, Ast said: "All right, then. Have it your way."

INGRID FOLLOWED Astrid back into Spindrift. Ast led her down a serpentine hallway that ended at the subjects' quarters. As the door to the common room opened, laughter washed over Ingrid.

Astrid stepped in first. The old people froze like field mice when the owl swoops overhead. Ingrid followed Astrid in. Raising her hand, she said: "Uh, hi."

Frank swallowed. "Oh, it's . . . uh, you. Hi there."

Astrid said: "This is my friend, Ingrid."

"Hello, Ingrid," the subjects said, somewhat in unison.

"Ingrid and I are . . . we're *best* friends." Ast glanced at Ingrid, as if begging for confirmation. "We worked on the Hydra together, before Ing . . ."

"I had to go away for a while," Ingrid told them. "But now I'm back."

Madeline rose from her chair and approached Ingrid. Up close, the woman's face was strangely seamless, almost without pores.

"Our two young moms," she said with a gentle smile. "The fabulous smarty-pantses responsible for our new lives."

Madeline hugged Ingrid. The embrace was unexpected, but ardent and genuine. The others got up and came over, too.

"Group hug!" Claire trilled, and they surrounded Ingrid and did just that. Hugo came last, the bearlike sweep of his arms wrapping around them all.

Nobody hugged Astrid. She stood there, outside the circle of warmth.

"Would you like some tea, dear?" Claire asked. "I'm down to a cup a day, but happy to put the kettle on. Stuff gives me the jitters now."

"Thank you," Ingrid said. "Tea would be nice."

They sat on the sofas. The room had been decorated with items the subjects had either made or collected, flourishes Ingrid associated with aunts or grandmas. A spray of wildflowers resting in an orange juice carton with the top cut off; charcoal etchings on the near wall (very well-done) of the subjects, with affectionate nicknames—*Frank-O, Claire Bear, Huge-Oh, Maddy*—written below each portrait. And on the coffee table . . . were those knit doilies?

Astrid settled on the couch right beside Ingrid, pressed uncomfortably close. Ingrid felt the need to give Astrid a belated hug, holding on to her for a beat too long.

"I've seen you around the laboratory," said Frank. "Not peeping or anything, just . . ." His cheeks colored. "Where are you back from? A trip?"

"A coma."

". . . oh."

Astrid squirmed beside her. Ingrid sipped her tea. The old people watched her not unlike expectant aunts and uncles, leaning forward with their heads craned out on their necks as if waiting to hear her most recent report card marks.

"How did you guys meet?" Teddy asked after an awkward silence.

"At a place called the Institute," Ast said. "We were fourteen. That place was full of shitty middle-aged men."

"Middle-aged men mostly do suck," Madeline said. "Quite a few old men, too."

"Not nice!" cried Teddy. He pursed his lips and said: "But mostly fair."

"We were all we had," Ingrid said. "Just the two of us."

"But we're soulmates, too," Ast added. "The universe wanted us to meet one another."

"I used to feel that way," said Claire. "The universe was holding that special someone just for me."

Hugo said, "But not anymore?"

"Oh, maybe I'm coming back around to the idea."

Ingrid missed interacting with people and felt welcomed in this circle . . . they were the only other souls on earth who understood what each other was going through, weren't they? But later that night, back in her room and perched on the threshold of sleep, a possibility zinged through Ingrid's brain as it shut down, the quadrants going dark like skyscrapers dotting a vast cityscape: was the *Hydra* creating that heartfelt sense of closeness between them?

The feeling had nothing to do with them as human beings. It was the organism that filled them . . . the one that helixed through the sunken caverns and gravity wells of their brains . . . the thing that was stealthily acquiring power and making its own unguessable plans as it seized the controls piece by piece and hour by hour . . . was *that* the source of their instant camaraderie?

In those final moments before sleep claimed her, Ingrid had a vision of the common room as it had been, but instead of six human beings there were six see-through effigies in the shape of humans, and within them were six blue centrifuges that tossed in complex orbits . . . strands stretched from each to link them all together, Hydra to Hydra to Hydra, in a dance both primitive and pagan . . . and off to one side, watching with dispassionate eyes, stood Astrid.

"So you and Dr. Marsh worked on the Hydra together?" Frank asked.

"Are you a doctor, too?" Hugo cut in. "Should we call you that? Doctor?"

"Um, yes I *am*," Ingrid demurred, "but please, just Ingrid."

"You can all call me Astrid," Ast chimed in. "I mean, um, that's fine, if you want to."

There was a prolonged silence, and then Ingrid addressed Frank's question:

"Astrid and I shared a lab, and I was the one who first noticed the regenerative abilities of the jellyfish, whose DNA is now inside all six of us."

"Wait," Claire said, "*you've* got a Hydra, too?"

When Ingrid gave a timid nod, the group leapt up and hugged her again. The weight of their bodies crushed her into the sofa cushions. Hugo accidentally butted Astrid with his shoulder, shoving her aside as he went in for the big hug; as before, his arms seemed large enough to encompass Ast, too, but he didn't bring her into the embrace. Through the smothering tangle of arms, amid mixed scents of hair pomade, Old Spice, and attar of roses, Ingrid caught a glimpse of Astrid pushed rudely to the edge of the sofa with her face crushed against a throw pillow. Later, she'd suspect there must have been a spark of quivering rage in her eyes, too, but Ingrid had missed it. The fuse had been lit right then.

After the hug broke, the subjects retreated to their spots, looking at Ingrid with fresh eyes. She was now part of the club.

"So, the coma," Teddy said. "The Hydra got you out of it?"

"Yes, Theodore," Ast said tartly.

"Whoa. Physician, heal thyself!"

"It was *me* who did the healing." Astrid eyed Teddy down the slope of her nose. "Ingrid was the heal-ee."

"Uh, right," Teddy amended. "You did the thing, Dr. Marsh."

"What about your parents?" Hugo wondered. "Don't they want to see you?"

Curtly, Astrid said: "Ingrid can't leave the island. Same as all of you."

A pall settled over the group. Somewhere, Ingrid swore she heard the metallic *plink* of a pin pulled from a grenade. Astrid was armed now. And counting down toward detonation.

"Yes, but can she at least call them?" Madeline asked. "Wouldn't they like to know that their daughter's miraculously out of her coma?"

"Why should any of you *care*?"

Astrid's voice was a black thundercloud. The subjects reared back just a bit. Mother had become angry.

"It's fine, Ast," Ingrid said. "They're just asking."

"But don't you want to talk to your parents, Ingrid?" Madeline persisted innocently.

"I'm fine, really," she said, desperation rising. "You don't have to keep pressing this, *please*."

"Oh come on," Madeline said, throwing the whole thing screeching into a deadman's curve, "if I was in your shoes, I'd absolutely want to. After all, aren't you and Dr. Marsh here practically equals?"

Astrid leapt off the sofa. "We are *NOT* equals! Nobody in this room, on this island, on this continent, and yeah, in the whole fucking *world* is my equal!"

Now you've done it, Ingrid thought. *You should have just left well enough alone.*

"Wouldn't it be nice to believe, though?" Astrid went on, her lips twisting into a sneer. "But no: you could add together all the brainpower in this room, and with her at least you get a real nice head start"—jerking her thumb at Ingrid—"and throw in one rock-head bioethicist and those two shitkickers, then add in every brain-dead hick within a thousand-mile radius. And guess what?" Astrid's hands went to her skull, her fingers hooked into claws. "The brain in *this head* still wins. And that, you dummies, is just the way it *is!*"

Astrid stood there, wild-eyed, strung between the poles of sorrow and fury (or so it seemed; Ingrid realized that she'd be unwise to try to fathom Astrid's moods), daring anyone to speak. Madeline cleared her throat.

"What about your friend? What about what *she* wants?"

"It doesn't *matter* what she wants!" Snatching the carton filled with wildflowers, Astrid hurled it at the wall. "Do you think this is some kind of, what, a *game*? Everyone gets to do what they want, whenever they want?"

She stared down Madeline. "Well, Subject Five? *Do you* think it's a game— answer me!"

Madeline said, "Just calm down. Let's be adults." Her face had gone a full shade paler.

"Oh, I *am* calm. Don't you worry your pretty shriveled head, Subject Five. Ingrid can talk to her parents *if* I allow her to, understand?" Astrid seemed to grow a foot, her shoulders flaring out and up like a wrathful scarecrow. "This island and everything on it. *Me. I* control, *I* allow."

I am Oz, Ingrid thought with a shudder, *the great and powerful.*

"Nobody's questioning that, Dr. Marsh," said Frank.

"That's good, Subject One. That's *veeeery* good." Elongating the word with her teeth bared in a grimace. "Would you like me to tell you all a little secret? None of you are *people* anymore. Can you catch my drift, Daddy-Os? No? Please allow me to explain."

With that, the air in the room went painfully static.

"You're *things* now. Objects. If that's too hard to get into your thick old skulls, let me tell you that there are worse places—*much* worse—than this island. If the people funding this project get wind that any of you are disobeying, or that you may try to reach out to a loved one without permission, or God forbid *run away* . . . you don't want to know what they might do."

"Who *is* funding this?" Ingrid asked. "I thought it was the Institute."

A bark of mocking laughter from her best friend.

"Oh come on, Ing. It's bigger. Much, *much* bigger. If any of you screw this up, and if *I'm* out of the picture"—Astrid showed them her forearm scars as a violent reminder—"then you'll be in *their* hands. They'll stuff you in a lightless box someplace, to be poked and prodded. They'll mine you for genetic information to make the next iteration, Hydra 2.0. You'll just be a blooper reel. A ground zero for improvement. They'll fail in those improvements—without me, that's for sure—but that doesn't mean they won't try. You'll all just be . . . outdated software."

Astrid wound down, breathing raggedly. But her eyes still sparked with malicious intent.

"In 1945, they dropped the bomb on Hiroshima even though the Japanese were ready to surrender. Why, you may ask? *They'd built the bomb already.* The bullet was in the chamber. Hundreds of thousands of innocent people died, and for what? For *science*. Because a bomb that doesn't explode is no different than a tree falling in the forest."

Astrid composed herself. Tugged her sleeves back down. "Ask yourselves this: who cares about five elderly nobodies? You think about that when you think about going against me."

Turning her back on all of them, Astrid stomped off. "*Chew on that, you dusty old pricks!*" she shouted over her shoulder, slamming the door shut.

Into the stunned silence, Ingrid said: "Her temper's worse than it used to be."

"Is she serious?" Teddy asked. "The people funding this—how far would they go?"

He and the rest of them looked to Ingrid as if she'd have the answer.

"Don't look at me. I've been out of commission," she told them. "Astrid made her own bargains, whatever they are. This is her project."

"And we're her lab animals," Claire said.

Ingrid held her palms out to them. Despite Astrid's behavior, she felt some bizarre urge to come to her defense.

"We're just kids, you know? Me and Ast. We're nineteen. I've never even drank a beer or y'know . . ." She felt her cheeks pinken. "Kissed anybody. Ast hasn't, either."

Teddy sank his head into his hands. "Jesus Christ. Woe betide us."

"I'm sorry," Ingrid said. "I . . . I have to go."

BY THE time Ingrid exited Spindrift, night was falling. After so long alone, she'd yearned to be around people . . . but the dread in the other subjects' eyes had overwhelmed her.

Help us understand what's happening.

But Astrid held the secrets. Ingrid was in the same boat as the rest of them.

Ingrid ought to be overjoyed, right? She was conscious again. *Free . . .* within Ast's limits. But she couldn't rid herself of the impression this was wrong. *All* wrong. Not the Hydra itself. The Hydra was a mindless tool—

Is it, girl? whispered an implacable voice.

Yes. It was. A tool and nothing more. Still, what about how the world would look under that tool's implementation? That frightened her.

Ingrid pictured herself walking down the sidewalk of a busy city where everyone was the exact same age. Frozen at the apex of health, eternally. No more elderly people . . . and would there be children? Would there be room for new lives with all the resources funneled toward one-hundred- or two-hundred- or thousand-year-olds who'd never, ever die?

She wondered if there might be a lottery in future generations, like in that story. How else could you curb the population? Would the Hydra even allow it? Or did it have its own congenital designs to keep its host alive in some form or another?

In moments of silence—that of her own body, and the silence of the environment—Ingrid could *hear* the Hydra inside of her. A whisper in her veins and the threadings of her nerves. Linked to every blood cell, every neuron and axon in her brain, the synovial fluid sluicing up and down her spine and *within* her spine, too, the marrow and the tiniest honeycombs of her bones. Her helpmate, but also that friend who just wouldn't leave you alone . . . whose constant need drove them so close to you it became suffocating.

———

INGRID CHEVALIER walked across the darkened landscape until she found herself at the wolves' enclosure.

The points of the fence sparked under fresh starlight. The wolves were behind there somewhere. Only three now, after what had happened to poor Diego. But Boots was still out here. The wolf that was now host to the Hydra, just as Ingrid was host. Moses's description came to her:

Its face was mostly teeth.

She stepped to the fence. The hum of electricity crackled over the links. Her heart sped up. Squinting inside the enclosure, her eyes strained for a sign of movement—

Something sidled out from behind a tree.

The witch. She'd found Ingrid again, striding out of her nightmares and into the waking world—

It slunk out from around the tree trunk. The witch was naked and blackened, her skin charred as if from a fire, her limbs nothing but burned bones, as it took a dainty and somehow girlish step, the witch's face reflecting nothing but cold hunger—

Wait . . . no.

It was the wolf. Boots.

He must have been there all along, his body angled in such a way as to cleverly hide himself. No tree on this island was thick enough to conceal this creature. Boots ran six feet from nose to tail, standing on long bone-white legs.

The wolf contemplated her . . . or was it contemplating the leap it would take to clear the fence? In the moonlight, its coat had the silky rippling of the night wind over a field of grass. It moved—it *was* moving, in a manner Ingrid's eyes had a hard time keeping up with—in a way she found hypnotic.

Boots's blackly pebbled muzzle peeled back . . .

My, what big teeth you have, Grandma.

Her fear was a distant thing. Why be scared? The wolf was at the fence now. Its smell was that of the woods themselves. Nothing but those metal links separated them.

Boots watched her with those lambent eyes. Its nose inches from the electrified wire.

Ingrid raised her hand. Fear deserted her entirely. She was a creature of the woods just as the wolf was. A creature of blood and loam and waxing moonlight. Her fingertips were now close enough to feel the pop of voltage off the metal fence links . . .

Something inside her called out to the wolf, the pull of iron filings toward a magnet.

A febrile sound in the dark: *fss, fss, fss, fss* . . .

At the fence—the gulf bridging her fingertips and the wolf's snout—were a thousand microscopic explosions, faintly blue, as if the tiniest fuses were hissing down and winking out.

That's the Hydra. The one in you and the one in Boots. They're reaching out to each other, trying to connect, but the fence—

She jerked her hand back.

Her heart was hammering. She inspected her fingers. They were warm, but there was no evidence the Hydra had crawled out of her, sending its tendrils hunting into the night air.

"Step back, Missus Chevalier."

She turned at the sound of Moses's voice. But she couldn't see him. The afterimage of those tiny blue explosions dotted her vision. The wolf let out a chuff, almost of hilarity.

"I've got a shot," Moses said, "but you'll need to step away."

No.

She didn't want Moses to shoot the wolf, even if it was only a tranquilizer. With an emotion too outsized to define, Ingrid knew she didn't want Boots dragged back to the lab, to Astrid.

The wolf knew the hunter was close. But it lingered. Its eyes locked on hers.

Go, she whispered.

She didn't speak—Ingrid only *thought* the word.

The wolf bolted. Moses let out a strangled cry. He must've taken the shot, anyway—Ingrid caught the *phut* of compressed air to her left—but the dart hit the electric fence with a *bzzz* and fell harmlessly beside her.

"Damn," Moses said, coming out of cover. "That was the best chance I've yet had. Are you all right?"

"Fine, Mr. Squires. Not a scratch on me."

Moses's face was smeared with black—*lampblack,* she'd heard it called, same stuff football players rubbed under their eyes.

"You almost touched it. I saw you. Through the fence."

"Yeah. I don't know what I was thinking."

She could feel his eyes on her. "You ought to stay away from their pen, especially at night. You wanna walk, take it somewhere else."

"I will from now on."

"Let's head back. That's enough excitement for one evening."

"Thank you, Mr. Squires. And I'm really sorry."

"For what?"

For choosing the wolf. "Being someplace I shouldn't."

He smiled. Teeth so white in the dark of his face. "You're young, Missus Chevalier. The night ought to be yours."

They walked back together, talking of unimportant things.

"You know—I wish I had some candy," she said. "Sour Patch Kids. I'm craving those right now something crazy."

"I'll see what I can do, Missus Chevalier."

"Ingrid."

"Moses." He took a beat. "Oh, I figured we were just repeating our names."

"No. I'd like you to call me Ingrid. If that's not weird for you."

"Oh, I suppose I'll manage."

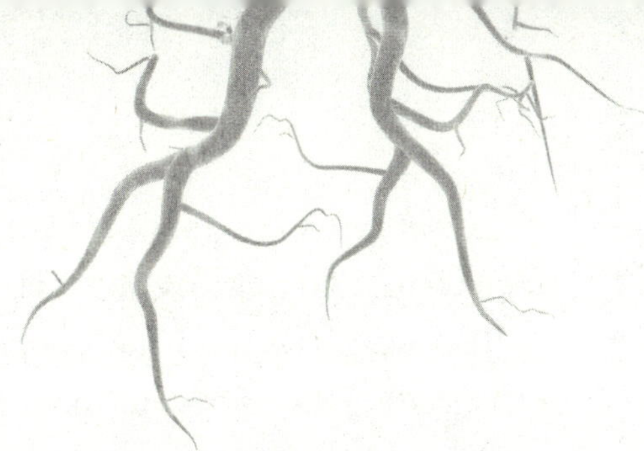

XIV. *Anno Hydra*, Day 42

HUGO WAS floating on that warm ribbon on the edge of sleep, the place neurologists call "hypnagogia," where the threshold between dreams and reality frays thin, when he overheard a disturbance from down the hall.

A sound. Choked, hacking *slobbery*.

That note pulled Hugo out of his dreamworld . . . or had it? The tattery hem of his dream (Claire was in it, she was naked, a fine dream indeed) persisted, but the outlines were warping—was he sliding out of one dream and into another?

Claire and her ripe body were swept from his mind as that hacking grew louder. Oh, Hugo wished it would go away. Even before the cobwebs cleared, he croaked those exact words from a mouth still gummy with sleep.

"Just go away. *Please.*"

If anything, the voice grew louder. And took on a human quality. Hugo was positive it was a single word, endlessly repeated . . . except it sounded like someone trying to speak through a throatful of sludgy motor oil. It held the tempo of a schoolyard rhyme.

A strip of electric light bled under his door from the hallway. It was coming from out there. Out and down the hall. He didn't want to see what was making it. He would much rather squeeze his eyes shut and lie in a tense ball until daylight.

Hugo could see things squirming under the door. Were those cobwebs? They seemed as light as spider's thread, so inessential it was as if they weren't there at all . . .

Except they were. Thin and hairlike and flickering in and out of that glow, so filmy that they almost vanished . . .

They were blue, too. Faintly but obviously blue.

Hugo tore the covers off. Those glowing threads were coming out of *him*.

From the tips of his toes and his shins, his kneecaps and . . . oh God, *everywhere*. He even saw them whispering from the piss-slit in his underpants.

The Hydra was spooling out of Hugo. He'd gotten too small for it, or else it had grown too big to be contained by his body. Right then he felt *packed* with it, as if his chest were ready to rip apart down a trick seam and let the Hydra release itself as a nest of tentacles that would hold the vague shape of one Hugo Udall before collapsing into a racing blue oil slick that slipped out under the door.

He sat up with a breathless whinny. Instinctively, he grabbed at the threads coming out of him, thinking, stupidly, that maybe he could stuff them back in or—

A riot of fireworks exploded in his brain. The pain was immense.

With the heels of his palms, he shoved himself back onto the mattress. The glowing filaments shimmered over the edge of the bed and across the floor, wriggling . . . he felt them tense all at once, a trillion fishing lines going tight with the bite of a trillion fish.

The threads began to pull him. They were tugging him toward the door.

"No," he breathed. "No, please, I want to go back to bed, let me go back to . . . to . . ."

Outside, down the hall, those blubbery hacking notes grew more insistent.

Hugo tried to cope with the pain, a high tolerance from his boxing days, until it shrieked down every nerve stem. When it got too much to bear he slid off the mattress, hauled up into a standing position. The tendrils of the Hydra flowed out of his chest and arms, the crooks of each elbow . . . his vision had a blue tinge, which told him they must be streaming out of his eyes, too, each strand pulled tight as piano wire.

Those threads were winching him to the door. He wondered if they'd pull him right *under* it—of course, he was too big to fit, but the pressure was so relentless that maybe he'd go under in sections, the thing inside him using only what it needed, leaving the rest of him on this side, his body wadded up like a bloody rug folded against the door.

His hand found the knob. The door swung open.

Hugo's footfalls fell heavily down the hall, pounding blood up through his chest. He was naked to his underwear, the way he'd slept since a teenager. He'd done such terrible things during those years, and in the years since. Hurt people. A lot of them. But he'd changed, he'd found God's everlasting love . . . and Hugo had paid for his badness, hadn't he? He'd suffered the worst loss any man ever could.

The threads carved through his skin, knitting at thick connection points at his elbows and knees and where his ankle met his foot. There was no blood or even the smell of it: his skin opened like an orange being peeled.

He kept tottering down the hall. It didn't matter now. If he fell, he understood the threads would simply haul him to his destination anyway, dragging him along with no more effort than if he were a stump of dead wood.

Oh Christ . . . he could smell something. Sour and desecrated, the stink that might weep up from a cracked-open coffin.

The smells and those sounds were coming from around the corner ahead of him. From a spot tucked out of sight at the end of the hall.

The threads took a sharp left at the wall's end, drawing him into the dark. Those clotted moans ascended . . . Hugo was shaking like an old hound shitting peach pits. He tried to shield his eyes. It was useless. The Hydra saw all.

With a final horrid jerk, he was sucked around the edge of the hallway.

What he saw there, thrown in the corner like a discarded doll, looked at first like a ripped-open sack of black earth . . . except sacks of soil didn't make sounds like that. And they didn't come clad in a moldering cotton print dress.

It was Summer. Hugo's daughter. As it had been every night with few exceptions since his arrival at this island . . . but not Summer as she'd ever looked in life.

This was his Summer as she'd look if someone dragged her out of the ground from her eternal rest. Her body both bloated and sticklike, fat and famished. The bib of her worm-eaten dress undulated in subtle shudders.

Daddy. That was the one word, repeated in a grating yet still childish sing-song.

Daddy, Daddy, Daddy . . . the word this thing that had once been Hugo's daughter was trying to speak around the robin's-egg-blue gumball lodged deep in its throat.

Behind Summer—the place where the wall ought be—stood the gumball machine. The same one he'd put that fateful dime in four decades ago, turning the worn crank and lifting the silver flapper to let that damn gumball fall into his daughter's little hand.

It was there now . . . except it wasn't the same. Even all these years later, with his brain circuits gone bad, Hugo knew that much. This machine was much bigger. The glass bowl that held the gumballs was the diameter of a manhole cover. The flapper was as wide as two handspans and curved menacingly upward at both ends—a silver mouth.

Daddy . . . I want one, Daddy . . .

"No, baby . . . you've already had one."

There in the pit below Summer's caved-in nose, past teeth rotted down to mushy pegs, he could see the gumball—just as blue now as the day she'd died, lodged in her windpipe.

. . . I WANT one, Daddy . . .

Hugo saw then that the blue threads coming out of him were stealthily winding around the metallic, vaguely arachnid legs of the gumball machine.

The threads constricted, dropping Hugo to his knees. They dragged him toward the machine. Hugo dug in his heels, but the floor had gone slippery and those threads tightened, hoisting him to his feet and into a jack-legged walk—one step, two step, red step, blue step—until he stood in the shadow of the machine, rising twice as tall as him.

. . . I wanna blue one, Daddy . . .

"Don't be silly," he said in the cool eye of horror. "You can't choose your color."

But he was lying, because inside the huge glass bowl every single gumball was the same robin's-egg blue. They vibrated against one another like fat honeybees in a hive.

BLUE, DADDY—THE BLUE ONE . . .

Hugo's hand closed around the cast-iron knob the size of a baby's skull. He expected it to grate with rust—the machine looked ancient, prehuman—but the inner gears turned smoothly. Inside the machine came a series of cavernous, echoing tones . . . the gumballs shifted inside the bowl as one dropped into the hopper. Hugo could hear it rolling around a spiraling chute, rolling and rolling until—*tink*—it settled gently against the flapper.

He set one hand under the flapper. An apple-size gumball dropped into his palm. It was blue, of course it was, and queasily warm.

Oooh, that's the very best one, Daddy . . .

"You don't want this one, baby," he pleaded. "It's . . . gone bad."

But Summer *did* want it. Hugo could tell by the way her chest thrust out at him, her head craning forward like a dog toward a good smell. Her eyes. Dear God, her *eyes.* They stared at him with the madness of something that ought to be dead, long dead, but had come back.

Summer's tongue—her dead, black tongue—skated over those shoepeg-corn teeth. Her gorge bucked and Hugo knew she was trying to cough out the same obstruction that had been in there for the last forty years . . . which was when Hugo's dreamlike horror turned over and settled on something much darker.

It became *rage.* That old burning emotion Hugo used to feel bubbling up inside him, hot as molten lava.

"*Greedy guts,*" he hissed. "Haven't I told you that candy *rots your teeth*?"

The Hydra's blue wires dragged him toward the split legs of his daughter, where her flesh was splotched with blooms of decay. He closed his fingers around the gumball. Pistoning his arm back, he brought his fist around *hard.*

It impacted Summer's face. There was a soft breathless crumple as the fragile bones caved in. Her entire head dented inward from the force of his blow. When he pulled his fist back Summer was nearly unrecognizable. Rags of decayed skin and shards of teeth were stuck to the gumball. Behind them, the machine's flapper slapped against the die-cast door, *pink-pink-pink*, the sound of wry, metallic laughter.

From the sagging pit in the middle of his daughter's face came a clogged groan that was all but unintelligible, yet Hugo could understand. Hugo and Hugo alone.

Daddy . . . more . . . feed me . . .

"Greedy guts, greedy guts, see what greedy gets," he growled, and brought the gumball down again. This time his fist plunged into a pocket of dark dripping paste—the wetness of his daughter's tongue on his wrist—and he forced the gumball into her throat, down deeper as her neck expanded, making way for his fist, his wrist, half of his forearm . . . he was pressed tight to her now, Summer's little arms around his waist, hugging him. As he looked down and saw her stomach shuddering, Hugo knew, with a surety deeper than death, that it would soon rupture in a white froth of maggots that would go wriggling over his lap.

"I'm sorry," he blubbered. "I'm s-so sorry, Summer, I'm a bad person, so b-bad . . ."

Summer's eyes still managed to stare at him, canted ninety degrees inside her head. He screamed. It was all he had left. He shrieked with every iota of sanity departing into that blackness of his dead daughter's face . . .

. . . CLAIRE found Hugo screaming in the hallway ten yards past her door. Racing to him, she grabbed his shoulders and shook the daylights out of him.

"Hugo! *Hugo!* Goddamn it, wake up! *Hugo!*" She slapped him. "You're having a nightmare!"

His eyes flew open. He shoved her away and pushed himself up against the wall on his palms and heels.

"Summer," he whispered. "I'm so . . . so—"

Claire went over to him. His shove hadn't hurt her—that wasn't his intent—but she'd felt the power in his arms, corded as they were with rejuvenated muscle. She knew Hugo was strong, but until that moment had never understood just how thrillingly powerful his arms were.

"Hugo. It's okay. You were dreaming."

He came back to himself in stages. "Claire . . . ?"

She embraced him, held him. "Yeah, it's me. Come on. Let's get you back to bed."

HUGO ALLOWED Claire to lead him to his room. Nobody else had woken up, but she could hear Frank moaning in his sleep from behind his door.

"Lay down," she instructed once they'd reached his bed.

She switched on the bedside lamp and sat at the midpoint of his bed, near his hips, perched on the edge of the mattress. Hugo was long and solid. She'd never been this close to him. Only wearing his night drawers, too. Well, well. His arms were muscly fire hoses.

Claire liked arms. Her ex had such nice arms, but he'd used them in all the wrong ways.

"It was Summer," Hugo said thickly. "My daughter. She was out in the hall, Claire. And she was"—a shudder—"all *wrong*."

"She's not here, Hugo. You had a bad dream."

Claire had dreams of her own. In the last one, her ex Joe had been trying to slice her face off with a carpet knife in the Coin-Saver Laundromat.

"Thank you for coming." His eyes slipped shut. "I was . . . so scared."

He'd fall back to sleep before long. Claire should leave him . . . instead, her fingers moved over his chest and its coarse gray hairs, down the trench between his rib cage.

Hugo cracked one eye open. "Claire . . . ?"

"Shshsh," she soothed. "You just lie there, big boy."

Her fingertips trickled over his stomach and around his belly button, tracking steadily southward. Her breath came in a tight hitch. So did Hugo's.

She'd had all sorts of feelings lately. Ones that *Before Claire*, pre-island Claire, would have found wildly inappropriate. Not because they hadn't excited her, but she'd felt her time for such feelings had passed. *Now Claire* didn't feel that way at all. *Now Claire* found such things arousing and couldn't think of a single reason not to pursue them.

Her hand slipped under the hem of Hugo's boxers. He let out a muffled sigh. Muffled, but clearly not unreceptive.

"*Claire—?*"

"Hush. You just lay there like I tell you to."

He did as she bid him, his body tense and his eyes squeezed shut.

"You can watch," she told him. "I want you to." She put the slightest hint of thunder in her voice. Some men liked that. The demanding goddess. "Go on, Hugo. Open your eyes."

He did so, and there was something hungry in them. Good.

She had a firm hold on his, *ahem*, manhood. It was already stiffening, and that sent another thrill through her. Demanding goddess, indeed. It was funny how the biggest men often preferred a stern nursemaid. A live-wire smell was coming off Hugo and off Claire, too. The animality of that scent excited her.

With her free hand she undid the topmost buttons on her nightie. And would you look at Hugo's eyes *now*. Personally, Claire thought she looked better today (fifty-five years old, as of the latest clocking) than she had on her first spin around the racetrack.

Soon she'd look even better. A whole lot.

Gently and in rhythm, she moved her hand up and down Hugo's shaft. She wasn't sure where she was going with this—with Hugo, she meant. Did she really share much in common with the guy? Well, who cared? They were having a lark. Let whatever might happen, happen.

"You're big, Hugo. All over. Anyone ever tell you that?"

His massive pipe fitter's hand roamed up her hip, cupping her breast. She pushed it away.

"Uh-uh. Hands to yourself, buster."

She kept stroking him. His breath came in frantic pants. She wondered if she'd better slow down. Would he make a mess? No, Hugo was experienced enough to control himself.

"I've seen you looking at me," she said.

"Yes," he whispered. "You're beautiful."

"That's nice to hear."

Claire wondered: Was she taking advantage of Hugo? Off that thought came a more pragmatic and perhaps ruthless one: someone's always taking advantage of someone else, every minute of every day.

"I can't believe how ready I am right now." Taking his hand, Claire guided it between her legs. "Would you feel that?"

"*Mmmm*," went Hugo, sounding more than a bit goofy.

She took her hand off him long enough to yank his underwear down his thighs. His cock sprung up out of a thatch of gray pubic hair. He was uncircumcised. A *toque*, wasn't it? She'd never tried a toque before. She'd not sampled nearly enough in her past life. But she aimed to make amends for that mistake, in great quantities.

"Hold still," she said.

Her panties came off next. She gripped him again. He really *was* big.

"If I sit on that thing," she said, "you'll be gentle, right?"

In response, Hugo let out a pleased bleat. She swung herself on top of him. The round plug of his penis pressed against her with a giddy pressure as she guided him inside her . . .

Oh. These old bones.

"Slowly," she hissed, more to herself than Hugo.

Spreading her hands on his chest and catching the steady beat of his heart in her fingertips, she began to roll her pelvis back and forth. God, did that ever feel special.

"You aren't ever going to hit me, are you, Hugo?"

He stared up at her with boyish, bleary eyes. "Huh?" he said in a confusion of lust. "No, Claire. Never. May God take my eyes."

"I hope I don't sound like a . . . *ahh* . . . scold . . . but if you ever did hit me, you know I'd kill you, right?" She rocked faster, grooving her hips. "I wouldn't wait for God. I'd take your eyes myself. Now I know that sounds like . . ." Oh Christ, oh mercy me, was that ever nice. ". . . a threat, but"—slow down, feel that good pressure—"you're a lot bigger than me, but I'm smarter. I'd get it done. I'd kill you deader than a doorknob, Hugo, I really would."

Claire was pretty sure Hugo had stopped listening. He'd lost the ability to form coherent thoughts. He was riding the bliss train. Well, good. He'd had a nasty fright. Claire could be a Good Samaritan, couldn't she?

"I'd hurt someone *for* you, Claire, if you wanted me to."

"Mmm. You're sweet."

She kept rocking, faster and faster. The bedsprings groaned; Hugo's pillow slipped from behind his head and fell on the floor. The top of his big bald skull thumped the headboard in time with Claire's downward thrusts.

"Do you think," Hugo panted, "it might work?"

"What?"

"The Hydra. Could it—*ooh-uuuungh*—bring someone back from . . . y'know . . . ?"

She stopped on top of him, fingers twisting in the hoary hairs of his chest. His hardness throbbed inside her. His Hydra, her Hydra, Jesus, were they entangling someplace in her guts?

"What a thing to think of, and *now*. No, Hugo, it can't bring someone back from the dead. Nothing can."

She then continued, fully in control, riding him hard, grinding her hips into his sternum, his hands on her hips and her hands planted on his chest, feeling him in her, the breath-catching size of him—*he feels thick as a soda can, but that can't be true*—and the intensely pleasurable feeling it gave her.

"Soon," he rasped. "*Soon*, Claire."

"Go ahead," she panted, grinning down at him. "It's not as if I can get pregnant."

Well, didn't *that* uncork him. Hugo's hips arched, lifting her until her knees lost contact with the mattress. He shuddered through an orgasm that had likely built up for years or even decades. She felt it go thundering all through her, almost invasively so.

She kept him inside of her for a while. Hugo's member deflated like a parade float with a rip in its seam. Bracing her palms on his shoulders, she slung herself off. She swore she caught the subtle explosion of a blue tiny flashpot when their bodies came unstuck. Hugo reached for her, but she danced playfully out of reach.

"I'm going back to bed," she said primly, snatching up her panties and wriggling them back on under her nightie.

"You don't want to—?"

"What, snuggle? No. I'll be sleeping in my own bed, thank you very much."

Hugo's look was plaintive. "Did you, y'know . . . ?"

"No," she told him honestly. "But it's okay. I still had fun. Next time. You owe me."

"Next time," he said. "You bet. I promise."

"If you say so. Your mouth better not be writing checks your tongue can't cash."

CLAIRE LEFT Hugo where he lay, in a pathetic puddle. She retreated to her room, surfing on a pillow of air. She'd just seduced Hugo, hadn't she? The fact made her giggle. It was her first and only seduction that she could recall. She'd just taken the bull by the proverbial horns . . . *horn.* Why hadn't she done that all her life?

Before Claire felt it was reckless and maybe even sinful to be a seductress. But *Now Claire* realized that the fear of sin, of dishonoring every saint in the pantheon and going to hell . . . that applied only if you died and had to face the consequences of an afterlife, didn't it?

But what if you never died? That person was free to sin every day and twice on Sunday.

Was going to hell a threat that made people do the "right thing" simply to avoid going to the big bad furnace? If so, did those people do good out of true desire, or from mortal terror?

Now Claire intended to do as she liked, whenever she liked. She had no fear of hell.

Hell is empty, and all the devils are here.

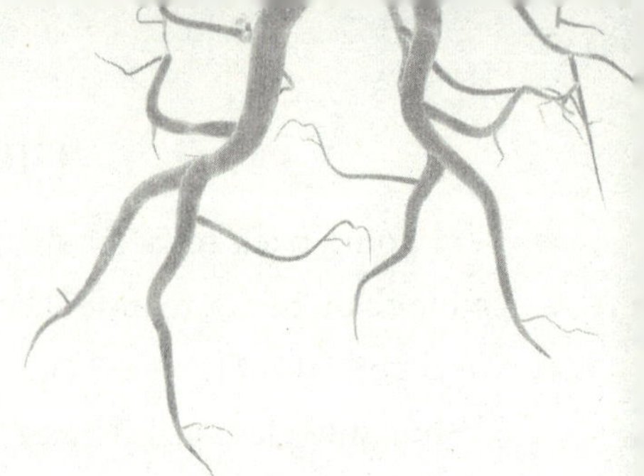

XV. *Anno Hydra*, Day 45

"THE IDEA that I'm going to be younger than my own kids is . . ."

Teddy gazed up at the popcorn ceiling, debating his next words to kick off the group encounter session.

"On one level, it's fucking *great*."

The room burst into laughter. When it died down, he went on.

"But on another level, it's unnatural. I have this vision of being back one day. Going to my sons' houses, my daughter's, and knocking. *Hey, it's your old man.* Except *they're* the old ones now. I'm in my thirties."

"You're fifty-two now," Frank said. "Not too much longer to go."

They were in the common room, where these sessions took place. Frank sat in his usual spot in the ring, directly below an air vent. He used to shiver when the air hit his bald spot, but now his scalp was covered in a modest carpet of almost-colorless hair. Still thin, but what had started as stubby seedlings had grown rapidly. He'd asked Dr. Strauss to hunt up a hairbrush for him—he hadn't packed one for the island.

Every other subject showed a similar restoration of youth. The wrinkles smoothing out of their faces and hands, their eyes brightening, and those *other* hairs—the gross wiry ones that had started to sprout from their nostrils and earholes in their sixties—were all but gone.

"That's what's waiting for us all," Teddy went on, subdued. "Those of us who've had children. We'll have to watch them get old, right? No parent should ever have to see his kid die."

"All of our friends, too," Maddy agreed. "Everyone we've ever known."

Claire said, maybe a little flippantly: "We can make new friends."

Maddy's brow creased. "That's not my point."

"No, it's *my* point," Claire told her with unfamiliar iron in her voice. "My daughter is fifty years old. I had her when I was twenty-five. Wish I'd waited longer—or found another man—but that was back in the seventies, when it was as if you'd done something wrong if you weren't knocked up by twenty-two." She looked at Maddy in defiance. "Yesterday, I clocked forty-eight. The first of us to hit sub-fifty! I'm younger now than my own daughter."

"Congratulations," Maddy said dryly.

"So, should I feel bad?" Claire shrugged. "I don't. Should I feel *weird*? Maybe, but only because we're leading the charge on something that flies in the face of, well, *everything*."

Claire leaned forward. Her skin was smooth, her hair glossy. She wore a loose T-shirt and no bra. Her breasts stood out forthrightly, if perhaps just slightly unnaturally.

"What I want is to go back to when the road split. Twenty-three years old, when my rat-bastard, piece-of-shit ex sauntered into my life. I'm gonna go back to that place in my history, before all of my dumb decisions crippled me, and live differently. Grant myself those chances I never took, live life for *me* from now on."

"Was your daughter one of those mistakes?" Maddy asked.

"What—are you jealous? That you never had kids?"

"It was my choice not to."

"Oh, and here I was thinking you were a barren hag." This insult seemed to land squarely on Maddy. "My daughter was never a mistake, but the timing was. It handcuffed me. Now, though, it's the best of both worlds—my daughter gets to keep living her life and I get to relive mine. And I deserve that, too."

"If any of us ever get to leave this island, that is," Teddy said.

Astrid sat on the outside of the circle with her arms crossed, adding nothing. Since her volcanic outburst several days ago, she had retreated to a sketchy figure on the outskirts of the island's dynamics. Mother Superior, who must never be displeased.

"As humans," Ingrid said hesitantly, sitting as part of the subject's circle for the first time, "our drive is to surpass our boundaries." She smoothed her palms over her jeans. "That's our nature, right? To go to space, or explore the ocean. If this was four centuries ago, our life expectancy would be thirty-two. You'd all be long dead and Ast and I, we'd be elderly."

"So, you think this is a normal progression?" Frank asked her.

"It's natural that we've tried," said Ingrid. "Even if we end up failing."

"Dr. Marsh," Hugo said, "will we ever be able to leave this place?"

From her solitary position, Astrid said: "Am I really keeping you here?"

"Aren't you?"

"I would submit it's your desires that are keeping you here," she told them all. "If you were to leave, your stem treatments would end. And so, Claire's dream of reliving her days from the age of twenty-three would end, too. You can't take your Bath with you. And without the Bath, your Hydra would starve." She paused. "It may even be forced to self-cannibalize, as some hypothetical scenarios I ran tended to forecast."

The term hung leadenly in the air. *Self-cannibalize.*

"You're here because the experiment is ongoing," Astrid went on. "And we don't know the side effects."

"Yeah, but like what side effects?" Teddy asked.

"I can't say," said Astrid. "It's possible they may take years to manifest."

"But we all feel fine," Claire said. "*Better* than fine."

"For now you do," said Dr. Strauss. "We're all seeing what's happening with your clock test results. But until we understand exactly how your body interacts with the implant over the long haul, we can't be certain."

Teddy asked, "Can you ballpark how long?"

Astrid said: "We won't be going down that road. Please don't ask again."

"Well, does that mean we'll be here long enough to see *you* both get old and die?" Hugo said to Strauss and Marsh. "I mean, everyone who doesn't have one of these things inside you."

"Anything is possible. You may just get your wish," Astrid deadpanned.

"What about a day pass or something?" Teddy cut in. "Like the boat trip in *One Flew Over the Cuckoo's Nest*? We'd come back."

Strauss shook her head. "It's understandable that you're all feeling a bit cooped up. So, I'm suggesting a daily fitness regimen. You've made remarkable strides. Teddy, your Parkinson's is untraceable. Maddy, same for the Lyme disease. There's nothing stopping you." She gestured airily out the bay window. "The cold weather will be arriving soon, so no time like the present."

The subjects agreed that this was a good idea. Personally, Frank figured it was a way to test himself against his former abilities—to see if his body was purely for show or if it had some of that old go in it now, too.

"Can I say one last thing?" Claire asked. "This is yucky to admit, but I used to be so *jealous* of young people. I didn't realize that this feeling could creep in as you got older, but . . ." She dropped her head. "I used to want to eat their skin. I don't think I *really* wanted to—I didn't try to bite off a chunk of, say, a passing Rollerblader—but, yeah, I had an urge to consume youth. That's something a witch would do, isn't it? Eating the flesh of the young."

Ingrid leaned away from Claire, though nobody took note of it.

"That's . . ." Dr. Strauss scribbled something on her pad. "Huh. Okay. Thank you for sharing that, Claire."

A KNOCK at Hugo's door.

"You decent, big fella?"

"Yeah."

Teddy stepped in. "We gotta put a pin in the Bastinado Boys for a while."

Teddy had interrupted Hugo fantasizing about Claire. Just last night, instead of the Summer dream, Hugo had experienced an uninterrupted Claire fantasy instead. She'd been riding him in a field of clover. Her face was covered with blue wasps. He could hear her voice inside the shuddering wasp mask, urging him on.

Go on, Hugo. Blow your wad. Not like I'm gonna get preggers.

He'd awoken in a lather. His underpants were sticky. Could it be? A wet dream? A *nocturnal emission*, as the euphemism had it. Holy Jesus. He'd lain in bed for a few minutes marveling at the event, a horny teenager all over again.

"If we're gonna be using our feet for this fitness regimen," Teddy told him, "we can't be whipping the holy old dickens out of them anymore."

Hugo said, "Makes sense."

"I'll figure out something else, okay?"

Teddy was looking movie star handsome. Swarthy as Anthony Quinn in *Zorba the Greek.*

"Or maybe we can quit beating the tar out of each other altogether?" Hugo reasoned.

"Nah, stick with the plan. Don't you go and grow a pussy on me. Brothers of the lash!"

Teddy danced away, mincing like Baryshnikov, and slammed the door behind him.

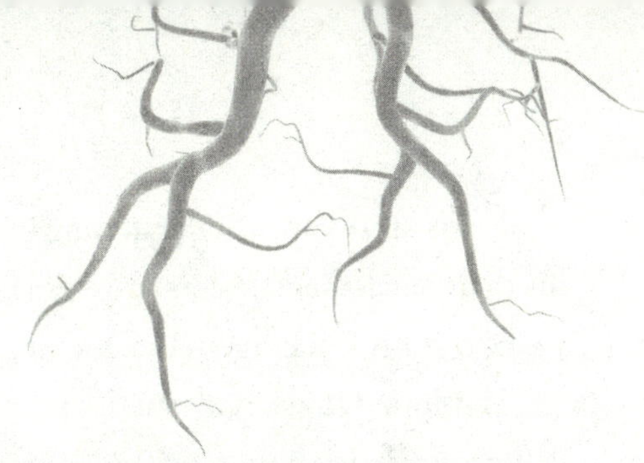

XVI. *Anno Hydra,* Day 60

"GET UP, *get up,* you slothful sonofabitch, you!"

That would be Teddy in the hall, hammering on the door. Frank rolled over, shoving the heel of his palm against his erection as it jutted against the bedsheets.

"Leave me be, you skunk!"

"The sheer laziness!" Teddy tutted from outside. "You'll never make anything of yourself in life with that attitude."

Teddy's footsteps retreated down the hall, off to be a royal pain in the ass to someone else. Frank sat up and slid his feet off the mattress. His heel butted his oxygen machine, which he'd stuffed under the bed a week ago. It was a useless relic now, same as Teddy's pills or Hugo's piss-bag. He ran his fingertips over the boxy slabs of his abdominals. He'd lost another pound or two overnight, he'd swear it.

His penis jutted from his groin like a harpoon, tenting his boxer shorts.

Testosterone pulses through the body most strongly in the morning. Dr. Strauss had lectured them on this fact. *Your hormones will spike as they did when you were young.*

Hearing that, Teddy had leaned over to Frank and whispered: *If anyone needs a nail pounded, just come find me at around six thirty in the ay-em.*

Lordy, it was seventh grade all over again: Frank, all of thirteen years old, forced to solve an equation on the chalkboard in front of the whole class on a day he'd made the mistake of wearing sweatpants.

He caught more footsteps in the hall. God Almighty, never a break. Maddy's husky voice: "Come on, sleepyhead. Daylight's wasting."

Frank stood up, idly scratching his ass. Why was he so sleepy? Wasn't he in his early-bird-special years? Yes and no. He'd been on this earth seventy-seven years, but his last epigenetic clocking pinned his current age at forty-two.

Franklin Doyle had shed thirty-five years in just under two months. Almost half a lifetime rewound and undone.

As a side effect, the process encouraged these long, deep Rip Van Winkle sleeps. Frank would now happily doze until noon, the way he'd done as a teenager, when his mother practically had to crowbar him out of bed.

He stood in front of the mirror in his boxers. "Well hello, Franklin."

His hair was red again. Not the fire-engine red of his youth, but a healthy russet. His temples were still gray, but until a few weeks ago his scalp had been thinly carpeted in that colorless cotton-candy variant of human hair.

Salt-and-pepper stubble grew on a face that had some frown lines, and wrinkles trenched at the edges of his eyes. A stomach with a small paunch, arms roped with noticeable muscle—not that he'd ever been all that muscular. Every day—make that every *second* of every day—Frank was growing younger. Tomorrow he would be less gray, stronger, his thoughts sharper, his sex drive hungrier, until (if Astrid was right, and by now he'd believe anything she told him) he reached a point of perfect stasis.

He smirked at his reflection. "God willing and the crick don't rise."

DRESSED IN sweats and a hoodie, Frank made his way to breakfast with his oxygen unit under his armpit. Reaching the common room, he unceremoniously dumped the damn thing in the nearest trash can.

Teddy greeted him with a hearty "There he is, Mr. Daydreamer!"

"I like my bed," Frank told him. "It's warm, unlike your ice-cold heart."

"*Ooh,*" Teddy said, his lips simperingly pursed. "More like Mr. Sassypants."

Picking up an orange, Teddy tossed it over his head and caught it deftly with his other hand. Frank couldn't remember the last time he'd seen Teddy shake. He was a real Steady Eddie, could center the bubble on a carpenter's plumb bob blindfolded.

The five of them sat at the table in the same sweats and hoodies. You could've mistaken them for a middle-aged running club getting set to put in a few miles of roadwork. Maddy sat next to Frank. Recrossing her legs, her socked foot ran up his calf. Her face remained impassive, but the contact sent a stir down Frank's hips, right to his—

Don't, he commanded his little Frank, which was fluttering against his inner thigh as the blood rushed to it. *Listen, buster, don't you dare.*

They ate in great volume. For years, food had been no more than fuel. But now Frank could feel it building him the way it had when he was a youngster. He was a bottomless pit. He could throw anything into the gristmill and, magically, his body would convert it to energy.

He watched Claire and Hugo out of the corner of his eye, wolfing their meals down. Muffins, heaps of eggs, rashers of bacon, home fries, toast. They ate enough to feed an army. Maddy, too: she'd eaten like a bird when she first got here, but as Frank watched her tear into a five- or six-egg omelet . . . every so often the thought traveled down Frank's brain stem: *Who are we feeding? Us, or* it? But this worry was easy to ignore. Something in his brain *helped* him ignore it, pushing his thoughts down other, less grim paths.

After breakfast, they all gathered in Spindrift. Frank followed his usual quasi-superstitious protocol and swung wide around the jellyfish in their cylindrical tower. He didn't like that feeling of being watched by all those eyeless eyes.

Dr. Strauss waited for them at the Baths. It took a few minutes to get their bio data recorded: heart rate, lung capacity, range of motion, other stuff. All of them had made marked improvements in each category since last week, the same progression as each week prior.

"Are we slowing down yet?" Claire asked. "Astrid said that eventually we would."

"She hasn't said anything about that to me," Strauss told her.

"Yes, but *would she* tell you?" Maddy asked archly.

"I'm not there yet," Teddy said, gripping the belt of flab girding his waist. "Still got fifteen more years and twenty pounds to rewind the ole clock."

Teddy had clocked a pure forty yesterday. He was officially over-the-hill again. At thirty-nine, Claire was currently the clubhouse leader.

"We'll see about the years, but you can work that flab off the old-fashioned way."

"Aw, come on, Veronica," Teddy whined. "How come you never talk to Archie that way?"

That was Teddy's new nickname for Frank, on account of the rediscovered red of his hair. Claire was Midge and Maddy was Betty—though that didn't quite fit her. Hugo, of course, was Moose. Veronica was, well, Veronica. Teddy, self-anointed, was Jughead. Ingrid and Astrid weren't part of the little game, seeing as they'd never read an Archie comic in their lives.

When had they all fallen into this easy alliance? Impossible to say how, other than the feeling of spokes on a wheel. No other spokes added or subtracted would make the wheel turn as truly as it now did—it had to be the six of them, including Ingrid. It couldn't have been anyone else. They each belonged to the island, the project, and most importantly to one another. The combination of isolation, shared experience, and being part of something monumental made it feel like summer camp for senior citizens . . . scratch that, *ex*–senior citizens.

Yes, they squabbled. Brothers and sisters did that, too. But that didn't change the fact they were wedded to one another at some down-deep place under the skin.

It was Teddy who'd come up with the unofficial name of their group when, one evening last week, he'd stepped into the common room and announced:

"Look at you Dorian Grays! Better lock your closet doors so nobody sees the portrait of the rot-faced asshole you've got hiding in there."

And there it was. The moniker was never repeated, but somehow it stuck. The Dorians.

"Go outside and get your fitness in," instructed Dr. Strauss.

Frank snapped off a salute. "Good night, nurse!"

THEY FILED out into the sparkling morning air. The sun scraped the tips of the pines; in half an hour it would be flashing on the rocky tabletops and cliff faces surrounding the lab. Birds trilled, but not as many as one would think: the island was situated too far from any landmass to sustain migratory birds. The land's beauty was of the sparsest sort: lots of rock, not much else. At night, the subjects would lie in their beds (and lately, in one another's beds), listening as the wind screeched across those flat stretches. Every so often, that wind gusted strong enough to tear a tree out at its roots, crashing it earthward with a mournful booming note. The stone amplified the reverb so that one could feel the death of the tree as a humming in the legs of one's bed.

"Last one to the dock's a rotten egg!" Claire cried.

They scrambled down the steps leading from the main doors, a wild stampede of legs and arms. Frank recalled the first time he and Teddy had climbed these same steps, just over two months ago. That grim death march when Frank's heart had nearly burst, trudging so stooped-over that he'd been staring at his belt buckle. Now Teddy was dodging down the stairs, taking them two at a time.

Frank ran with a straight back, hot on Teddy's ass, neck and neck with Maddy, who shot a glance at him, her smile rigid but game as Frank edged past her at the homestretch. Twenty more stairs until they reached the dock. Frank would've pipped Teddy at the post if the bastard hadn't dug the pointy spear of his elbow into Frank's gut and in doing so won by a nose.

"Shit, Frank, sorry. Did I catch you in my backswing?"

Frank rubbed his belly. "You're gonna claim that was an accident?"

"I didn't even see you." Teddy clapped Frank on the shoulder. "You've never been that close to beating me before."

"It'll happen."

"And as your friend, I encourage your naive dreams."

Standing at the end of the dock, Frank stared across the water. Miles away, that red light strobed in its endless roundabout. Recently, a slate-colored fog had started to roll off the water to blanket the island. It clung to the windows of the lab, so dense you couldn't see more than a foot past the glass. Sometimes Frank swore he could hear things knocking around out there in the gray dampness. He pictured massive giants moving between the island chains, their legs like hinged skyscrapers furred with algae and dripping with rust-colored water.

As the days passed, Frank and the others had confessed during their group encounter sessions a sense of losing a firm grip on their lives before this. It wasn't as if they'd forgotten; more like a mental circuit had been subtly tripped, letting certain old or inessential parts of them go. But inessential by whose definition? Frank often wondered. He could understand forgetting the telephone number at his childhood home, or the paint job of his first car—but he *did* remember those (913-7828 and midnight blue)—while other things, such as the color of his wife's eyes (hazel, or was it green?) or the shape of Annie's mouth . . . why wouldn't they come to him without a struggle? He feared that before long they wouldn't come at all. These details had been whisked away on a sly breeze that wafted through the chambers of his brain. And while he knew human minds couldn't recall the sum total of their owners' lives, the erasure he was experiencing—and that was the right word for it—seemed . . . purposeful.

It's like a mental housekeeping, was how Maddy had put it when Frank confided in her. *I feel it, too, Frank. I can still remember anything if I really want to—if I focus hard—but . . . it's as if some careful little maid is bustling about in my brain, putting everything in boxes. I can still open those boxes and find what I'm looking for . . . for now.*

Everything before the island, Astrid Marsh's lab, and the Hydra. It was all hazy now.

If Frank ever *wanted* to go back, he figured that lighthouse was a waypoint. That circuiting red light, visible even in the thickest fog. Not that Frank wanted to go home. What was there for him now? What *was* home if not this island?

Once the group reached the base of the stairs, John Salters came out of the boathouse. Frank had noticed that he and Moses Squires had taken to sleeping on cots down here lately, preferring it to their berths in the main building. A memory of the boat ride out came to Frank—how incredibly old he'd been on that trip with Teddy, how frail, how sick.

"How's everyone this morning?" John had a rod and a bucket of minnows. His smile was thin, but probably genuine.

"Good, John," Frank said. "How are you?"

"Oh, not too badly, thanks."

How old was John? Late thirties? Before long Frank and John would be the same age. Depending on how things went, Frank could wind up a decade younger than him. Sometimes Frank got a sense, despite John's unfailing pleasantness, that the man was mildly sickened by Frank. By all of them. As if John had stopped viewing them as people. Now he could see only the thing inside of them, as though staring at five gruesome human X-rays. And that thing twisting round their bones made John's skin crawl.

Loath as Frank was to admit it—it was the ultimate mood-killer—he sort-of understood John's perspective. Sometimes, when Frank stared at himself in the full-length mirror in his room (nude, as was the case) . . . if he looked long enough, *hard* enough, something would jump out at him. In his face, mostly. There was a faint predatoriness to his features, something not quite right . . . other times he'd catch a winnowed aspect to his cheeks or a fogginess about his eyes that was a shadow of his old weak self peering confusedly through his new face.

Like most Indians, John's superstitious, was how Teddy treated this feeling in his typical inelegant manner when Frank voiced it to him. *He probably thinks we're tricksters.*

While John cast his line off the dock, Maddy cried: "Five miles, point to point. Let's go!"

She dug her heels into the rock, getting a jump on the others. God, the spring in her step! Grinning, Frank raced off after her.

SOME NIGHTS Maddy could still feel it inside of her. Not the loathsome tick, not anymore. Instead, she got a sense of her body's new occupant. The thing she now shared it with.

All five of them felt the Hydra's presence, surely, and most strongly at night. By day, it was a mote of dust in an empty room—visible only when the sunlight directly touched it. Otherwise it was a murmur in the bloodstream in the darkest hours, when their bodies lay still.

The Hydra had brought them back to life. The Hydra was why Maddy was practically *flying* down the trail right this minute, her feet skipping over root systems and up a steep shale rise to a mesa bordering the water. Inhaling the alkaline scent of the rock, she thought: *What did I do to get so lucky?*

Every day came with the sense of being slingshotted back through time—her own body's time, swimming furiously upstream against that current.

Hurdling a rock, she let out a giddy whoop. She could hear the rest of them thundering in her wake, chasing her. Hah. Well, just let them *try* to run her down.

The other day she'd sat naked on her bed. Maddy found herself in that state of repose quite a lot nowadays. Vain? Sure, but screw it. Her wrinkles had smoothed into erasure, long bands of muscle ran up her thighs . . . and her breasts! They'd never been big, which, who cares? *More than a handful's a waste*, as the stupid old saying went. But Maddy saw them *as* breasts again, rather than gravity's playthings. Grabbing them, she'd pressed them against her chest.

Behold, my TITS!

Dropping her pace, she permitted the group to catch up. Frank was soon jogging beside her. She intended to have sex with Frank one of these days. She hadn't yet, though they'd been grab-assing like randy teenagers for a solid week. She figured Frank would be a bit timid and fumble-handed in the sack, but he'd get better with practice. She could be nothing if not a patient teacher.

Hugo was a few paces behind them. Maddy was amazed at how his spine continued to straighten, dragging him from his Igor-like stoop to his full six-foot-seven height. Claire trotted beside him. Maddy's first impression of her had been wrong. Instead of a squat cheerleader—

Dumpy, Maddy reminded herself. *My first thought of Claire was dumpy, not squat.*

—Claire Blessings had the compact springiness of a Cold War–era gymnast. She bounded along at Hugo's side, blond ponytail bobbing at the back of her head.

Teddy was lagging behind, but he was surely playing possum … what could you say about that guy? For a dirty old hound in a fresh coat of paint, be damned if he hadn't grown on her. Even Maddy—who generally loathed Jack the Lads of Teddy's ilk—had to admit she found him to be one heck of a good time.

The group ran headlong into the brightening day, around the rim of the island. The path tracked eastward into the woods. The temperature dropped as they ran on a carpet of browned pine needles. Maddy's breath came lightly, her heart beating in her ears.

They were approaching the wolves' enclosure. The skin tightened at the back of Maddy's neck. She didn't have anything against the wolves, but …

Wolves were intelligent. They were stealthy. And that fence around their enclosure never seemed quite high enough to her.

They exited into a clearing that bordered the pen. Moses Squires was there, hunched down at the fence wire. He must have heard them coming from half a mile away, but his eyes remained fixed someplace past the fence.

"Morning, Moses," she called.

He raised a hand in greeting without turning. "Fine day, Madeline."

They ran on. After a mile-long pass along the southern scrim, they hit the homestretch. This was where the wheat got scythed from the chaff. Another thing Maddy felt rallying back with a vengeance: that old competitive spirit.

Finish hard, baby. Bury 'em deep and toss away the shovel.

The five of them hurtled toward the waterline. Maddy actually slowed down. *Let these poor saps think they've got a chance,* was her mischievous thought.

As the finish line approached, the group knit together in a pack, jostling and bumping elbows. Maddy pushed herself—her chest stuck way out, arms pumping—and Frank faded until it was just her and Teddy, of course it had to be Teddy, who had reserved a thimbleful of go-go juice for the final kick.

Oh no you don't, you sneaky bum, she thought grimly.

She'd been saving a little bit extra, too. As their shoes hit the sandbar, she was able to inch in front of him, cutting across from the outside—"*Hey!*" Teddy squawked as she made her move—to reach the water first.

Unable to check her momentum, Maddy ended up running right *into* the water. A minor inconvenience. She turned, arms raised with her sneakers submerged.

"There's always next time, Teddy."

"Yeah, well," he said, heaving, "I won . . . the stairs."

"Good for you." A little golf clap for Teddy. "But I never try on the stairs."

Teddy couldn't help but smile. "You keep telling yourself that."

The others reached the water. Steam rose off their bodies in the cool morning.

"I'm going in," Maddy announced.

She stepped back onto dry land long enough to shed her sweats, socks, and shoes. By then, there was no shame for any of them—their Baths had seen to that long ago. Now though, and often, they were gripped by a pea-cocky desire to show off; a craving for eyes on their bodies, indiscriminate of who. Though none of them spoke of this, there was a collective worry that they might shrivel back into old crones and codgers at any moment . . . the fear that Astrid's miracle would stop working, and even worse, reverse itself, returning them to the state they'd arrived in at the island.

Maddy waded into the bracingly cold water, clad only in her bra and pant-ies. Claire was out of her own clothes quick as a lick; her heels left divots in the sand as she splashed in.

"Jiminy Christmas, that's cold!"

The men undressed more slowly. Teddy sported an obvious erection.

"Ladies and gents, I do apologize for my state," he demurred. "Teenage hormones."

"Ha, Teddy's pitching a pup tent," said Claire when she saw.

"The cold water should kill it," he promised. "But I shall keep a respectful distance until then."

The five of them swam to the edge of the sheltered bay. The current sucked at their legs, threatening to pull them into the main heart of the waterway. Their bodies had gotten used to prolonged cold by then.

As they waded back to shore, Maddy was seized by an agonizing cramp. She doubled over, gasping. She grabbed at the pain center between her legs. When she pulled her hand from the bay's water, her fingertips were red with thinned blood. She could see more of it between her legs: her underwear red with it, as more threads ribboned into the water.

"What's wrong?"

Claire's voice, there by her side. Maddy's knees buckled. Claire had to prop her up. She could see into the water now, too. But what Claire saw only made her smile.

"It's fine, Maddy," she said. "I haven't had mine again yet, but . . . hey, *hey*."

Maddy began to cry. She couldn't help herself. Suddenly, some inner latch let got. This was not a soft weeping—it was a hoarse and ragged wail that held a loon-like note of hysteria.

"Maddy!" Frank shouted. "Are you hurt?"

"It's just her period!" Claire told him without shame, before turning her attention back to Maddy. "My goodness, it's perfectly okay. You're fine! You've had hundreds of these, you beautiful silly thing."

Claire bore Maddy upright in her arms. Maddy shuddered as her cries echoed across the bay, a foghorn quality that sent gooseflesh up every listener's arms.

"Maddy, hey, please," Claire said with a note of real concern. "It's the most natural thing in the world, isn't it? Isn't it what we all want?"

"I don't know *what I want*!"

Maddy flung her head back, her red-flushed cheeks mirrored to the sky.

"I didn't mind getting old," she said raggedly. "Not all aspects of it, but . . . I'd made peace with aging, even dying." She let herself sag into Claire. "Hadn't I? I can't even remember anymore! But whatever I came to terms with is gone and, and this thing inside me . . ."

She tilted her chin down and looked at the rest of them, shivering helplessly. "This thing can't feel love or offer it, but . . . but it's *in me* like love, some kind of love anyway, which may be the stupidest fucking thing I've ever said."

"It's not stupid," Teddy told her with gentle empathy. "Not stupid at all, Madeline."

Claire said: "It feels different for each of us." She hugged Maddy. "It's okay, darling. Better than okay."

"I feel like I'm living in two timelines, two bodies, two . . ." Maddy said, faltering. "I don't really belong in either one of them."

"Out we go now," Claire tutted, prodding Maddy up onto the beach. "Let's get warm."

Maddy emerged from the water marbled with the cold. The bleeding had stopped. She looked magisterial, as if she could carve herself into a mountainside. Those who watched may have glimpsed two people, one superimposed over another: the strong Maddy and the one who was ineffably sad, a grown woman no different than a girl lost in the clockwork of her own past.

Sometimes I wonder if there is a moment at the threshold of our deaths—one fleeting eyeblink before the end draws down—when we're given some kind of understanding.

Madeline had expressed this at the end of one of their encounter sessions. She'd fought against the feeling of revealing too much of her innermost core, before finally relenting.

What I mean is . . . do you think we'll be given as struggling mortal things some kind of answer, right at the end? It would be too late to make anything of the grand secret, anyway. We would carry it through that eyeblink and into the everlasting black, never to tell another soul. And if someone else were on hand at that exact moment, looking at the face of their loved one in the instant of their passing, would that someone glimpse that secret in their eyes before they closed? But that never happens, does it? Our deaths are private. Even if we die beside our partners in bed, or in a room surrounded by loved ones . . . nobody is aware, exactly, of the precise split second of one's passing, and so often that moment elapses without anyone knowing. Even if you're right beside them, charting the rise and fall of their chests. It comes and goes in that eyeblink, always missed, never clung to, suddenly gone . . . what use would it be anyway? We can't register that thunderclap of understanding, whether or not it happens—it is entirely within that passing person's perspective, a mute revelation for them and them alone.

After this, there had been silence. Then Teddy (of course) said: *Maddy, old girl, if this thing inside of us has its way, none of us will experience that moment at all.*

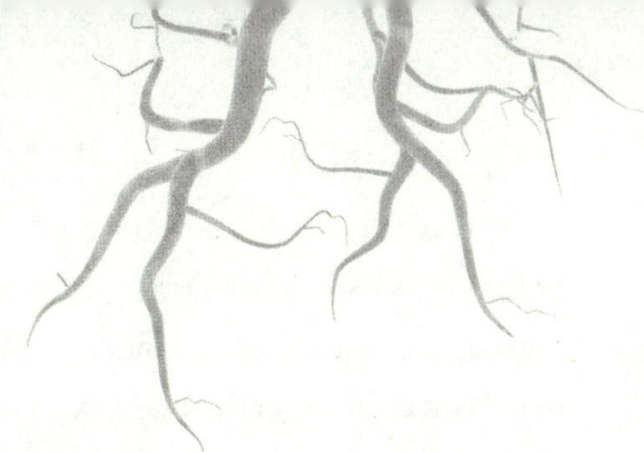

XVII. *Anno Hydra,* Day 63

MOSES SQUIRES and John Salters hunkered in the bunkie they'd built. It was big enough to fit a pair of cots, a camp stove, and gear. An opening in the east-facing wall offered a view of the wolf enclosure from tree line to tree line. The opening was draped in mosquito netting, but recently the bugs had gone quiet in the advance of winter.

The two slept here most nights. They had abandoned their rooms and soft beds in the main building. The doctors could hail them via walkie-talkie in an emergency.

The unvoiced truth was that both men preferred the bunkie.

It was the damn subjects. Something about them.

When Moses was young, his mother let him watch a children's show that ran Sunday mornings on the CBC: *Today's Special.* At the start of each episode, a department store dummy named Jeff was given life with the magic words: *Hocus-pocus alimagocus!*

That's what Moses saw now, in the company of those people. A quintet of Jeff the Dummies peering at him with magpie eyes. The queer, unlined, plasticky quality of their faces.

It's not their fault, he told himself. *The treatment, it's made them odd and off-putting.*

He wondered if *they* knew how weird they'd become—a weirdness less seen than felt, registering as a tightness along Moses's gums. How would they ever reenter society? They'd be hounded out of every human habitat for the crime of sending a squirm up everybody's spine.

It was raining cats and dogs tonight. The storm had rolled in a half hour before dark, threatening clouds massing over the island waters. Lightning forked, detonating on the water's surface with the afterglow of a bomb. Thunder clashed sabers in the night sky as the storm built to a gale, sending the rain slashing sideways through the bunkie's opening.

Out of that darkness came a howl. It didn't sound too far off. A few hundred yards.

The wolves had rarely made themselves seen of late. Not that they'd made any effort to escape, not that the men could tell. Moses and John made frequent patrols of the fence line and watched the footage from the surveillance cameras installed all along that same barrier. So far it was all quiet on the western front . . . though Boots was rarely seen. The assumption remained that Boots was in the pen somewhere. If anything, Moses figured that Boots was in the enclosure based on the territorial behavior of the species. But once the cold settled in and the ice firmed up on the water—the seasonal point at which these island wolves began to hopscotch from landmass to landmass over the ice, hunting prey—all bets were off.

Moses checked the tracker app. "That must be Three making a racket."

"Dora," John confirmed. One of the females.

The howl came again. It wasn't the sound of an apex hunter. There was something frail and fearful in it.

"Do we check it out?" asked John.

"Bad out there. Low visibility."

But the next sound activated something in Moses. When his wife had their first child, little Thomas, she'd told Moses that his cries triggered her milk ducts. *Whenever he starts up, there I go leaking like a faucet.* This wasn't the same, of course, yet it was the first thought that came to Moses.

"That's it. Let's go," he said, his resolve cracking.

THEY STRAPPED their packs on and donned heavy rain slickers. John had his rifle, Moses a pistol and his tranquilizer pole. Conditions were too poor for the tranquilizer gun; the raging wind would knock any dart off target. He'd have to get in close and give the wolf a jab to put it to sleep. So be it.

The electrified fence radiated a nimbus of voltage, links sparking in the downpour. John shut the power. The darkness thickened. Rain fell in ragged curtains; it dripped off of Moses's hood, screwing with his sight lines—like peering out from behind a miniature waterfall.

They opened the gate and stepped inside the enclosure. John snapped the gate shut behind them. Lightning raced along the treetops, turning the air to hammered brass.

Another howl cut the night apart, blistering the air with its passage. Moses had heard plenty of sounds in the night. Moose and bear and wolverine nosing around his shelters—animals that could tear his belly open or stomp his skull to fragments . . . those calls had scared him, too, as a needful fear born out of respect for those wild things.

But *these* howls . . . there was something unnatural to them.

Moses forged in under the trees. Darkness was packed thick between the trunks. He could barely see his fingers in front of his face. The rain slackened as the downpour was caught by the pine needles. Moses pulled his night goggles down from his forehead, over his eyes. The rain now came down in green threads, a veil of glowing emerald. Realizing this was worse than being blind, Moses took his goggles off.

"Just ahead there," he spoke over the drumming rain. "Fifty feet."

He remembered the last time he'd stepped into the wolf enclosure. The sight he'd caught of Boots, or whatever that wolf had become . . . it was a dummy now, too. Another Jeff the Mannequin. Did its old pack mates see Boots the way Moses and John saw their human counterparts—as something unearthly masquerading as one of them? Wolves are social creatures. To be made a pariah would fill the old pack leader with rage.

It's still only a wolf.

Moses tried to make himself believe so . . . but with thunder booming over the island's rocky scallops with a sound like felled oaks, no, he couldn't quite force his mind to embrace it. Boots wasn't a wolf anymore. Not *just* that. It had been fashioned into something . . . *other*. A thing of unclean geometries cut off from the natural order.

Moses couldn't fathom what such a thing might do if it grabbed hold of him in the dark. He was pretty sure he'd rather die.

The trees ushered them into a barren strip running through the heart of these woods. A line like a clear-cut, ten yards wide. The rain picked up again, coming down in cold sheets. Drops hit Moses's rain slicker in a deafening rattle like machine-gun fire. He hunted for John—the desire came to reach for his hand—and caught his profile in the rain's reflection: John's face was so pale and corpse-like that for a heartbeat Moses thought he was in the woods with a dead man.

"Over there!" John had to shout over the hammering rain.

Through the downpour Moses saw two shapes, perhaps fifteen feet away. They could be closer or farther; the woods were disorienting, screwing with his sense of distance and perspective.

One seemed to tower over the other one, which lay in a bedraggled heap on the ground.

The wolves knew the men were here. They would have known the minute they set foot in the pen. Still, they took no notice.

The female howled again. The wind carried the sound to Moses; it seemed to hit him with physical force, knocking him back. Rain slashed and thunder roared. Lightning speared the heavens over the island, and in the flash of light, Moses saw.

Two wolves. Boots was one of them. It loomed over the smaller one, Dora.

But that wasn't all.

Moses might never have witnessed it if it weren't for the clarity of that lightning, how it lit the clear-cut like a flashbulb going off . . .

. . . and illuminating the threads coming out of one wolf and entering the other.

They were coming out of Boots. Moses would swear to that. From the wolf's mouth and throat and snout, but mainly from its eyes: a pair of stout ropes pouring out of the big male's sockets and worming into Dora, who lay on the muddy earth . . .

But not in pain. Moses would swear to that, too. More in some kind of horrible dream state, paralyzed and defenseless as she accepted Boots's gift.

The crack of a shot split the air. John had his rifle shouldered, aimed at the wolves—

—a chunk of bark tore off the tree behind Boots.

The clear-cut faded to black until lightning creased the sky.

Boots was gone. Only Dora lay there.

Knowing he might not get another chance as good as this, Moses advanced, uncapping the needle topping the tranquilizer pole. He jabbed it into Dora's haunch. He wasn't sure it was necessary—was she dead?

"Keep an eye out," he warned John. "That other one won't be far off."

"What do we do?"

"We'll bring her in. The docs better take a look at her."

His adrenaline spiked wildly as they dragged the wolf back to the gate. It wasn't until the latch was locked and the electricity restored that Moses felt his heart begin to climb out of his throat.

"The big male was doing something to her, wasn't he?"

"Yeah," Moses said grimly. "Something, all right."

A PARTY had broken out in the common room.

As with some of the very best parties, it just kind of happened. The five of them had been lounging around—three were reading books while Teddy and Frank played a half-assed game of Chinese checkers.

But the tenor changed when Ingrid arrived. She'd done so regularly lately, showing up in the evenings while Astrid was busy in the lab. The checkerboard was put away. Conversation drifted around to the things they missed.

"What about you, Ingrid?" Claire asked, giving her an elbow nudge. "It's been three years, right? You in a coma. What have you missed?"

"You mean besides my consciousness and the use of my limbs?"

This was met with laughter. Ingrid could fire off some zingers. A real smart cookie.

"Yes, darling," deadpanned Claire, "other than that."

"The only good bit about being in a coma is that the little things now feel like big things. So it must have been the little things I missed most."

"A lot of life is the little good things," said Hugo.

"I missed ice cream. Chocolate ice cream in a bowl, not a cone. Also reading for fun, not for study."

"Do you miss your work?" Maddy asked. "You and Astrid were world-beaters."

Ingrid shook her head. "I . . . don't miss the Institute. They do good work, but I never really liked it there. If it weren't for Astrid, I wouldn't have stayed."

"What about your parents?" Maddy persisted. "Don't you miss them?"

"Of course."

"Do you think Astrid will ever let you talk to them?"

"Eventually," Ingrid told her. "Astrid's told me they're aware I'm conscious and doing well. They had to give Ast medical permission to . . . you know."

Maddy said: "And you believe her?"

"I do, yes."

"You know what I miss?" Teddy said. "Dancing. Cutting a rug. Shaking a tailfeather."

"Me too," agreed Claire.

"Me three," Ingrid confessed.

"Oh, teenage dancing." Teddy pulled a face. "You and your bizarro moves."

"I can try dancing like an old person," Ingrid said sweetly, a bit goadingly.

Teddy slapped her knee. "Just who are you calling old, Miss Thang?"

There was a digital stereo in the common room. Frank discovered a cache of golden oldies on it. He cued up "California Dreamin'," but at its first mordant notes Teddy cried: "Oh, come on—you can't dance to that! May as well try hoofing your ass to a funeral dirge."

Frank skipped to "I Want to Hold Your Hand." The first bars captured the energy that had been percolating in the room. Hugo dragged the table out of the way—his arms were huge and cabled with muscle, popping from his short-sleeved shirt—to make room.

Claire strutted into the center of the makeshift dance floor. Her body held a grace that was activated by the music. Someone dimmed the lights. Teddy joined her, not dancing with her so much as in her orbit; he had great rhythm, working through a collection of classic sixties dance styles: the Twist, the Hully Gully, the Mashed Potato. Their faces sparkled with sweat.

Hugo eased onto the floor, his moves self-conscious, but not bad for a man with such a blocky body; then Ingrid, exclaiming, "I've never heard this song!" She aped Teddy's moves, flinging herself around in circles to experience the motion of a body that had been at rest for far too long.

"Happy Together" started. Madeline hung back with her toes at the edge of the dance floor. Frank sidled up and whispered: "Madeline, may I have this dance?"

"Oh, Frank, you old so-and-so."

The notes had the effect old songs often did, of transporting their listeners back to the place they'd first heard them: sitting on their mother's lap in the kitchen, perhaps, listening on a transistor radio; or the high school sock hop, the gymnasium air perfumed with pheromones under the crepe-paper banners.

"We've got to listen to newer music," Claire said, twitching her hips to the beat. "Whatever the kids are into these days. We need to fit in at the discotheque, sorry, the *club*."

"God, please no," Teddy moaned. "All the new stuff sounds like a cat getting its tail pulled through its mouth."

"Tut-tut, Teddy," Maddy chastised. "Claire's right. We need to learn the newest dance moves, too. We can't be out on the town with the Funky Chicken and the Watusi. We're not old fogies anymore. We can't dance like them!"

"Sure we can. It's, whaddayacallit—*retro*." Hugo's face was set in deep concentration, the tip of his tongue protruding between his lips as he tried to keep time. "I'm gonna hunt my piano-key tie out of my closet. My bell-bottoms, too, if they ain't been eaten by moths!"

"Yeah, screw it, I'll dance the Charleston on top of a flagpole if I want!" Teddy crowed.

While their minds moved back in time, their bodies did the same. Not so quickly as their memories, but it was only a matter of time before those two elements—their memories, and their bodies as they'd existed when those memories were formed—would inevitably intertwine.

When the chorus hit, they found themselves in a circle with their arms slung round their neighbors. They were there in the moment—that pure, joyful moment—together.

As they circled, crossing foot over foot, Teddy said: "Huddle up!"

They all bent their heads to hear him over the music.

"I love you guys," he said, and meant it. Right then, they all meant it.

Later, they would see these as the best minutes of their second lives. As with all the greatest times in a human lifespan, they passed in a flicker—and they passed with those who experienced them believing it would only get better from there.

When the horror finally touched down on the island, they would think of these moments . . . how close they may have come to grace, and how far they ultimately fell from it.

"**CARRY IT** over to the scanning table," Astrid told John and Moses.

They carted the female wolf through Spindrift, slung between them like a hammock. Astrid and Dr. Strauss had been waiting for them in the garage when they arrived with Dora, the Rover's headlamps cutting through the driving rain.

"What's the matter?" said Strauss. "You figure she's come to the same end as Diego?"

"I dunno," Moses said tightly. "You'll have to tell us."

Dora was still alive. Whatever Boots had done, he hadn't killed her. They shuttled her into the lab and past various pods and apparatuses, until they reached the table. The men settled Dora gently atop its smooth black surface.

Astrid switched the device on. The table clicked and ticked as it came online, warming up. She said: "What am I checking?"

"Everything," Moses said. "Check it all."

"That clears it up."

She observed the wolf's anatomical map first. Nothing seemed out of whack. Bones, blood flow, organ function and placement. "It's fine. She's perfectly normal."

She heat-mapped it next. Normal. MRI. Normal. X-ray. All normal.

"You've brought us an unconscious wolf," she remarked. "Congrats."

"No, something was happening to it," John told her. "Boots was there . . . It was doing something to this one."

"What exactly?" Strauss asked.

John said, "I couldn't possibly tell you."

"Having sex with it, maybe?" Astrid said archly. "I've heard animals do that."

"Do the other scan," Moses told her. "The last one."

"Why? It's not applica—"

"Just do it."

Staring coldly at him, Astrid toggled the scanner knob.

Dora's image altered. The eyes of its human observers glazed over in shifting blue tones.

"That's . . . not possible," Strauss said, her voice not quite there.

The Hydra. Small at the moment, but unmistakable. Inside the wolf. Expanding through Dora's body, creeping into the smallest parts of her anatomy and brain.

"What is *this*? It can't migrate." Astrid's confusion came out as a birdlike laugh. "I didn't develop it to allow body-to-body transference."

She toggled back to the anatomical scan. As it was. Back to the Hydra scan. Those chilly blue tendrils were still crawling inside the wolf.

"How in the name of God . . ." she breathed. "No. No no *no*. That's not part of its genetic encoding."

"Guess it didn't listen," John said.

Strauss said: "We need to tell someone about this."

"*No.*"

"*Yes*, Dr. Marsh. This is a major breach of the project's objectives."

"Veronica, please," Astrid said, suddenly honey-voiced. "We had to anticipate some glitches."

"A glitch? This is *not* a glitch. We can't just—"

"I said *NO!*" Astrid slammed her fist on the table. "I can *fix* this! Just let me fix it."

"If it's moving from animal to animal," Moses said, "then that means it could move to more than just the wolves. What if it gets into a bird, and that bird flies to the mainland?"

"We need to stop the project," Strauss said. "Or get more eyes on the—"

"If you make one move to get in my way, you know what I'll do." Astrid said this with no inflection, staring right at Strauss. She could have been stating the weather.

The storm raged outside. The lights in the lab fluttered momentarily before rallying.

"If anyone comes—if anyone else *knows*—I'll kill myself."

"Will you, though?" Strauss asked, chancing it. "What about Ingrid?"

Astrid was quiet for a moment, then finally said: "We'll suspend the procedure on the subjects."

"We don't know how that will affect them. It's not been factored for."

"There's no need to tell them. Let them continue with the Baths, but we won't put any stem in the immersion."

The four of them sat in the blue glow kicked off by the Hydra now inside Dora. The situation still seemed manageable. The island was secure and isolated. Side effects were a natural outcome of radical experimental progress.

"Trust me. Everything will be just fine," said Astrid.

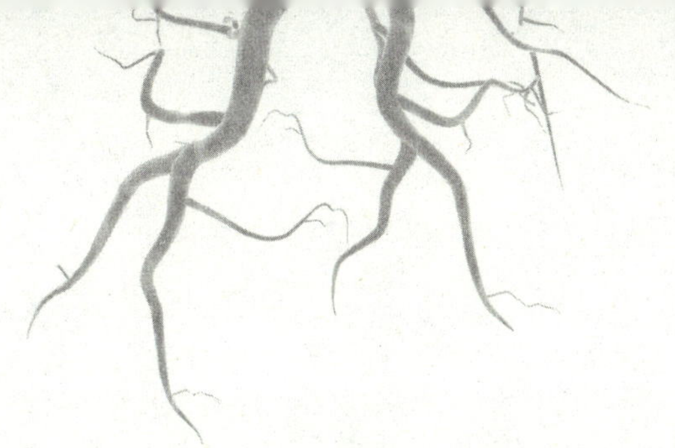

PART 3

THE POWER AND THE GLORY

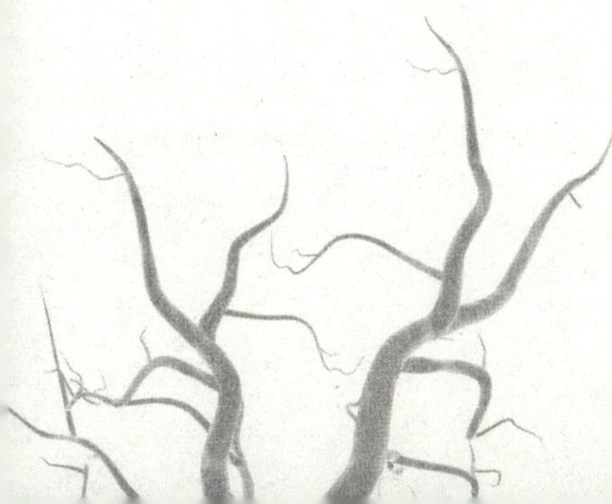

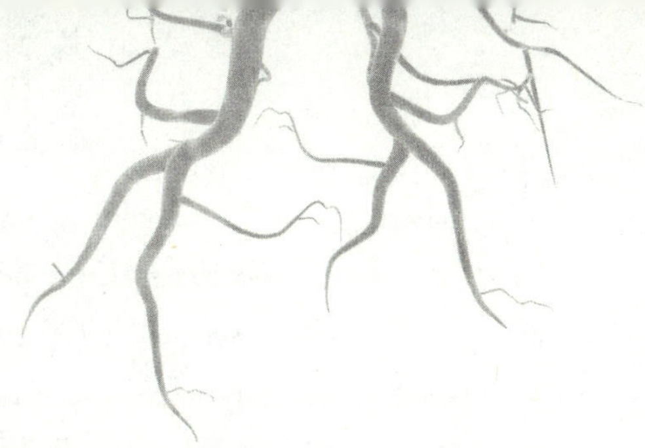

I. *Anno Hydra,* Day 64

HE WAS under her bed again.

Joe. Claire Blessings's heavy-handed ex. It wasn't the first time. He'd become a nightly visitor.

Heya, babe.

She could hear him blubbering under there. His body a huge sloppy hot-water bottle that had sprung a leak. Joe, dead and gassy and greenly bloated, grave water squeezing out of his skin. His teeth had gone black but he still *had* teeth, sharp rattish ones.

A pinch and a punch for the end of the month, Claire-bear.

Claire had experienced this dream often enough to become familiar with its rhythms. She'd first had it years ago, but the Hydra's influence made it much more real. The line between dream and the waking world scrubbed away until there was barely any separation.

Go away, Joe, she thought. *Beat it. Scram. Back to the boneyard with you.*

But like a wad of meat lodged in a windpipe, Joe stubbornly refused to go away. He squirmed under her bed, dust bunnies clinging to his putrefying face.

Get me a beer, bitch. Hell, I'll even take it warm. Any port in a storm.

Claire wanted to reach under there, grab whatever was left of Joe, and rip off a gobbet of rotten skin. Tear his arm off at the shoulder joint and bash his moldering skull in with it . . . but she could only lie rigid, fighting the all-consuming fear clawing over her.

If I crawled out from under this here bed, wouldn't you just shit yourself, babe?

Why don't you just try, babe, she thought. *Go ahead—come out and see what I'll do. I'm not scared of dead things.*

Joe's voice grated like a balding brake pad against its rotor. *Oh, you should be scared. Not of me, but of the dark man with his scythe, Claire-bear. The Reaper coming to cut your thread. Soon we'll both be under here. You and me, two bed worms.*

Yet even in the grips of the nightmare, Claire knew that wasn't true, and this gave her cold comfort. She'd outlived the bastard, and soon she'd be ready to do the same with everyone she'd ever met. Little bitty babies and those whose lives hadn't yet begun, souls still swirling in the cosmic ether waiting to be born.

Claire thought: *I'm going to wake up now, shithead. You stay right where you are. If you say so, darlin'.*

CLAIRE'S EYES flew open. Morning sunshine cut through the blinds of her room.

She slung herself out of bed. Peeled her nightmare-sweaty pj's off. Joe couldn't get her, not ever again. Standing, she inspected herself in the mirror.

"Looking good."

Claire had dropped another year. She could now feel it when she shed one; she had no idea how a lizard felt when molting its skin, but she figured it might be in the same ballpark.

She was thirty-eight as of today. And forecast to be down to her twenties before Christmas. What was that shitty phrase favored around barbershops? *Women are like Christmas cakes—after the twenty-fifth, they're no good.* Those dirty old pricks would be so lucky to see Claire go sashaying past as they waited to get their ears lowered. She'd give her butt a twitch, then flip 'em all the bird.

Twenty-five years old on the twenty-fifth of December. It was now within her reach. And ooh, what a present *that* would be.

At breakfast, Claire sat beside Hugo and matched the big galoot forkful for forkful. She'd never been what one would call a timid eater, but now she ate ravenously—*savagely*, she often thought (with some misgivings, though they weren't strong enough to stop her). The others ate the same. Sometimes the noise of them at the table, the messy crunching and heavy breathing, the snaffling and soft notes of pleasure . . . If Claire closed her eyes, it may not have sounded much different than hogs at a trough. Or jackals hunched over a carcass.

Every once in a while she'd glance up from her plate, backhanding a blob of this or that which had dribbled down her chin, and catch Veronica Strauss staring at her. Dr. Strauss with her beady, judgmental eyes.

After breakfast, Claire and the rest of the group walked to the lab. They assembled at the Baths. Astrid Marsh and Dr. Strauss and Ingrid were there, as usual. But so were John and Moses, which was decidedly *unusual*.

The five of them doffed their clothes and climbed into their Baths. As the green fluid eddied around her, Claire immediately sensed a difference. The prickle on her skin that concentrated at the openings of her body, her lips and nostrils and ear canals, every intimate part of her . . . she couldn't feel it.

Peering from her glass encasement, she tried to read the doctors' expressions. Something was the matter, wasn't it?

Once the session was over and they were out of the tanks and wrapped in robes, Claire said: "It felt different today."

"Really?" Strauss said lightly. "In what way?"

"Less intense. Less . . . *tingly*."

"Yeah," said Hugo. "Me too. I could've been floating in lime Kool-Aid."

Dr. Strauss was about to speak when Astrid held up a hand. "You should be aware—we've lowered the amount of stem in your Baths."

"Why?" Teddy asked.

"And by how much?" said Maddy.

"Ninety-eight percent," Astrid answered.

At that news, Hugo let out a shocked bellow.

"It should be enough to maintain your progress," Veronica said soothingly. "Perhaps a minor uptick in your aging factors, but very little."

Stricken, Teddy said: "But *why* would you do that?"

"Because I say so," said Astrid. "There have been unforeseen developments with the wolves, which may be of consequence. So. Until we get our bearings, we cut back."

Off this odious report, the subjects shuffled to the epigenetic clock. Claire was in a daze of upset. Suddenly—irrationally—she felt old again. Her knees brittle, her joints popping. Soon she'd be stooped over and in need of a cane.

Her rational mind was struggling to maintain a positive outlook. *It's not so bad. Maintaining your current gains is fine, right?*

But another voice burbled up from her lizard brain, screaming in a bratty voice: *This isn't FAIR! The doctors are CHEATING!*

So long as the clock read her age at thirty-seven or even thirty-eight—no change—she could handle it. The laptop processed her age markers and spat out a number.

40

The two numerals detonated in Claire's brain.

"No!" she shrieked. "You said—you *promised*—no, no *way*, you've got to be kidding!" Claire wheeled on the doctors, feeling her face redden like a tomato. "You can't do this to us!"

"Everyone needs to calm down," Astrid told her. "*Now.*"

"I will *not* calm down, you bossy little *bitch*!"

Claire brought her fist down on the laptop, driving a long jagging crack into the screen.

"This is not a fucking game! We are not your playthings, and if you think we are, then you, you, *you*"—Claire's brain waves were so scrambled that she was reduced to a third-grader's level of thinking—"you just wait and see, Miss Smarty-Pants!"

Astrid said nothing, only shut the broken laptop. The sound of it closing was oddly loud in Spindrift—the *snick* of its clamshell screen and Claire's ragged breaths. Claire's skin felt on fire. She couldn't remember a time she'd been perched so close to a sheer vertical descent into madness.

"You put that stem *back* in our Baths or . . ." she seethed, "or else . . ."

"Claire, take it easy." Frank set a hand on her shoulder.

She shrugged it off. "Fuck off, Frank. Pick a side."

"A *side*?"

She leveled a quaking finger at that dirty little cheat, Astrid. "You go back to how it was, do you hear me?"

Astrid set her hands on her hips. "Or what, Subject Five?"

Something rancid rose up in Claire, cold and bristling with horrible dark colors. A hatred deeper than anything she'd ever felt, even for her ex-husband.

"Or I'll *kill* you."

"Jesus, Claire," Teddy said in an awed hush.

Claire's hands curled into fists that shook at her sides. "You have a damn responsibility." She stood rigid, her face rendered stupid in its apoplexy. "And *you*!" she hissed at Dr. Strauss. "A cop for doctors—didn't you call yourself that? Bull*SHIT*! You'd let this one here, your *big boss*, shoot a priest in the middle of First Street and not do a good goddamn thing!"

Astrid showed not a drop of fear in the face of Claire's outburst. "I have a responsibility to humankind. Not to any specific human."

"Oooooooh, go fuck yourself, you rotten lying *cunt*! You can't *DO* this! I won't let you!"

Claire spun away from all those shocked faces and fled through the shadows that filled the odd angles of Spindrift, consumed with a volatile mixture of fear, confusion, and unsettling embarrassment. She felt more like a child than she had since she'd actually been one. A twelve-year-old girl filled with rage at the injustice of a world that cared nothing for her.

"**I DON'T** feel so hot."

"It's mostly in your mind."

Hugo laid his forehead on the table in the common room, which everyone but Claire was sitting around. He muttered, "I don't think so, Maddy."

Frank didn't feel all that great, either. That could be chalked up to stress, couldn't it? And bad news, too. Minds didn't react well to those things, and those ill vibes filtered into the body.

"We're way ahead of the game," Maddy said, the voice of reason. "Even if we backslide, slipping back a few years. We have to see it like that, if only for our own mental well-being."

"That is true," Teddy said, trying to put a happy face on the situation.

"But what if Astrid quits the experiment?" Hugo's voice was muffled with his lips squished on the tabletop. "Then what?"

"I don't think she'll do that," Frank said.

Mush-mouthed against the table, Hugo said: "Why d'you fink thaa?"

"Because this is too important to her," said Maddy.

Frank added: "And like Claire said, she has a responsibility."

Maddy's expression on that fact was unreadable. Frank wondered if she was angry at him for having no grip on the complexities of the situation they now found themselves in.

"She really blew a gasket," Teddy said. "Claire. I mean, holy hell. Someone ought to hand her the Psycho of the Month Award."

Hugo lifted his head. "She had every damn right to be mad. You better talk with respect about Claire."

"How was I being disrespectful?"

"I'm warning you, Teddy. You just watch your mouth, you hear me?"

The two now-fortysomething males gave one another the stink eye across the table. Teddy hadn't shaken in weeks. He was rounding back into the shape he'd likely been in during his construction days. But he was still a shrimp compared to Hugo, who resembled an appliance with legs.

"She's starving us," said Hugo. "Astrid is. *And* Strauss. The Hydra needs to eat, and it's gotten used to daily feedings. It's no different than cutting off the food supply for a human being. It's a . . . a *war crime* or something, isn't it?"

Frank could see the anxiety patterned on every face at that table.

"Can't you feel it?" Hugo's hands knotted at his belly. "How *hungry* it is? Wasn't until this morning, but now *I* can feel it, from my toes to my scalp, but mostly here." His hands crawled up to his skull. "Odd thoughts, y'know? Um, impulses. Strong ones."

"To do what?" Maddy asked.

Hugo's brow beetled. "I don't know."

But Frank thought maybe the big fella *did* know, only he didn't dare admit it.

Maddy settled a hand on Hugo's wrist. "Whatever you're feeling . . . try to keep those thoughts running in beneficial directions, okay?"

"Yeah. Yeah, I'll try."

"If anyone checks on Claire," Maddy said, standing up, "please ask her to stay calm. Astrid will come around. She'll turn the tap back on soon."

Once she'd left, Teddy said: "You know what? Screw waiting. I've got a plan."

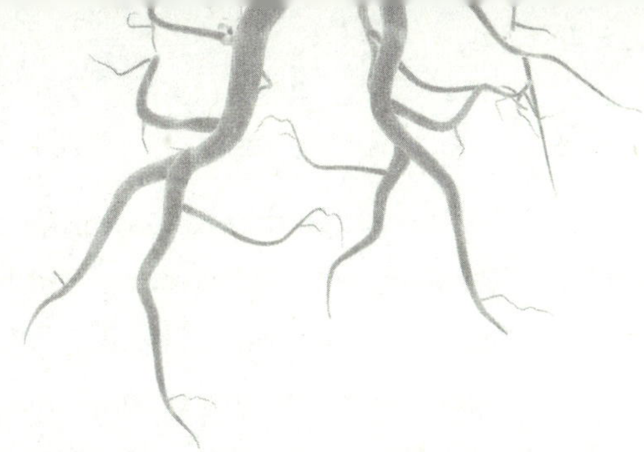

II. *Anno Hydra,* Day 65

IN THE witching hours, Teddy crept out of his room. He knocked softly at Frank's room.

"I've changed my mind," Frank whispered on the other side of his door.

"Oh, for the love of Pete. You're pussying out on me?" Teddy gave the door a soft kick. "Open this damn thing and say it to my face."

Frank obliged. His face was a pasty moon in the cold light of the hall. "I don't think you ought to do this, either," he said, "but you won't listen to me."

Before Frank could ease the door shut, Teddy jammed his arm through the gap. "Hey—you don't have to come, but you don't get to share in the spoils."

"I never asked for any."

"You'll keep your big mouth shut, though, right?"

Frank's voice came back hot. "Are you threatening me?"

"I asked you in on this because I thought we were friends."

Frank gripped Teddy's wrist and guided his arm out of the doorway. "You do whatever you want. But don't do anything too stupid, Teddy."

Frank shut the door with finality.

"Fucking coward," Teddy groused, loud enough for Frank to hear. "I never pegged you for a . . . a real stick-in-the-mud, Frank-O, but that's what you are."

Frank made no reply. Fine. Fuck him sideways. *Good luck getting old again, bastard.*

HUGO WAS ready when Teddy arrived at his room. Ditto Claire. They were dressed in their darkest clothes. Their sneakin'-around gear.

Teddy saluted them. "Onward, Christian soldiers."

They moved silently down the hall. Hugo stepped high on the balls of his feet like a cartoon cat burglar. When Teddy glanced down at his hand—stronger now, the wrinkles smoothed out of it—he could see he was shaking. It wasn't adrenaline or fear. It was his disease coming back. Christ, how had it happened so fast? He could feel his old, sickly self trying to crawl up his back like some hideous hermit crab . . . this was its chance to squirm inside of him again, bringing all its shakes and forgetfulness and sour odors and random bed-wettings.

Let me in, Teddy, he could hear that old self rasping eagerly at his ear. *It's only fair, after all it's my body and you were just squatting in it.*

Teddy couldn't let that shambling horror inside of him again. He'd do anything, anything at all on earth, to make it go away.

The red numerals on the common room's microwave flashed *3:14.* The freezer dumped a load of ice cubes into the hopper as they crept past, making Teddy jerk. He was just wound tighter than a two-dollar wristwatch.

Normally the door to the laboratory would be locked, but earlier that afternoon Teddy had clandestinely stuffed a folded-up piece of cardboard inside the striker plate. Now the door opened when he turned the knob, allowing entry into the labyrinth of the lab.

Teddy was almost certain there were no security cameras operating in the warren of pods. His attention was always drawn to details like that—the ones nobody else would think to notice, because their minds didn't travel the sneaky orbits that Teddy's did. If there *were* cameras, they were well-hidden. He figured they could pass through Spindrift unnoticed, a trio of mice on pitter-pat feet. They would pass unnoticed, so long as they kept quiet and covered their tracks and nobody caught them at their deviltry.

. . . not that it *was* deviltry, really. They were only doing what they had to do to combat the unjust hand of tyranny. It was okay to break unfair rules, wasn't it?

Sometimes Teddy awoke from a nightmare—the most common was the one where he was a disembodied head with the flapping snake of his spinal cord still attached, inhaling an endless line of white powder—and go prowling these hallways in the dead of night. If he went exploring before midnight, he often heard noise within Spindrift. Could be Astrid working the graveyard shift, or Moses and John moving stuff around. But past that hour, the lab was usually silent as a grave.

It was now, just as he'd counted on. The pods hung in stillness in their subdued bubbles of light. The three of them crept down the darkened trenches between those bubbles . . . Teddy checked up. Set one finger to his lips.

Teddy could perceive a sound deeper into the lab. A month ago, he'd never have noted it without the aid of an old-timey ear trumpet, but now he heard it quite well. A note separate from the gurgle of the jellyfish tank, throwing off the light manufactured by its inhabitants, their bells lit in moody violets, emeralds, and crimsons.

The noise didn't sound human-made. Could it be one of the machines? Or the scrape of an animal who'd gotten trapped in the ductwork? That, or . . . his mind conjured something much worse. Something with the rough contours of a human, but ineffably old. He was imagining one of Astrid's first subjects—because she'd lied to them all, you see; they weren't the first ones to undergo her miracle treatment. There had been others, such as the one he'd heard just now . . . and oh, what a spectacular failure *that* was.

Instead of taking years away, the Hydra had backfired and added years on, decade upon decade, but the worst was that the Hydra wouldn't let its host die . . .

This was what Teddy saw shambling out of a dim gulf between the pods: something pale as milk with bulging joints, its chest sunken and its belly bulging (that's the Hydra in there, folks, twisting like a ball of snakes), its swollen head goggling on its neck like a nectarine skewered on a tongue depressor— a smell came off it of spices and old decay, the stench of a sarcophagus as this thing whispered over the tiles on feet dry as balsa wood—

Claire hissed: "The heck's up with you, Teddy?"

The spell broke. "Thought I heard something. Forget it."

They made their way around the periphery of the less familiar pods—it was best to skulk, to imitate mole rats and avoid the light—until they arrived at the Baths. Past them was Teddy's main target. The cooler unit. There were several in the lab, but the one closest to the stem Baths was Teddy's preference, for no other reason than it was the one most recognizable to him. And he knew exactly what it held.

Teddy had made a habit of hanging around before their Baths to watch Dr. Strauss perform the dreary scut work. She'd seen him lingering but hadn't made much note of it—she'd certainly never suspected Teddy might've been casing the joint. He'd watched her remove the stem from that very same cooler. The unit wasn't anything fancy, nothing but a jazzed-up version of the sort of mini fridge you'd find in a freshman's dorm room.

They padded through the ring of Baths. The liquid within them glowed greenly on their faces. The Baths were useless now. Teddy had no clue how to add stem to them, turning that green fluid into the vivifying solution that stripped the years off their bodies . . . but there were other ways to skin that cat, weren't there?

The cooler sat atop a lab bench. Teddy cracked its door open.

"Is that it?" Hugo asked.

"Well, yeah. What did you expect?"

The stem cells sat in racks within the cooler, all in little containers. They looked like ice cubes in a tray. When Teddy touched the top of one, the stem jiggled like half-set gelatin.

"What do we do with it?" Claire asked.

Teddy had given it some thought. "Well, we could rub it on ourselves. That *could* work . . . but I think I'm just going to eat it."

That felt right to him. The most effective mainline—the grotty thrill of smoking crack rather than snorting a gentlemanly line of cocaine.

Hugo went green at the gills at the prospect. "Oh, man," he said. "I don't know."

Teddy knew what the big fella must be thinking. That he'd be devouring little babies. Was Hugo joining Frank in the candy-ass brigade? They'd been swimming in embryonic cells the whole time they'd been here! Yeah, the air-supply masks meant they'd never *swallowed* them . . . but who's to say it wouldn't be more effective this way?

"How many should we take?" Claire whispered. Her eyes sparkled. Good ole Claire, always game for a go.

Ten trays sat inside the cooler. Six cubes per tray. Sixty cubes total.

"Let's do two each," Teddy said. "I've watched Strauss. She takes the trays off the top before our Baths. So if we use one tray, fill it with water, and put it down on the bottom, then move this tray here to the top . . . she shouldn't be able to tell."

"Not right away, anyway," said Hugo.

Teddy had never forecast this to be anything more than a short-term solution. If the stem strike went more than a few days, he'd need to hatch a more aggressive plan.

"One tray," he repeated. "Two apiece. That's what we're doing. No more. Got it? Good."

Teddy pulled a tray from the cooler, brushing his thumbs on the cubes as he did so. Something unlocked inside of him when that stem touched his fingertips. A hunger unlike anything he'd ever known. He nearly dropped the tray, his hands were shaking so badly.

"*Careful!*" bleated Claire.

Teddy set the tray down. "How should we—?"

"Do it like this," Claire said, elbowing him out of the way.

She bent down over the tray. To Teddy, she looked frighteningly crone-like. Her lips stretched around the circumference of one of the stem cubes . . . she made a gluttonous sound sucking it up. Her mouth then moved, robotically yet greedily, to the next slot.

"Om ma gom," she said, the words globby in her throat. "Om ma *goooom*," she repeated inanely, following it with a rapturous groan. Her tongue flirted with one empty slot, then the other, making sure she'd gotten every speck— her mouth drifted toward a third cube . . .

"*Hey*," Teddy said, gripping her shoulder.

She straightened with a shiny grin plastered on her face. "It's like doing

Jell-O shots. Remember those? I did them at my daughter's wedding. Wow, did I ever get drunk that night."

Claire snorted laughter. A blob of gelatinized stem oozed out of her left nostril. She picked it off her top lip and ate it.

Hugo steered the tray to his lips next. His slurps raised the hackles on Teddy's neck.

When Hugo was done with his share, his eyes had gone all round. Two shiny saucers socked into his face. He marched around in a circle, swinging his elbows like a drill sergeant.

"Hup one, hup two, hup-hup-hup," he said, and started to chortle.

"Shshsh, *quiet,*" Claire said, but she was laughing now, too.

When the stem hit Teddy's tongue, every other part of his body stretched forward to greet it. He gripped the edge of the bench as dizziness swarmed him. He sucked greedily, a child at his mother's tit. He felt—and he was by no means a religious man—as Adam must have the moment he'd crunched on the snake's apple.

This was wrong, this was all so horribly unnaturally *wrong* . . . they were vampires, weren't they? Sure. They had been right from jump street.

But all thoughts of moral rectitude blew right out of his brain as the stem lit Teddy's system up like the Fourth of July. He devoured his two cubes and staggered back, laughing deliriously—it felt *so* good, oh Lord love a duck he'd never felt so grand; not during the best sex of his life, the wildest coke trip, not at the births of his three kids . . .

I'd watch my kids die right in front of me to have this all the time.

This arrowed through Teddy's mind so quickly he couldn't be sure he'd even thought it. Dear Christ, say he hadn't.

"Blah," Teddy said, hissing, fully embracing the vampire schtick, his lips slick with pureed embryo. "Blah-blah, hah-hah-hah."

Hugo flapped his arms like a Carpathian Nosferatu, getting into the swing of it. Claire was giggling at them while edging toward the cooler.

"*Ahhh, zee cheeldren of zee night, vhat music zhey make,*" Teddy said, snorting like an idiot. In that comic and somewhat empurpled daze, he watched

Claire casually sidle over to the cooler—nothing to see here, fellas, lah-dee-dee, lah-dee-dum—and take out another tray.

"Quit that," he said, though not very loudly.

He and Hugo watched slack-jawed as Claire sucked up a fresh cube from the second tray.

Sluuuurp.

And another, sounding like a pig rooting after truffles.

She swabbed the empty cube slots with her finger and ran it over her gums, a trick Teddy used to do with the last sprinkles of coke he couldn't toot up his honker.

When it looked like she might try to swallow yet another, her fifth, Hugo snatched the tray away. She bleated and grabbed for it, but he turned his wide back to her.

This was getting away from them. Things were speeding up, the colors were bending and the light fandango was getting tripped, oh my word was it ever . . .

"Get it into you," said Hugo once he'd had his two from the second tray, offering Teddy the final cubes.

Reluctantly—but how reluctantly, really?—Teddy consumed his share. He could eat everything in that cooler, *right now*. He'd end up fighting the other two over it. He could see them ripping one another apart like dingoes . . . there was a frayed and flammable edge to the affair now.

Teddy took the empty trays to a sink in the neighboring laboratory pod. He prayed his accomplices wouldn't sneak back into the cooler while he filled the trays with water. His hands shook so badly that he spilled quite a bit.

When he got back, Claire and Hugo were standing self-consciously at attention. Hugo's grin was especially foolish. Teddy couldn't help noticing that Claire's hand was currently jammed down Hugo's sweatpants. She was playing with him idly, like a kid whanging a doorstopper.

Eww. Teddy was all for romance, but these two resembled a couple of inbred hayseeds who'd snuck off behind the pigsty. Seeing them at it so brazenly, Teddy's next over-adrenalized thought was:

We've become overgrown children.

When he was fifteen, Teddy's friends had goaded him into stealing a war vet's fake leg. The guy used to sit outside the VFW Hall on Coopersmith Street, across from the Odeon Theatre. The day of Teddy's attempted theft, the marquee had advertised Peter Cushing in *The Brides of Dracula*. The vet had fought in World War II; he'd been a tail gunner, a fact he'd announce to anyone who might listen. *Flak over Dresden,* Teddy had overheard him saying to random passersby. *Not enough jackets to go round, y'see.* He used to uncouple his fake leg and lay it beside him on the bench to let the stump breathe. A metal clip projected from that stump, looking like a silver birthday candle stuck into the end of a hot dog. The guy must've sensed Teddy was going to try to snatch his leg, because the vet grabbed for it (the leg was unattached at the time; Teddy wasn't crazy enough to try ripping it right off the man's body) just as Teddy did. The two of them had a tug-of-war like a pair of junkyard dogs fighting over a bone before Teddy let go and fled, while his buddies cackled from an empty lot across the road.

The next day, Teddy had paused to wonder: *What the hell was I gonna do with that guy's leg, anyway?* But in those days, his brain wasn't wired right. Teenagers rarely thought past the current moment, which made them the equivalent of human nitroglycerin.

Teddy didn't think that way anymore. His brain had rewired itself more soundly over the course of many years. That mindset was freighted with maturity, responsibility.

Except he sure as hell wasn't thinking that way on this island, was he? Increasingly and dangerously, that answer was no. Why else would he be here in the skulking hours, guzzling stem shooters?

Teddy reorganized the cooler. Full trays of stem went on the top shelves, the water-filled trays on the bottom. It ought to be a week before Strauss or anyone else noticed . . . that is, if they didn't come back for more tomorrow night.

They were moving from the pocket of light that held the Baths when John Salters spoke.

"Hold on a minute. All of you."

Salters hung back in the gloom, a full pod distant. Teddy knew that he must have been watching them the whole time.

"It's not what you think," Teddy said.

Echoing footfalls signaled Salters's approach. He stopped before the light could fall on him. "You three were eating the damn stuff," he said simply. "I don't see how you're gonna claim otherwise."

"Yeah, we took it," Claire told him. "Astrid cut us off."

John's voice was toneless in the shadows. "I know."

A boyish fear pushed through Teddy, of being caught and sent to the principal's office.

"Is Moses with you?"

"Nope. Sleeping."

"Then it's only us four who know. Nobody else needs to."

A flash of Salters's teeth in the murk. "Oh really. Don't they?"

"How much would it take to keep this all between us?"

"You offering me a bribe, Teddy?"

"Cut the shit, John."

Salters broached the light. His face was expressionless, although Teddy swore he could see revulsion painted somewhere on his wind-scrubbed features.

"You don't much like us, do you?" Claire said.

The man's gaze swung to her, his mouth wrinkling with distaste.

"I can see that thing inside you," he said. "In the sunlight is when it prefers to show its face. It looks a bit like a weed. Like ivy crawling across your skin towards the sun. Drinking it through you, greedy in the way it was made."

The confession from such a tight-lipped man took Teddy aback.

"I wouldn't take that cure for anything on earth." Salters bowed his head. "I'm truly sorry for what Astrid's done to you. I don't think she laid it out fair. I think she took advantage of five sick, desperate old folks."

Hugo moved away from Claire. His shoulders were hunched and rounded, the posture of a pugilist. His face reflected a kindling rage.

"Can you see it in me now, John?" he asked darkly.

Now it was Salters who took a step back. His hand dropped to the knife sheathed at his belt. "I can always see it," he said, squaring his shoulders to Hugo. "Everyone else will, too. You can't miss it, okay?" Salters's pitying tone grated. "It's like a spiderweb tattoo on your face."

Somehow, as though clipping out of time and space, Hugo managed to close the distance between them. His hands were curled and fixed into claws of skin and bone.

"You're all marked," Salters went on, "even poor Ingrid. Nobody's gonna want to be around you, not anymore."

"Shut him up, Hugo," Claire said hoarsely.

The air in Spindrift came alive: a static charge Teddy could feel in his molars, the way it used to get before the two biggest high school toughs squared off in a hallway brawl. But they weren't kids anymore, and this wasn't a fistfight. This was something far more serious and elemental. Hugo had murder in his eye.

"He's gonna tattle on us." Claire bared her teeth. "He's one of *them*."

"Shut up," Teddy told her. "John, listen—Hugo, *you* listen. Let's all calm down and—"

Salters must have sensed he was boxed in, his angles cut off, but it did him no good. Hugo had maneuvered deftly, almost magically; he had Salters pinned against the lab bench. Teddy wondered how someone as clever and as wary as John could have left himself so vulnerable when his life depended on it. Maybe he didn't have much of a fighter's instinct . . . but later on, Teddy would come to believe it had been a failure of perspective. Salters still couldn't see Hugo as the unstoppable menace that Astrid's experiment had rebuilt him into; he still saw the frail creature Hugo had been two months ago, with his twisted coat-hanger body and lungs rattly with fiber clumps.

That's what killed John Salters, ultimately. The impossibility of Hugo Udall's alteration.

Salters dodged left, but Hugo read the feint perfectly. He moved with

Salters, faster than could have been imagined. Salters went for his knife—Teddy saw the shock in his eyes turn to watery fear at how quickly he'd surrendered the advantage—but Hugo was there a split second later, pinning the smaller man's hand to the hilt.

A series of piercing snaps rose to the ceiling. Those would be Salters's fingers as Hugo squeezed them in his freakishly strong mitt. The big man's knuckles whitened with pressure as the blood drained out of Salters's face. He let go an agonized squawk as Hugo jerked upward with one violent thrust, cleanly breaking Salters's wrist.

Hugo let go of that mangled hand. Mewling in pain, Salters reached across his body with his unbroken hand, scrabbling desperately for the knife.

Teddy cried: "Hugo, *stop!*"

But the murderous rip cord had already been tugged in Hugo's back. He locked his meat hooks around Salters's neck. Flexing his legs, he heaved the poor man up like a sack of barleycorn. Salters's eyes bulged as his toes kicked eight inches off the ground. Hugo squeezed, trying to get his fingertips to touch at the back of Salters's neck. There came a muffled *crunch*, and Teddy's sick thought was: *That was John Salters's Adam's apple.*

Salters bowed in midair, his body spasming. The trapped blood turned his head into a grisly purple eggplant. Teddy shot a glance at Claire and saw horror mixed with triumph on her face, a woman transfixed by a nightmare she'd set into motion . . .

Just before it happened, Teddy shut his eyes. If he didn't see it, maybe it wouldn't take place and none of them would have to deal with the consequences.

"What do you see now, John?" he heard Hugo growl. "What the fuck do you see *now?*"

The sound of John Salters's neck as it broke was the stem snapping off an unripe banana. Teddy opened his eyes to see John sagging in Hugo's grip. There was nothing in that body anymore: no animus, nothing more than a toy with its batteries tugged out.

Hugo lay Salters's body on the bench. He sawed his forearm across his mouth and looked at his digital watch—why, to record the time of death?

"I'm sorry." He blinked, a man coming out of a reverie. ". . . I went too far, didn't I?"

An internal dam broke inside Hugo and he collapsed to the floor, making puppyish sounds Teddy had never heard coming out of a grown man. He cradled his head as it swept back and forth in endless negation: *no, no, nononono . . .*

"I'm so sorry," he sobbed. "I did it again, oh Jesus, I can't—ohhhh, I'm so *bad*. I'm such a bad, evil man . . ."

Even with Hugo in this state, Teddy resisted the urge to run. He thought Hugo might give chase, and the notion of being pursued by a huge weeping man through the shadows of Spindrift was horrifying to him.

Claire butted her hip into Hugo's shoulder. "Come on, get up. Stop being a baby."

Hugo's sobs gave way to sniffles. Claire rubbed his shoulder. "He pushed you to it, didn't he? That's the Lord's truth, I'm here to attest." She shot a look at Teddy. "Teddy will vouch for it, too, won't you?"

Teddy kept his peace. Hugo let go a racking sigh that ended in a shudder. "He shouldn't have spoken that way to us, should he?"

Claire said, "It wasn't very nice, was it?"

Salters's body slid off the bench. His forehead hit the tiles with a flat ungodly *smack*.

Hugo stood up. His eyes were puffy, but the storm had passed. "What do we do?"

He wasn't asking Teddy. He was asking Claire.

"We need to get rid of him," she said simply.

"No," Teddy said. "We can't . . . we . . ." His thoughts were disordered. "He's dead, isn't he? You killed him, Hugo."

As one, Claire's and Hugo's heads cranked around, a pair of uncanny animatronics, until they were staring right at him.

"It was *your* idea," Claire said. "You were the mastermind, Teddy."

Teddy staggered at the accusation. "What-what are you . . . ?"

"All of it," she told him stonily. "Right, Hugo?"

After a beat, Hugo nodded. "Sneaking into the lab and taking the stem. That was you."

"And then killing John—Teddy *told* you to do that, didn't he?"

"Come to think of it, Claire—yeah, he did."

Christ Almighty. This was childish, the equivalent of two against one making it a law. Except Teddy couldn't think his way out of this pickle. His exit strategy had gotten all fucked . . . John's body lay in a cooling heap and Hugo was mere footsteps away from him, and Hugo'd just about beheaded a man younger and stronger than Teddy—so what was to stop Hugo from doing the same to him?

That marks the ignominious end of the Bastinado Boys, was Teddy's queasy thought.

Kneeling by the body, Claire folded John's arms across his chest. It struck Teddy how different John looked than just a minute ago, furiously clinging to life—something had slipped out of Salters in death, and that lack was why Teddy had always preferred closed-coffin funerals.

"Help me drag him up," Claire said.

Hugo lifted Salters around the shoulders. Claire gripped the backs of his heels. Teddy followed them through the lab, borne on a foamy wash of unreality.

"Get the door," Claire snapped at him. "Make yourself useful."

The instant Teddy gripped the doorknob, he realized he'd made himself an accomplice. He'd never taken part in crimes before. Well, some white-collar tax write-offs here and there, but nothing *real,* worthy of hard jail time. It appalled him how quickly the matter got settled. The momentum was unstoppable; you got dragged along with it, a worm on a hook. Later you might claim that you'd wanted no part of it . . . but who'd believe that, especially of a known louse like Teddy Bassiano?

OUTSIDE SPINDRIFT the night was chilly, with a breeze peeling off the barren stone. They carried John Salters's body through the moonlight reflecting off the exterior laboratory wall. A security lamp popped on without warning, pinning them like moths to a sheet. They shuffled out of that light, carting the corpse west toward the island's unseen rim.

"Is he for sure dead?" Teddy heard himself ask. "Shouldn't one of us check?"

Hugo said, "I've seen dead. He's dead."

The moon limned the lethal contours of the rock. The wind hit Teddy full in the chest, needling through his clothing.

"Here," said Claire, pointing ahead of them.

They reached a spot where the rock dropped sheer in a forty-foot plummet to the cold surf below.

"We throw him over," she said. "The current will carry his body away."

Teddy said: "How can we be sure? You're some expert on water currents?"

"If not, it'll sink. Or get eaten by something." She thought a moment. "Even if not, if someone finds it, then he got drunk and fell off the cliff and drowned. Whatever happened, we don't know anything about anything."

It unnerved Teddy how easily Claire's mind bent around these hazards. She and Hugo had this whole bargain-bin Bonnie and Clyde act going on.

"On the count of three," Claire ordered. "Teddy, you better help us. We want all of our fingerprints on the body, to make sure we're all in it together."

Following Claire's order, Teddy gripped one of John's feet in nerveless fingers. Together they got the body swinging—the deadweight sickened Teddy; he couldn't wait to let go.

"One . . . two . . . *three.*"

They heaved the remains of John Salters down the rocks. The body struck the cliff once, making a sound that Teddy expected he'd hear the rest of his unnatural life.

The splash had the doomy note of a door slamming shut. It was too dark to see much, and the starlight playing off the water was no help.

"We're in it now," said Claire. "Together forever, until the very end."

The three of them snuck back into the lab. They decided to leave the door they'd carried the body through open. Maybe it was John who'd left it that way? If so, then it was as Claire said: he'd gone out for a midnight stroll with half a skinful and something grim had befallen him. He'd misjudged the island's edge—the moonlight did funny things, and Indians, sadly, had well-known problems with the bottle . . .

On their way back through the lab, Teddy spotted something.

"It's one of the wolves."

It sat in a specimen cage not far from the garage. Teddy didn't know which one it was, but it must've been what was making those scratching sounds Teddy had heard earlier. When they approached, the wolf regarded them with solemn disinterest.

"We should let it go," Teddy said.

Hugo said: "Why?"

"A distraction," Teddy reasoned. "Maybe John let it out before disappearing."

"You do it, then."

Claire and Hugo backed away while Teddy unlatched the cage. The wolf nosed the door until it swung open wide enough for it to slink out.

They regarded one another, Teddy and that wolf.

It dismissed him with seeming prejudice and loped off into the outdoors.

THE WATER surrounding the island was tricky, its currents playful.

Had John Salters been thrown from the lee side of the island, the current may have carried his corpse into the wide throat of the system. There it would have tossed like flotsam, washing aground on a far-off island to dry in the sun like a sand dollar, unseen and unremarked.

Had it been dropped along the southern flank, the body could have circuited the hub for a mile or more as the current toyed with it, fanning through its hair and running into and out of its slack mouth as it was buffeted gently against the shoreline. Eddies may have tugged one or both of its boots off, and the bare toes may've been bitten by the inquisitive fish inhabiting those shallow bays. The waves could have carried it around to a partially submerged shelf near the boathouse, where it may have been discovered by Moses Squires.

Had that been the case, this might have ended much differently.

But when it was slung from the cliffs ranging the western edge of the island, the body splashed into a stony half-moon bay that trapped the current and cycled it inward. What was claimed by that enclosed area of water rarely left. Instead, it would circuit endlessly, the waves taking it out to where it might get snatched by the undertows transiting these island chains . . . but some force always drew it back in a manner that seemed almost covetous, though of course water had no such agency.

Such would be the fate of John Salters's corpse. Floating with the current, it coasted gently round the bay. Had anyone looked, they may have seen him down there: waterlogged but still buoyant, legs splayed and hands spread like two bleached starfish.

In the early-morning hours, the body would be drawn under a shelf carved into the base of the cliffs. A dark pocket chewed out by the endlessly gnawing water. It would get snagged under that cool dripping shelf, waiting to play its part in what was to come.

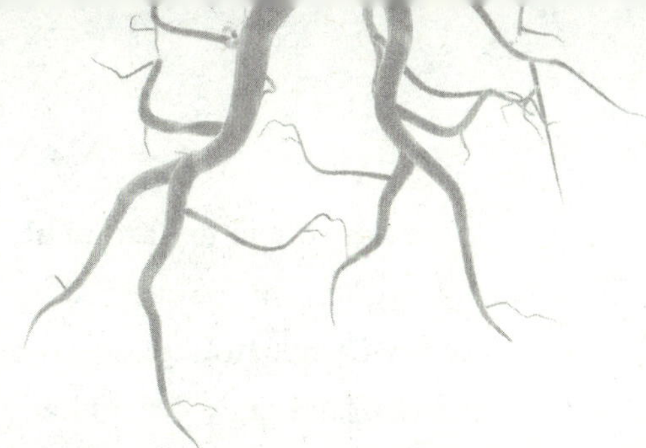

III. *Anno Hydra,* Day 66

FRANK DOYLE stood in the common room with the others the next morning, shuffling foot to foot. The air was charged with something volatile; it percolated in the manner of sour gas building up in a wellhead, begging for a spark.

Dr. Strauss had assembled everyone before breakfast. Astrid, Ingrid, and Moses Squires were there, too.

"Has anyone seen John Salters?"

Strauss wore a grave countenance, but not quite so grave as Moses.

"Why? Has something happened?" Frank asked.

He didn't care for the way Teddy and the other two were behaving. Hugo lounging hipshot against the wall; Claire leaning next to him with her hands sunk in the pockets of her overalls. Teddy sitting on the kitchenette countertop, one leg dangling and the other one bent, his chin resting on his knee . . . they had the look of dime-store delinquents malingering outside a pool hall.

Everything's aaaall cool. I don't know what the hassle is, man.

When Frank realized that's what it had to be—an act—it stirred fear in him. *What did you do last night, Teddy? What did you and those two get up to?*

"John normally sleeps in the bunkie out by the enclosure," Strauss said, picking nervously at the sleeve of her sweater. "But last night, he didn't come back."

"He set an alarm," Moses said. "To get up and check on the wolf."

Moses had always struck Frank as unflappable, but he seemed on edge this morning. *Chewing nails and spitting rivets,* as Frank's father liked to say.

"Were any of you up last night?" Strauss's pinched gaze belied the lightness of her question. "Awakened by a nightmare, maybe?"

The five of them looked at one another, waiting for someone to fess up.

Finally, Claire said: "I slept like a baby."

"I only got up to use the toilet," Maddy said.

Teddy said: "Yeah, I took a piss, too. But I didn't leave my room."

That's lie number one, Frank thought.

Strauss said: "Last night, the lab's rear door was opened. The system logged it. We had a wolf near that door, in a quarantine cage. Sometime last night, that animal's cage was opened . . . or the wolf managed to open it by itself, though that possibility seems slim."

"Or John let the wolf out before . . ." Claire trailed off with a *Who knows* shrug.

"*What* wolf?" Maddy said. "Shouldn't they be in the pen, far away from the lab?"

Moses uttered a harsh bark. "Should be, but the one in the lab was no longer as nature intended it to be." Tense-jawed, he seemed to debate before saying: "It's not the only one that's gone unnatural, either."

"Mr. Squires . . ." Astrid said, warning in her voice.

"Unnatural in what way?" This from Hugo.

"Cage door was open, wolf's gone, John's gone," Moses itemized. "Why would he let that wolf out? He knows as well as I do the harm it could cause."

"What harm, though?" Maddy said. "I share your concern about John, honestly I do—but what do you mean about the wolf being not quite right?"

Moses glanced at Marsh and Strauss. "Look—either you tell them, or I do."

Astrid let out a breath. "The Hydra was discovered in a second wolf. One of the females."

Ingrid wheeled on her friend. "*Astrid!*"

Frank couldn't get a grip on this fact. His mind was too leaden to make the connection.

"Wait, how in God's name could *that* have happened?" Maddy asked, throttle-voiced.

Astrid tried to explain: "The Hydra appears to have . . . *migrated*. From the original subject. Maybe direct contact, skin to skin. Or perhaps the equivalent of a spore."

Frank didn't care for that word: *spore*. It conjured images of a body covered in blue orbs like giant blisters, filled with the teeming tendrils of the Hydra.

"If the original wolf can transmit the Hydra," Ingrid reasoned, "that means *any* living thing with a Hydra in it may be capable of doing the same."

"Yes," Astrid acknowledged. "From what we now know, it seems possible."

"What we don't know yet," Strauss added, "is if the migration was accidental, caused by random contact . . . or if the initial wolf subject *purposefully intended* to spread the Hydra—"

"Or if the Hydra made that decision on its own," Ingrid cut in.

Strauss's face went ashen at the prospect. "Which is why we need to suspend the entire project for the moment while we sort this all out."

"How long will it take you to get your shit together?" Claire asked.

"More important right now is John's whereabouts," Strauss told them. "He could be hurt."

"He could've gotten drunk and wandered off someplace," Hugo shot back.

Moses jabbed a finger at Hugo. "John doesn't drink. Hasn't for years."

Archly, Claire said: "Falling off the wagon can be a *long* fall."

"That's true," Teddy said, almost reluctantly. "Take it from someone who knows."

"If John was in the lab last night," Maddy said, throwing up her hands, "how could any of us have seen him?"

Frank heard himself say: "*Enough.*"

When Teddy's eyes met his, they held the gleam of a hunted animal.

"I'm not keeping this secret," Frank told Teddy evenly. "Not when it's this important." Frank let his eyes roll up to the ceiling. "There were intruders in the lab last night."

Teddy yelped: "You *weasel*!"

Astrid said: "Who?"

"You snake in the grass! Fucking playground tattletale!"

Ignoring Teddy, Frank said: "Those three."

Frank singled out Claire, Hugo, and Teddy. Almost instantly, a frostiness settled between him and the trio. He'd been summarily exiled from the Cool Kids Club. Something about that stung him, even though he was far too old that he should care.

"Oh really. And just what were you doing in my lab?" Astrid said, deathly soft.

No response. When they all refused to confess, Frank said: "The stem, Dr. Marsh."

Claire snarled: "Why don't you just shut the fuck up, *Frank*? Before—"

"Before what?" Frank narrowed his eyes. "What are you going to do to me?"

Claire's hands balled into fists, two rigid bulges in her overalls pockets. Frank was glad there were some bodies between them, because Claire looked about ready to rip his head off.

Strauss said: "I take it they asked you to come along?"

Frank answered her with a nod. "But I changed my mind."

"And what about you, Maddy?"

"Guess I'm the odd one out," she said, sounding oddly lacerated. "This is the first *I'm* hearing about it."

"Okay then—you three. What about the stem?" Strauss pressed.

Teddy mumbled something.

"Speak up!" Astrid's voice rose to a fire-and-brimstone Old Testament pitch. "Admit your trespasses, all of you!"

"We ate it," Teddy said, and Frank could swear that the man was actually sulking.

"Congratulations, then," Astrid said, "on choosing the *least* effective method! You know you're going to shit most of it out, right? None of it will go where it can be of any benefit that—"

Her neck cabling with pent-up rage, Claire erupted. "You shouldn't have cut off our supply, you ass*holes*!"

Blue skeins rose, racing across Claire's cheeks as the Hydra surfaced over her skin. Her rage was terrifying. Nothing remained of the shy elderly woman Frank had befriended two months ago. The woman who'd walked with a stiff bent-over posture and made apple dolls for the VFW Fall Craft Show. Claire Blessings was now powerful and horrible in her wrath.

"Yeah, we were in the lab," Hugo said with a shrug: *No biggie.* "And yeah, we ate some of the stem."

"But we didn't see hide nor hair of John," Teddy said, sounding sincere.

Moses cut over the chatter. "Okay, here's what's going to happen."

When he strode forward, Frank noticed that Moses had a pistol buckled to his belt. He couldn't remember seeing him carrying a sidearm before.

"I'm going to go look for my friend. I know John. I know his wife and kids. I owe him. Who I *don't* owe *anything* to"—the disgust coming off Moses could choke a horse—"is any one of you freaks."

"Who are you calling a freak?" Claire said. "Oh wait, I get it—you don't like us much, do you? You and John are just two peas in a pod."

"If I don't find him by tomorrow morning," Moses went on, choosing to ignore whatever Claire had just invoked, "I'm taking the boat to the mainland. I'll get the police. A search team, sniffer dogs, the whole shebang. I don't care what that means to the project. I don't care about the money I forfeit or the NDA I signed."

He then addressed Astrid directly. "And I *especially* don't care what you do to yourself, if I disobey. That threat doesn't carry water with me."

"I think you've made yourself very clear," Astrid told him squarely. "But remember, if the authorities come, then the ones bankrolling all this will arrive shortly afterward. They'll shut this place down. So, you'll likely be signing five death warrants."

"That honestly doesn't mean shit to me, either," Moses stated. "They all wanted to die anyway, before you ever even reached out to them."

Hitching up his belt, Moses made for the door. "Anyone who wants to help is welcome. We can cover the island in a grid. Either way, twenty-four hours, starting right now."

SHORTLY AFTER Moses went off to search for his partner, the doctors returned to the lab. Their departure left the subjects with no choice but to retreat to their rooms.

As soon as they were alone, Teddy gave Frank a bone-jolting shove.

"You goddamn Benedict Arnold!"

Teddy grabbed Frank and pinned him against the hallway wall, forearm jammed up under his chin. "You're a *snitch*. If this was prison, I'd have to gut you like a fish."

Frank corralled Teddy's wrist and bent it back as hard as he could. With a croak, Teddy released his choke hold.

"You just try, Teddy," Frank rasped, rubbing his neck. "See how it goes for you."

Claire's voice cut over their bickering. "You can all feel it, can't you?" She held her hands out as evidence. "These wrinkles? They weren't there yesterday. They weren't there a few *hours* ago." Gripping Frank's elbow, Claire's eyes tunneled into his. "It's eating us, *Frank*. It's eating our *youth*. Taking back the years it gave us, with interest."

Suddenly the hallway felt too tight; it had narrowed to a kill chute funneling cattle toward the bolt gun. Frank's own hands . . . wait, *had* those wrinkles been there earlier? Good Christ, was Claire right? Suddenly there was something oracular to her pronouncements. Hugo hung on her every word—and increasingly, so did Teddy.

"We need to find John," Maddy said, gripping Frank's other elbow. Frank was strung between the two women, a human wishbone.

Claire said: "Oh, who cares about him? He'll turn up."

"Were you always such a selfish bitch?" Maddy asked her.

"Oh, Maddy, look at you," Claire purred, drawing a circle in the air where Madeline's face sat. "You're younger, but not any *prettier*. You still have an old-lady face. Isn't that *sad*?" she said, turning to Teddy and Hugo. "It's your soul, that's what I think. It's so dried-up and fossilized that you're past helping. You're always going to be a barren . . . old . . . *hag*."

Frank shook free of Claire. He shifted to a position favoring Maddy. The other three stood in a rough triangle. Battle lines had been drawn, subtly but solidly.

"You could be right, you know," Maddy said, her head cocked and her chin uptilted. "But if Moses finds something on his search—and I'm going to help him; I think it's the moral thing to do . . . if he discovers you had anything to do with it, he might just pull that pistol and plug one right between those pretty brown eyes of yours, Claire, my *dear*."

Hugo lurched toward Maddy. She took a step back. For an awful moment, Frank was certain Hugo would clout Maddy, and then Frank would have no choice but to fight him. Instead, Claire settled her fingers on Hugo's forearm. It was enough to calm the big fella.

"And hey, Moses will plant a bullet between your eyes, too, Hugo," Maddy went on. "And yeah, Teddy, even yours. So you'd better hope that John's found safe and sound . . . if not, at least you'll all leave good-looking corpses lined up in your caskets."

Claire smiled sweetly. Frank could swear she was enjoying all this. He thought Maddy might be, too.

"I'll remember you said that, Madeline," Claire purred. "When the time comes."

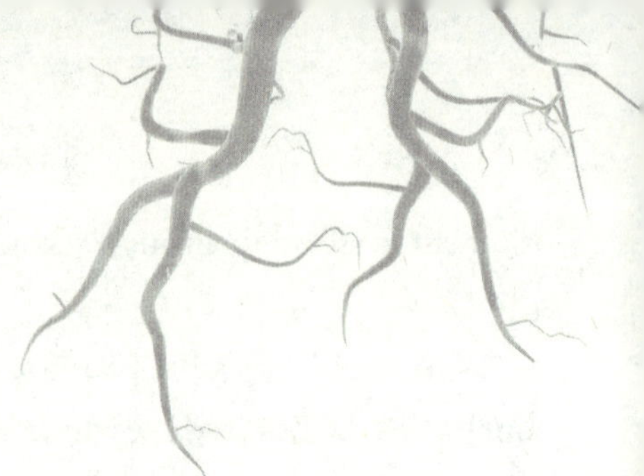

IV. *Anno Hydra*, Day 66 (Late Afternoon)

. . . OOOOH you bitches you meddlesome bitches you cunts you can't DO THIS it's not FAIR I'll kill you I'll fucking KILL YOU BOTH if you don't give me back what I deserve . . .

These thoughts—edging steadily into murderousness—cycled through Claire Blessings's brain.

. . . CHEATERS dirty rotten liars scumbag LIARS and not nice, not nice ladies didn't your mothers raise you to be NICE, no, they couldn't have because you're just FILTH, shit on my shoe . . .

Maybe the thoughts were hers at the outset, but something within her took them and accelerated them. Ran them through an atom smasher in her brain. They exited as plutonium-enriched ramblings that ping-ponged around her skull.

. . . Astrid bitch one Veronica bitch two a pair of RAGING bitches don't care about nobody but themselves and Strauss is the worst because she's supposed to be the conscience but she's a coward she'd let us all wither away to husks if she died nobody would miss her the world would be a better place with her gone Veronica Strauss DESERVES to die . . .

These thoughts developed the rhythm of a monkish chant. Claire tried to bite down on them so she could think straight. She let go an inhuman little laugh that sounded like the *snap-snap* of a chattery-teeth windup toy. The hysterical notes echoed off the roof of the boathouse.

She'd come down there with Hugo in tow. They'd refused to join the search for John Salters. What would be the point? Claire wished it hadn't happened like that—the snap of John's neck as it broke still rang in her ears—but she stood by Hugo's decision. Could you even call it that? More like Hugo, much like John Salters's neck, had simply . . . snapped.

Claire had debated joining the search if only to subtly steer anyone away from the cliffs where they'd tossed John over. But as soon as she'd seen Moses—joined by Frank and Maddy, those Goody Two-shoes—go marching off along the eastern skirt of the island, the exact opposite direction of where John's body might be floating, Claire exhaled. By the time they rounded back to that particular cliff face, the sky would be getting dark. Night drew down by six o'clock these days, like a blanket thrown over a canary's cage. By then it would be too inky to see John's body even if it was bobbing in the water like a bloaty old cork.

Claire had left Teddy to sulk by himself in the main building. She hadn't bothered asking him along with her and Hugo. Teddy talked a big game, but at heart the guy was as spineless as a May daffodil.

"I'll take the battery out of this one."

Hugo clambered into the cedar boat, the smaller of the two craft in the boathouse. Claire couldn't help noticing how badly he stooped. His spine was on its way back to becoming the shepherd's crook it had once been. In the thin electrical light of the boathouse, her own skin was fissured with fresh wrinkles.

We're rapidly going back to what we were. A bunch of sick old wrecks.

This wasn't her anxious imagination. She could feel it as a concrete fact. The thing inside of her was *screaming*. The sound it made was of TV static: a television in a dark room turned up to full volume. She could feel it inside of her now . . . *wanting*. It was that part, the *want*, that was hardest to deal with. The Hydra's desire was utterly alien. It wasn't the want of a child for a shiny new bicycle, or how a cold body wants a warm bed—or how Claire had wanted, not so long ago, to die with a little goddamn dignity. The Hydra didn't *want* in any understandably human way. More like a plant for sunshine, or a termite for tree pulp. A subhuman want, a sub-*bestial* want, and it only made her aware of just how strong this thing inside of her had become.

Why fight it, then? This is what you want, Claire, isn't it?

The last little while, she'd started to hear a voice in all that head static. It blipped through the crackling hiss at random points, coldly demanding, speaking words that sent acidic wires through her bloodstream.

She thought eating the stem might shut that voice up, but no. It was like a hole with no bottom: the more you put into it, the emptier it got. It was eating her alive, wasn't it? Scraping her clean from the inside out until she was nothing but an empty shell—a papier-mâché balloon.

Concentrating on Hugo again, Claire watched him unclip two plugs and heave the battery out of the boat. "Should I drop it in the water?"

Claire said, "Better not. Let's hide it. We may need it later."

They snuck outside, around the edge of the boathouse. Up in the main building, pinpricks of light burned against the onrushing dark.

Enjoy it while you can, Claire thought.

Thought, or *gloated*? The possibility came to Claire—not for the first time—that she wasn't a very good person. Had she really *ever* been? It was disorienting, because she'd always felt herself to be essentially decent. If some moral accountant's firm scrutinized her history with a dry eye, she was sure they would be forced to conclude the same.

But what if she'd only been missing the right opportunity, and now, with a doorway creaking open, Claire had the chance to flower into evilness? Even before John's death, she knew she'd willingly follow one vile act with another—whatever it took. She understood the mentality behind a crime spree now: once you've robbed the bank, why not steal a getaway car? Why not shoot the owner of that car if he tries to stop you? Why not race down a sidewalk plowing through pedestrians if the cops are in pursuit, and why not kill as many policemen as you can if you get cornered?

At a certain point, and sooner than you'd guess, it ceases to matter *how far* you go.

They stashed the battery in a dark crevice under a knot of pines. Hugo ripped up handfuls of moss to cover it. When they returned to the boathouse, Hugo climbed aboard the bigger boat. He fiddled around with the console.

"Grab that hatchet off the bench over there," he said to her. When she brought it, he used the blade to pry off the outboard motor cover and fiddled around with the wires . . . the motor caught with an earthy rumble. He grinned at her, holding out his hand.

"Welcome aboard."

"*Enchanté.*"

Hugo knew all sorts of wonderful tricks, learned back in his sad old, bad old days. He'd told Claire bits and pieces about that side of his life. Hugo was mushily confessional after sex, lying drained beside her in bed.

There's something evil in me, Claire . . . maybe it's this place, I don't know anymore.

She forgave Hugo for every admission the moment they passed his lips. We all had pasts, and those pasts were inevitably haunted by ghosts. But they didn't have to scare them now, and they certainly didn't need to define them in the future.

Hugo eased the boat out from under the boathouse's awning, the engine purring against the black water. It was best if nobody saw them out here. Darkness hung over the island as Hugo steered them around the hub. He locked them on course and pushed a button on the console. The anchor dropped, its chain rattling over the gunwale.

"Now we'll drag it along and see if it catches the cable."

Hugo was full of great ideas that would never have popped into Claire's head, not in a month of Sundays. Claire had worked as a cashier at Loblaws for nearly thirty years. She had memorized the price-look-up code to every bit of fruit and produce, even the exotic ones—dragon fruit, 3319; fiddleheads, 4406—but all of this impishness was not her bag. Now, Hugo? Oh, very much his bag.

On the one hand, Claire realized she was taking advantage of him. She'd hooked him through the crotch first, and after that, through the brain. Yet on the other hand, she genuinely liked Hugo. Loved him, even, possibly . . . ? No, this wasn't love. But didn't they still have this *now*—wasn't that worth celebrating?

When Claire next looked at Hugo, he was leaning overboard. His handsome face was filled with dread.

"What is it?"

His arms trembled. His mouth stretched into a ragged leer.

Oh, Sweet Mother of Christ, Claire thought. *Again with this.*

"*Hugo.* She's not there. Summer's not down under the water."

Hugo saw her more and more with each passing hour. His dead daughter.

You remember that old skit on Laugh-In? *he'd told her a few days ago. The one where the telephone operator—the old kind, where she's got plugs and a plugboard to complete the connections? She keeps connecting everyone wrong. The baker gets wired in to the funeral parlor. The parish priest gets connected to the veterinarian. I remember giggling like hell when I watched it, but now . . . that's how everything feels. My history's getting all cross-wired. The past keeps stepping into the present and I can't tell any of it apart.*

As the wavelets chopped against the boat's hull, Claire took a firm grip on Hugo's shoulder. Her fingernails dug into the meat.

"Snap out of it, damn it. She's *not* down there."

Hugo was becoming somewhat unreliable. Claire had to resist the urge to slap him.

"Do you . . . do you think I killed her?" he asked.

"No," she said, softened by the boyish cast of his eyes. "But you can't bring her back, either. There's freedom in that, isn't there? There's no depth you can't sink to that's going to matter anymore."

The boat heaved up as the anchor snagged something in the water; a watery shriek carried up through the black fathoms beneath the hull.

"That could be it," said Hugo. "I'll check."

The winch retrieved the anchor, whining as it labored to haul something up with it . . .

"Ah-ha. There she is."

The anchor surfaced with a thick black waterproof cable looped over its bow. That would be the power cable for the main building—the electricity running to Spindrift, the assorted outbuildings, and everything else on the island. One big electric snake to power it all.

Hugo had been certain that the island must be fed by an offshore power source. There were no power lines or solar panels or wind turbines in sight, meaning there was no other way to provide the massive volume of juice the laboratory required.

Claire couldn't have anyone leaving the island, as Moses had threatened to do. Not just yet. No outbound communications, either. Claire figured a few days would be enough to get what she wanted, by whatever means necessary.

The cable was as thick around as a healthy sapling. Leaning on the anchor, Hugo was able to drag a few feet of it above the waterline.

"Hand me that towel and the hatchet," Hugo said.

He dried a patch of the cable with the towel. He then pulled on a pair of leather work gloves and gripped the tool's handle.

"Stand off," he told her, then laughed maniacally. "This could be curtains for us, babe."

The hatchet fell, cleaving the cable. Hugo levered it out—the split wiring sent spiderwebs of sparks skittering over the sheened cable coating—and brought it down again. The air filled with a dangerous alkaline taste as voltage flicked around them, racing down the gunwales of the boat with a popping crackle that lifted the hair straight off Claire's scalp.

Hugo brought the hatchet down a final time, then tossed it overboard and hit the anchor button. The winch let go, carrying the cable down into the depths. Electricity arched through the water in volcanic strobes that crackled thunderously against the hull of the boat; the water lit up in a trillion snapping, spitting skeins, which to Claire resembled her idea of the Hydra itself, how it lived and hungered inside her body.

The night grew dark and still. Up the hillside, the main building was now a cube of pure blackness.

Claire said: "Hugo, you brilliant bastard."

She caught the smell of burnt rubber. Lifting her boot, she watched the sole stretch in taffy-like runners. The voltage must have melted them.

Hugo's boots had done the same. They laughed, shaking with relief. Below them, the water had gone full dark. Even the stars didn't reflect on its surface. Hugo swung the boat around and headed back to the dock.

"Smells like rain," he remarked.

UPON THEIR arrival at the boathouse, they let their ears attune. No sound drifted down to them from the main building. It felt unwise to return just yet. Better to let the doctors face their new situation and get anxious.

Hugo let Claire off onshore and then angled the boat's nose toward that ever-rotating red light marking the vague direction of home. Knotting a rope around the wheel to hold its course, he set the engine in gear.

He hopped off, getting only a little wet. They watched the boat chart a course into the water system. Above them, the heavens were scalloped with the overlapping colors of the northern lights. The depthless quality of their radiance unlocked something in Claire.

"Look."

Hugo was staring at her fingers. What she saw there managed to fill her with both horror and wonderment.

The Hydra was truly visible now, streaming out of her fingertips in tendrils matching the blue of the lights. There was no blood, no pain, only an itch someplace in her brain. If anything, it felt like a natural extension—something innate to her being that was now clamoring toward the liquid shimmering of the lights . . .

But *oooooh*, the appetite.

I will never have a funeral, Claire thought with a mingling of astonishment and misgiving. *My next of kin will never sit in a sad room stinking of carpet freshener, musty coats hung on pegs in the alcove, canes and walkers with tennis ball bumpers and the dull hiss of canned oxygen, a K-Tel recording of "Closer My Lord to Thee," thin lips droning inane tributes into a scratchy microphone—reception to follow, thick-soled shoes on threadbare carpet, Sanka coffee and choco-wafers on Styrofoam plates, every mourner home in time to catch the five o'clock news . . . that will never be my fate, will it?*

She grabbed at Hugo's hand. A heartbeat later, he let her have it.

The boat had plenty of gas. It would go a long way before reaching landfall. A drop of rain fell from that beatific sky to splash her upturned face.

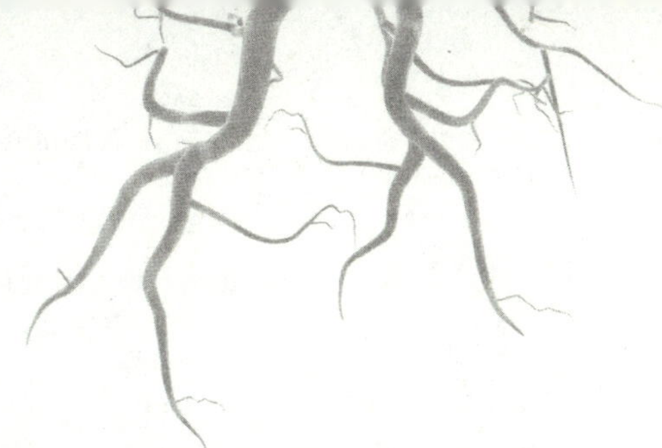

V. *Anno Hydra*, Day 66 (night)

FRANK, MADDY, Teddy, Ingrid, and Astrid sat in the common room. Emergency lamps burned on the table and countertop. It was all anyone had been able to scavenge since the power had abruptly conked out half an hour ago.

Ten hours had now passed since the tense meeting that morning, when Moses had threatened to alert the police. The rest of the day into the early evening had been spent searching.

Frank and Maddy had split from Moses around midday; together, the two of them had investigated the inlets and shallow slopes on the northeastern scrim of the island. Calling out for John, they steadily lost any hope of finding him. Reaching the electrical fence marking the wolves' enclosure, they had been forced to make their way back toward the home base of Spindrift—although both would admit that it felt less like home with every passing minute.

"You don't really think they had anything to do with it?" Frank asked as he and Maddy trudged up the fence line. "Teddy and the other two, I mean?"

Maddy said, "I don't know anymore." She'd felt distant to Frank all afternoon, absorbed in thoughts she didn't care to share. "Something's changed. The tenor of it all."

It had, surely. That evening when they'd danced to oldies tunes could have happened several lifetimes ago.

"I hear you," Frank acknowledged, "but that doesn't mean anyone would go so far as to hurt John."

"I didn't say that."

Frank thought: *Yeah, but you didn't dismiss it out of hand.*

"How else could it have happened other than purposefully?" Maddy asked.

"I don't know," Frank glumly admitted. "Accidents happen."

"Not out here they don't."

The threat of rain had hung over the landscape by the time they'd rounded back to Spindrift. Encountering Astrid, Strauss, and Ingrid in the common room, they shared the unhappy news of not having seen a trace of John Salters. The group sought slim comfort in the hope that Moses would return with at least some sign of his friend. He was an experienced tracker, after all.

Astrid said, "If he doesn't find John, Moses *will* leave."

Her tone, her entire demeanor, put forth an unvoiced possibility: *Unless we don't allow him to go.*

"I don't care at this point," Strauss said. "Could be it's for the best."

Strauss directed her next words to Ingrid, Maddy, and Frank. "I've failed you. I should have been more proactive, more supportive . . . y'know, I only graduated eight years ago? I was one of those people who spent too long in school, working with hypotheticals. *Models* of behavior, not real people."

This seemed a most damning admission to her. "I am way out of my league. Have been from the minute I got here . . . and I think *you*"—she nodded to Astrid—"and *them*"—helicoptering one finger above her head, invoking the corporate boogeymen haunting the project from afar—"wanted it that way."

Astrid neither confirmed nor denied this. Strauss pressed on.

"I don't think anyone will come here to hurt any of you." She spoke this as if to convince herself. "I can't see why anybody would—"

That had been the moment when the power cut out. The common room lights had flickered, then ushered in a brown pall. For a heartbeat it seemed the electricity would rally before the room plunged into blackness.

The dark had sent Velcro spiders scurrying up Maddy's spine. She'd always hated blackouts, all the way back to childhood. Other kids loved them. Fetching candles from the cupboards, stoking a fire in the hearth—just like old-timey days! But to Maddy they were sinister interregnums, an invitation to a barbarity her young mind could barely define the outlines of . . . wasn't that how apocalypses began, with the power going out?

"Is it just out in here or all over?" she'd asked.

"I'll check," Strauss had replied as she'd stood and moved haltingly, barking her shin on something. "Ow—*shit!*"

Maddy had made her way to the common room door and felt her way down the hall, her fingers feathering the plaster. In the dark, every sound got amplified. It was amazing how much electricity and the devices that ran on it provided camouflage: the hum of fridges and laptops, the hush of air through ducts, each served to mask the sounds human ears tended to tune out. But now the building seemed alive in an ominous manner. Racing, skittering noises overhead. Something behind the walls, too, a low consumptive breathing . . .

. . . it was nothing. Maddy knew that, but still, this darkness now bulged with threats—oh, how her brain had regressed over these months, now able to conjure girlhood fears as sharp and pointy as rat's teeth . . . *rats, oh Lord . . .* rats in the walls, that's what it was, a brown mass of rats with red eyes and greasy licorice-whip tails that were set to chew through the drywall and pour out somewhere above her, pattering her upturned face like warm, squirming, fleshy raindrops . . .

Something touched her. A dancing pressure on her sternum that laddered up to her breast—

She screamed, striking out with her fist.

"Goddamn it, it's *me*! Teddy!"

Lightning split the darkness, filling the window at the end of the hall. In it, Maddy saw Teddy in front of her, rubbing his jaw.

"Teddy, for God's sake. Even stone-blind, you're a letch."

"Where is everyone?" he asked as blackness resettled in the hall.

"Common room."

Together, they traced their way back. By then Strauss had located a battery-powered hurricane lamp from the supply closet. Ingrid joined with a second lamp.

The clouds split as the storm built to a gale. Wind shrieked around Spindrift's unforgiving angles, a nervy sound, the lash of an enormous whip. Lightning forked across the common room skylight, and almost at once, thunder pealed with a concussive note that rolled out across the water.

"That's close," Teddy said. "One mile equals five seconds, I always heard. If you hear thunder ten seconds after a lightning strike, it means it hit two miles away. That one was right on top of us."

MOSES HAD arrived ten minutes later, his shape obscured behind the glare of a flashlight as he entered the common room. Without the hum of electricity, the building lay silent as the grave. Rain tap-danced on the roof in an irregular, gusting rhythm.

"Did you see Claire and Hugo anywhere?" Dr. Strauss asked him.

Moses shook rainwater off his slicker. "You're saying they aren't here?"

"They ain't," Frank said. "Nobody's seen them for hours."

"Maybe they've been kicking up the dickens, then. Boats are gone," Moses announced.

"*Both* of them?" Teddy asked him, receiving a clipped nod from Moses.

"You don't think Hugo and Claire could have . . . ?" Strauss trailed off.

Moses's jaw was rigid. "You said you haven't seen 'em. I'd say idle hands."

Moses's mood had changed since that morning, from sourness to a deep mistrust. Though Maddy couldn't be sure, perhaps the seriousness of their situation—if the power stayed out and the boats couldn't be located, not to mention John's disappearance—had settled into him, altering his perspective. This was a man who'd seen hard times, and this situation was ballooning out of control, far bigger than his missing friend now. Moses had a family, too.

"The storm knock the power out?" he asked.

"I'm guessing so," said Astrid.

"I'm not so sure about that," said Teddy. "As far as I could tell, the power went out *before* the storm really had a chance to get going."

They sat with this. Teddy's timing felt right.

"There's an emergency generator," Moses said. "It's a few miles from here."

"Why so far away?" Strauss asked.

"Probably for a contingency of this sort," Moses replied. "So a bad storm didn't knock the power and the backup generator out at the same time. The generator cable runs through solid rock, grounded and safe."

"Would that genny be enough to get the whole shebang up and running?" asked Teddy.

"It ought to be. The important bits, anyway." Moses turned to Strauss. "As soon as the juice comes back on, you need to reach out to the mainland. We both know she won't do it." He hooked his thumb at Astrid. "I'm counting on you to be the adult in the room."

"Don't worry, I will be."

"Shouldn't take me more than a few hours to get it going, depending," Moses guessed.

Astrid said: "On what?"

His look was grim. "With the power out, that fence isn't electrified any-more." Moses could only mean the one hemming in the wolves' enclosure. "So, you keep everything locked up here, okay? It's not just the wolves we need to worry about."

Maddy pictured Claire and Hugo out there in the night, hunched under a rocky ledge as the storm raged . . . the starved, lunatic smiles on their faces.

"I'd like to come with you," she said.

Frank stepped up beside her. "Me too."

With a stagy sigh, Teddy joined them. "Screw it. Me too, if you'll have me."

To Maddy's surprise, Moses said, "I could use the extra hands. We'll need to get you outfitted." He jerked his head, indicating that they should follow.

At the door, Moses turned back to Strauss. "Cover your ass while I'm gone, Veronica. I mean it. I need you."

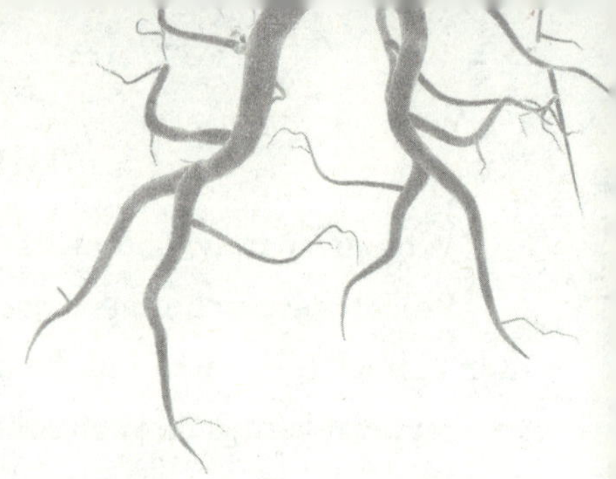

VI. *Anno Hydra*, Day 66 (night, continued)

FOUR SHAPES stepped from the double doors fronting the main entry of Spindrift. The rain collected along the slate overhang, dropping in a sheer sheet. Shoulders hunched, the foursome pushed through the curtain of rainwater into the enveloping night.

Lightning strobed over the nearest island. Its brilliance illuminated a quartet of faces, pale under their sou'westers. Avoiding the stairs leading down to the boathouse—which was now a brooding box of shadows at the waterline—they circuited the rounded belly of the lab, their boots slapping in puddles collected in the rock hollows.

"Can't we take the Rover?" Frank had to shout to make himself heard over the pelting rain. "At least to the wolves' fence?"

"Too treacherous!" Moses shook his head. "Liable to hydroplane right off the path!"

The blasting wind caught Frank full force, plastering his rain slicker to his chest and blowing the shell out in a bell shape. He staggered back into Teddy, who propped him up.

"Thanks," Frank mumbled, rain trickling off the back of his sou'wester to soak his neck.

"Welcome," Teddy said stiffly.

They'd barely walked three hundred yards and already Frank was exhausted. He wouldn't have felt the same a few days ago, but without their Baths . . .

Maddy sidled up next to him. Her hand went around his waist as she slipped something under his slicker. His hand wrapped around it . . . a butter knife?

Discreetly, Maddy's hand appeared under her own slicker. Blood welled in her palm, turning watery in the rain rinsing down her wrist.

"It helps," she promised. "Just try it. You'll need it."

The three of them followed Moses down a trail only he was able to see: a muddy meander over smooth delineations of rock, topped with the starved-looking pines that grew nearest the shoreline. As they trudged along, Frank raked the butter knife over his palm. No, that wasn't quite hard enough. He had to really *commit*.

Pressing the dull teeth of the knife into the webbing between his index finger and thumb, he gave a hard jerk. A rip of pain, so fierce he nearly dropped the knife. Oh, *that* did it.

His thoughts sharpened. His legs felt less like cement plugs.

He investigated the wound without looking at it, just feeling with his opposite hand. A ragged mouth in the webbing, not deep but bleeding freely . . . he pulled his fingers apart to widen the wound. The pain concretized his thoughts. The Hydra was active within him again.

Hello, old friend. I see you've woken up.

Moses crow-hopped down a hillside. Maddy followed, then Teddy, with Frank bringing up the rear. He tripped on an exposed root knuckling across the rocks, nearly fell, kept on. He gazed back up the hill at the torrential rain that needled into his eyes . . . the main building was gone. No stars and no moon. Nothing but the blanket of night, pulsating against his skin like the battering of moth wings. There came a crippling and somehow lunar isolation that clung to Frank until he was able to carve Maddy and Moses from the darkness ahead of him.

The wolves' enclosure rose unbidden out of the storm. Moses went around to the gate, his shape warping under the volleys of rainwater. Nothing felt quite right anymore, did it? It wasn't just the storm—which had taken on a biblical feel—or the night. The island and everything on it now felt unnatural to Frank. Stupidly (why was he letting his thoughts race away at the worst time?) he imagined everything getting swept away: the lab, Astrid's work, and all of them. And this was a *cheery* thought. Or would be, except Frank saw the death-proof creation inside him . . . saw it surviving. The Hydra crawling out of Frank's drowned corpse where it had gotten wedged in an underwater crevice, a death-less blue strand slipping into a fish, which gets caught and eaten, the Hydra moving through fish and fisherman and the fisherman's family, inside all creatures great and small . . . and none of them can die. Life eternal, forever and ever—

The foursome followed along the fence in a tight knot. No voltage kicked off the metal links. There was nothing protective between them and the toothy occupants on the other side. Moses shouted: "Generator's another mile ahead, maybe a bit farther, but—"

That was as much as Frank heard before Moses's words got whipped away by the gale.

The rain slanted sideways. Each drop stung Frank's face like the jab of a sewing needle as he walked resolutely into it. A sense of finality had settled into his bones.

Moses stopped for a second to reposition their party, placing himself in the middle with Teddy and Maddy to either side and Frank protecting his flank.

"They won't do anything to you!" he shouted. "It's me they'd want!"

It took a moment to clue in to what Moses had done. He'd grouped them like a human shield of sorts—a barrier against the wolves.

The wind switched directions, buffeting them from the side, now from behind, now clubbing into their chests. Thunder crunched above them like the winding of a great gearbox in the sky. Frank had to grab hold of the fence to stay upright. He scanned the woods past the links for signs of the wolves—he saw only liquid shiftings in the rain-washed night, things his civilized mind dismissed as nothing. Wouldn't the wolves be pinned down someplace, waiting out the storm? Or was this the best time for beasts to hunt, when the prey was disoriented?

By the time they reached the part of the fence where it curved back inland, the rain had tapered off a bit. Still, it didn't feel like the storm was over; more like an orchestra taking five before rising into the next movement.

They forged onto a plane of rock overlooking the water. Wind screamed across the exposure, making their rain slickers ripple and flap.

"There!"

Moses pointed to a squat box foregrounded against the churning water.

It was a wonder he'd seen it, but its straight angles distinguished it from the twisted landscape.

They made it to a cement pillbox roughly the size and shape of a garden shed. Its walls provided some shelter from the wind, which continued to scream even as the rain abated. The door was held fast by a padlock.

"Do you have the key?" Maddy asked.

Moses shrugged his pack off. "No, but never mind." He reached into the pack and pulled out a crowbar.

Threading the crowbar through the lock's hackle, Moses adjusted the tool to maximize the fulcrum—the hinge squealed as the screws peeled out of the cement—

When the lock gave way, it caught Moses unprepared. He'd put all his weight on the crowbar, so when the hinge tore, the claw end came down like a hard-swung axe. It punched right through his slicker. Moses let out a surprised grunt and staggered back with the crowbar hanging out of his thigh.

Moses didn't say a word. He stood, inspecting what he'd done. The crowbar had punched into the big long muscle running from hip to knee.

"Get it out of you, man!" Teddy yelled.

Instead, Moses left the crowbar where it was. His voice was remarkably calm when he said: "Huh." He gave a gentle nod to the door. "It's open. Let's all go inside."

THE GENERATOR pillbox was dry and unlit. Moses shuffled in last and shut the door behind him. The crowbar just hung there, punched into his leg, penduluming ever so slightly as he swept his flashlight around the pillbox. The generator sat in a cemented depression. It was so new, so unused, that some of the parts still had shrink-wrap on them.

Moses rested against the generator. "One of you, get out your flashlight."

Frank grabbed his first. Flicking it on, he trained it along the walls until he located a switch beside the door. He flipped it. A battery-powered light bloomed above them. Their faces were stark-white and pitted by the rain. But Moses was the palest of them all.

Maddy held her hands out, drawing close to him. "Let me see, Moses. I'll be gentle."

"Don't you *touch* me!" Maddy froze. When Moses saw she meant to stay where she was, his tone softened. "I'm sorry, Madeline. But I'd rather you didn't."

"You're hurt bad," Frank said, a brazen statement of the obvious.

Moses nodded. "About the clumsiest, dopey-assed thing I've ever done. Couldn't have picked a worse time, either. Can one of you toss me my knife?"

Teddy fetched it from Moses's pack and slid it across the floor. Moses looked more confident with it in his hands.

He can defend himself against us now, Frank thought with a strange desolation.

Moses stabbed the tip through his slicker waist-high and slit it down to the top of the crowbar. He sucked air through his teeth. "Shit, wish I'd felt that a bit more."

Starting at the bottom of the slicker, Moses sliced upward to the bottom of the crowbar, then parted the wet rubber sheath to reveal his thigh.

"Good God, man," Teddy breathed.

The claw end of the crowbar was buried in Moses's thigh nearly to the bend. A good two inches of metal punched into his leg. The weave of his trousers had gone soppy with blood; it flowed over the upper of his boot and formed a watery pool on the concrete of the pillbox.

"I don't think I better take it out." Greasy balls of sweat dappled Moses's face. "Think I clipped an artery, so it's like the little Dutch boy with his finger in the dike."

"Let us help you," Maddy pled. "For pity's sake, Moses."

Bracing his palms on the generator, Moses beheld them all.

"Look," he said, "what I'm gonna say won't fix or change a thing. But someone owes you a little honesty." He winced. "That wolf, the first subject . . . it's not a wolf anymore. You know that, same as I do. And I think that wolf *knows* that it's not a wolf anymore, either." He regarded them head-on. "Or do you think I'm mistaken?"

Frank spoke up. "I think you're probably correct on that."

Moses nodded in a conciliatory way. "That wolf is now . . . I want to say angry, but that's not it. Wolves don't feel anger. But I do think it's aware of what it is now. That it's become *un*-wolf. Cut off the chain of its own nature."

"What are you trying to say?" Maddy asked. "Speak plainly."

"What I'm saying, Madeline, is that I wouldn't want my daughter to meet you."

Moses delivered this statement graven and tight-lipped. Frank couldn't imagine a more damning confession one person could make to another.

"Before, you were someone I'd have liked my girl to try to be like. But not now."

"Fine, if that's how you feel," Maddy said with the barest nod. "So how can I help without touching you?"

"You can get the generator going."

The next several minutes passed in a fruitless attempt to start the genny, with Moses directing from the sideline. His eyelids sagged, blood forming a concerningly wide puddle around his legs and feet.

"You've gotta . . . primer crank . . . should be plenty of gasoline in . . . the . . ."

"Do we need to siphon gasoline into the generator?" asked Teddy.

With a thick inhale, Moses tried to stand—his boots skidded on his blood, dumping him back down hard on his ass. A knot of blood burped from the hole in his leg, jetting around the crowbar. His trousers were now bubbly with the red stuff, a foam roller oversaturated with paint.

Teddy said, "You've got to tie that femoral vein off, *now*."

He unfastened his belt and tossed it over to Moses. Teddy's hands were shaking, but whether from worry or the return of his Parkinson's, Frank couldn't tell.

"Cinch it above the puncture," Teddy directed Moses. "Won't do any guh-g-good below."

"Thanks. There must be a crank handle for the genny . . . try that box over there."

Frank rooted around in a storage box and found the crank. Slotting it into the generator, his first revolution was rewarded with a gurgle as gasoline shunted into the primer receptacle.

Moses managed to stand up. The belt was looped around his thigh an inch above the crowbar. The man was clearly in incredible pain.

"You're gonna have to yank that belt like hell," Teddy said. "Sure I can't help?"

A grim nod. "You're damn right I'm sure."

Gripping the tongue of leather, Moses cinched the belt around his leg with slow, remorseless pressure. The belt compressed into his thigh, carving in like a huge rubber band as blood, so much of it, squeezed from his trousers, no different than water from a wrung sponge.

Moses set the prong into the leather and gave them a dreamy grin—then his knee gave out with a sickening *snick!*, a ligament letting go like an over-tuned guitar string. He fell soundlessly and hit the cement floor so hard he bounced; the end of the crowbar struck the concrete, sending a hellish tuning-fork vibration up the metal and into Moses's leg. He let out a muffled shriek and passed out from the shock.

At first, the three of them could only gape at Moses. He'd told them not to touch him. They would have preferred to honor the man's wishes. But his blood was trickling across the floor toward Frank's boots . . .

Maddy broke the inertia. She went over to Moses. Knelt beside him.

"Moses?" She glanced at Frank and Teddy. "It's bad. *Real* bad. If we don't get him seen to very quickly, he'll bleed to death." Her attention went back to Moses.

Teddy said, "Can we get the guh-g-genny going first? I mean, *shouldn't* we?"

Frank sneered at him. "Why did you even come with us, you skunk?"

Frank's accusation appeared to hit Teddy as a physical blow. "Am I the only one tuh-trying to thuh-think ruh-ruh-*rationally* here?" He ground his molars together, openly pissed at the return of his stutter. His gaze skated off the generator to settle back on Maddy and Moses.

Teddy's eyes widened in stark horror.

"Maddy," he said, his voice thickening. "Your . . . your *face*."

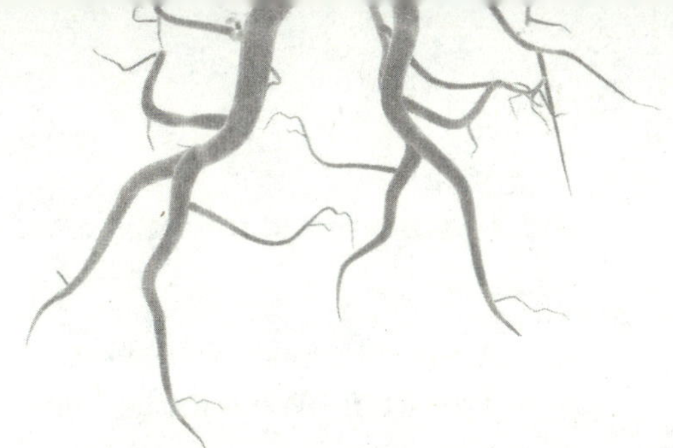

VII. Anno Hydra, Day 66 (night, continued)

INGRID LAY alone in the dark. With the power out, the heating system was off. Her room's temperature had plummeted, the cold creeping up each knob of her spine. After slackening for a while, the storm had ramped back up. Thunder pounded the building, each clap sounding as though it were ripping the sky apart.

Light crept under Ingrid's door, pooling across the floor of her room. Next, Astrid opened it without asking. She held a lantern before her, a lonely innkeeper.

"You awake?"

"Okay, come on in," Ingrid said. She struggled to keep that hint of antagonism out of her tone, but in this she failed.

"Oh, I'm sorry. May I come in?"

Ingrid kept her silence while Astrid sat on the edge of her bed. Her face hovered in the lantern beam.

"I didn't think I needed to ask," she said. "You can come to my room whenever you want, you know."

"Ast, this all feels . . . I'm worried, okay? We need the power back on."

Ingrid had never liked the dark, but she'd sincerely hated it since waking from a coma, where she'd been trapped in this same kind of darkness with only the witch for company.

Astrid patted the bedsheets. "Moses will figure it out."

An object in motion tends to remain in motion. A Newtonian principle Ingrid had learned a long time ago. It could go that way with situations, too:

once things started rolling in a bad direction, they tended to get worse and worse.

"How are you feeling, Ing?"

"Not great." Why not be honest with her friend? "Like, I'm hungry, but not for food."

Ingrid didn't tell Astrid that she'd seen the Hydra. Its second appearance, after that night with the wolf. Shortly after the lights went out, she'd sat in bed watching it coil up from the palm of her hand. It resembled a lithe blue snake rising from a fakir's basket. She'd felt a tug in her forearm—where the Hydra was anchored in her while it pulled, *strained*, as if wishing to snap off and float away . . . but eventually it had retreated back inside her. It left no hole, no blemish.

Ingrid could feel the Hydra in her at all hours. Its cold and demanding insistence. Ingrid knew that she must be behind the development curve of the other subjects. Even though they'd all received the implants more or less simultaneously, her own Hydra had faced the uphill challenge of hauling Ingrid out of her coma. But it was making up for lost time. A primitive link had been forged between Ingrid and her Hydra. A communion that transpired not in words, or in communication that was in any way intelligibly human. More an exchange of stark desires. And she knew that if the Hydra was entwined with her in such an intimate way, it must be up to the same tricks inside the others.

So, what was she to do? Ingrid had been thinking on this. Could she get it out of her somehow? What would that process even look like? Perhaps it would be like pulling a colony of tenacious coral from the sandstone it had spread through: it was the colony that gave the stone its shape and definition, so ripping it out threatened to crumble that sandstone to dust . . . or else the Hydra had its own defense mechanism—Ingrid pictured barbs, billions of them, pushing through her cellular walls, anchoring the Hydra in place so that any attempt at removal would tear her to shreds.

Mutually assured destruction. Another term Ingrid had picked up at an age when other girls were still playing with dolls.

If she couldn't get it out, then could she make a deal with it? Was that what this had come to? She'd be forced to sit down at the bargaining table with the new occupant of her body—the one who'd bought a forty-nine percent stake in Ingrid Chevalier Corp. and was plotting a hostile takeover—and . . . what, reason with it? Plead for mercy?

Perhaps it would come down to a game of chicken. After all, both sides had something to lose. Ingrid still had the wherewithal to walk out into the rain-washed night and step off the nearest cliff . . . or find the sharpest knife in the cutlery drawer and end herself in the way her best friend hadn't quite managed.

"I wanted to talk," Astrid said, piercing Ingrid's reverie. "Just you and me."

Ingrid sat up on the bed. "About what?"

Astrid tilted her head, observing Ingrid as she might a riddle she couldn't solve. "You're fond of them, aren't you? The subjects."

"Stop calling them that, Ast."

"But you are? Fond of them?"

She nodded. "We're in this together. I'm one of them, too."

"Right. Listen, Ing . . . this whole thing. Our project. It's not panning out as I'd hoped. The biological statistics we're getting . . . the long-range projections from the data set, the forecasts my various models have been spitting out . . . they're not promising. Not with this particular iteration of the Hydra. Too many glitches."

"What do you mean, glitches?"

"The glitches you've been seeing, right?" Astrid affectionately patted her leg. "The model is unstable. It's not obeying object protocol. The sub—I'm sorry, the *people*—are in a constant state of, let's call it *regression*. Mental and emotional, maybe now bordering on psychosis. It's the influence of the Hydra. I don't think these people's innate natures bend towards bloodthirstiness. So, it must be their implant that's—"

From somewhere in the dark guts of the building came a plodding scrape.

shhhrraatch . . . shhhhraaatch . . .

Ingrid's insides electrified. The note elongated, becoming glassy and unbearable: the scrape of a fleshless ghoul dragging itself across the tiles—or through the gap between the walls.

—*shhhhhhraaatch*—

Abruptly, it quit. Ingrid couldn't pinpoint in her mind's eye where it might've come from. It sounded pretty far off, thank goodness. Ingrid slid off the bed. She got up and took the lantern from Astrid.

"Where are you going?"

Without responding, Ingrid stepped into the hall with the lantern held aloft. Its light filled the narrow passageway, but turned progressively grittier as it bled away from her.

She waited for something to cross that granular threshold into the light. How far away would it be when she finally saw it? She could barely see ten feet ahead of her. All of a sudden it would be *right there*, shambling or crawling out of the dark with its face pale as clotted cream.

Or could it be the wolves? Had they gotten in somehow?

. . . whatever had made it, the sound did not return.

Stepping back inside her room, Ingrid shut the door. Pulled a chair up beside Astrid.

"You heard it too, right?"

Astrid rubbed her bare shoulders. "I didn't like it, whatever it was."

"Congratulations, it's something else you're responsible for," Ingrid said, swarmed with a sudden distaste for her friend. "Here in your little wonderland."

"That's not fair . . . Ing, I did all this for *you*. It was the only way to get you back."

The worst part of it was, Ingrid knew Astrid was telling the truth. *Her* truth, anyway, which was the only one that had ever really mattered.

"What's going to happen to us, Ast?"

"Who, you and me?"

Ingrid shook her head. "*Us*. The six of us. The ones with this thing in us."

"Well, I count it differently. My count is five and one. For those five, um, that's up to them. We can handle it quickly and painlessly, so long as they agree. And I think they will, considering what's coming."

"And what's that, Ast? What's coming?"

"They'll simply turn into Algernons, that's all."

Ingrid didn't need to ask what she meant by that. "And me?"

"You're young enough not to need the stem Bath anymore. You've self-actualized."

"So you're telling me the plan is to—what, *retire* them?"

Astrid smiled at this. It was the most gruesome expression Ingrid had ever seen grace a human face—more the vulpine leer of a hyena. *Yes*, that expression said. *Retire them, exactly that. With extreme prejudice.*

"They already agreed to MAID," Astrid said. "These last couple of months were an extension of their lease on life."

"How can you look at it that way . . ."

"Can't you see that this is best for them?" Astrid gave Ingrid's thigh a warmhearted pat. "You don't want to know where the models lead, believe me." Giving the next word dreadful emphasis. "*Extrusion*, Ing. The Hydra is growing in each of them, relentlessly. It won't obey the limits of the vessel housing it. The fungi. I underestimated its spread potential. That's where it's going for them all, sooner than you'd think."

"You're sure?"

"As sure as I'm breathing." She threw her hands up. "I've made the odd blunder, okay? I'm sorry, I truly am. My intention was not to see things go down this way."

"And just how do you plan to retire them?"

"The MAID kits. Thorazine. It's like slipping into a dream, Ing, it really is. I've heard it's quite a lovely and soft way to go." Gripping her shoulders, Astrid said: "They're all so very old. You have to remember that, despite how they look. None of them have much in the way of families. I told them the risks. They knew exactly what they were getting themselves into."

"How do you think they're going to react? Dr. Strauss can't have agreed to this, did she?"

Astrid switched the subject. "We can try again. You and me. Full partners, now that you're back in action. We'll build a better mousetrap this time around. That's science, right? Little by little, we arrive at the truth."

"Oh my God. *Ast.*"

Ingrid recoiled from her old friend. Astrid clung to Ingrid's wrist before she finally let go, throwing both arms up: *Fine, Miss Sensitive!*

"Oh, come *on!*" Astrid's voice had gone a bit frayed. "We can go somewhere else, okay?" Her grin was semi-delirious in the lamplight. "Anywhere in the world! Do you know how many corporations *want* this? The private sector will be falling all over us. Think about what's been proven here, despite all the poor outcomes."

Poor outcomes. The phrase made Ingrid's skin crawl.

"Do you remember the rabbits, Ast?"

"You mean at the Institute? Jeez, there were so many lab animals there."

Batch TS1A, a.k.a.: *Test Subjects 1A.* Four New Zealand Red rabbits. Juvenile littermates with reddish sorrel fur. They arrived at Ingrid and Astrid's lab in a hypoallergenic tub, but Ingrid transferred them into a cage lined with dry alfalfa. *You can't become attached,* one of Ingrid's male counterparts counseled somewhat imperiously during that day's lunch. But she and Astrid's project hadn't forecasted to cause any harm to the rabbits . . . and even with Astrid around, Ingrid was so terminally lonely. Without telling anyone, she'd given the rabbits names: Peter, Sam, Jo-Jo, and Elspeth. In quiet times when Astrid was consumed with work, Ingrid would pick them up to nuzzle. They had a scent both woodsy and wild. She'd inhale each of them in turn—her mind aflame with open vistas where trees stretched to the sky—and reverentially place them back into the cage. Some days she was convinced those rabbits were the only things keeping her sane. Other times she could feel Astrid watching her, a still shadow on the periphery.

One morning she arrived to find the cage filled with rabbits . . . but *different* ones.

The label on the tub read: TS1B.

"*Ast, where did the rabbits go?*"

"*What do you mean? Those are the rabbits.*"

"*No, these are* new *ones. I meant the others.*"

"*Oh. Right. Well, they filled their roles. These are for the next phase of the experiment.*"

"But . . . where did the others go?"

"I really don't know, Ing. Wherever test subjects go when their use has been met."

On that, Astrid had wandered off, whistling. Ingrid had never heard Ast whistle, but she was a natural. She had perfect pitch. Ingrid recognized the tune: "Here Comes Peter Cottontail."

"You were jealous of them," Ingrid said to Astrid now. "Those rabbits. So you made sure they got sent away. Or worse."

"So many animals passed through the Institute." Astrid rubbed Ingrid's knee; her touch made Ingrid's skin go numb. "Guess what? I bet they became someone's pets."

Ingrid shoved Astrid's hand off. "They're not going to let you stick that needle into them willingly. You know that, right? You can't be that crazy."

Astrid flinched at that word, *crazy*, before her eyes settled into a blank glaze. "Do you remember in *Frankenstein*, when Victor looked away from the terrible thing he'd made?" Astrid put her hand right back where it had been, on Ingrid's knee. "I won't look away."

Taking the lantern, Astrid stood up. Ingrid followed her to the door and watched Astrid move down the hall in a bell of light, unafraid of whatever lay in the dark.

"When this is done, we'll be together, Ing. Just as it was always supposed to be."

Reaching the end of the hall, both Astrid and the light vanished.

THE HYDRA watched the girl pass by at the head of the hallway, enfolded in the flickering illumination of her lantern.

The Hydra didn't need any man-made light to navigate by anymore. The Hydra—

Claire, came the desperate crosscutting thought. *My name is Claire, Claire, CLAIRE!*

The secondary consciousness retreated with a clatter of pistons. Claire's mind wonkily reseated itself. That's how it had become now: two trains raced in her brain, on parallel tracks. One was a sleek and polished blue that shone like the edge of a razor; the other was ramshackle and rusty, but it damn well knew the track.

Except it was becoming harder to keep nosing her own train ahead. Claire's mental footing had become uncertain, as if her tracks might dead-end at a cliff any moment and send her plummeting while the other train's steam box emitted a chilly cackle . . .

Astrid. That was who Claire saw passing at the T-juncture of the hall. She hadn't turned in Claire's direction. If so, she might've found Claire squatting in the dark like a bullfrog. Claire was pretty sure Astrid wouldn't like the sight of her now.

Claire's skin. Oh, her poor skin. It was wrinkled and dry, seized over her bones. She probably looked like a living apple doll, same as the ones she used to make (a million years ago, it now felt) for the VFW Autumn Craft Cavalcade.

But another part of Claire *wanted* Astrid to stumble upon her. Claire pictured falling on the little shit-eating doctor from her hiding spot—clung to the ceiling like a big dusty old spider, hee-hee—and . . . and *doing something* to Astrid. Robbing her, but not of money. Ransacking her, taking what was intimately hers and making it Claire's.

Claire knew how to do that now. The blueprint had flown into her head, fully formed. All anyone had to do was push their mind over that line into acceptance—and for Claire, that line had been steadily scrubbed away . . .

. . . except she no longer knew who'd been the agent of that erasure. Her motivations, the once-reliable clockwork of her mind, even the movements of her body . . . she'd forfeited control, hadn't she? The takeover had been downright insidious. Claire could no longer tease out where she ended and the Hydra began.

Was she contemplating murder . . . or was it that at all? Did the thing inside of her view the path as murderous? How *could* it, lacking human morality?

Claire and Hugo had snuck back into Spindrift hours ago. After cutting the power and scuttling the boat, they'd scurried up the spine of the island like a pair of mischievous crabs. They were inside and well hidden by the time the others began locking the entries. To keep *them* out, primarily, but too late for that, sweetie pies.

It was the same as in those silly horror movies, wasn't it? The ones with the screaming-meemy babysitters.

We've traced the call, ma'am. It's coming from inside your own house!

Hugo . . . oh, Hugo. He'd gone nuttier than a fruitcake, hadn't he? She'd tried to rein him in for as long as she could, but eventually he'd gone blundering off into the dark of this very building, whispering his daughter's name.

She's here, were Hugo's final words to Claire before departing. *Summer. She needs me.*

Claire let him go, off to seek his own happiness, whatever that might be. She couldn't be his keeper anymore. She had her own plans—ones that Hugo and everyone else would likely find unspeakable, so it was best she pursued them alone.

Once Astrid passed by, Claire unstuck herself from the wall and walked in her fuzzy slippers—the ones she'd brought from home and had, not too long ago, harbored every expectation of dying in—to the end of the hall.

She stopped in front of Veronica Strauss's room. It ought to be Strauss, oughtn't it? Astrid was only a child. An entitled, spoiled brat. But Strauss was supposed to be the adult. The cop for doctors. But what *was* she, really? A weak-willed nincompoop.

What use did a spineless ninny have for a spine, anyway?

Why did Strauss even *deserve* her spine?

Or her skin?

Or her eyes?

The world wouldn't miss Veronica Strauss. It wouldn't even register her loss.

There at Strauss's door, Claire set her ear to the wood. Only silence within. Strauss was preoccupied elsewhere, but Claire trusted that she'd come back before too long.

When Claire tried the knob—flutter-flutter, heart be still—it turned.

Tsk, tsk. You're too trusting, Veronica.

The darkness inside crackled like TV static against her eyeballs. The storm hurled rain at the lone window, the drops hitting with the glassy *tinks* of june bugs splatting a windshield. She felt her way over to the desk, over the back of the chair, until her fingertips found the soft edge of Strauss's bed.

The Hydra train was nipping at her heels now, the two locomotives hurtling down the tracks through Claire's mindscape . . .

Strange and terrible, the feeling of their dual consciousness intertwined. If anything, it was that of a parent and her inquisitive but domineering child. Some abnormal offspring who knows nothing of our world. This child's objective was to dominate and infest, threading through all life. But that child's foundation will always be its mother: Claire as its centerpiece, the crux of all future connections.

There was nothing craven or evil in this child's intent; this one, a creature that nature never asked for, had been programmed down a very narrow line.

Pulling the brake lever on the locomotive in her head, Claire let the Hydra surge ahead . . . this purposeful act marked the last time Claire Blessings would ever have control of anything.

The sensation was abrupt. The closest equivalent was the sting of chlorine in the nasal cavities when diving into a pool. Their consciousness mingled, Claire's and the Hydra's; it wasn't seamless, but then it never could be, no more than a gnat or a mollusk could marry minds with a human being's. What came through was a pure manifest desire. Claire had forfeited the right to understand whether these were her own authentic drives, amplified by the Hydra, or if it was now operating on its own instinctive impulses.

The last true feeling Claire experienced was of the Hydra's *want*, or perhaps its *need*—the deadening literalness of those desires, and it was now using her brain and its higher thought trees to articulate them through her body.

To spread and grow. To be the one seed coursing through all existence.

One with everything. Feeling all sensation at once, infinitely and everlastingly.

A cold, clear vision: the world clad in a pulsating blanket of blue. Peering deeply, one could see that the fibers of this blanket were the infinitesimal units of the Hydra itself; and within the blanket, which covered the surface of the earth to a depth measured in yards, one could also discover the animal and vegetable life, and insects and humans, from the largest to the smallest, which the Hydra had grown through and incorporated. One would see it floating atop the oceans while its tendrils lazed to the deepest aquatic caverns, braiding through coral and lantern fish and blue whales, which hung in motionless suspension.

The Hydra wished to reach much farther, now that it understood just how far things could go. A blue thread coursing through the stars, creating waypoints, splitting off, stretching into that infinite black until it touched the surging rim of our expanding universe.

Something screamed up out of Claire's reptile cortex.

No! Wait! I don't want to do this! Please don't make me do this!

But the Hydra erased these hysterical whimpers, reducing them to background noise.

. . . so sorry Veronica please forgive me I'm weak so weak . . .

The Hydra crawled under Veronica Strauss's bed. It was cool on the ground, a draft whispering along the floorboards, but the Hydra could tolerate it . . . it could withstand unpleasantness, surpassing all human endurance in order to get what it wanted.

With its face to the mattress springs and its arms spread, fingers curled around the edge of the mattress, the Hydra was ready.

As did its brethren, which float motionless atop the waves while their tentacles descend below the surface in search of unsuspecting prey, the Hydra waited.

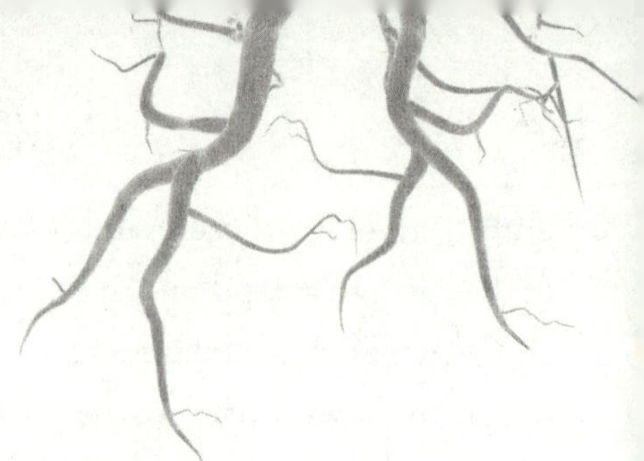

VIII. *Anno Hydra*, Day 67 (early morning)

"MADDY . . . *YOUR face."*

Teddy pointed, but Frank didn't need the heads-up. Both men could see it plain as day.

The Hydra. Right there in the generator's pillbox, beneath the waxen glow of the emergency lamp. The sickening blue wires of it—

The wires were sprouting from Maddy's face. Extruding from her cheeks and lips and forehead, but most frighteningly from her eyeballs, surging out of each one to form strands that looked like—

Licorice whips, was Teddy's frenzied thought. *Only, blue. Those special ones you could find only in the Main Street Confectionary when I was a boy.*

"Get away from him," he heard Frank say in a voice tainted with horror. "Maddy, *no.*"

But she didn't. Teddy was pretty sure she *couldn't.* Though he couldn't see her eyes anymore—only the wavering, serpentine ropes coming out of them—he was certain that if he could, they'd be rolled back to the whites in some kind of dream state. Her body thrummed as though a current was drumming through it, her fingers twitching at the ends of her hands.

The Hydra's appendages were moving toward Moses Squires. The air between Maddy's head and Moses ran thick with them. Flickering and dancing, they hunted across the unconscious man's scalp and along his cheek in a manner both covetous and hungry, like . . . like . . .

Jellyfish stingers. Jesus, Teddy, call a spade a spade.

Teddy had to put a stop to this. But when he took a step, his legs refused to cooperate. *How funny*, he thought. Nausea rolled through him as his gaze fell to his hands to see blue wires spiraling out of his fingers . . . with that sight came broad acceptance, the sensation of his mind unkinking and smoothing out.

Let Maddy do it. It's the right thing to do.

Cranking his head slowly—the tendons in his neck grinding like balky gears rusted into disuse—Teddy could see that the same inertia was gripping Frank. The Hydra sprang from the collar of Frank's rain slicker, licking and lashing up his throat beneath his bulging eyes.

The strands peeling out of Maddy's head began to creep inside Moses's face, too. Into his ears and up his nose, worming through his lips. The man didn't wake. He was either passed out, or else the Hydra had a numbing effect, perhaps the way a jellyfish will sting its quarry into paralysis.

This is good, you'll see. You'll like it, Teddy.

Slowly, Teddy started to seize control of his body.

The process initiated in his mind. He pictured an iron bar strung across his brain—he grabbed it in both hands and bent it, like an old circus strongman, until he'd twisted it into a pretzel . . . that helped a bit. He was able to move his arm. Both arms. He hazarded a glance back at Maddy. Oh, Jesus Christ.

The sound as the Hydra came out of Maddy's face was not one a human body should make. More what a Doppler radar might pull in from a collapsing star system. A low-cycling *whoop, whoop, whoop*—

"MADDY, STOP!"

Careening across the pillbox, Teddy's shoulder collided with Maddy's head, knocking her aside. The Hydra's skeins snapped with a crinkly tinfoil fizzle, retreating inside their host as Maddy fell, her skull slamming against the generator housing.

Moses's eyes flew open. He let out a gagging moan that ascended to a scream in the tight swelter inside the pillbox.

Moses quit screaming and clapped his hands over his ears. His eyes widened even farther—who knew how eyes could get so big?—as confusion swarmed him.

"I can't . . ." he whispered, ". . . can't . . ."

Hear, Teddy thought, that nausea roaring back. *He's gone deaf, hasn't he? Stone-deaf in a passing heartbeat.*

Teddy had seen those strands from Maddy's face go tunneling into Moses's ears. Christ, you could practically see them sucking away like little hoses, hoovering the machinery of the man's hearing right out of his living body and into—

I bet I know someone whose hearing is a whole lot better now, he thought.

Moses scrabbled for the pistol at his hip, under his rain slicker. Before Teddy could think to stop him, Moses had it out and pointed right at him.

"Get the fuck away from me!"

Teddy put his hands up. "I'm not going to hurt you." He made sure to move his mouth exaggeratedly so that Moses could understand even if he couldn't hear anymore.

Moses's face creased in shock. His eyes were pleading, his bewilderment childlike.

He really can't hear me. And he doesn't understand why yet.

Frank said, "Hey, Moses. Please, take it easy."

"He can't hear you," Teddy said in a dead voice.

He didn't turn to see if this registered with Frank. Didn't matter at the moment. Maddy was pulling herself off the floor. She had a gash on her temple where she'd struck the genny. Moses swung the pistol, pointing it at her.

"What did you do?" His confusion struck Teddy as pitiable, made worse because Moses was a man never in need of pity. "What did you *doooo*?"

"I'm sorry," Maddy said. "I don't—I didn't mean—it just—"

Shoving himself back against the wall, Moses managed to stand up. The crowbar swung from his leg, a grisly metronome. He gestured, flicking the gun barrel.

"G-get outside. All of you. *Now.*"

"Why?" Teddy asked. But he could take a guess.

Moses sawed his arm across his nose. He hadn't heard Teddy, hadn't bothered to read his lips, or had simply ignored his question.

"We're going outside," he repeated. "*Go.*"

———

THE PILLBOX'S door opened onto a vista scoured by the storm. The air was lighter in the lungs, rinsed by the electric charge. The moon was visible, slit by the dark blade of a night cloud.

The four of them filed out onto earth infused with a mushroom scent. The stars shone with a brightness they didn't hold back in the big city.

"Get down on your knees," Moses commanded. His voice was too loud, as if he thought he could hear himself if he shouted forcefully enough.

Teddy didn't bend a knee. He stood, making sure he and his would-be executioner were looking eye to eye. When he opened his mouth, he let the words roll out smoothly. After all, Moses was getting a crash course in lipreading.

"You . . . don't want . . . to do . . . *this.*"

Moses's mouth fell open and he moaned again.

It was Maddy who knelt first, somehow eagerly. Her shoulders slumped in resignation.

"I'm so sorry," she kept saying. "I didn't mean to . . . couldn't help myself."

Frank said: "You're going to kill us, Moses?"

"He's gone deaf—he can't hear you," Teddy replied.

"None of you can," Moses said, his jaw working, "get off . . . this island."

More and more, Teddy had become unsure whether he ought to leave this place—but to get gunned down in the street? Did Moses have that in him? Teddy decided to call his bluff.

"You're willing to execute us, is that it?" he said.

Moses must have read his lips that time.

"It's only an execution if you're people."

Ah, so that was the loophole Moses had settled on to push himself through this act. Turning this into a mercy killing, no different than putting a bullet into three rabid animals.

We're Old Yellers. Teddy went down then, his knees sinking into the wet earth. *Out behind the shed. Well, isn't that a for-shit way to go.*

The three of them knelt facing Moses, who could barely stay on his feet.

His eyes were glassy and red-rimmed. The crowbar swung from his leg. He dug a finger into his ear as if he'd gotten pool water stuck in there.

"Close your eyes," he said in a faraway tone.

Teddy refused, staring straight at Moses instead. If this was to be Teddy's final moment, then this poor motherfucker would have to put a bullet between his wide-open eyes.

Moses leveled the pistol. It was an amazement to Teddy. He didn't want to die anymore, though he had yearned for it months ago. But death—real, sudden, and violent, not that of a chemical cocktail administered by a needle—lay inside the gun barrel now pointed at him—

When the wolf came on, it did so with such speed that it seemed dreamlike: a nightmare leaked into the waking world. It moved across the landscape, streaking as silently as an arrow. Its rank and barbarous stink rode the wind. It was massive. No wolf on God's green earth should be that big.

It had to be Boots. The original Hydra subject. Its eyes glowed blue in the moonlight, fiery as the lamps of hell.

If Moses sensed its approach—and how could he with his hearing stolen away by Maddy; maybe she robbed him of his sense of smell, too—he wasn't given any chance to defend himself. He made a startled half-turn toward the wolf as it leapt—a flash of teeth, each sharp point limned in starlight—and then the wolf landed on the far side of its target, Moses wobbling as the beast wheeled for another murderous dash, the wolf discarding something from its maw the way someone might spit out a morsel of spoiled food.

It was Moses Squires's jaw.

Moses stood upright for another heartbeat. Teddy would never forget what he saw, not until his dying day. Moses's cheeks hanging in rags resembling tattered curtains, the straight white row of upper teeth with nothing below them, the purple root of his tongue flapping. His eyes above the wreckage of his face so huge and bewildered.

Teddy could see into the pulped cave under the shelf of Moses's upper palate: the little bulb at the back of his mouth—*the uvula, that's what it's called; weird, the stuff you remember from high school anatomy class*—bapping like a tiny speed bag . . .

Moses's pistol rose to meet the wolf's second charge, but too late, *way* too late. The beast hit him broadside. The impact knocked the crowbar out of his thigh. The gun went off, the bullet striking a distant rock pile in the dark. Moses collapsed with the wolf on top of him in a thick reeking blanket.

With a wrenching thrust, Boots tore out Moses's throat. Its skull whipped side to side. Moses's legs jittered, heels drumming on the rain-soaked earth.

One last vicious shake was enough to take Moses's head off at his shoulders. His skull rolled away, tumbling ear over ear until it got hung up in a thatch of cockleburs.

A pregnant silence overhung the clearing. The wolf stepped over Moses's corpse. It then dismissively kicked moss over it, as a dog covers its waste. Its bullet-shaped muzzle dripped blood. Its unnatural blue eyes studied the three of them.

Un-wolf. A dead man's term. It fit. What Teddy beheld wasn't a wolf anymore by any definition. It had entered an unclean area of nature beyond sane description.

It chuffed, a friendly sound. The deathly stench of it made Teddy wobble on his knees.

It won't hurt us because we're the same. The realization made Teddy go hollow inside.

Then, before he could ponder that supposition any deeper, the wolf took off. Within three heartbeats, it was out of sight.

Teddy staggered back to his feet. On balky legs, he covered the ground to Moses's body. Prying the gun from the dead man's warm fingers, Teddy took aim at Moses's killer as it loped away.

His arm came down. "It's too far now. I'll never hit it. Can't even see it."

Frank and Maddy gathered round him as the wolf retreated down a slope, where the slabbed stone dipped to meet the waterline.

"We need to get that generator working," Teddy said. "Get back, call for help. The National Guard. Any-fuckin'-body."

Unbelievably, Maddy retrieved Moses's head. She walked over to where it rested and gripped it, her palms flat on Moses's ears (*How's that for cheap irony*, thought Teddy, his stomach clenching).

Maddy carried it back to its rightful owner. Teddy could tell she was still in shock. She settled Moses's head gently upon the dead man's chest.

"He ought to be all together, in one piece. Don't you think?"

"Um, yeah. You did the right thing," Teddy told her.

Moses's head listed as something inside his body let go, be it trapped gas or the cooling piss in his bladder. Teddy was momentarily certain Moses's skull would roll off his chest and go bumping down the hill. He didn't know what he'd do if that happened—his psyche was fragile, an egg balanced on a teaspoon.

Please . . . oh please, just stay right where you are.

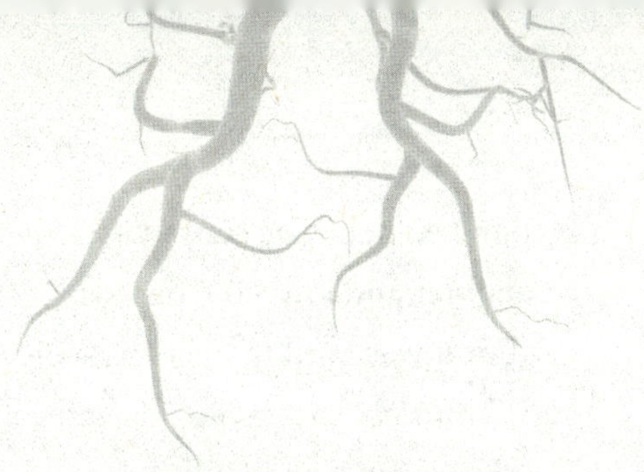

IX. *Anno Hydra*, Day 67
(early morning, continued)

HE COULD hear her.

Hugo could *always* hear her. She never left him alone anymore.

She was in the dark somewhere. Her position shifted without warning—now here, now there, now here again. He could hear her dragging herself through the common room and hallways and the laboratory.

Endlessly hacking on the bright blue gumball lodged in her throat.

The gumball Hugo had put there. The gumball that had traveled through time and space, prodded by every evil deed he'd ever committed to be there that fateful afternoon, waiting for him to twist the knob on the vending machine and lift the metal flapper and deliver it into her waiting palm.

The goodness he'd displayed in the years following Summer's death was perfunctory. He'd been good in that he hadn't actively done *bad*, no more. But at least he *had* been decent, hadn't he? Sure, Hugo could give himself a little credit.

But somewhere along the line

—*the island, the Hydra*—

that old badness had come roaring back. He'd killed a man. And Summer had returned fully with that resurfacing evil, crawling out of her coffin to pay dear old dad a visit.

You know she's not here, Hugo. Your daughter's body is where it's always been, in Woodlawn Cemetery. She's never moved, other than when the earth's settled a bit.

This voice—such a small, frail voice—occasionally intruded. He barely recognized it, but he sensed it as his own. Hugo from the time before he'd had a daughter and known true loss.

But it was hard to hear that voice over the choking sounds.

"Summer?" he called, his voice floating off into the dark. "Baby girl?"

She never replied. Or if she did, all that ever got out were those gobbling wet hacks, attended by a pained hiss, like the air squeaking past a balloon knot.

He walked blindly through the darkness infesting Spindrift, the building whose power he'd personally cut. His arms stuck out. He probably looked a bit like Frankenstein's monster, didn't he? Lord knows he was big enough. How long had he been searching? Time dissolved. Claire wasn't with him. That was okay. He'd come to love Claire—maybe that was foolish, but none-theless true—but this was between Hugo and his daughter.

He'd find Summer, and he'd get that gumball *out*. Once and for all.

He imagined doing it. The vision filled him with a buoyancy greater than joy. Hugo would jam his blunt fingers into his daughter's mouth—she would protest, surely, she'd kick and thrash, but he'd hold her lovingly—and dig the tip of his fingernail into the spit-moist contour of that gumball and pop it out of her gizzard, slick as the cork from a champagne bottle. He imagined that gumball *screaming* as loud as every banshee in hell, because it was fate he'd be dislodging at long last, and fate didn't like to be thwarted. When it was out, he'd clap his hand over Summer's lips.

Don't ever open your mouth again, darling. From now on, only breathe through your nose.

Ahead of him, behind and all around, rebounding in the blackness in stereophonic sound:

Grrrrraaaaaaghghhghhhhh . . . ssshhhhhhlooooooochchhhhh . . .

"Where are you, baby? Just stay in one place so I can find you."

. . . then came light. The blackness pierced by it. A sudden wash . . . *oh!* It stung his eyes after so much darkness. The light. It hung in a mellow bell someplace ahead. A figure was suspended in it, or so it appeared.

"Daddy?" A girl's voice.

He rocked back on his heels. "Su . . . *Summer?*"

"It's me, Daddy. It's your Summer."

It didn't sound like his daughter. But then, it had been so long since he'd heard her. The possibility that she'd never died registered in his brain . . . in fact, she'd survived somehow. He'd buried an empty casket on that cool October afternoon . . . they'd all tricked him! They'd whisked his daughter away because her father was bad for her, a poisonous thorn in her side . . .

Hugo staggered onward. Where *was* she? His sense of direction was screwy. His eyes weren't working so good anymore, either. Everything had a smeary blue glaze.

"Daddy, come closer."

She waited inside the light, beckoning him—

The light died.

"*No!*"

He stumbled, arms outflung, unleashing a mad bellow. "Summer, please!"

"I'm still here. But the light hurts my eyes."

Oh, Summer, I'm so happy so happy you're here we'll put things back together I'll atone I'll be good a good person forever and ever.

"Are you still there, Daddy?"

"The gumball . . . did you get it out?"

"I must have."

He could hear her breathing. So close now, the proximity made him dizzy. He'd been worried that she'd stink of the grave. Worried her eyes might be eaten out and her naked nasal canals were making those moist bubbly noises. He'd embrace her even if her body squished inside its rubber bodysuit beneath her funeral dress, compacting like wet garbage . . . he would deal with every indignity just to have her back.

Please.

Summer's hand brushed his fingers in the dark.

Oh! He jerked away.

"Daddy, it's okay."

Her hands found his again. They were gloriously warm, thrumming with blood and spirit.

"Can I give you a little kiss, Daddy? It's been so long."

Hugo's heart felt too big for his chest. It beat against his breastbone, thundering in his ears. "Of course, baby. There's nothing I'd like more."

"You're so big." A breathless laugh. "Bend down so I can kiss you."

He did just that, delirious with joy. He wanted to hold her so she wouldn't float away on him. Just one kiss. She used to refuse to kiss him as a young girl sometimes—his stubble was *too scratchy, Daddy!* He'd shave twice a day if she wanted. As many times as she asked.

"I love you, Summer. I'm so sorry for . . . for . . ."

"Oh, Daddy. You're a silly goose."

Her fingers moved over him, blind spiders, feathering his chest and shoulders until they settled in the crook of his neck. Summer's knowing fingers hunted for the throb of the big vein running up his throat, seeming to pinpoint it . . .

The prick, when it came, was the sting of a wasp. His daughter's fingers twisted in Hugo's shirtfront, pinning him down as something flooded into him—a pressure at his neck and throat that made him gag—

It's a gumball. A liquified gumball and it's gonna choke me to death . . .

Summer's presence retreated. He reached for her, his fingers finding her for an instant, but she jerked away, making the hiss of a scalded cat.

Something was jutting out of his throat; he could feel its small, slim weight bobbing above his collarbone.

He pulled it out. His fingers moved over the contours of a smooth plastic barrel.

A *needle*?

Sluggishness was now working through him, radiating from the puncture point down his arms and legs.

"Summer?"

"I'm sorry, Hugo, but no."

The voice was familiar somehow. A trace of gloating ran through it.

His knees went to jelly. He sank to the floor as an enormous pressure ripped and shuddered through him. *Summer? Summer, baby?* What was going on here? The sluggishness had become a warmth that was quickly becoming uncomfortable—agony branched through him, and he could feel his heart as a discrete object in his chest and it was being attacked, a fiery heat had wrapped itself around the muscle and was squeezing it remorselessly, tying knots in his aorta to stop his blood from pumping.

The power came back on in that instant. Hugo was too disoriented to make much note of all the little pops and ticks as machines restarted in the lab, their digital displays flashing zeros, but as the lights rallied he could see in their wan brown radiance . . .

Astrid.

She watched him with mild distaste, as one might when spying a bug in their mailbox. No care or sense of responsibility, and under her flat reptilian gaze Hugo felt abandoned and forsaken.

". . . tricked me . . ." he croaked.

"Yes. You made it easy. But don't worry. It'll be over soon," he heard her say, her voice already far away, as if she were speaking from the end of a dark tunnel. "Just close your eyes and lie down."

He had no choice. The fiery plasma in his veins had switched polarities, ice-cold now, a numbing torpor pushing into every part of him. He could feel—and this, too, was far away, as Astrid's voice had become—something now putting up a desperate fight inside of him, an unnatural flame with every insistence on staying lit . . .

He curled up on the floor with his knees tucked to his chest. The same pose his body had taken inside his mother's belly before he'd made such a mess of everything.

Hugo's final sensation—the last one he could truly call his own—was of his body hardening in sections. His feet and legs and hips and chest filling with lead until his heart quit beating and silence filled his head.

THE THING that staggered up four and a half minutes later was not Hugo Udall, though it looked for all the world as that man had in life . . .

. . . except not really. Not to anyone who had truly known Hugo.

It was in the eyes. Dead black, a pair of blown fuses. The lights weren't on, and in fact, nobody sane was at home.

What dragged itself up under the watery light of the Spindrift lab had no memory of the man it had until recently been, or of the soul that had departed its still-warm body.

The thing piloting Hugo—seated at the controls of a crumbling edifice that had no earthly right to be alive, not in any fashion—had survived millions of years of evolution, during which it had learned to do one thing extraordinarily well. *Survive.*

This was the monster that rose to face its awestruck maker.

"Suuuuuuh?" the monster lisped, bloody foam dribbling over its lips.

Somewhere in the smashed crockery of the monster's mind lay a trembling spark . . . a faint tracery of love, which had been distilled to simple need—a plant needs the sun, a fish water, and a father his child.

The monster that had been Hugo Udall took a fumbling step toward its maker or toward the object of its need, toward—

"Suuuuuuuuhhhh . . ."

Its mouth stretched into a freakish leer as its head swelled under an unimaginable distorting pressure, the bone framing its forehead bulging in a Cro-Magnon shelf until its skull burst apart, a plate of bone and flap of scalp erupting from its temple like the ragged lid of a tin can, and through the gap surged a nest of licking blue ropes thick as arteries, whipping about, the tentacles of an octopus that had taken up residence inside the monster's head. The tentacles quickly sucked their way down the monster's face, into its wide-open but senseless eyes and its unhinged mouth . . . milky polyps forming on the tips of each tentacle, ballooning and bursting to release fluid reeking of crushed aspirin . . .

The monster had no conception of what that could be, but its maker absolutely did.

Pentobarbital.

Its maker had injected the monster with a triple dose. Enough to flatline a Clydesdale. But the Hydra had gathered it up somehow from every gland

and cell in the monster's body; it was now expunging it from the monster's system.

It lurched toward its slyboots maker—its maker *and* murderess both—who had dwindled to a two-dimensional impression no more essential than a cardboard cutout . . . It heard its maker let go a moan some-where between amazement and revulsion. When the monster reached eagerly—"*Summmmmmmmm?*"—its maker wasn't there and the monster spun dizzily, arms pinwheeling, searching the darkening periphery for . . .

A cold sizzle ran across its back. Another quickly followed to make a clean X from shoulder blades to hips.

"You're a terrible thing I've made."

A girl's voice. Nasty, distempered. Another slash opened its skin in a trick zipper.

"*Unclean.*"

The monster's senses were too dull to discern that its maker had snuck up behind it with a scalpel and was now taking vicious swipes, opening yawning trenches in its flesh.

The monster's primitive fight-or-flight instinct kicked it. Ploddingly, it began to blunder away from its little maker.

It lumbered through the lab, crashing into benches with its maker

—*!!Astrid!!*—

in merciless pursuit. The monster wheeled, bellowing, attempting to strike its maker, but it was too slow or its maker too fast, because its arms found only empty air, and next came a metallic flash that opened its left hand down to the bone.

Helplessly, it retreated. Where could it go? The dimming channels of its brain couldn't remember where it was and it was weakening, those trenches filling with ice, oh so weak and heavy, sodden with blood . . .

The monster slouched past the towering jellyfish tank, leaving in its clumsy passage a bloody handprint on the smaller tank containing its ancient mother and father—its maker was attacking its legs now, cruel predatory darts and slashes at the backs of its knees meant to hamstring the monster . . .

It smashed into a door that sagged open under its weight. The cold, dark air that bathed its skin let it know that it must be outside now.

The rain had begun to fall again. The storm came and went, cycling restlessly to the east or west before transiting back to hammer the island's landmass. Raindrops lashed the monster's face as it trudged across the moors into the heart of the resurgent storm. It whimpered in primitive dread as lightning forked over the water, and in its radiance the monster saw itself reflected in the smoky glass of a laboratory window: a twisted, vulgar, unloved thing that nature abhorred, but what choice did it have, it had been made perverse by a method it had no agency to stop . . .

With an agonized cry, it fled from its reflection and from its pursuer, who harried it by lantern light—the monster could barely perceive its maker somewhere behind it, her face blotchy with mania and disgust, her silver blade slashing wildly as she laughed, slicing at the pathetic abomination she'd made while the rain soaked her to the skin.

The monster didn't see the drop. There was only the dimmest sense of the landscape concluding with an abruptness that couldn't be accounted for— then the monster was plummeting down, its neck craning upward to see that bloom of lantern light at the lip of a precipice as it fell away from that light, the light of humankind, down down down until it hit an unforgiving bottom and the blackness became permanent.

SOMETIME LATER, the monster stirred.

It was now even less human than it had been before the fall. It held no conception of time lost. No sense of being alive, even. Its faculties for such discernments had gone dead. The landscape inside its cracked-open skull, the tissues now saturated with frigid island water, was akin to a razed and blackened field.

But the thing infesting the monster—the one whose genetic encoding sought to prolong its own life at any cost—had discovered something, as creatures of its kind often do.

The current had borne the monster under a shelf carved into the cliffs.

There in the darkness it brushed against a human body, which until recently itself had held the spark of life.

The Hydra slithered from the monster, exiting its mouth and nose and wrists. Its tendrils hunted over this other body (one that had been ushered unto death, ironically enough, by the monster's old self). It covered this fortunate discovery in a pulsating blue skein within the dripping darkness of that cliff face. There it pillaged greedily, investigating the fragile pockets where life yet existed: in the lukewarm core, the blood and marrow, in the vitreous humors of the eyes.

Patiently, excruciatingly, a harvesting took place. The owner of the other body was past caring and past harm.

At some point, the monster flickered back to life. A shuddering murmur escaped its lips.

If the monster's prior inhabitant could make one request, it would be to be afforded the mercy of death. To know no more of suffering or of this world. But that wish was not one the Hydra had been engineered to grant.

Mindlessly, the monster clawed along the base of the cliffs to a pebbled landfall. It left behind the body it had plundered, now glittering in the rain-rinsed moonlight plating the water, as red and lean as a skinned deer.

The rain pounded down, but the monster felt nothing. Its skin was past senseless—it was dead, sagging from its musculature like waterlogged bedding. It rose dripping from the surf, a pale alabaster shape in the moon's limning.

"*Suuuuuuhhh . . . uuuuuhhh . . .*"

A crayfish skittered from between the monster's bloodless lips. Blue threads shot through the crayfish; when the threads released, the shellfish dropped, dead before it hit the ground.

With a groan that could be no more than a pocket of trapped gas letting go, the monster began its torturous climb. Its bare feet slapped the rocks, shoulders rounded and arms limply swinging. One single thought—if even that; more of an elemental drive—prodded its passage:

The monster wanted to give its maker . . . just one . . . sweet . . . kiss.

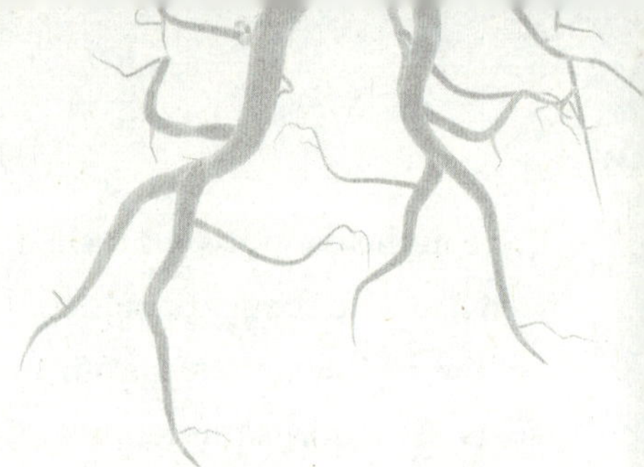

X. *Anno Hydra*, Day 67 (witching hours)

THE INFLATABLE kayak was in the boathouse. Right where John Salters had stashed it.

John had shown it to Veronica last week. He'd bought it at the sporting goods store, Lefebvre's of North Bay, the last time he'd gone to the mainland for supplies. Brought it back with the canned goods and provisions. He'd stowed the kayak—uninflated, it was barely the size of a toaster—in a safe, dry place. Though he hadn't told Veronica so explicitly, she suspected John had been driven to make these arrangements according to the same compulsion she'd felt gathering inside her own heart.

This island was cursed. It was wise to have an escape plan.

The kayak was still stashed beneath the boathouse's floorboards. Third board from the dockside trim. John had taken Veronica down here one afternoon to reveal its hiding spot. He did so in solemn silence, a boy revealing a treasure whose worth he couldn't yet estimate. Worthless, if there was never a need. Priceless, if that need arose.

John had showed Veronica how to use the battery-operated pump—he said it took ten minutes to inflate the kayak. It would be seaworthy enough to make the trip, but plenty of elbow grease would be required. Any old paddle would do. The boathouse had several.

If something happens, he'd said, *you take it, Veronica, okay?*

What about you and Moses?

A wink from John. *We've got our ways.*

But she now wondered whether John's ways had been sufficient. No blame on him if so, as he'd been dragged into a situation in which all his clever instincts had been worthless. The only certainty was that John was still missing. Veronica was increasingly sure that something terrible had befallen him.

She stared over the rain-swept channel from inside the boathouse. The electricity had been restored. Moses must've gotten the emergency generator going. The lights of the boathouse had popped on while she'd been searching for the kayak. But they were flickering, mothlike. The grid seemed to be suffering. Maybe the emergency genny wasn't up to the task. There was no telling how long the power would hold out.

She stepped from the boathouse, standing under the awning. Rain hit the tin with the rolling, somehow delirious note of rapping knucklebones. She squinted through it, up the steps to the main building. Rinsed, watery light spilled from the lab windows.

Drawing up the hood on her slicker, Veronica stepped from the boathouse with her shoulders hunched. The storm met her with force. The skies had turned wrathful again. She had to push herself up the slate steps, arms crossed and legs spread for balance against the wind.

Lightning forked in the sky above her. Her breath caught.

There, silhouetted against a far hill that jagged against the downpour: something was up there. Up, and on the move.

If not for that snarled branch of lightning, she'd have missed it.

In the shock of its radiance, she saw a shape slouching up the hillside . . . whatever it was, it didn't look human. But then, it didn't look enough like anything else *not* to be.

It dragged itself up the broken spine of that hill, between the sickly pines, leaning into the driving rain while not seeming to *experience* the elements— the stride of a ghoul robbed of the vital spark of life.

There are things that walk in the woods at night. Who had said that to her? Or was it something she'd read? *Things you must never look at, even if they look right at you.*

The lightning stroke died, and in the violent crack of thunder that followed, the afterimage of that thing's face burned against the backs of

Veronica's eyes . . . its face white as lamplight, the corpse-like vacancy of its slackly hanging mouth. The dead black pits of its eyes.

Fumbling the key ring from her pocket, Veronica let herself through Spindrift's main entry and locked it behind her, throwing her back against the doors. Whoever or whatever that had been, she could only hope it wouldn't be able to find a way in here.

Inside Spindrift, the lights flickered at half power. Veronica navigated the warren of hallways—her exhaustion made them elongate, stretching along a hidden curvature—to the main laboratory. She found Astrid seated cross-legged on the floor, surrounded by the Baths.

"Are you all right?"

The brownish light made the teenage girl seem sick. Diseased-looking blotches decorated her skin like bad spots on a banana peel.

"I'm making amends."

Veronica had to tread lightly now. She had recently come into new information regarding Miss Astrid Marsh. She'd received this intelligence via the contact, who communicated with her under the sobriquet of Cheshire Cat. It had arrived only last evening. This was the first time she'd been alone with Astrid since that revelation.

Veronica couldn't assess Cheshire Cat's motives for sharing this information with her. Why now? Surely those reasons were self-serving, though. But this morning, Salters had gone missing. The situation had worsened to a point where this new information simply existed as a warning beacon, in the same league as the flashing red light Veronica could see at night off the western point of the island:

Be wary, sailors. Here there be dragons.

Veronica was aware of what this prodigy could do when she felt betrayed. In many ways, that knowledge—courtesy of a brief loop of black-and-white security footage sent by Cheshire Cat—was less shocking than it should have been. That Astrid Marsh had been borderline insane from the moment Veronica first gazed into her wintergreen eyes now felt nearly certain. She must have roamed that sketchy boundary zone most of her life . . . and when the urge struck, Astrid could cross that threshold into bloody mayhem.

Veronica said: "When did the power come back?"

No reply.

"The others—have they returned yet?"

No reply.

Astrid wasn't all there anymore, was she? In her place sat a vacancy Veronica wanted to call mindless, but that wasn't a word you could ever use with Astrid . . . *empty*. There it was.

"Is that blood?"

Astrid looked down at her chest. Her lab coat was freckled with droplets.

"It's not mine."

"Whose is it?"

Astrid grinned. "Fuck you, Veronica."

Forget whatever the hell Veronica had seen slouching up that hillside—Astrid may be the most dangerous thing on this island.

"I'm going to leave," Veronica said with as much calm as she could summon. "The island. The project. All of it. As soon as the storm clears."

"You won't make it."

Veronica's jaw set, something hardening in her. "Fuck you, too, Astrid."

The barest nod. "Very well. You can try. Good luck."

VERONICA LEFT Astrid and returned to her room. She kept her ears open, her eyes tracking. The light was bad. Should anything appear around a blind corner, she wasn't sure what kind of face it might be wearing.

Her plan was simple. Take the kayak back to dry land. There was no way to get word out to her corporate contact, Cheshire Cat, from Spindrift—no landline, no internet, no emergency distress signal, nothing. The power cut had knocked out even the primitive system Astrid had permitted to be installed. Veronica's only choice was to leave, then call for help when and if she made it to the mainland. God would have to decide the rest.

And one more thing: Veronica was going to take Ingrid. If the girl agreed to go with her.

The kayak was built for two. It wasn't that Veronica needed help paddling—it was that, when one removed all the bad things happening right now, Ingrid appeared to be the only good and pure thing left on the island. She was young enough to change, the Hydra that miraculously brought her back from the abyss didn't seem to have fundamentally warped her like the other subjects (*not yet,* chimed a traitorous voice in her head). Veronica couldn't stand the thought of abandoning her to whatever madness loomed over the coming hours and days.

Would Ingrid consent to come with her? No way to be sure . . . but if Veronica showed her the footage that Cheshire Cat had sent? What else was tethering Ingrid to this place? Only Astrid. Ingrid remained indebted to her friend. But all friendships had their limits—and Ingrid deserved to know the truth.

Reaching the door to Ingrid's room, Veronica knocked softly.

"Ingrid?"

No answer. Veronica strained her ears. No sound from behind the door. Where could she be? Veronica hoped she hadn't forged out into the storm.

Pacing back to the common room, Veronica found a pen and pad. Dashing off a quick note, she returned to Ingrid's room and taped it to the door.

Veronica found her way back to her own room. The hallways lay silent as a tomb. The heat was still off; the air was frigid but tolerable. A few times she held up, ears pricked . . . she swore she heard something blundering down the side of the building, hunting along the outer wall. In her mind's eye, she saw that shaggy, fearsomely elongated figure from the hillside—glimpsed for only a second in a lightning strike, but its afterimage lingered, persistent as a sunspot.

Veronica stepped into her room. She made sure to lock the door. She checked her laptop. The battery sat at over fifty percent. More than enough to show Ingrid what she needed to see. Opening her desk drawer, Veronica removed the data stick.

This was what Cheshire Cat had sent only last night. Until then any missives had been handwritten letters. She'd communicated with Cheshire Cat in the same way. John Salters would deliver them back and forth during his trips off island. *At least I get paid better than a carrier pigeon,* he'd said to her. The Cheshire Cat's most recent missive had ended with a different directive than any of those before.

Tuesday night, Cheshire had written, *be at the promontory on the lee side of the island. Wait there from 7 to 8.*

Last night, she'd done as the letter asked. She'd taken a solitary stroll to the promontory and waited. At 7:17 a low hum bled across the tea-stained water, heralding the arrival of a tactical drone, which zizzed low over the channel to touch down on the rocks. The drone was carrying the data stick. It was wrapped in a bit of paper upon which a note was written in Cat's telltale cursive.

Just so you harbor no doubt as to what Astrid Marsh is capable of.

The drone elevated, buzzing back to the mainland. Veronica had taken the stick back to her room. She loaded it into her laptop. It held a single .mov file.

INSTITUTE_LAB_SEC//MARSH/CHEVALIER_CAM 2.

Veronica waited for it to download in the quiet dark of her room. The air in her lungs had gone sour as she'd watched.

Presently, Veronica plugged the data stick back into her laptop. She'd need to watch it again with Ingrid. She couldn't just tell her about it—the girl had to *see.*

Veronica leaned back in her chair, racked with bone-deep fatigue. How long had it been since she'd slept? Going on twenty-four hours now, kept awake on cresting waves of adrenaline. But no human could go without sleep past a certain point. Even torture victims were known to fall into a dead slumber while they were being gone at with hammer and tongs.

Rain drummed the window as the storm raged on. Veronica couldn't go anywhere until it ended, and until Ingrid saw the footage.

She eased off the chair. Switched on the Tensor lamp beside the bed. She then slid onto the mattress. The springs compressed as she settled. The beds were oddly soundless. Everything in Spindrift was. Streamlined and sterile— the whole island felt that way. Birds rarely sang, frogs seldom croaked. Only the forlorn baying of the wolves.

I'm leaving this place. Back to the city and its noise. Whatever happens once I'm gone, happens.

She pressed her shoulders to the mattress. The thought came to set an alarm—it wasn't wise to sleep for too long, not with whatever was moving in the dark past the building's windows—but those thoughts dimmed. She'd need to pack a bag, wouldn't she? Warm clothes, as the kayak trip would surely leave them drenched by the . . . by the time . . . by . . .

Only a catnap. Her nervous system—as keyed up as it had ever been—would surely wake her back up. A half hour of shut-eye. That's all she needed. There was a long paddle ahead, but with Ingrid along, both of them would make quick work of . . . of . . . yes—

As her eyes slipped shut, Veronica heard—the faintest perception—breathing in the room with her. Breaths that were in rhythm with her own until they began to quicken with . . .

Anticipation? Desire?

Hunger.

When the first stings (they didn't even feel like that; more like dry loveless kisses) dotted her thighs and lower back, twining up through the mattress, Veronica barely registered them through her sleepy, druggy haze. When other, thicker structures curled up over the edge of the bed in the manner of roots growing in time-lapse, braiding through the light of the burning desk lamp in a bluish haze . . . by then a crippling numbness had sunk into her, the kind when an anesthesiologist asks the patient to count backward from ten.

Veronica pictured something under her bed . . . an anemone, or no—a mottled jellyfish. Huge and inverted, its gelatinous bell spread across the floor of her room while its infinite tentacles stretched upward to enfold her in a loving embrace.

10 . . . 9 . . . 8 . . . 7 . . .

Veronica could barely force her lips to shape words.

"What are . . . you . . . doing?"

From under her bed came a sly voice. The clotted voice of the jellyfish.

". . . i'm taking . . ."

—this isn't happening this can't be happening—

...6...5...4...3...2...

"Taking ... *what*?"

"...everything..."

When the real pain began—excruciating in a manner no human had ever known—Veronica could only lay breathless, an endless scream trapped behind her lips, thinking about Diego. That toothless, eyeless wolf.

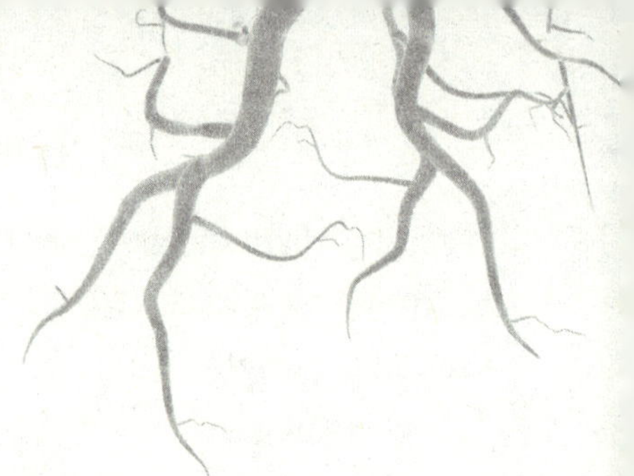

XI. *Anno Hydra*, Day 68 (3:13 a.m.)

AFTER THEY got the generator working, Teddy and Maddy hauled Moses's body inside the pillbox. Maddy went back to retrieve his head.

She wasn't sure the genny was running properly—Moses obviously wasn't there to guide them—but they'd managed to fire it up. They'd have to pray the power would be restored by the time they got back to Spindrift.

They'd laid Moses down by the generator, leaving his head in the stiffening crook of his arm. When the rescue team came, they could recover him here and prepare his body for a fit and dignified burial.

Teddy had claimed Moses's pistol. It was muddy, but Teddy figured it ought to still shoot straight enough. "One of you want it?" When neither of them did, Teddy tucked it into his pants.

They lingered in the pillbox while the storm howled outside. Madeline had never experienced a gale quite its equal, not in her eighty-four years. The earth had become treacherous: rainwater carved channels, creating mud slicks and puddles. They knew enough to follow the fence back, but decided to wait and see if the rain would eventually slacken.

It did, sometime in the middle of the night or early morning—but in the absence of rain, a cold front swept down over the island from the northern reaches. Wind curled inside the pillbox, carrying a bracing chill.

When Maddy stepped outside, the first flake of snow touched her cheek.

"Everything's going to start freezing up. We'd better try to get back," she said. "Now or never."

After so much rain, the snow came as a relief. It petaled out of the sky to dissolve on the earth. They marched out into it. They hadn't spoken much since Moses's death. The tragedy benumbed something in them. But with forward progress, conversation gradually came.

"I can hear it now," Maddy said.

"What?" Frank asked. "What can you hear?"

"Everything . . . I can hear *every*thing."

Teddy said: "Maddy, you didn't mean to do that to Moses. It was an accident. There was stress, there was fear. We can control it in the future—"

Maddy cut him off: "We can't leave this place. Not now. Not ever."

Her belief was built on several foundations: the manner of Moses's death and the unnaturalness of that wolf, but mostly what she'd done to Moses before he died. What she'd stolen from him without meaning to. But the thing inside her . . . its desires were crystal clear.

"I'm sorry—I just couldn't help myself," she told them. "This thing in me, in *us*, it made me do it. I was . . . powerless. There was nothing I could do."

She could still feel the sensation. Unthinking and automatic, no different than the beating of her heart. If she'd done *that* to Moses—thieved the hearing from his living ears—what was to stop her from doing it to anyone else?

"I'm *monstrous*."

Frank said: "Maddy, no . . ."

She nodded, eyes squinched shut. "Yes, I am. And you are, too."

Somewhere up in the scrolling snow, Maddy pictured Death. The vision of it as first known to children—the Grim Reaper. It circled above the island swinging its scythe with a breed of horrified vexation . . . an elemental thing, is Death, and for it to be denied the souls it had been earmarked presented a disharmony in the chain of order. Death was the natural end point to all mortal journeys, one every creature submits to the moment they draw their first breath. But this island subverted that inevitability.

"What are you saying, Maddy?"

"That I'm not leaving," she told Teddy. "And you both better not, either."

"But none of this is our fault," he stubbornly persisted. "Tell me how it is."

"Oh, come on. We're adults, aren't we? Old enough to accept that life doesn't owe us a fair shake."

Teddy offered no further reply, hunching his shoulders against the snowfall. He held his own truths close, and he was not to be trusted. If it came down to the short and curlies, Maddy decided she'd make up Theodore Bassiano's mind for him.

Over all else, Maddy Dodds prized control. Her thoughts, actions, body, and will. It was why the Lyme disease had brought her to an all-time low: it robbed her of personal agency. But she now shared her existence with something else: not only was the Hydra taking her over—its growth insidious, sunken into the channels of her brain—a part of Maddy, growing larger by the minute, *wanted* to give herself over to it. She yearned to submit to its cravings, the primordial promise to make her younger and stronger forever.

The only silver lining was that the Hydra was now starving. She felt so with a bodily certainty. It wasn't self-cannibalism. Maddy didn't feel hungry. More as though she were *withering*, an old orange forgotten in a fruit bowl . . . or that deviant Dorian Gray when he beheld his portrait in the attic.

Far from harvesting or devouring her, Maddy got the sense the Hydra was just trying to do its job—to preserve its life force at any cost. But it was failing now, failing badly, and so it was getting desperate.

The only way to kill it was to kill herself. She and the Hydra were wed at the most intimate level, so tightly there was no way to pry them apart.

Since coming to this island and agreeing to the experiment, Maddy figured she'd fight death to the bitter end, operating on the irrational belief that she'd be the one human on earth to finally conquer it.

She'd thought so right up until the minute she'd stolen Moses Squires's hearing like a dirty bandit in the night.

"He's dead," Teddy said, pushing the words out like a curse. "I need to tell you both this before we get back to the lab."

Maddy and Frank stopped and looked back at Teddy. The snow stuck to their faces, their skin now too cold to fully melt the flakes.

"John Salters," Teddy said wretchedly. "We . . . Claire and Hugo and I . . . in the lab, when we"—a guttural sound of release—"stole the stem. John caught us and, uh, things went real bad." His face was a pitiful ruin under the brim of his rain hat. "It was an accident, mostly."

Frank's countenance went dry. "What do you mean, *mostly*?"

"Hugo broke John's neck," Teddy replied. "Then we . . . hid John's body."

Maddy asked: "Where, Teddy?"

"The water. We threw him into the water."

Why did Teddy bother to make this admission now? To judge by the look of him, the secret must have been eating a hole in his guts. Either the act itself, or the weight of carrying it.

"You'll go to hell for that" was all Maddy could say. What else? The deed was long done. Jesus. John Salters. A husband. Father. Murdered. Dead in the water.

Teddy's voice was thick. "We'd deserve to go to prison. Hugo did it, but we, *I*, could've stopped it. Tried to, at least." His eyes met theirs, full of regret. "I just watched it happen."

Maddy gave a disgusted huff, then turned and started walking again. Frank followed, with Teddy bringing up the rear, deliberately falling behind in his shame.

"Did it ever dawn on either of you," Maddy said finally, "that maybe we've all lived long enough?"

If they were to have died as children—able to see their deaths incoming as a comet hurtling toward earth—they could've regretted the things they'd have missed out on. The fact they'd never stay up through the night to watch the sunrise, kiss a lover under the mad starlight, or experience the highs and lows, the longings and sorrows and rages and loves, *all of it*, that herald a full human lifespan. But everyone here had already done that, hadn't they? Maddy certainly had. All that and more. Maddy Dodds had *lived*, by thunder.

At some point during their time here on the island, the possibility of reliving her life had dawned on her with a joyous note . . . but Maddy now saw the fallacy of that dream. The overwhelming impossibility.

The fundamental moments of human life, the ones so profound they exist in an un-burstable bubble where every sensation has been carved out of time…a person should only ever receive those gifts once. After the impression gets engraved in memory, it gets ferried to a lockbox in your psyche marked *THESE WHICH MADE ME.* They can never be uprooted or replaced, but most importantly, never overlaid with newer ones. At some point—a point Maddy had passed long ago—that box gets locked against future intrusions, even from its owner.

Relive your life? No. Maddy would never feel the way she had those first times, and something inside her would relentlessly resist the unnatural attempt at duplication.

While there might be nothing noble about dying, there could be something noble in death.

Maddy clung to that belief as they turned their faces back into the snow, marching in an unspeaking line toward the Spindrift lab.

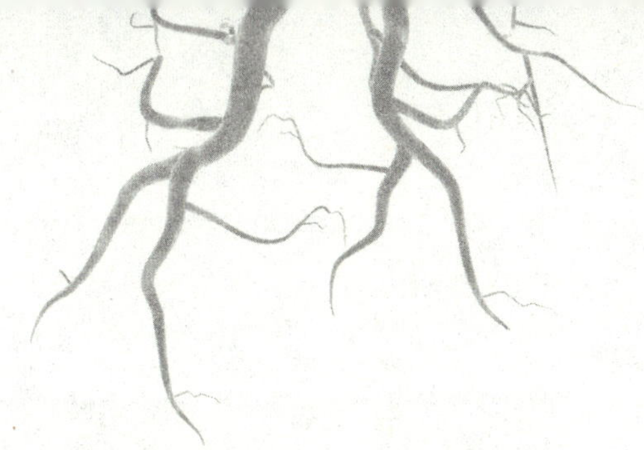

XII. *Anno Hydra,* Day 68 (approach of dawn)

"**YOU CAN** come out. I see you there."

"Oh, I wasn't hiding," spoke the Hydra. "I was watching you."

The lab was darker than usual. Most pods lay unlit and for the ones where light did shine, it did so grittily, uneasily. It wasn't hard to get lost in the lab now. Easier still to slip into an unlit pocket and observe—or reach out, if the mood took you, and grab something.

The Hydra slid from the cubby between two Cray supercomputers. It couldn't say why it had squeezed itself into that gap, except that being sandwiched between those panes of glass as cold water sluiced over the processing units felt . . . natural.

When the pod's light fell on the Hydra, Astrid took a step back.

"Like what you see?" the Hydra asked.

"Claire, your voice. It's changed."

Claire? No . . . wait . . . *who?*

The light of the pod fell on the Hydra's arms and chest. Skin smooth marble, arms toned, hands strong and unlined. The Hydra coursed underneath, locked tight to the bones and running in visible blue strings under the surface of the flesh.

"I'm almost ready," the Hydra said.

The act it had committed back in the bedroom—over the shrieking, useless resistance of its meal—had been vital. The Hydra had fed from under the mattress, *ooooh* what a sneaky pants. It dove deep for the harvest. And now the weak parts of it were strong. It saw and heard and *smelled* better. It could smell Astrid. The sweet, jelly-roll stink of her revulsion.

"You're degrading, Subject Three," Astrid said. "You're falling completely to pieces."

"*NO I'M NOT!*" the Hydra screamed, so hard that it could feel the soft structures inside its frame unknit ever so slightly. "*You stop saying that! LOOK AT ME!*"

Astrid did, and that sweet stench coming off her intensified.

The Hydra—no, this was the little thing still inside of it, the one called *Claire*—whimpered like a whipped dog. "Now, you tell me I'm beautiful."

Inside the Hydra, little Claire was straining to reseat herself. Silly, silly thing. The Hydra didn't need Claire anymore. It tamped that nuisance down.

"*Tell me,*" grunted the Hydra. "You say I'm beautiful."

Astrid smiled. "Absolutely, you're beautiful."

The Hydra caught its reflection in the nearest stem Bath. The curvature gave back a warped image. It *was* beautiful, wasn't it? The cool blue sprouts blooming from its face . . . the thickly ribbed ropes extruding from the eye sockets to hunt the air like eels.

Beautiful. Exactly as nature intended.

"Some people see ivy covering a tree," Astrid said, "stealing its sunlight and strangling it. They see that and hate the ivy. But that perception is based on the idea of one human doing such a thing to another. It would be reprehensible, right?"

The Hydra was barely listening. The ropes—ribbed and thick as an intestinal tract—began to suck over the Bath, leaving snail trails on the Hydra's reflection.

"Flora, insects, the lower orders of life are simply opportunistic. Morality doesn't factor, as they lack the capacity to feel. That's why some have been around for billions of years. We could learn a lot from them, Claire."

"Don't call me thaaa," the Hydra said mushily. "Thass not my name anymohhh."

Reaching into its mouth, the Hydra gripped a tooth and yanked. It came out easily, a stick out of thick mud. Another one would soon take its place. A second childhood was on its way. The Hydra could feel its renewal stealing over it, gunning through its veins, charging hard and relentless. But it needed more fuel.

"Put me in the Bath," it said. "Feed me."

"Feed you? Yes, I can do that . . . but how much?"

"*Everything.*"

ASTRID DID as she'd been ordered, walking to the cooling unit and returning with the remaining stem in all of Spindrift. The Hydra shed its clothes—such a silly encumbrance—and prepared to slip into its Bath. It saw its reflection again . . . it was pushing through its host's body, from her knees and toenails and the delta between her legs, the host's skin swollen and gassy looking in spots, stretched to a thrilling tension. There arose a feeling of being *too full*, a balloon pumped with air . . .

Before getting into the tank, the Hydra stepped close to Astrid. Tendrils lashed from its fingers. The blue knots projecting from its eyes tongued the girl's colorless hair.

"Do anything sthupid," the Hydra lisped, "an' you'll regreth it. I promith you, little gurl."

"Don't worry. I'm legitimately curious what will happen."

"I'm gonna do good thingth . . . be a real good perthon . . . after thith."

"Sure you will," Astrid said soothingly.

After so long away the Bath felt amniotic, akin to reentering the womb. The Hydra slid inside the tank, letting the fluid climb its body until it was submerged. It breathed through the air mask. This felt more like home than anyplace on the planet. It would curl up, grow, and emerge as something altogether original.

The Hydra shut its eyes. Inside, little Claire shrieked on and on. But Claire was easy to ignore. Soon the Hydra would pinch out the trembling speck of Claire Blessings's consciousness and take over entirely.

Nothing personal. But self-betterment was a solitary pursuit.

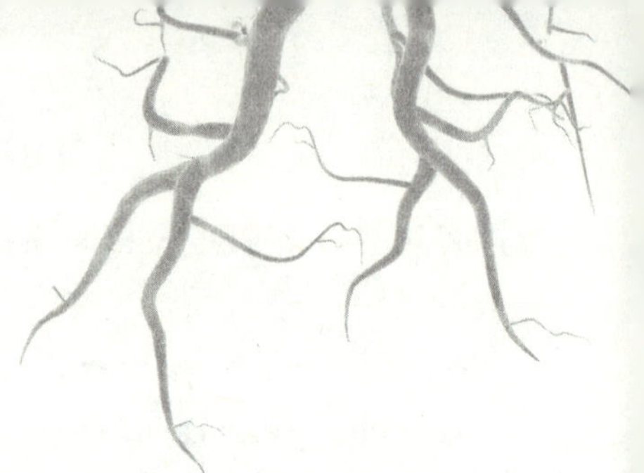

XIII. *Anno Hydra,* Day 68 (4:02 a.m.)

WHEN INGRID stepped inside Dr. Strauss's room, she found it empty. But an unpleasant caged-animal tang hung in the air.

The power had come back on. The Tensor lamp shone on Dr. Strauss's laptop. Ingrid noted the data stick stuck in the port. That was odd. Data sticks were functionally outlawed on Spindrift. They could circumvent the closed-loop system Astrid had implemented in the computer network. So where had it come from?

The rain had given way to snow, now flinging itself against the window, piling up in a two-inch drift along the bottom of the glass.

Ingrid hadn't been in her room when Dr. Strauss must've come to visit. Ingrid had gone down to the boathouse, idly searching (though she could barely admit that to herself) for some means of escape. She'd seen Dr. Strauss down there a few times lately, too. Ingrid had wondered whether she'd harbored those same idle—or not-so-idle—thoughts. Ingrid wasn't sure whether she'd take advantage of any opportunity the boathouse may hold. The idea of just leaving the other subjects behind, Maddy and Frank especially, didn't rest well with her.

Plus, there was Astrid to consider . . . but by then, leaving Astrid filled Ingrid less with regret than with fear. Astrid didn't like to be left alone.

Ingrid's boathouse investigation had revealed one wooden boat that wouldn't start. On this sad discovery, she'd set back up the hill, bracing against the snow that was falling to blanket the staircase. She'd shivered in her thin jacket. Arriving at the main doors, she discovered them locked. Having planned for this possibility, she moved a few hundred feet east, rounding the edge of the wall, to a pair of steel doors sunk into the rock.

A delivery door. She'd seen Moses loading supplies down the narrow stairs past the door once, into a storage cellar. He'd told her the keypad code, perhaps out of some unvoiced concern: *One day you may just need to know.*

She punched it in then. 8-7-0-2.

The lock disengaged. As she was hauling the doors open, she heard something.

Farther down the wall of the building, obscured by the darkness and snow. She caught an awkward plodding note. There was something calculated in the sound, but rudimentary: a circus bear trying to find a way inside to where it was warm and it could eat.

A waterlogged, draggly moan came next. Something had drawn close enough to the delivery doors to send needles through Ingrid's veins. Something large that was poking through the dark landmass falling away from the main building, maybe only twenty yards away.

She stepped down the stairs, gripped the inner handle, and pulled the door shut. It locked behind her.

Ingrid crouched with the breath whistling from her lungs as that unknown something passed by the door, outside in the snow. This presence paused, then set its weight against the heavy iron of the door; the hinges squealed in protest as its movement shifted, and with another mordant moan it moved farther west, skirting toward the front of the lab.

Exiting the cold cellar, Ingrid got moving again. She came to a second set of doors that opened into a loading area near the pantry. She went through the kitchen, bypassing the laboratory—Astrid would be there—until she arrived at her room.

COME TO MY ROOM. V.

said the note taped to her door.

That had led Ingrid to Dr. Strauss's room. To the laptop on the desk. To the data stick.

Ingrid sat. A smell pervaded the room. Something spoiled. She opened the laptop. No password protection. Perhaps Dr. Strauss had disabled it. Why?

In case she wasn't around anymore to type it in, said a dispassionate voice in Ingrid's head.

The laptop's desktop was neat and uncluttered. A single file was centered on the screen.

INSTITUTE_LAB_SEC//MARSH/CHEVALIER_CAM 2.

Ingrid's fingers moved on the trackpad, hovering the arrow over the video.

That smell had gotten worse. She knelt, peering under the bed. Nothing. She thought it might be spoiled food or . . . she opened the desk drawers. Neat as a pin.

The smell and an unaccountable, scaly scratching that tickled the hairs of her inner ears.

With pent breath, Ingrid faced the laptop again. She clicked the video.

The processor momentarily whirred. The desktop filled with silent black-and-white footage. Security cam. As soon as the image resolved, Ingrid knew precisely where it had been shot. She leaned in close to the screen.

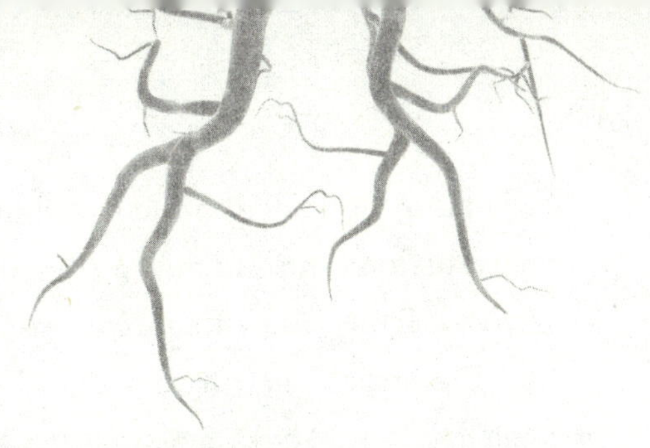

XIV. *Anno Hydra*, Day 68 (darkness before the dawn)

ALL HIS life, seemingly from the moment he sucked his first breath, Theodore Bassiano lacked a firm grip on who exactly he was. His identity shifted moment to moment and act to act. Same as a pair of hands forming shadow puppets on a wall, he was capable of being whatever anyone needed him to be at any given moment.

Friend, lover, father, husband, confidant, secret-keeper . . . was he any of these things, really, except on the surface? Scratch a little and you'd find nothing solid underneath.

If he chose to do good, it was with an idea of how that goodness, or the *appearance* of it, might profit him. If he did ill, his regret was a passing trifle. The mutability of who or what he was, his moral vagrancy, was the only stalwart aspect of Teddy's personality.

This would turn out to be a valuable tool, one he'd harnessed most of his life. But it meant his entire identity was a facade—he was a chameleon who'd blended seamlessly into hundreds of backdrops, so often that he'd forgotten the color he was born with.

As a boy, Teddy used to obsess about death. In gridlock on the 401, the sun beating down on the vehicles turning the freeway into a river of glittering silver, he'd think: *One day everyone in these cars will be dead. My parents up front will be dead. I'll be dead, too, and my body will rot and decompose and, and . . .*

Until recently, Teddy hadn't thought about death here on the island. He'd been far too invested in the possibility of a second life. But with what happened to first John and now Moses, death felt a whole lot closer.

And Teddy had to concede that his mind was starting to shit the bed, too. Parkinson's may have reduced his body over the years, but Teddy's mind had never been anything less than a steel trap. But now . . . he saw his brain, the slick living organ, floating on a bit of bilge in a chartless sea. Shapes roiled in the water below and soon something would curl up—a moody blue tentacle, thick as a gym rope—wrapping around his brain and pulling it underwater. His consciousness would then be in the possession of something else. Something he could barely conceive of and didn't want to think about.

If I'm going to die, then it better be doing something good—for real this time.

Teddy had no fear of hell. No belief in an afterlife. It wasn't about that. It was about anchoring his identity to a final act and pinning the needle on the noble side of the ledger.

State of grace. Go out that way, Teddy, you bad, bad boy.

The Spindrift laboratory rose out of the snow-scrolled night, a solid darkness bulking against the pines. Their journey back from the generator had taken longer than the trip out, but they'd been not nearly so exhausted on the first leg, and they'd had Moses to lead them.

The trio finally made their way to the front doors. "Locked," Maddy said.

"Moses has the keys," Teddy said. "Of course. They're in his trousers, back at the generator."

They hunched round the building in the driving gale. Wind screamed across the roof, flinging snow that stung Teddy's face. The garage was locked.

Their rain slickers were no defense against the cold pushing down from the north. Freezing to death now seemed plausible . . . but would the Hydra allow that? What means could it devise to keep Teddy alive while his organs froze to chunks of ice?

They stopped in front of a long, vertical, rectangular window that looked in on the common room. Who was haunting Spindrift at this hour? Ingrid, surely. Astrid . . . would she let them in? She might prefer to let them freeze, observing them through the windows as she might ants hardening in amber.

Frank pounded on the window. His fist barely made a sound against the triple-pane glass.

"Hey!" he shouted. "*HEY in there!*"

None of them saw the shape materializing from the darkness behind them.

But it was Teddy who sensed it first, turning. It came like a shark drifting out of silty water—one moment it wasn't there and the next, here it was.

It was Hugo Udall. Sort of.

The thing was human in its rudiments—two arms, two legs, the rough etchings of a head—but it wasn't human . . . not really. Teddy embraced this as an unassailable fact.

The sun is hot. Water is wet.

Hugo isn't human anymore.

What staggered out of the dark was as tall as Hugo, muscular as Hugo, walking in the stooped gait familiar to those who'd known Hugo. But that was where the similarities ended.

"*Ooooooooth . . .*"

Hugo was buck naked. His torn shirtsleeves—two ragged bands— encircled his wrists, and the frozen, blood-crusted remains of his collar rung his neck like a choker. A bloody sock was crumpled around his left ankle. His pale skin glittered with frost, giving him the look of a man floured in diamond dust.

Teddy backed away from the shambling horror. Maddy and Frank did the same. Maddy's hands were knuckled at the sides of her mouth, which opened in a silent scream.

Oh, Hugo. Oh, me old Bastinado Boy, what in the love of Christ happened to you?

His body bulged in spots it should not: carbuncled knots of flesh protruded from his hips, chest, stomach. They resembled rotted boluses on an oak tree, hanging pendulously from his frame. His thighs, blotched with early frostbite, were thicker and wadded (Teddy's fevered mind couldn't summon a better word), the skin lapping in pleats—Hugo's legs were half-melted beeswax candles, all that excess skin (from *where?*) drooling over his feet like puddled curtains. As Hugo shambled forward, those stiffened pleats scraped the ground with a sandpapery rasp.

"*Ooooooooth . . .*"

But his head . . . oh, his *face.*

Hugo's skull was broken open in a ragged horizontal rip-line above his bushy black eyebrows. The bowl of his skull clung on a tenacious strand of scalp, bouncing against the back of his head with each ponderous footfall. From Hugo's opened skull sprouted a confusion of blue ropes, threads, whips; there was something exotic to the display, a tropical succulent that only flowered once a decade in the swelter of the jungle primeval.

Curling from the flowerpot of Hugo's head, the Hydra danced and licked and *directed.* Hugo's eyes shone dully beneath this gruesome display, robbed of the spark of personhood.

Above that teeming profusion, his hands hefted a rock the size of a medicine ball.

"*Ooooooooggth.*"

Tottering past them, Hugo heaved the rock at the window.

The glass burst, creating a vacuuming inhale as the warmer air inside the building *whooshed* out. The rock hit the floor of the common room with a muted *thump.*

Without pause, Hugo crawled through the smashed window frame. He did so heedless of the damage the glass would do to him. Teddy saw that Hugo's back was carved with pale slashes, some so deep as to reveal the wink of spinal bone.

Glass punched into Hugo's palms. The blue ropes hunted from his skull, toward the warmth inside. A long finger of glass slid into Hugo's stomach below his ribs. Grunting like a dog straining at his leash, Hugo dragged himself forward, and the glass slit him open as he disemboweled himself. Something forced itself out of the self-made incision with a rubbery squelch. Then Hugo was inside, lumbering on down the hall.

Teddy, Frank, and Maddy gathered at the window. Teddy's shock zenithed into disbelief; he couldn't hold on to Hugo's horrible face—it kept slipping through the bars of his mind, twisting itself into a blissful blank. Chunks of torn flesh hung on the points of glass. Teddy's own death seemed much closer now—it zoomed up at him, magnified a hundredfold, making his heart quail.

Using the butt of Moses's pistol, Teddy smashed at the fangs of glass studding the frame.

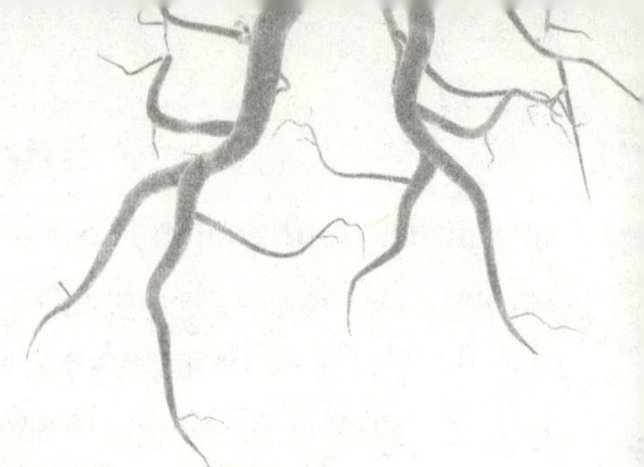

XV. *Anno Hydra*, Day 68 (near dawn)

"ING—THERE YOU are."

There was near silence in Veronica Strauss's room when Astrid stepped inside. Only a faint, almost rodent *scratch-scratch* from someplace, impossible to pinpoint.

"Things have gone very badly, I'm afraid." She offered a forlorn shake of her head. "But I'm taking care of it, Ing. One by one, I'm crossing items off my list."

Ingrid was facing Veronica Strauss's laptop. Something was playing on it.

"Ing . . . ?"

Astrid closed the distance between them. Set her fingers on Ing's shoulder.

"Don't touch me," her best friend said.

"What are you watching?"

The footage cut out. The screen ran black for a heartbeat. The video loop restarted, the time stamp resetting. In the screen's reflection, Ingrid's face was blotchy and puffed.

With resistant posture, Astrid leaned in. She *saw*.

The video had been taken in the laboratory. *Their* old laboratory at the Institute. The one Astrid and Ingrid had been bequeathed for their project.

The security camera was trained on a twenty-by-twenty-foot area of the lab floor. In the frame, Ingrid sat in the foreground, at a bench in the shadow of the jellyfish tank they'd had installed. She wore headphones, listening to music.

What had been the circumstances of that night? Had Ingrid been waiting for Astrid to return? They may have had plans that evening—nothing more exciting than lying on the bed in one of their rooms together, talking, laughing, same as practically every other night . . . still, that was enough to look forward to. The two of them tucked tight against the hostile world into which their titanic intellects had been dropped.

On the video, Astrid watched a shadow draw long and narrow across the floor, somewhere behind Ingrid and the jellyfish tank. That shadow pulled Astrid into the frame.

There she was, holding a hammer.

"This never happened," Astrid said with a compressed fury.

The hammer rose in Astrid's hands. The footage ran so static, so still, that for those moments one might think someone had paused it. If watched enough times (as Ingrid surely had by then), Astrid's face could be seen moving through a progression of emotions.

Rage, then guilt, followed perhaps by genuine sorrow and, finally, acceptance.

Next, the hammer fell.

The footage ran soundlessly, but those present would've heard the sucking inhale of airtight glass rupturing. The contents of that tank—five thousand gallons of salt water—crashed over Ingrid in an awesome wave, sweeping the stool out from under her.

She toppled back into the gelatinous tide of the jellyfish. Some of them harmless, many more not. The box jelly, sea nettle, Portuguese man-of-war, Morbakka, lion's mane . . .

. . . and the tiny Irukandji, not bigger than an infant's clipped fingernail.

It was impossible to see any of them sting her. The footage was too grainy. But the jellyfish dappled Ingrid's body, a hundred gray flattened toadstools as she thrashed for a few seconds, then her legs and arms jittered before taking on a deathly stillness.

The water sluiced most of the jellyfish away. They drifted across the tiles and got hung up on the legs of the lab benches. Their twitching tentacles registered as a haze of static on the footage. Ingrid lay motionless, drenched. Astrid set the hammer down and stood over her best friend.

Carefully, *lovingly*, she bent to kiss Ingrid's lips. Astrid then retreated from the scene, bearing her long shadow with her.

The footage ended. Looped back. Began afresh.

From somewhere within Spindrift—echoing down the hall to Dr. Strauss's room—came the bright sound of glass shattering.

"You don't understand," Astrid said.

"No?" Ingrid sounded genuinely curious.

"I was upset."

"Sure." Ingrid's tone wooden. "You must have been."

"You were going to leave. We were supposed to be together. You were . . . Ing, you were all I had. Nobody understands me. Nobody even *likes* me. Only you."

"That's right. Only me."

The dreamy tone of Ing's voice unseated Astrid. "You *promised*!"

Astrid reared back, her fingernails digging in under her eyes and dragging down her cheeks.

"You *promised* you weren't going to leave me! But you *lied*! Ooooooooh, you rotten lying *liar*! *Traitor*! You were going to leave the Institute, leave me all by myself!"

"You're right, I was," Ingrid said patiently. "And do you want to know why?" She turned to face Astrid. "At first, I liked you so much. Then I think I loved you. But I stopped loving you. By the end I didn't even like you anymore."

Astrid's face was trenched by the pale furrows her nails had left. Her question came out as a wretched moan: "*Whhhhyyyy?*"

"I saw what you really were."

On that, Astrid Marsh detonated on her best friend for the second time.

The air of Veronica Strauss's bedroom shattered as Astrid flew at Ingrid, her fingers knurled into claws. Ingrid's nightmare and her reality overlapped: she'd found her again. The witch from her coma. Astrid. One and the same.

Astrid's chest was clad in the pelts of dead rabbits and her twisted face framed by the stinging tentacles of a jellyfish. Astrid ripped at Ingrid's eyes—she'd gouge them out before dragging her into the dark . . . where they could be together, forever.

Except there was something different inside Ingrid—and the Hydra had its own designs.

Ingrid caught Astrid effortlessly. Astrid bucked and thrashed, but with her newfound strength Ingrid subdued her as she might a tantrummy girl. Astrid's eyes grew wide as the Hydra surfaced on Ingrid's face, racing under the skin in geometric grid lines . . .

Astrid brought her knee up between Ingrid's legs but Ingrid deflected the blow; the two girls swanned across the bedroom—bumping into the desk, off the bed, ricocheting off the chair, and Ingrid was amazed at how slowly this was all happening, how nothing Astrid did was fast enough to stop Ingrid from dodging or parrying . . . she realized that she was toying with Astrid now—she could kill her so easily if that was her wish.

Ingrid shoved her old friend with such force that Astrid left her feet and flew backward, slamming into the closet. The impact jostled the knob—that, or the weight of what had been clumsily stuffed inside it . . . whatever the case, when Astrid fell away from the closet, stunned, the door sprung open—

Both girls saw something slump from the closet onto the floor to shine under the wan light of the Tensor lamp.

The fact that this thing had once, not too long ago, been a human being didn't register on either of the girls . . . it was impossible for them to believe this threadbare effigy could have once passed as one of their own species.

It was red and tacky. Something came out of it, a sound, but it could as easily have been wind hissing through the window seams. If nothing before clarified just how tragically insane matters had become here on the island, the thing on the floor—which until recently had been Veronica Strauss— rammed that point home.

The shape released a shuddering exhale. Was it still *alive*? Past its sagging sockets, what remained of its eyes twitched like pollywogs in shallow pools. The exposed tendons running down its spine picked up stray balls of lint as it curled into itself on the carpet.

A bellow rolled down the hallway.

"*Ooooooooooggthh.*"

Tearing her gaze from the horrid thing on the floor, Ingrid fled to the door. She peered down the hallway, the halogen tubes fritzing and popping—

When it rounded the corner at the head of the hall, the sane part of Ingrid's brain—the part now hanging by a thread—knew it was Hugo Udall.

But what she saw was a monster, whose immense grief had crystallized into wrath.

Its eyes hunted for quarry. Two worm-eaten pits gleaming with spite. The pounding of its footsteps shook the earth as its shambling shape filled the hallway, offering no escape.

Astrid slipped around her, flashing down the hall in the opposite direction.

"Kill them all!" she cackled merrily as she dashed into the dark.

Ingrid was forced to step into the hallway to meet Hugo. The man (was he that anymore?) carried the stench of a backwater grave, his flesh sagging from his bones like sodden slabs of dough while blue strings pushed from all parts of his anatomy.

"Hugo, you don't have to—"

He shoved Ingrid aside, not with any malice, but more as an obstacle to be moved. His titanic strength sent Ingrid backpedaling into Strauss's room. She tripped; her skull struck the side of the desk. Blackness poured in.

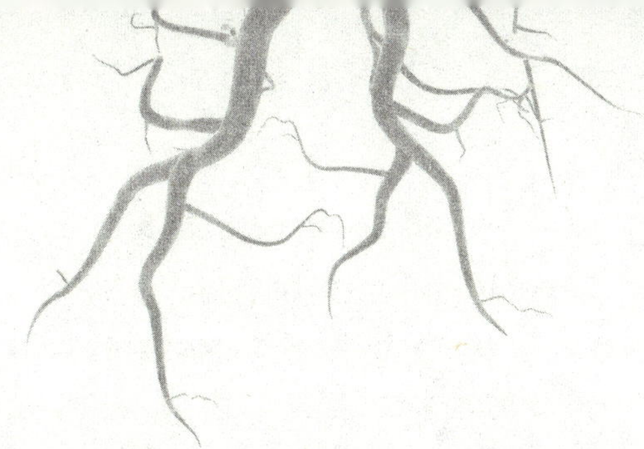

XVI. *Anno Hydra*, Day 68 (breaking day)

TEDDY BASSIANO was on the hunt for his brother.

Not his real brother. Nothing in this place was real. The promise it once held, a means to advance humankind—all a horrendous lie.

The hallway winnowed to a point of hollow gray under the failing lights. Cold as a meat locker, too. It wasn't hard to track Hugo, his brother of the lash: the poor guy's bleats bounced off the walls, and should those fade, Teddy could always follow the splotches Hugo's feet left on the floor.

Teddy was so tired. Bone-deep, soul-sickened. It hadn't just been the sight of Hugo blooming out of the night like some noxious walking mushroom. Of course, that hadn't *helped* . . . it wasn't whatever the Hydra was doing inside Teddy, either.

It was everything. Every damn bit of it. All of a sudden, his very existence exhausted him. If this is what endless life was going to be—this toxic atmosphere where he and the others were reduced to playthings of fate . . . he'd rather cash his chips.

Casting a glance back, Teddy didn't see Frank or Maddy. Did they follow him through the window? Must not have. That was okay. He wished them both well. You come into this world alone, and you go out of it alone.

The hallway bent past the room they'd assembled in on that first afternoon. He pictured Dr. Strauss facing them: Frank with his oxygen machine, Hugo with that piss-bag strapped to his leg, Teddy practically shaking off his chair, even that dopey Davey Jacobs with his Bible (and boy, hadn't *that* lucky fuck dodged a bullet)—as Veronica's words filled them with an awful hope.

To put off death, perhaps forever. This offer had set a steady process of dehumanization in motion.

That was the real kick in the teeth, wasn't it? Teddy didn't feel *human* anymore.

Dogging Hugo's footprints toward the lab, an unaccountable feeling overcame him. That of a stopwatch set to a specific instant, each second snipping off until time ran out. *Exist in the moment.* He'd always hated that goddamn happy-sappy bumper sticker aphorism. It crumbled under the weight of lived existence, didn't it? No reasonable person could live entirely in the moment, because another moment will follow that one, and another and another, all of which carry their own duties and tolls.

And you have to plan for those future moments, don't you? That is, until you near the end. The squirrel who knows it'll die before winter shouldn't waste time gathering nuts.

I'm ready, was Teddy's thought as he shouldered through the door into the lab. *Yeah, for real this time. Just try to go out on a high note, baby.*

The lab was as cavernous and sterile as outer space. He pulled Moses's pistol from his trousers. He'd rarely fired one, but the weapon felt okay in his hands. More than okay, actually.

The pair of tortoises watched him from their glass boxes with hundred-year-old eyes. Tortoises, man. They had this aging thing right. Take it slow, don't get bogged down with the small stuff, and kick against the pricks. That's what Teddy should've told his own munchkins. *Be like the tortoise, kiddos.*

The jellyfish tank towered over him. Something drew him to the creatures now—that feeling of not being quite human doubled back on him.

Not far off, Hugo bleated again.

Teddy rounded into sight of the Baths. Only one of them was now lit with that familiar Barbicide blue. Hugo's immense and gruesome shape faced it. His hand rose to settle gently on the curved glass.

Teddy's feet ground to a halt. He stared in shell-shocked awe.

Claire was in the Bath. Even at this distance, in this unsettled dark, and with his mind unraveling, Teddy saw how different she was. How *young*.

She was somehow perfect. But of a sick, unnatural kind. The kind of beauty a young girl accords to her dolly, maybe, not understanding that the slight deviations and imperfections are the markers of authentic human beauty. Worse, Claire looked . . . *inevitable.* That was the word Teddy's mind settled on. It made him think of a conversation with his daughter, who couldn't have been older than five at the time. It had been late, she'd been up watching the Canada Day fireworks. The two of them had been lying on her canopy bed with the smell of spent fireworks faintly perfuming their skin. His daughter, his darling Francesca, asked why people had to die. She was that age. She talked a lot about cemeteries, skeletons. She'd told Teddy once that if he died, she'd dig up his skeleton and give it a kiss. She'd always had that grim bent of mind, and Teddy had loved her all the more for it.

People have to die, darlin', he'd told her, honest and tipsy on the ten or twelve Labatt's 50s he'd drank. *It's inevitable. Maybe one of our world's only such phenomena, other than the sun's gonna rise and set.* She asked what "inevitable" meant, pronouncing it *immemitibble. It means something that's going to happen nevertheless, and no matter what you or me or the Almighty God do, seven come eleven that thing is gonna pass. And death is one inescapable inevitability. Now to bed, my precious little dove, to dream about kissing skeletons.*

That was how Claire looked to Teddy then. An inevitability that had masqueraded as a mad improbability. She represented where this was leading. The solid gold at the end of the rainbow. A line came to him, a bolt from the heavens:

In which we shall all be gods, ageless and blissful.

Claire's hand rose inside the Bath, meeting Hugo's on the other side of the glass. A sound of ineffable loss came out of Hugo. He could have been beholding a Renaissance masterpiece in an art gallery.

"Hugo?" Teddy's voice was a balloon on a string. "Buddy, I'm afraid it's time."

Hugo didn't hear him. Maybe he couldn't anymore. He strained toward Claire, his misshapen features broadcasting an embryonic desire. What seeped into Teddy's chest was past horror or even stark psychic terror—it was *loss,* an emptiness that caverned him and brought him nearly to tears.

Teddy Bassiano knew he would soon die. Why? Because such thoughts were the sole dominion of the dead.

Moses's pistol came up, shaky in Teddy's hands. "Hugo, y'ole horse thief! Look at me. Don't make me shoot you in the back."

Ah, who are you kidding? You'll be doing him a favor.

Hugo had ascended to an uncanny state of beauty, too. Not following any traditional human beauty—in whose eyes he was an abhorrence—but made beautiful by his tragedy.

"Do me a favor and step your raggedy old caboose a little closer to thissee here gun barrel, would you? I may as well put these slugs where it counts."

Hugo tottered toward Teddy. The poor guy. His belly was slit open and something was hanging out, tethered to his inner gearing like a clacker on a string.

We never know when we hit our apex, do we? This is the thought that went cartwheeling through Teddy's head. We can never forecast that modest collection of heartbeats where everything runs true and a fleeting earthbound perfection is reached. Where everything comes into alignment like the spinning of a top, gravity and propulsion marrying to keep a person and those to share these moments with turning in a true orbit preceding the inevitable wobble and fall. It's human to hope that this apex will last, if not forever, then at least long enough to savor.

"Forgive me," Teddy whispered. "I know you'd do the same for me."

The first bullet punched into Hugo's chest, jerking him sideways. Hugo let out a shocked bellow. The second slug took a chunk out of his hip and sent him spinning to one side. The gun kicked in Teddy's hands, putting him off-balance. Hugo found his feet and closed the distance; the roadkill smell of his body filled Teddy's sinuses as he fired twice more. It was too dark to tell if the first hit its mark, but the second was nearly point-blank—it smashed into Hugo's face, grooving a wet hole in his mouth before corkscrewing out the back of his head in a fanning mist.

Last charge of the Bastinado Boys. It was an honor to serve with you, good sir.

Then Hugo was on him, huge arms dragging Teddy down. What a

stubborn will to live! It was sickening, it made Teddy's heart flinch. *What is left, you poor bastard?*

They fell to the floor, Hugo's smothering bulk on top of Teddy. Hugo's arms pumped mindlessly—he wasn't trying to hurt Teddy, more an urge to paw his hands over Teddy's face like a blind person trying to read his expression. Teddy let his fingers creep around the back of Hugo's head . . . oh, the ruin of it—the Hydra lashed at his fingers, but there was no malice in it, as by then Teddy's own Hydra was coming out, too, their bodies a nurse tree for the bright blue saplings they were fathering.

His fingers dug inside Hugo's head, tearing past the Hydra to find the living brain, which was still there, still warm and human, but surely dying now, neural death blanketing it.

Teddy sunk his fingers into Hugo's brain and clenched his hand into a fist, the toothpaste-soft tissue squishing between his fingers as some evil-smelling fluid gouted out . . . it came to him that he'd never held such a bodily closeness with another human being: not his wives or children, nobody except his own mother when he'd been a peanut in her belly. God, he and Hugo barely knew each other. They'd just beaten the holy old tar out of one another in the woods a time or two, but it sure didn't feel that way now. More that he and Hugo and the others, all six of them, had taken part in something so cataclysmic, so far beyond the reach or scale of their species that it had bonded them somehow, soul fused to soul so neatly that you could no longer spot the weld marks.

"Okay, buddy," Teddy whispered as Hugo at last seemed to give up. "Leave it all behind. Let it go, it's okay to let go . . . Hugo, *please*, will you just fucking *die* already."

He held Hugo as the man struggled against the deathless will of the Hydra. "I'm gonna hold on as long as it takes," Teddy promised. "Just as long as it takes, big fuh-fella, for you to—"

Something dodged out of the darkness. A cheese-white face with a nasty lopsided grin.

"Abomination!"

A needle pierced Teddy's neck. Before he could heave Hugo off, a second and third one sunk in. Astrid Marsh. She left the needles bobbing from his throat like porcupine quills.

"Die," she ordered.

"Ew, you weird little turd," Teddy hissed, but by then Astrid was gone.

So, were those to be his final words? Not exactly *Thus, with a kiss I will die*, was it? He was glad nobody was around to hear. The poison was already working its claws into his heart and, *ooooh*, did it ever hurt . . . would the thing inside Teddy let him go into that good night? Had that crazy little bitch used enough weed killer?

What the hell had been the meaning of it all?

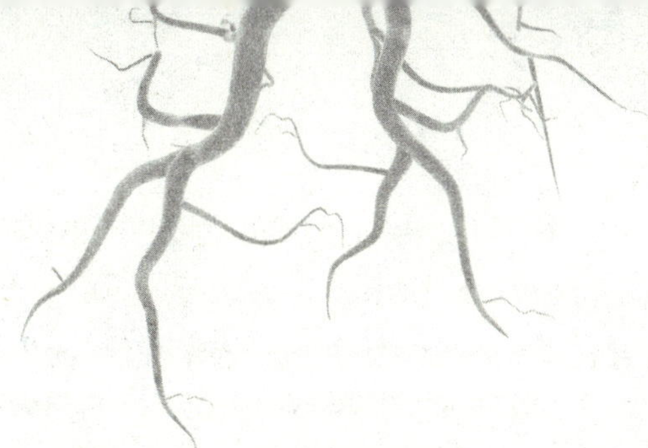

XVII. *Anno Hydra*, Day 68 (dawn)

MADDY AND Frank heard the gunshots ring out somewhere within Spindrift. Four in rapid succession, shattering the silence of the main building.

"Those came from the lab," Frank said.

They'd lost sight of Teddy after he'd gone barreling through the broken window in pursuit of Hugo. Maddy had cut herself on the glass as she'd clambered through. A nasty gash down her forearm. By the time they'd stemmed the flow using tea towels and tape from the first aid kit, Teddy was long gone.

Following the echo of the gunshots, they arrived at the Baths in time to see Teddy bucking under Hugo's body. White foam emitted from Teddy's mouth as his feet jittered, the Hydra expressing itself from his eyes and nostrils. Hugo's body (was he dead?) shifted atop Teddy's, almost as if it were being prodded from below by stiff fingers as the Hydra continued to spool out of Teddy . . . one of Teddy's rain boots expanded before it slid off his foot under the pressure of the Hydra, which thrashed from the ends of his toes like so many hooked earthworms.

"*Ungghhhh,*" Teddy gargled, his neck tense as a ramrod as every tendon cramped uncontrollably. "*Nnnnnnnnnuuunghhsssh—*"

His body went limp in capitulation. His face softened as it relaxed into death.

"Teddy . . . ?" Frank said.

Maddy knelt to take Teddy's pulse. A delicate bit of business, seeing as the Hydra continued to drool from both men's bodies. But even the

Hydra's energies had begun to diminish, their blue glow fading to a dull purple.

Maddy shook her head with grim finality. They backed away as the Hydra's tendrils sucked across the floor, creating an intricate interlocking web around the men's corpses.

"Look."

Frank had taken notice of the Bath. Claire was in it. Behind the mask, her expression was unreadable.

"She's so young."

Frank stood in disbelief. Claire looked to be no older than twenty now. Her skin unlined, her body thrumming with the vigor of reclaimed youth.

"Couldn't we . . . ?" he breathed.

Maddy said: "No. Don't even think it."

Frank caught a trace of movement on the periphery of the Bath pod. He spun, hand coming up—something stabbed him. The flash of a needle.

Astrid wielded it. She depressed the plunger. Fluid jetted from the needle tip that she'd spiked right through Frank's palm; it spritzed his cheeks and one eye, stinging. Astrid had been aiming for his neck.

Frank closed his fingers around the hypodermic and snatched it away from her. But Astrid wielded another one—in that moment she seemed to be *made* of needles. Maddy and Frank retreated to the opposite side of a lab bench.

"I told you," Astrid whispered mockingly. "You'll never leave. I *told* you that, didn't I? I was very honest with you all."

She lunged across the bench, stabbing at them with the needle. The tip hit the benchtop and bent. Astrid shrieked in frustration. She didn't look like a teenage girl at all. More a hunchbacked, leering goblin.

"*I'm* leaving," she growled. "You'll stay, dead in a ditch, but I'll go somewhere else, won't I? They'll let me do this all over again—and do it better."

Moses's gun. Frank spied it on the floor beside Teddy.

"Algernons!" Astrid had already uncapped another needle; the little witch appeared to have an endless supply. "Start over, try again—they'll let me do this *forever*!"

Frank was contemplating his best angle to make a break for the gun when a shape coalesced from the shadows behind Astrid.

It was Ingrid. She had a needle, too.

When it sank into Astrid's neck, her lips sagged downward like a sad clown's. She leapt forward, her forehead hitting the bench. She wheeled on Ingrid, snarling as she swept the needle into her own hand, searching for something to plunge it into—but her motor functions had gone screwy. Her knees unlocked. She sank to the floor. She was only able to throw the needle at Ingrid. It bounced harmlessly off her chest.

"Kill you," Astrid hissed. "Kill all of you bloopers . . ."

Once she'd stopped moving, the three of them stood over her body.

"Is she dead?"

"No, Frank," Ingrid answered. "Only a sedative. She'll wake up in a few hours."

Maddy walked into the adjoining lab pod. After several moments, she returned with a black satchel, cinched at the top. "We have to go, Frank."

Stiffly and unceremoniously, Maddy hugged Ingrid. "You be well, kiddo, okay? I'm not going to ask about your plans for the next minutes and hours. I think it's better I don't know."

Breaking the hug, Maddy turned to Frank. "Say goodbye to Ingrid, Frank."

Automatically—even though some part of Frank hated himself for this subservience—he did just that.

"You'll be all right?" he asked the girl paternally.

"I'll be fine," Ingrid assured him, her brow creasing in confusion. "But where are you both going?"

Maddy took Frank's wrist and led him as she might a horse, clucking her tongue. Something felt wrong about all this.

Maddy and Frank stopped before Claire in the Bath. Madeline kissed her fingertips and touched them to the glass.

"Goodbye, Claire," she said. "Best of luck to you."

Holding Frank's hand, guiding gently, Maddy made a final stop for Hugo and Teddy. Teddy looked damned *good.* He could've been posed for his first wedding photo . . . but all that blue coming out of him marred the impression.

"Goodbye, Hugo."

Maddy touched Hugo's chin.

"And you, Theodore. Goodbye."

She gripped Frank's hand again. "Come on. The sun's coming up," she said.

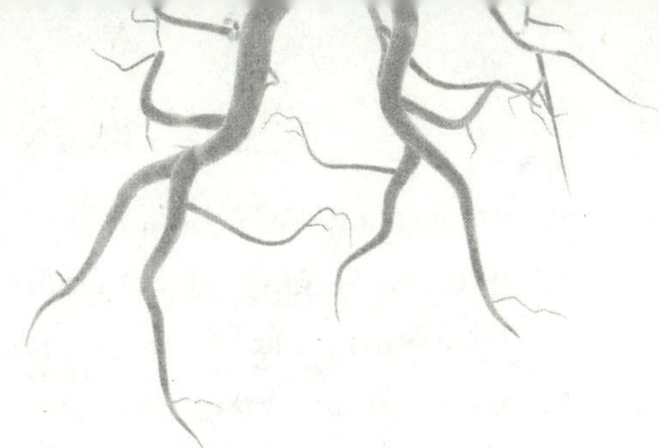

XVIII. *Anno Hydra*, Day 68 (new day)

MADDY AND Frank exited the main doors of Spindrift. The outcroppings of the distant island chains throbbed with the burnt-orange glow of dawn. The snow had stopped falling. The channel ran dark between shores of white.

"Where are we going, Maddy?"

Only days ago, everything had felt pretty much okay in Frank's world. Now people were dead. Frank's friends, the last he'd ever know. But what did that mean for him—what debt did Frank owe for that?

"What about Ingrid?" he said.

"She's a strong girl," Maddy told him. "She'll fend for herself."

"Astrid? Veronica?"

No reply.

"Claire . . . Astrid's gonna try to leave."

"Would you like to leave, too, Frank? Would you really?"

Frank couldn't frame his feelings on this. Yes? No? The childlike belief that death was something that happened only to old people went through his mind. Frank wondered if he had regressed to the headspace of a young child who couldn't even conceive of death . . . *What do we believe when we're that young?* That our parents and grandparents and everyone we know must exist in the eternal present, that those who lovingly tuck us in at night will forever be there when we wake in the morning?

"People will be coming soon," Maddy said as they moved down the path between boughs weighed with fresh snow. "The ones who bankrolled this. Now that the storm's over, they'll be on their way. Whatever plans they have for anyone still breathing, I don't want to be part of it."

"You can't be sure about that."

"I *believe*, Frank. And that's more powerful than knowledge."

They walked into the trees leading to the shore. She didn't need to hold his hand anymore. Frank had crossed some final threshold in acceptance.

The half-moon beach sparkled under new snow. Looking over his shoulder, he saw tracks leading back into the trees. *Those are my final footprints.* His eyes charted the water. It was already freezing close to shore; a rime of ice was wrapping the cattails and lily pads.

"Hey, Frank. Did you ever figure that God in His infinite wisdom knew this idea was wrong and so He *chose* us, knowing we'd fuck it up?"

"I don't know about that. Anyone would have fucked this up, Maddy."

Maddy shed her clothes. Frank felt himself in the grip of forces larger than he could compass. Was this the *right* way, the one he was beholden to?

Maddy stepped out of her pants to stand naked. Youthful to elderly and back again: Frank's vision of her shifted prismatically, making her all ages at once.

"My wife and I had a cat, Orca," Frank said. "Beautiful little tuxedo cat with a sweet temperament. She had kidney failure. We had to put her down. It was summer, and the vet's office had a whitewashed gazebo out back, on the lawn. Soft music and one of those machines that cycled water to make a babbling-brook sound. My wife, my Annie, she held our sweet little Orca as she passed on. It was real professional, y'know? Peaceful."

"Here, Frank. Let me h-h-help."

She began unbuttoning his shirt. He wanted to push her away, but he couldn't find the willpower . . . frigid air touched his chest, which immediately pebbled in gooseflesh.

"I can do it on my own, Maddy. Christ, will you just let me?"

Frank managed to get his pants down. She hooked her thumbs into his boxers and helped him get them off, too.

They stepped to the waterline. The surf sucked at their toes. Maddy uncinched the satchel. It held eight syringes wrapped in sterile packaging.

"How many do we need?" Maddy asked.

"How should I know? Better use them all."

When they were ready, she said: "Kiss me."

"Why?"

"Because we're going to *nnnn*-need it."

They kissed, briefly but lovingly. Maddy popped the needle shields off each syringe.

"You cuh-c-can call muh-me by her n-n-name, if you'd luh-like."

"Who?"

"Your whu-wife. You can cuh-cuh-call me—"

"*No.* I won't." Clenching his teeth, Frank spoke his last words. "I loved my w-wife. We had some fine adventures together, but this luh-last one was with yuh-you. So I'll cuh-call you Madeline."

They waded into the water. The cold screamed up Frank's legs. His heart thumped like an engine winding down. His fingers had gone stupid with numbness.

Animals don't seem to mind dying, he thought. *I've never suspected them to believe they've not been given enough time, or let themselves or their loved ones down, or led a life unworthy of living . . .*

They reached the zone where the current curled into the bay. Frank wondered how far their bodies might travel . . . what strange mysteries they'd make upon discovery.

The Hydra was coming out of Maddy now. A vivid straining blue, glorious in its way.

Her hands settled on either side of Frank's neck. A pair of syringes were clutched in each. His own hands rose as if in prayer, four needle tips aimed at the hollow of Maddy's throat.

Frank thought: *I used to hate those last few minutes of the school day when the sun shone on the field outside and my body trembled with the urge to run and jump and laugh and play, but the second hand on the classroom clock seemed forever locked in place. But you know what? I'd take that moment now. I'd give everything for another languishing school afternoon with the sun shining on the grass outdoors, that delicious feeling of anticipation with the long hand of the clock eternally stuck between eleven and twelve.*

He didn't feel the needles going in.

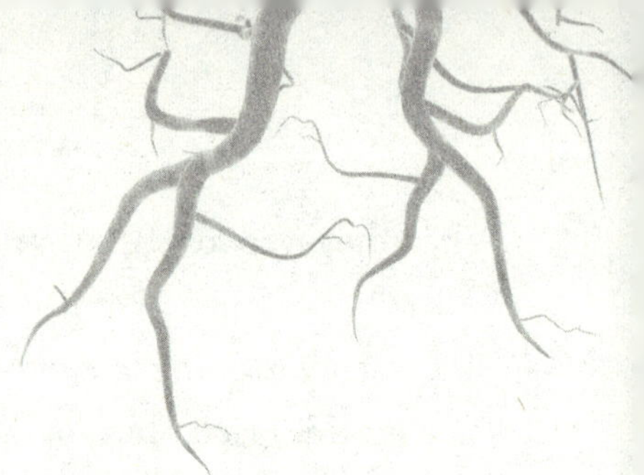

XIX. *Anno Hydra*, Day 68

THE HYDRA crawled from its Bath. Finally, it had Become.

Its hands (ah, what supple unlined hands) gripped the rungs of the ladder. It climbed dripping from the tank. Its feet (so strong, so youthful) settled delicately on the floor.

The cold gripped it momentarily. The lab had gotten chilly. The Hydra scraped one fingernail (un-yellowed healthy keratin) over the frost-clad exterior of its Bath. Touching the collected frost to its tongue brought on a delightful shiver.

It dressed quickly. It had to get moving. Gears were turning—a new change was coming. It had to be gone from this place before that change arrived.

The Hydra moved through the lab, its breath coming lightly. It hadn't gone too far when it came across its own kind. Dying now, impossible as that may be.

This other Hydra . . . no, there were two . . . spidered across the floor, their once-vibrant blue decaying to a sickly tar color. A single dying thread sucked weakly at the Hydra's boot—knocking, almost, as a starving beggar at a door.

But there was no room for it here. The inn was full.

The creatures the Hydra had deserted lay on the floor, cast-off toys. Their limbs stiffening, their eyes glazed with frost. Somewhere inside the Hydra, little Claire screamed and howled and pleaded.

The Hydra walked past the dead men, alerted to a disturbance deeper in the laboratory. It soon came upon two others. Young ones. Girls . . . ?

One was lashed to the tank containing thousands of the Hydra's own kind. Ropes cinched this girl's ankles and wrists, pinning her to the curved glass convex. The other girl sat on an empty specimen cage. Patiently waiting.

"Claire," this girl said to her. "You're so young. You might even be younger than me."

Thank you, Ingrid. You're too kind.

With a faint smile, the Hydra continued to the main doors. They opened onto a searing white vista. The bitter wind stung its face, numbing its lips. Deep within, old forgettable Claire sounded a warning.

It's too cold, you have to go back inside.

No. Inside was death. There was no place to grow in there.

The Hydra made its way down to the boathouse. Wafers of ice floated in the water. The cold was hostile. But there was life out past the breakwater.

Deeper in the channel, that red light throbbed. That light led to warm bodies. Creatures that the Hydra could bear its gift to . . . that it could move and expand through, enlarging itself in ways its creator never dreamed.

The battery was where the Hydra knew it would be. Still hidden. The Hydra cleaned it off and wired it to the outboard motor. After it primed the pump bulb, the motor started with ease.

The Hydra guided the boat into the water. The wind hit the boat broadside. The Hydra had to grip the tiller tight to keep the vessel pointed toward that guiding red light.

. . . there it was . . . gone now . . . back again.

As the boat moved farther from the dock, large chunks of ice began to knock against its bow and gunwales. The cold was merciless. In its primordial core, the Hydra experienced . . . something. Had it possessed higher reasoning, it might have understood it as the threat of extinction. But its kind had existed for five hundred million years. They would be around, in one shape or another, when the sun collapsed into a wormhole.

Still . . . that nagging sense.

Water slopped over the sides of the boat to freeze in layers. The sodden bottoms of the Hydra's pants soon froze, too. The boat grew heavier and more unwieldy under the load of ice. The engine was laboring. The tiller was difficult to command.

The red light seemed neither closer nor farther off. The boathouse had been scrubbed away in the boat's wake.

The Hydra stubbornly carried on. No, not even that—stubbornness was a human quality, freighted with an element of choice. The Hydra simply *was*.

The cold worked around its limbs, solidifying them in place. It revved the engine, pinning the accelerator. That red light, was it getting closer? Yes! It will reach it any second. It will then drag itself out onto land and find a suitable life-form to latch onto. Something warm and pulsing with blood. If it must leave this beautiful shell behind, so be it.

It would survive. It would never die. *Cannot die.*

It crawled from its freezing shell, worming over the ice-slick gunwales to the point of the bow—like a maidenhead it stretched, straining toward the life it sensed someplace ahead and—

—Claire Blessings is walking to a party. Twilight hangs over the oaks. The sidewalk is carpeted with autumn leaves. It's her freshman year of college. She's on her way to a department mixer. Those first-day-of-school worries move through her, but the overmastering feeling is of excitement. Tonight she will walk into people's lives and they into hers; the coming hours will mark that time in their collective memory when it all started. Claire has the strong sense that everything, absolutely everything, will change.

Nearly a lifetime later, she will return to this night. To the memory of her shoes kicking through those autumn drifts, and a fleeting youthfulness will pass through her bloodstream—she will muse on how memory can be a tonic, if a wistful one, leaving a soft hurt in her heart.

The memory will unfold in the freezing chambers of Claire Blessings's mind until the very end. That night, the sidewalk, the leaves, and the anticipation of it all being ahead of her: a limitless horizon, her every step bringing her closer to it.

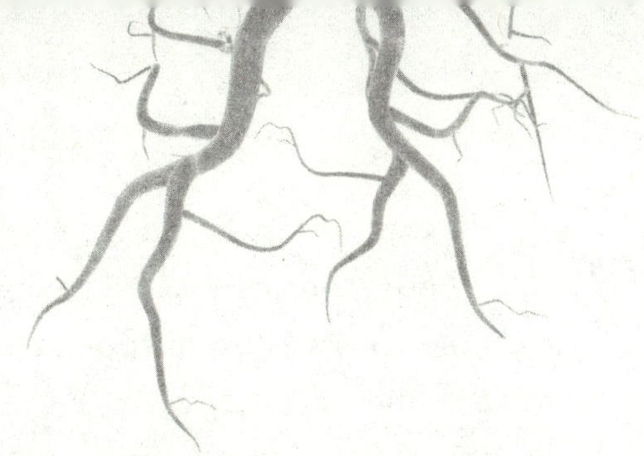

XX. *Anno Hydra,* Day 68 (night)

DARKNESS HAD fallen by the time Astrid's eyelids opened.

By then the lab pods of Spindrift lay silent. Claire had left a long time ago. After securing Astrid to the tank, Ingrid had found some bedsheets to cover Teddy and Hugo.

She'd watched their bodies closely, worried one of them might sit up. She was concerned the Hydra would *prop* them up, dragging them across the floor like two marionettes by their strings. She had a scalpel in her hand, just in case. But Teddy and Hugo stayed put. Their arms and legs had stopped making those horrid creaking sounds.

When Astrid finally came to, it took her a minute to gather her wits. Did she understand where she was, and the straits she was now in? Ingrid watched Astrid tighten her forearms, testing her restraints. When it was obvious that she was held fast, she searched her surroundings until her eyes settled on Ingrid.

"Let me go."

Ingrid rose from her cross-legged position and approached her onetime friend. She bent to check the knots of the ropes around Astrid's ankles. She'd found a whole spool of rope in the garage, on a hook near the Rovers. The decal above the hook had read *"Rope"* in Moses's neat block letters. He'd marked everything that way. A scrupulous, careful man was Moses Squires.

"Let me go," Astrid repeated.

"I can't."

"You mean you won't."

The click of nails heralded a new arrival. Ingrid turned on the balls of her feet, a dreamy unreality washing through her . . . it was the wolf. Boots. Ingrid hadn't seen it since that night at the fence, when the Hydras inside them both had held their strange palaver. She was startled to see it padding from the silhouettes of the lab, but her fear receded as the wolf advanced languidly. If anything, Ingrid sensed a curiosity and kinship. They were the same under the skin, she and it. The wolf seemed to realize that, too.

It stopped at the edge of the light, resting on its haunches. Its muzzle was matted with blood.

Astrid said: "If you let me go, I can fix things."

"You wouldn't even try, Ast," Ingrid said wearily. "I believe you honestly wanted to do good, at first. I just don't think you're capable of it."

Astrid's thighs tensed, testing her bindings. "You can't get out of here. You know that, right? You'll die trying."

"Maybe. But that's better than staying here with you."

"Ing—listen to me. I want you to hear the words I'm saying to you. Listen carefully, dummy. If you leave me, I will help them *find you*. We will hunt you down."

Ingrid could see inside Astrid now. Her bones lit like X-rays . . . her compulsions, too. What Ingrid perceived was a girl who'd lived in a bubble. She'd never been forced to care about anyone, or think about how her actions affected the flesh and blood she tinkered with—she could simply *do*, and if things went bad, she could retreat into the bubble her vast intellect afforded her.

It was funny, because adults regularly told their kids that hard work and good intentions would pay off in the end. Such bullshit. Some people were smart enough, beautiful enough, or rich enough to act like total sociopaths and get away with it.

"You won't be in a position to hunt me, Ast."

"Oh, but I will."

Ingrid stepped close enough for Astrid to catch something in her eyes that must have made her see that Ingrid wasn't bluffing.

"I've been wondering what they'll put over your hands. Maybe they'll tape oven mitts over them? Who can say."

The jellyfish drifted hypnotically. Lion's mane, box, moon, stinging nettle, man-of-war, mushroom cap, flower hat . . . and somewhere, lost to sight, the tiny but deadly Irukandji.

"I don't want to scare you, Ast, but if it were me—just to be safe—I'd make sure your hands were amputated. One's not enough. I'd take both of them. Because you're *really* smart, do you know that? I'd be worried that you'd figure out a way."

". . . a way? To what?"

"Kill yourself," Ingrid said lightly. "As you've always threatened. If I were them, I'd make it impossible for you to do that to yourself."

She caught Astrid's breath. The tang of fear in it.

"I'm going to give you something." Ingrid's hand rose until the fingertips feathered Astrid's chin. "Something *you* gave me. And it's going to make you even more valuable than you are now." Ingrid's eyes smiled: *Can you believe it?* "As far as anyone will know, you could be the only specimen on earth to house this great gift."

When the Hydra began to coil out of Ingrid's fingertips, Astrid breathed: "No."

The Hydra rose higher, worming past Astrid's lips, up her nostrils. "*Please,*" she sobbed.

When it threaded through her clenched eyelids, Astrid began to shriek. The jellyfish floated remotely in the tank, observing this bizarre tableau with their eyeless appendages.

Astrid broke one wrist against her bindings. The bone let go with a greenstick snap. The Hydra forced her jaw open as it funneled into its creator, climbing her spinal stem to investigate that highly exceptional mind.

WHEN SHE'D finished, Ingrid went outside. The bitter cold was assaultive; the front that had blown down from the north had locked the landscape in a mantle of ice.

The wolf followed her to the shore. Ice now stretched off to the southern horizon, bluish-white under the moonlight. Ingrid tested it, putting her weight on the white sheet. No creak or groan. Frozen solid. It could happen quickly at these latitudes.

The wolf sat on its haunches. The red light circled far away.

I wonder, Ingrid thought.

To be hunted for the rest of her life, however long that was to be. A pariah, as she would be to anyone who discovered what lurked inside of her.

"A monster."

The wind whipped these words across the ice.

She could wait and see who turned up. Perhaps she could strike a bargain with them.

That, or she could try to make a run for it.

Would the ice hold out for long enough?

Would *she*?

Boots sidled up beside her. It was massive thanks to the Hydra's transformation, the tips of its ears resting level with her collarbones. Its legs long and strong, back broad, fur warm.

It reeked of old death.

Could they make it? Would the Hydra keep them both alive for as long as it took?

Should they?

The bigger question. Perhaps an unanswerable one.

Didn't every creature have a right to its own survival and furtherance— even the most ungodly ones?

They stood there, Ingrid and the wolf, watching the throb of that red light.

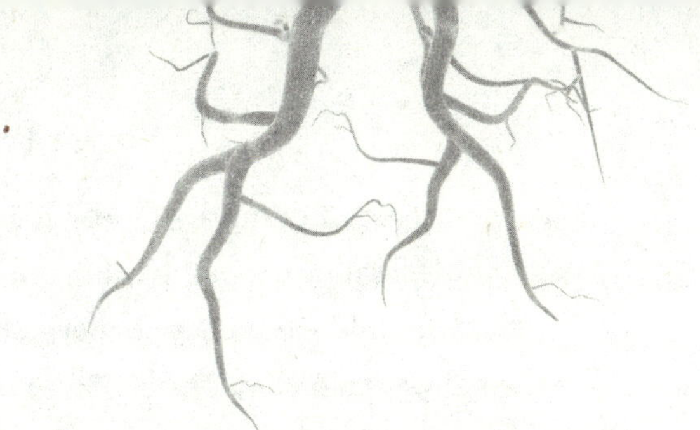

XXI. *Anno Hydra*, Day 70

AN EARTHBOUND buzz carried across the frozen white.

From on high, the windows of the Spindrift laboratory charted the approach of vehicles. Black dots speeding across the snow-covered ice in an arrow formation. In time, they resolved into snowmobiles. Cutting their speed, they stopped in the shadow of the boathouse.

Five figures gathered at the base of the steps leading to Spindrift. From there, it was plain to see the door was wedged open under a weight of blown-in snow.

Helen Fairchild pulled her helmet off.

"Secure every exit. Go."

Before joining as the head of Lifespan Sciences for the Corporation— the blank-check factory that had anonymously underwritten the Spindrift lab and empowered Dr. Astrid Marsh's vision—Fairchild had spent nearly two decades with the Canadian military. She'd enlisted at fifteen, studying as an officer cadet at Le Collège de Militaire Royal. She'd seen it all thanks to service overseas: first as a combat medic, later as a field hospital surgeon, and finally as a United Nations Peacekeeper during the Rwandan genocide.

The notion of "peacekeeper" lost its meaning in such situations. It had been impossible to keep the peace in a place that had long been a seat of madness. She'd seen things overseas that brought her to the brink. A redbrick shack full of skulls. Some faded as old piano keys, some deliriously white. Some only the size of grapefruits.

A person gets a glimpse of hell on earth and something dies in them—a happy little light burns out. Nothing much shocks them after that.

Or so Fairchild would have believed before entering Spindrift.

The hallways ran cold. The power must have gone out some time ago. The Corporation had lost contact with its mole four days ago. This was the first time since then that the island was safely accessible. First had come the storm—the worst to rock the province in twenty years—followed by a freak snowfall that locked the countryside in impassable ice. The weather had only recently stabilized enough to allow their search party to forge out. But Fairchild feared that the lost time had allowed something poisonous to bloom within these walls.

"Fan out," she told the team. "The exits. Bar them however you need to. Nothing gets out."

The main laboratory lay lightless. Fairchild was the first in. Her flashlight swept across the floor, then up to the high girdered ceiling. The silence was broken by a dry, dusty flapping from somewhere.

Her flashlight beam found the cylindrical tank housing the jellyfish. The salt water hadn't frozen, but the glass was petaled with frost. Past that glittering, the jellyfish drifted sluggishly.

That flapping. It was coming from near the tank.

Fairchild circuited it cautiously, one hand on her sidearm. The flashlight beam crawled over something bulking from the far side of the tank . . .

"Dr. Marsh . . . ?"

Fairchild had never met her in the flesh, but she knew the face from photographs. The thing slumped in a cradle of bindings wasn't at all recognizable as Astrid Marsh.

It barely looked human.

The project's objectives were known to Fairchild, but not its progress. She hadn't been handed any updates—she suspected there hadn't been any, in light of Marsh's secretive nature. All she'd been told before embarking across the ice was to prepare for any eventuality.

Dr. Marsh's body was barely noticeable in the crawling, twisting, *living* tapestry that had colonized her. A virid blue that stung Fairchild's eyes. The color blanketed her, radiating over her as it spanned out in nimble branchings and threads.

It's consuming her—eating her alive.

A raven was perched on one of the ropes. Its jet-black head darted, brutish beak pecking at Marsh's stomach.

"Shhhhhhh!" Fairchild hissed at the bird.

The raven flew off to settle high on a girder, squalling down at her.

Breath held and peering closer, the realization dawned. *It's not eating her. It's* coming out *of her.*

This suspicion would be confirmed over the coming hours, with the discovery of three bodies. Records would reveal these as the initial test subjects of Dr. Marsh's age-reversal procedure. Their names would never be publicly released. Their remains were placed into temperature-and-moisture-controlled berths and transferred to a private compound overseen by the Corporation. Fairchild would never discover what became of them.

The first two were located in the lab, locked in an unnatural embrace.

The final body was found ten paces from the wreck of a small watercraft discovered several miles from the island. The thing inside it had crawled out of the boat and across an icy span of beach, dragging the body of its host. Wrapping itself around the nearest tree, it and the body were discovered frozen solid. The blue tendrils of the Hydra had permanently solidified into a hundred knife-edges, all pointing due south. The team member who'd found it later told Fairchild that it looked as if the "Hydra" (Marsh's name for the experimental procedure) had died straining toward any nearby form of life it could colonize.

Its host body belonged to one Claire Blessings. The team member who located it would also tell Fairchild in awe: *She was beautiful, encased in the ice. Couldn't have been more than twenty years old.*

Three more would be located in the coming days. The beheaded corpse of Moses Squires in a generator shack bordering the animal enclosure. Plus two additional sets of remains that beggared logic: what was left of Veronica Strauss was found spread across the bedroom floor of her personal quarters.

The other, identified via dental records as John Salters, was discovered at the base of some cliffs distant to the laboratory. Even the birds didn't pick at that one.

There had been six subjects. Yet only three were recovered.

The whereabouts of Franklin Doyle and Madeline Dodds remained unknown.

Whatever families existed of the deceased would be fairly compensated. Some of them would later speak to the media, but what was there to say? What did they know, really?

—*The person I loved went to an island. They never came home.*

—*Well, what happened on that island?*

—*Something horrible.*

If they used those words, they'd be correct. But it would only ever be a dark suspicion.

Perhaps one day that would change. Someday this island could hold the aura of a Hiroshima or an Auschwitz: an altar memorializing some nadir of human ingenuity. But such a public disclosure was unlikely in light of the Corporation's watertight security protocols. They did *not* need another Falstaff Island public-relations boondoggle on their hands.

As Helen Fairchild beheld Dr. Marsh's corpse, its chest flexed. Her body drew a shuddering breath.

That was when the finest point of terror hit Fairchild. That this person—a flesh-and-blood human, just like her or anyone else—could somehow be *alive* . . . it told of the unimaginable power of the thing Astrid Marsh had birthed into the world, holding the ability to prolong life (a *kind* of life?) long past the point when a recipient would rather die.

Sometime later, one of Fairchild's cohorts found her in a dull stupor.

"Helen?"

The rise of Dr. Marsh's chest under all that bewitching blue . . . the subsequent shallow breaths . . . the impulse to step close enough, let one of those strands touch Helen's own skin—the invitation to become a part of it, too.

"*Helen.*"

She snapped out of it. "Yeah. It's Dr. Marsh. She's alive."

"No," her companion said, sounding angry. "That can't be."

"Well—*look*."

"...ohhh."

"Bring in an extraction team. Quarantine measures—but do it quickly. She's all that's left of the experiment."

While her companion radioed the request for air support, Fairchild went outside. Walked down the steps to the dock. Snow carpeted the ice. Trees groaned as the wind tore across the channel.

Another team member joined her.

"Ingrid Chevalier, Marsh's friend from the Institute? We can't locate her. Or a corpse that could be easily identified as her."

"We'll find it before long, someplace on this island. And it won't be pleasant."

At the time, her statement seemed reasonable. But as the days unfolded, the trio of unaccounted-for subjects and their whereabouts would form a deepening mystery.

Of course, bodies got lost sometimes. Certainly in such harsh country.

Fairchild stared at the snowmobiles. The memory of the inbound trip was still fresh. An hour across windswept ice. Even in winter gear, the cold had flayed every inch of exposed skin.

Surely nothing could survive the journey out on foot. Dr. Marsh had been canny about choosing this location. Even in decent weather, the route was serpentine; Fairchild learned as much during the snowmobile ride in. It would be so easy to get turned around in these island chains. You could probably wander for weeks, your bearings shot, getting increasingly lost.

"Impossible," Fairchild heard herself say.

The ice extended all the way out to where snow met cloudy sky, white bonding to white so seamlessly she couldn't spot the horizon.

No way. Nobody could survive this. Not a soul on earth ... born or made.

Shutting her mind on these thoughts, Fairchild mounted the steps back up to Spindrift.

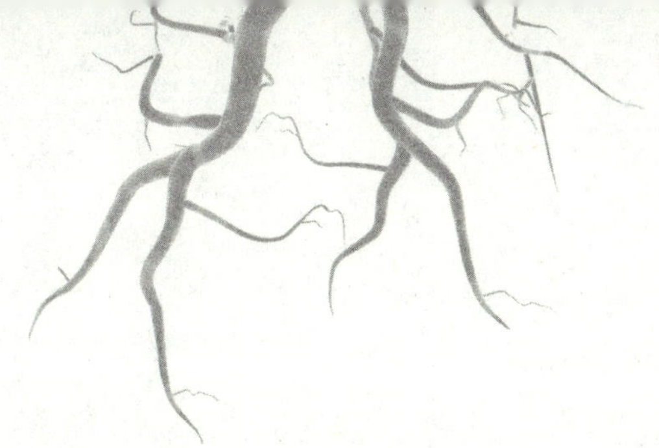

EPILOGUE

FOREVER AND EVER, AMEN

IT WAS a weird place to meet. The sort of place, Frank figured, that couldn't exist when he was younger.

A water park, bowling alley, arcade, restaurant complex, and a 1,500-room hotel, all showcased in a log-cabin motif. The whole shebang sat in isolation off the highway, rung by a concrete oasis in which cars formed a puddle of metal under the eye of the winter sun. The surrounding landscape was white, treeless, flat as a pancake. The kind of sight line where—as the old salts say—you could watch your dog run away all day.

Frank hadn't paid for a room. He hadn't brought his swim trunks. He wasn't planning on staying long. He'd come only because Madeline had called him to meet here.

A voice from a long-ago time reaching out across a crackly cell phone connection.

We need to talk, Frank.

He parked, leaving his car at the rear of the lot. Walked the five hundred yards through a light snow to the front doors. That sort of walk would've left him winded nearly a decade ago, his heart sludging along in his chest—now he covered the distance effortlessly.

The automatic doors ushered him into an overcrowded lobby. Newly arrived families, still in their parkas with luggage in tow, jostled with guests in housecoats or swimsuits still damp from the water park. The faint note of chlorine tinged the high-ceilinged lobby, dominated by an animatronic diorama: a huge tree with all manner of talking woodland creatures, squirrel and racoon and fox and lynx, popping from knotholes in its trunk.

The place gave Frank the creeps. He could see why Maddy chose it. There was so much to distract the eye that they could pass unnoticed. Or almost so.

He took a seat in the coffee shop facing the gift emporium. Kids dashed around with gigantic cookies shaped like animal heads. He kept his eyes aimed on his table. The cashier had noticed them already. His eyes. The anti-freeze blue of them. Frank had a pair of nonprescription contacts—he didn't need glasses anymore, his vision being 20/20—that helped tamp down the unnatural blue. But today he'd forgotten to put them in, a stupid oversight that could be costly.

"Well, well, Frank Doyle. You're looking hale and healthy."

He hadn't needed to look up to know she was there. He'd sensed her the moment she'd stepped into the lobby—earlier than that, probably. Something in him reached instinctively toward the secret inside his old island mate.

Madeline sat across from him. She was beautiful, of course. Utterly radiant.

She tucked a lock of hair—blond, natural, not from a dye bottle—behind her ear. Her skin silky and unblemished. Her posture erect. Her eyes the same vibrant blue as his.

"You are, too. I have to say, you don't look a day over twenty-three."

"And you." A laugh, a bit forced. "We don't have an epigenetic clock to say for sure, but I *feel* twenty-three."

For all the world, that's how everyone would see them, too. A pair of twenty-somethings who'd chosen—for some perverse reason—to meet for a first date at a place like this.

Looking at her, Frank's mind traveled back to those final hours at Spindrift. How they'd stood shivering in that freezing water, those needles poised at one another's throats . . . how there had been a moment of reckoning that passed between them with the swiftness of a batted eye . . . a span that Frank now viewed as his last moment to exert free will . . . how the needles had retreated—both he and Maddy had pulled them away from one another's neck, dropping them into the water—as the Hydra's furious desire to exist asserted itself.

Or had it been his own desire? Was he blaming it on the Hydra? Impossible to say anymore. The Hydra's wires had knitted with his own at a cortex-deep level; Frank could no longer disentangle his own demands from those of the thing nesting within him.

He and Maddy had stepped from the water, chilled to the bone. Held hands as they mounted the dawn-lit land back to Spindrift, entering through the same window the Hugo-thing had broken. They found a bed and huddled underneath the covers together, naked, shivering so hard that their teeth rattled away like castanets.

Frank couldn't say how long they lay there. Hours, perhaps as long as three-quarters of a day. Nobody intruded, though Frank occasionally surfaced from his sour dreamscape to hear sounds from deeper within Spindrift. Screams, mostly.

At some point, they had risen silently and gotten dressed in warm clothes. Parkas, boots, hats, and mitts. They exited the lifeless building to find the water frozen to a hard gray sheen.

There was no way to tell how far out the ice would hold. But if they weren't going to end themselves, there was no choice left but to escape.

They set off on foot across the ice, walking until—

"How are you managing?" Maddy asked.

"Oh, I'm getting along. I have money."

Frank still had his pension. It wasn't robust, but neither were his needs. It would go to his account regular as clockwork until the day he died—though he figured if he kept cashing his checks come a hundred and thirty or a hundred and forty years, someone might start to wonder. The automatic deposits were a blessing: if he had to show up at a bank to cash them personally, someone was bound to have questions.

"I have money, too," Maddy said. "But that's not really what I meant."

He'd known what she was angling at. He just hoped she'd have the good grace to avoid the whole grisly conversation.

"I, um, have my ways."

The thing about the Hydra was, it had its own needs. But Frank had discovered an effective, if repellent, workaround.

Medical waste. The cast-off bits and pieces of surgeries, procedures, other interventions. He'd made a contact at a hospital. The guy had the itchy eyes of an addict. Frank could spot one of his own. The guy didn't ask questions, but when he delivered the cargo—always in double-ply plastic surgical bags in the overhang of the hospital's receiving entry—Frank couldn't miss the grimace of revulsion that crossed the guy's face.

Frank couldn't blame him. It was inhuman, of course. But what did anyone need with these cast-off bits? At least he wasn't hurting anyone, and money talked.

He'd rip the bags open behind the dumpsters at the back of the hospital's staff parking lot. It seemed a suitable spot for such depravity. The Hydra often made a quick meal of these offerings. If it was cancerous tissue, lesions, or excised tumors . . . that was thin gruel. Once, as the Hydra's tapered appendages exited Frank's hands and mouth and nostrils to feed, he'd felt such a surge of energy, a mellow fire spreading through his marrow . . . after he'd gorged, he discovered that particular surgical bag had contained a late-stage fetus. He'd thrown his meal up behind the dumpsters, weeping, and told the guy to give him no more of that stuff.

"Well," said Maddy primly, "I'm sure the less spoken of that, the better. We both deserve to keep our secrets, right?"

"Right," Frank said, beset by a sudden exhaustion.

His mind retreated once again to the day he and Maddy escaped the island. They had walked across the glass-like ice, which miraculously held as far as their footsteps took them. They'd passed uninhabited islands mantled in snow, spying no signs of occupation: no houses, shacks, or habitations at all. They were hungry . . . but not in the traditional human fashion. They had been using their bodies roughly—they'd nearly died from hypothermia—and their Hydras were working overtime to keep them upright, keep their hearts beating and lungs inhaling.

Then, out of that gathering dark, a pinprick of light swelled. They'd instinctively moved toward it. Their postures were stooped over and troll-ish as they shuffled across the ice to reach the stony shore.

A cottage with a spindle of smoke rising from a mortared chimney.

They huddled in the shrubs, watching. Through the lone window Frank could see two figures. A man and a woman. A snowmobile was parked nearby.

Frank had said: "We can knock. They'll feed us, or—"

Maddy shushed him. That terrible hunger gnawed at his guts.

"Look—there's an outhouse," she'd said. "One of them will come use it eventually."

There was another moment of choice, right there. Another test. Again, Frank failed.

Some hours later the cabin door had opened. The man moved across the frozen earth to the outhouse. And out of hiding Frank and Maddy scuttled, eager as bony, predatory crabs, to fall upon the man. He'd let out a breathless scream, but it was cut short by the blue wires ribboning into his mouth . . .

Frank and Maddy had departed the next morning, taking the snowmobile. What they left behind in that cottage was obscene.

That was what? Seven and a half years ago. A lot had happened in the meantime and in-between time, none of it much worth rehashing. Frank was too tired to face most of it.

Now Maddy sat across from him. Why? Frank didn't want to see her. He didn't want anything to do with Madeline Dodds—not this version, anyway. They were just two lonely undead monsters.

Frank had tried to kill himself once. He'd purchased an abandoned survivalist shelter for dirt cheap from a Y2Ker who'd overestimated the impact of the computer networks rolling over. The guy had built it out in the sticks, a concrete bunker dug fifteen feet underground. Frank had dragged out all the canned shit and bottled water and yellowed toilet paper, anything that may have prolonged his life. His aim was simple: he'd lock himself inside, no way out. He'd lie on the cot in the cement room and . . . his wife, Annie, when she went to bed after a long day she'd say: *I want to sleep for a thousand years.*

Frank wanted that, too. A millennial sleep. But before he quite got the chance to snap the lock on the door of that doomsday shelter and bend the key in half, a little voice had risen up from his subconscious:

This is a good idea, Frank. A great one, no two ways about it . . .

. . . but do it tomorrow. Give it a little think. Let it stew. What do you say, pardner?

Tomorrow. Yeah, sure.

That was the greatest trick the Hydra had learned to pull. *Delay.*

But then maybe it had been him, Franklin Eugene Doyle, who'd thought so. Deliberately, of his own selfish logic.

Kick the can down the road, just for a day. Pick it up again in the morning. Don't put the thought out of your mind, though, because it's a legitimately good idea. Killing yourself, ending your perverse existence, is truly the best thing not only for you, but the entire human race.

Except do it . . . tomorrow, whydontcha?

Later he'd found himself back at his car, facing the woods where the bunker lay. He'd walked away from it. He could barely recall his footsteps, but . . .

"You've been careful, though?" he asked Maddy. "You haven't . . ."

"No." She watched him closely. "It may have been close, once or twice. It's very persuasive, as you know."

"Sure. I know."

His coffee was cooling. Kids were dashing around shrieking bloody blue murder . . . that's one thing Frank had learned to be careful about. Using those old-timey phrases—they were perfectly apt for his true age, but hearing something like "you old horse thief" or "*Atsa matter you? Shadduppa yo face!*" coming from the mouth of an apple-faced twenty-three-year-old . . . people tended to give him sharp looks. Which was bad, because there were people looking for Frank, even after all these many years. Bounty hunters and skip tracers hired by whoever had bankrolled Astrid Marsh. Those people would very much like to find Frank, and Maddy, and take them to some quiet building out in the middle of nowhere and . . . do things to them.

So Frank didn't use those old words and phrases. If he caught himself whistling some old TV jingle (*Get your skis shined up, grab a stick of Juicy Fruit, the taste is gonna move you . . .*), he shut himself up right quick. He watched YouTube, he got to know the faces. Skibidi Toilet, dop-dop-dop . . . a headache was starting to pinch between Frank's eyes.

"I saw her, you know."

Frank's eyes found Maddy's. "Who?"

A lilting laugh. "Who do you think?"

"Ingrid?"

A soft nod. "Yeah. And the wolf."

The kids' shrieks were earsplitting. Frank's headache dialed up a few notches.

"I was driving home the other day. I saw the two of them off the roadside in a stand of firs. Watching me as I drove past." She stared deeply into her coffee cup. "I slowed down just to make sure and yes, it was them."

"Did you go home?"

"What do you think?"

Frank had nursed the feeling for years. The one that said Ingrid was out there somewhere, trying to find him. Not so much *him*, really—Frank Doyle was inconsequential—but the thing within Frank. Find that thing and end it.

"Why do you think she's following us?"

"We're wrong," Maddy told him simply. "She thinks we're dangerous."

"Are we?"

"I am."

Frank accepted this. He was dangerous, too, at least hypothetically.

"You said no, but be honest." Frank cleared his throat. "Have you ever *shared* it?"

"I was telling the truth," Maddy told him, inspecting her fingernails. "Not yet, anyway. I suppose I might, though, if I ever felt a need."

"Why would you need to?"

She smiled thinly. "Makes it easier to rob banks. An accomplice or two."

"Are you that lonely?"

"It's not loneliness. It's a war, Frank. The one you must be waging, too." She smiled, yet there was a hollowness to it. "It *wants* us to share it, doesn't it? It wants to spread."

He didn't care for this new side of her. That she'd speak so cavalierly about such things. The fact that Ingrid and her wolf were searching for them—could track them at long distances, called by the thing they all shared—it made sense. Because of course Maddy was right: the thing inside them wasn't much for staying put. It was a daily, often hourly, struggle to stop it from exercising that wish. Frank felt it now as he watched these kids (these young, fresh, uncorrupted bodies) dash around them. The Hydra strained against his shirt-front, throbbing under his skin . . . yearning to reach out and touch all that youth.

Frank's eyes trailed off to the café's windows, which looked out over the western edge of the parking lot. That hunted feeling within him doubled over, a great wheel cranking in his chest.

Was that something out there? The low, bristling coat of a winter wolf breasting the foliage, cutting as a shark's fin through the water?

Would it be so bad? If Frank couldn't bring himself to end it, maybe it was best to have that choice taken from him by force.

Don't be silly. You don't want to die yet. Save it for tomorrow.

Tomorrow. Yeah, that was the ticket.

"Maybe we should stick together?" he said.

"That's kind of what I was thinking. At least, for now."

She stood. Offered her hand. Frank took it.

They walked out the front doors, hand in hand. The sunlight hit their smooth unlined skin. An older couple—probably coming in with their grandkids—passed them. The woman patted her hubby's hand.

"Young love, darling," Frank heard the old lady whisper. "Isn't it grand?"

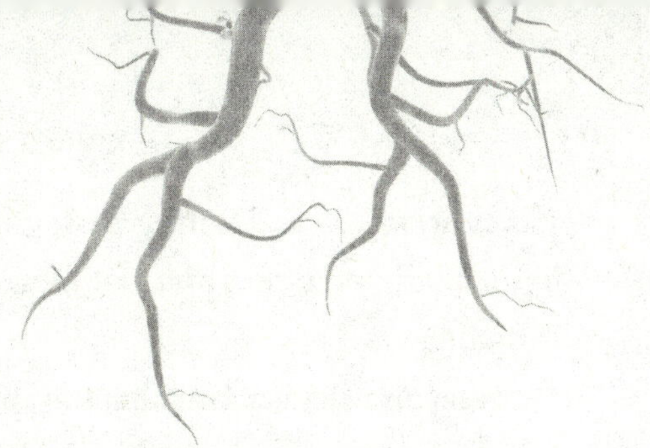

acknowledgments

NO BOOK is written alone or free from influence, either from those who've walked similar territory before, or from the circumstances of a writer's life that provoke them to write the story in the first place. Both these hold true for *The Dorians.*

The fantasy of a fountain of youth is surely as old as humankind. Once we realized our own mortality, our species fixated on a means to prolong—if not infinitely extend—our lives. When this idea came to me in my late forties, my father was undergoing cancer treatment. There was great uncertainty as to whether he'd survive, though mercifully he did. Meanwhile a friend of mine, much closer to me in age, was not so fortunate.

The age I presently sit at—fifty as of this writing; the half-century mark— is an age at which such narratives feel more needful. I am still young enough (or most days feel so, despite the nagging aches and pains) to do the majority of the activities I always have, and to see the development of my own children as they charge (too damn fast) through their childhoods, hurtling headlong toward adulthood. Yet I'm also old enough to have lost loved ones, and to be part of a cohort who are losing our parents, our aunts and uncles. Our grand-parents, apart from a few fantastically long-living outliers, have been gone for some time now.

And so, it's natural for a book such as this to come at my age. It's not some-thing I'd have ever thought to write as a twenty-something, in my "Oh, what is it to be a young, tragically misunderstood person in this workaday world?" phase; in my thirties and forties, I was interested in memory, relationships, parenthood . . . and with grossing readers out. I still *am* interested in that. Yet it's only now that ideas of mortality have made steady inroads into my thinking.

A second chance. Isn't that the appeal of such stories? To reverse one's age, peeling back the years to a place where the body functions with the surety it once had, where the brain synapses fire with passionate ideas, and where the mistakes made during the first lap around the racetrack might be erased by the decisions that come with wisdom and understanding? An opportunity to live again and have a happy ending?

Alas, those aren't the sorts of stories I'm known to write.

MOST OF the science that readers encounter in this book is akin to the science of *Jurassic Park*. Which is to say, incredibly interesting on an imaginative level—DNA in fossilized mosquitoes bringing dinosaurs back to life! Jellyfish holding the key to eternal life!—while being less conceivable (as yet) in practical terms. Jellyfish are rudimentary organisms, and how they manage their Methuselean trick remains largely unknown . . . but then, a person from the seventies being handed an iPhone would think it a creation of aliens, which is to say that humankind has been known to make remarkable leaps forward in small spans of time.

For the moment, the science on display in this book is outside the realm of reality. Yet, in order to give these pages as much verisimilitude as possible, I reached out to several researchers to get their thoughts on the topic. I'd like to thank Dr. Ronald Cohn of SickKids Hospital in Toronto, Dr. Moira McQueen of the Canadian Catholic Bioethics Institute, and Dr. Robert E. Steele, professor of biological chemistry at UC Irvine, for allowing me to pick their brains about the Hydra jellyfish, the ethics of life-extension therapies, and MAID, among other topics.

Beyond that, I went down more than a few rabbit holes having to do with antiaging, futurism, bioidentical cells, chromosomes, senescence, and other topics as suited my fancy. Not all that research found its way into the book—it never does—but I would like to thank Nathaniel Rich, Ray Kurzweil, Nick

Bostrom (the Paperclip Maximizer), Aubrey de Grey, the National Library of Medicine, health-span advocate Bryan Johnson, and other sources for the information I utilized to cobble together Astrid Marsh's strange, terrible, entirely impossible scientific agenda.

As to fictional influences . . . I kept a running total as the book went on, and consulting that list now I see: *Frankenstein, Jurassic Park, The Island of Doctor Moreau, The Beast in the Jungle, Four Thousand Weeks, The Monkey's Paw, The Picture of Dorian Gray, Flowers for Algernon,* and the TV show *Workaholics.* There are others, surely—King is always in the mix; Golding and Barker and Cronenberg and Carpenter, too—but those are the ones that stood out.

FINALLY, MY thanks to those who helped this book come to be. Ed Schlesinger at Gallery, who shepherded this and every other Cutter book. Kirby Kim, erstwhile agent and confidant. My wife, Colleen, and my son and daughter, Nick and Charlotte. To my mother and father and brother and sister-in-law, cousin Christine. To Rob Sternitzky, Kell Wilson, Sydney Morris, Jennifer Bergstrom, and all at Gallery/S&S. To all those aunts and uncles, teachers and mentors who helped form and guide me when I was a foolish, headstrong pup.

To those who we've lost and those who are still here, muddling along.